THE
HUNT

THE MOON BLOOD SAGA

The Bite

The Hunt

THE
HUNT

Z.W. TAYLOR

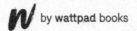 by wattpad books

An imprint of Wattpad WEBTOON Book Group

Copyright © 2024 Z.W. Taylor

Published in Canada by Wattpad WEBTOON Book Group, a division of Wattpad WEBTOON Studios, Inc.

36 Wellington Street E., Suite 200, Toronto, ON M5E 1C7 Canada

www.wattpad.com

First W by Wattpad Books edition: March 2024

ISBN 978-1-99885-424-0 (Trade Paper original)
ISBN 978-1-99885-425-7 (eBook edition)

Library and Archives Canada Cataloguing in Publication information is available upon request.

Printed and bound in Canada

1 3 5 7 9 10 8 6 4 2

Cover design by Laura Klynstra
Author Photo by Jordan Heddins
Images © Trevillion; ©NeMaria, ©Demja, ©Chereliss via Shutterstock
Typesetting by Delaney Anderson

For my father, who taught me
that it was okay to have wild dreams.

"When one is alone at night in the depths of these woods, the stillness is at once awful and sublime. Every leaf seems to speak."

—John Muir, *The Unpublished Journals of John Muir*

CHAPTER ONE

"Shift."

I ran through the snow-dusted forest as the dim mid-morning sun streaked through the trees. My bare feet pounded against the ground, as I tried to block out the feeling of ice against my toes.

Levi had me shifting back and forth and back and forth between my wolf and my human form. He said I would do this until it was like breathing. He made it look so effortless when he shifted into his fur, a black-as-night coat with a dust of silver on the top rolling over his body like a wave as bones easily snapped into place. I tried to mimic his swift motions, but all my clumsy steps found were the hard snow, remnants from the raging winter's wrath, waiting for me each time I fell to the ground.

Although I reminded myself to be grateful—because with every disjointed shift I was making progress, little by little, doing the very thing that had almost killed me only a few weeks ago when I was just a human.

"*Shift*," he ordered across the telepathic channel that linked our minds.

I took a large step then jumped in hopes that I would dive right into the shift. Cracking sounded while my muscles screamed for mercy, and then the pure clusterfuck of my awkward shift had me sliding across the frozen ground.

My wolf got up with a groan and shook out her coffee-colored fur. She darted forward and jumped over a fallen log, following the trail down the creek that Levi had sent us on. I was growing tired; we had been at this for hours and I could feel my handle on this "beast" starting to thin. Usually she let me drive while we were in four legs, but with my mind feeling like the oatmeal I'd had for breakfast, I found myself taking a reluctant backseat.

"*Shift*."

She growled lowly. A sentiment I agreed with. I wasn't sure if I was going to be able to do anything but crawl back to the house. In two strides we jumped into the air, reaching for skin. It rolled over us in a graceful wave, but right as the cold air hit my back, I felt little shards of ice dig into my skin.

My lungs burned as I gulped. "Shit." I wheezed.

"*Shift*."

With my eyes clenched shut, I stood up, then started to run again. Levi was in a mood today.

But he had saved me, helping me through each gruesome moon until I finally shifted successfully for the first time. If there was anyone I trusted to help me embrace this new life, it was him.

So I took a step, then sprang into the air while reaching mentally for my wolf form. My bones snapped in a brutal chorus that carried through the forest, ending when my paws landed firm on the hard ground.

Both my beast and I were shocked, but both of us were too tired to dwell on it. We wound around brush and boulders with ease while the wind nipped at our paws. She curled around a set of trees and broke through the thicket into a pristine meadow.

My paws littered the perfect blanket of snow on the ground with prints until I felt the beast lock her legs. Snow flared on the path as we skidded to a halt. I felt the fur on my neck rise when it hit me—the quiet. A silence that constricted itself around my lungs.

There were no creatures, no birds, no squirrels, no anything making any noise at all. Faintly in the background the snow fell quietly, and even that sounded more hushed than usual.

The wind picked up, carrying past me like a whisper that made my head snap toward the tree line that was thick with darkness, almost like it was sucking out all the light. It felt like a sick trap, yet something about it piqued my curiosity.

My hackles rising, I stepped forward. A breeze blew through the limbs and danced its way to me. It smelled of magic, like burning sugar, but something was off—this wasn't the scent of hot caramel; this smelled dusty, burned. Like it had been left to crust over itself in a humid room.

I stopped when I realized that I was only a step away

from entering the mouth the darkness had laid wide open, ready to swallow me whole.

My beast cocked her head while we both waited, as if we were waiting for it to say something to us. But nothing spoke. Instead, it felt like the darkness was reaching its fingers forward so it could pull us into its embrace. My lip curled as a growl rumbled through my chest, disturbing the false sense of peace that the snow provided.

"Charlotte!" I turned to see Levi loping toward me, snow contrasting his black fur. *"Get back from there."*

"What is this place?"

He paused next to me. *"It's the Trapper's Forest. Come on—I didn't think you'd make it all the way over here."*

"We can't go in?"

"No," he said. His familiar silver eyes glowed with a hard gaze. *"It's dangerous. You don't go in alone. Ever."*

"Why? It's just a forest."

"No, Charlotte, it's not just a forest." He pawed at the snow before turning and darting back the way we had both come. *"We're going home."*

I took one last look, wondering if the forest would finally speak to me instead of holding its breath. But it said nothing, so I ran after Levi.

When we reached home, he shifted into his skin and jogged easily up the stairs. "You know the rules, no fur in the house," he called over his shoulder, brushing his hands on his shifters, long black running pants that had been magicked so he could shift with them on.

Shifting back into my skin, I cursed his name over and over as my vertebrae cracked one by one while I rose to stand. My yoga pants clung to my skin and my black sports bra felt like it was a sweaty cage around my lungs.

"I hate you," I stammered.

He shrugged. "I know. Let's get some lunch. You're chopping wood after."

I rolled my eyes. Of fucking course I was. It didn't matter that I had to pull myself up the stairs by the railing or that my legs felt like they would give out at any moment. With my luck, I'd be chopping wood until the end of time.

Elliot sat in the living room with his notebook spread out over the coffee table while he furiously typed away on his laptop. He paused to take a sip from a wineglass with a lid on it. The iron scent of the thick blood in the glass made my stomach curl. Levi had told me once that it smelled rotten to wolves because it was human.

"How did it go today?" the vampire asked me, eyes not leaving his computer.

"I found the Trapper's Forest."

Elliot paused, green eyes lifting to study me closely. Running a hand through his thick red locks, he looked at Levi's closed door.

"Elliot, what is that place?"

I blinked and the door to Levi's room opened. Elliot closed his mouth as Levi strolled out in a pair of old jeans and a faded navy sweatshirt. He had his silver hair tied back in a low ponytail, tired gray eyes hard like he was pissed off at the air in the room.

Elliot bit his lip and offered me an apologetic shrug. The topic wasn't dropped. I put a giant bookmark on that page and decided to wait until the right time; not very long ago,

I would have let it go. I would have nodded and said *Fine*, because it was what I was supposed to do.

Elliot's mate, Derek, stormed through the front door, a scowl contorting his perfectly symmetrical face. His dark-mahogany hair was windblown, olive skin a shade paler than usual. Although now that I'd shifted fully into a wolf, I realized that he had always been pale—my old human eyes just never picked that up.

Derek's dark eyes were steady as he took deliberate steps to where Levi was leaning on the counter next to the refrigerator, opening a beer. He tossed a thick letter with his name written in old-style calligraphy onto the counter.

"Leo's summoned me—well, us," Derek stated, nudging his chin at Elliot.

Elliot groaned, sinking farther into the couch. Levi set his beer down and looked through the papers. He shook his head. "Why? Seems weird to call the coven home this time of year."

Derek rubbed his tight jaw. "Rules are rules."

"And you have to go?" I asked, sliding onto one of the barstools that lined the kitchen counter.

Derek turned to me, his shoulders instantly relaxing. "Yes," he offered with a sad smile. "We have to go back once a year to check in, the whole coven does. Although usually Leo waits for spring. Maybe he wants to do Christmas with all of us?"

"Doubt it," Elliot griped. "It's going to be a bunch of ring kissing and soddy tossers hoping to get up Leo's ass." He marched into the kitchen.

Levi eyed me. "You eat?"

"Not yet."

He pushed off the counter. "Better get on it, you're about to be on your own." He snickered, taking a long pull from his beer as he strode into the living room. I shook my head, wondering how I was going to last an entire winter without the two vampires.

Derek rolled his eyes. "I'll do it. Might as well treat you while I can."

"I'm sorry you have to go," I offered.

Derek shook his head. "Don't be. Leo is the best sire I could have asked for. He's abundantly kind and understanding—he takes very good care of his coven. He even took Elliot in even though he's not one of his by blood."

Elliot slid onto the stool next to me. "You'd probably love him. You know, we could always take her—"

"No." Levi's cold voice sliced through the warmth the small fireplace had created in the room. He was stoking it, eyes watching the flames as a few embers crackled, like they were angry at Elliot's idea too.

Elliot waved him off. "It will be fine. Besides, you'll be plenty busy with pack things." Elliot looked over his shoulder at Levi. "Oy! Have you decided what her offering will be?"

"Offering?" I arched a brow.

Derek slid a sandwich in front of me. "If you want to be in the pack you have to make an offering to be considered. You still want to do that, right?"

I did. In my gut I felt a faint longing, but still, saying yes felt harder than it should. "What does the offering have to be?"

Levi walked back to the sink to wash his hands. "The pack works because everyone contributes to it."

"And beer cans are your contribution, eh?" Elliot teased.

Levi flicked water at him. "To officially be a member of this pack, the Thunderhead Pack, you have to have a role or a job you perform. Each member of the pack council oversees a function. We have people who manage our livestock and harvest, guards who protect our borders, and there's the trackers, our scouts. They scope out where the game is for hunting, help patrol the borders, monitor any security issues alongside our guard," he explained. He turned the sink off and picked up a dishtowel with sunflowers on it, drying his hands before tossing the towel to the side.

My beast perked up in the back of my mind, as if her ears were flicking forward.

"Usually, what happens is one of two cases: a wolf transfers in from another pack for whatever reason, or we have young wolves that mature to be adults, out of their parents' guardianship, and can assume a proper role in the pack.

"Regardless of which case, you have to be approved by pack council and seen fit to perform the role of your choosing. If they approve you, then usually it's a fast process if you're already trained in the role. For new pups, like you," Levi explained, "they decide what they want to do, then train for it. Once they complete the training and have approval from the pack leads, then they can be sworn in."

"Who's all on this council?" I asked.

"Besides me and Lander, there's Bowie and David," Levi answered. He snatched a bag of potato chips next to him. "Bowie is our head tracker or Head of the Hunt, as she likes to be called, and David is the Head of Security and Agriculture. They're both good wolves."

Elliot handed me another bag that I quickly grabbed a handful of chips from. "What are typical offerings?"

Levi shrugged. "Some people have brought bushels of apples, others have brought a herd of goats, one woman brought hand-stitched quilts. Usually people bring something that is indicative of what they want to do. Trackers usually bring a kill, the gardeners bring crops—you get the fucking idea."

Elliot bumped his shoulder against mine. "So what do you want to do, Char?"

Wasn't that the million-dollar question? I hadn't thought much past beyond trying to survive a few weeks ago.

"You know, I think she may have a nose to be a tracker," he went on.

I looked at him, eyes narrowed. "Why do you think that?"

Elliot snickered. "Because when I say *hunt* your beast lights up like it's a bloody holiday. And somehow you've found all of Levi's socks, which seems like a sign."

He wasn't wrong. The idea of hunting, of letting my wolf run through the forest in search of her prey, seemed like heaven to her. But I had been transformed not long ago and joined a world that I'd thought before was only make-believe. Before all this, I'd sat behind a desk, played the perfect girlfriend to a foul man, and paid a high price for it. I wasn't sure if I was ready to charge into the wilderness and bring back the whole hog. I had just learned to shift without crying each time. But still, the idea did seem to stir something in me.

9

"So what would I have to do to be a tracker?"

Levi's eyes narrowed in almost a warning. "Tracker camp."

Elliot smiled. "Bowie runs the best one in the state. She's probably one of the best trackers that I've seen in over a hundred years. Other packs send their trackers here to train because of how well her program is crafted. You could learn from no one better. Give it a think."

I drummed my fingers on the counter. "And to be sworn into the pack, that's after?"

Levi nodded. "There's usually a ceremony. You swear loyalty to the pack and the pack swears it to you before you're added to the larger pack link."

"Who adds you?" I asked.

"I do," he replied. Levi stared at the floor for a moment, eyes unfocused. He blinked, lifting them to me. "Lander said your new paperwork and ID got mailed in."

Levi's brother, Lander, had come by after I'd shifted the first time and told me that we had to kill me. Levi had not been amused. Their attorney fixed me up with a whole new identity—which he'd emphasized was still subject to taxes. He'd said looking normal so we could fit into the system was the best way to stay hidden. Apparently, in thirty or so years they'd fake my death, but until then, they did not want me to leave a paper trail.

"Glad I can still buy beer."

Elliot snickered. "Lucky that our lawyer is good at his job."

Levi had told me the law firm—the "business"—was passed down through one very human family. They handled legal affairs for most of the packs in the area.

"He was . . . interesting." The guy was a creep. When I told him I wanted to take my mother's maiden name, Stevenson, as my last name, his response had been, and I quote, "Precious."

Levi snorted. "He's a fucking worm is what he is, but he's useful. His dad was a good man." Levi shoved off the counter and walked back to the fire, leaving me to my own thoughts, which followed me outside while I chopped log after log until the sun started to dip in the sky, the afternoon quickly fading away.

I found myself watching the rest of the sunlight fade over the trees through the window in my room. My hair was still dripping beads of water, wet from the shower that I had taken a few extra minutes in. I clutched the towel around my body and tried to open my underwear drawer, only to find it caught on something. "Come on," I groaned, trying to jiggle it loose. I wiggled my fingers into the small space that was open, feeling around until I touched something that felt like it was hanging down from the top. "What are you?" I asked, now energized to get the damn drawer open. I jiggled it a little more before it finally gave way. My hands reached back in and felt along the top of the drawer until I found a little piece of twine to grasp.

The false top opened with an easy tug, and a small cigar box fell into the main drawer. The box read, "Lucas's shit," in blue marker on the top.

I curled my fingers away from it. It felt wrong to disturb the box that belonged to Levi's dead son. But the beast in me felt bold. It was like she was moving my fingers to delicately turn the latch then lift the lid open.

The contents looked like they would for any teenager. There were a few toy cars and a signed baseball. A few baggies of weed were sitting in the corner. I rolled my eyes. I would have paid money to see Lucas trying to keep that away from his dad. There was a pocket watch that was broken, the front of it cracked. I tucked it away carefully then picked up a thick stack of papers, turning them over to see that they were photos.

The first was one of all of them—Lucas with Levi and a woman who had to be Eve. She was so beautiful, with hair red like it was on fire and full of lively curls. They were sitting on the front steps, laughing. Eve had dimples that made her smile even more contagious—I found myself smiling with her too.

Levi had his arm around her shoulders. He had short hair and wore jeans without holes in them. He was laughing, smiling in a way that felt like it would break his face today.

Lucas could have been his twin. He looked about eighteen in the photo, with white-blond hair and silver eyes that felt abnormal. He had a gray T-shirt on and was barefoot, pointing at someone in front of him with a giant smile, showing dimples just like his mother's.

My eyes watered. It was no wonder Levi lost his mind and almost went rogue when his family was murdered. Because he looked so damned happy. Less hard—not like a block of ice that would never thaw out. Although how could anyone blame him? They were his true mate and his son. Two pieces of himself that he was never going to get back.

I wiped my eyes then tucked the photos back into the box and stowed it in its hidden compartment, taking the memories of the photos with me to bed—although I couldn't sleep at all.

Nate still visited my dreams. You would think after everything that I could forget the man I had originally run from—the one who'd driven me into the hands of rogue wolves that almost killed me. Rogues that Levi saved me from.

In my dream, Nate took me to one of our favorite beaches. One moment we were walking in the moonlight, and the next he had buried me in the sand up to my neck. He tilted his head down to look at me. His eyes were yellow with a hazy redness around them, like that of a rogue wolf's—like the ones that had attacked me. He left me for the high tide to drown me, but the water turned to blood, and when I screamed, all I saw was a Blood Moon like the one I had transformed under, high above me with crimson tears running down Her face.

I sat up in bed with a growl.

Monsters should be able to sleep.

In the kitchen the fire was almost out; embers burned sleepily in the ash. Outside, snow was spiraling, whipping through the trees and around the stone columns that lined the perimeter of the yard. The pillars created the boundary line that had been built when Levi lost his mind years ago. The storm had left a thick coat of ice around each of them, giving each the aura of a gargoyle rather than a column. They were supposed to the keep the pack safe, but tonight they felt more dangerous than Levi.

Someone was sitting on the porch in one of the rocking chairs; I immediately recognized the red hair above the chair back. There was a bottle next to him.

I grabbed a coffee mug and stepped outside, catching Elliot's sparkling green eyes. "Can I join?"

"Misery loves company." He laughed easily.

I sat next to him and held my cup out. He poured me a healthy portion of whiskey, eyes glancing over me. "The nightmares are still bad, aren't they?"

"Tonight they were," I admitted. He hummed next to me and took a sip from his glass. "Do they ever get better?" I asked.

"The demons in our hearts never sleep, unfortunately."

I took a sip of the amber liquid, letting the burn warm me up like a soft blanket. "How long will you be gone?"

He sighed. "Not sure, to be honest. Sometimes it's only a month, sometimes six. The problem, and I guess benefit, is that Derek is one of Leo's favorites. How could he not be?" he added with a lazy shrug. "Although with winter setting in, we probably won't be able to get back home until after the melt starts. Would be a proper bitch to hike through."

I groaned. "So it's me and him all winter."

"It's you and him all winter," he echoed. "His bark is worse than his bite. Never forget that."

I took another sip and watched the snow dance down as the light of the moon reflected on the crystal flakes before they landed in a soft bed of white on the ground.

Leaning back in my seat, I turned to Elliot. "That forest, why is it dangerous?"

"He didn't tell you?"

I shook my head.

Elliot sat forward and let out a long breath that looked like dragon's smoke coming out his nose. "It used to be a playground for werewolf hunters, fur traders, and really any nefarious blokes out for a werewolf. It became notorious back in the day when the fur trade was at its height, it's where trappers would hunt werewolves. They would skin their pelts and then ship the fur down the main creeks to the river. This was before the Timber Pack, Talia's pack down south, owned that land—the Timber Pack is honestly who everyone has to thank for ending the trade. They destroyed all the ports and drove the trappers north for the wolves there to handle them as they saw fit."

"You say it like you were there," I mused.

Elliot breathed a laugh. He took a sip from his cup. "Derek and I are very old. I know you know that."

"I know," I acknowledged, although I never got around to asking how old. Every time I danced around the subject Derek dipped into this place of sadness that wrapped its arms around him for hours. Elliot usually deflected, and I decided that for now, whatever painful memories they had weren't worth sating my curiosity.

"We've seen so much, Charlotte. Too much. Those were such dark days. They brutalized wolves. Hunted so many people. Forced them to shift and skinned them alive. You see, when a wolf dies, they shift back into their human form, so the fur traders had to keep them alive to harvest the fur."

I felt sick. My beast snapped at the idea of it—the horror of it.

"Your fur is gorgeous—and soft. They could have passed it off as something else, but believe me, there's an underground market for everything. Depravity's appetite is a bottomless pit." His eyes tipped down, like he was watching a weary memory. "That forest is laced with traps. I helped Levi's father try to clean it out a long time ago. But it's such a big forest, so much territory to cover, even today there's probably parts of it that are unexplored. Levi and Lander tried to clean parts of it with their father, and they lost their uncle to it."

My mouth went dry. I drank more whiskey hoping it would help, but all I could think about was the black fingers of that forest reaching for me.

"There's something else about that forest. It's foul, Charlotte. So many have died there, too much bad magic has been used there, blood magic. There's nothing good about a place where so much blood has been spilled. Do you understand? Too many blood memories, too much evil in one place will corrupt anything and everything around it. Everything from small birds to great trees," he said, his voice quiet, like he was trying not to disturb the snow. "They're corrupted with the sickness that has a hold over that place."

"It felt bad when I was in front of it." I paused and licked my lips. "What are you not telling me?"

He traced the rim of his mug. "Eight years ago when Levi's family died, when the packs were attacked, rogues came in numbers that had been unheard of for a long time. Do you know where they came from?"

My heart stopped. "The forest."

He nodded, looking up at me with sad eyes. "They came down the mountains and out of the forest." He paused and wiped his mouth. "I combed that forest with Bowie. I took the better hunters in our coven and scoured it." He paused and stared into his glass. "And we found nothing. There was nothing there. Just old traps, remnants of rogues, silver, and dead magic."

I glanced at the porch steps, imagining Levi's family in the photo I'd seen earlier. "I'm sorry," I told Elliot. "So I'm assuming the forest is off-limits then?"

"No." He snickered. "It's where the Hunt is. The final challenge of the tracker training. You'll have seven days with a team to find a deer painted with your team's chosen color in the Trapper's Forest. Bring the deer back, with your team, and you my darling, will be an official Tracker."

"In the Trapper's Forest? You're joking?"

He shook his head. "Few are not afraid of it. Bowie is one of them, as is her boy. But she's a breed of her own. Her thought is trackers go where others can't—trailblazers, fearlessly walking into an unknown."

"And you think I may have a knack for this?"

He turned to me, green eyes growing vibrant, like the fauna in a rainforest coming to life at night. "You, my sweet, sweet monster, have survived what many would think impossible. Humans rarely enter our world and survive the way you have. I would say if I knew anyone who could walk into the darkness of the forest and come out alive, it would be you."

I felt my throat twist. I could feel it in my bones. I could feel her need to hunt—my need to hunt. I could feel her desire to walk right into that forest and rip open what the darkness was hiding. I could feel our desire to run with the wind, let it comb through our fur. Elliot wasn't wrong earlier; the word *hunt* made my heart flutter like a crush.

Elliot took my hand, leaning closer to me. "It's what you

want that matters. Not what others think you're good at or could be good at. It's your choice. You fought hard enough for it, remember that."

My heart stilled as my wolf howled in the back of my mind. Because he was so right. I hadn't come this far to just sit behind another fucking desk. I hadn't survived Nate's poisonous love and three fucked-up months of transforming into a werewolf to just roll over again.

"I will." And I meant it. His lips pulled into a smile that looked anything but happy. I tilted my head. "Elliot, is there something else going on?"

He shook his head. "Just let me have a melancholy night, yeah?"

I let out a long breath as he squeezed my hand. "More whiskey, then?"

"Always more whiskey, love," he answered, pouring us each a big helping as snow kept falling in the front yard.

CHAPTER
TWO

Before the first real snow hit, the vampires left.

Derek had worked day in and day out to stock the freezer with plenty of meals, which he left along with a notebook of recipes and a house that felt too big for Levi, me, and our ghosts. It was then that I felt the longing in me start to truly howl. It stoked my desire to run outside and find the other wolves that I had been faintly smelling and hearing around the house.

I hadn't seen Liam since I'd shifted, although he kept leaving me little gifts. I always searched for him in the woods at night through my window, hoping to spot his familiar dimpled smile or silver eyes. But Lander's oldest son kept his distance except for the small tokens I received, like this morning on my windowsill. I found a bundle of evergreen limbs tied together with brown twine. It wasn't flowers, but the little red berries and pine cones that decorated the limbs like ornaments felt more precious than any rose I had ever received. I hid the bouquet under my pillow before I left my room and went to the empty kitchen. I didn't want it out in the open where I would have to answer questions about why Levi's nephew was leaving things for me.

Eventually, Levi joined me, walking straight to the coffeepot to pour himself a cup. Like every other morning, he didn't say a thing about the vampires' absence. Taking a long sip, he looked outside like he was already annoyed at the audacity of the dawning sun breaking over the tree line. The ground was a blanket of white, beautiful and clean. I loved the sight of it. Levi told me I would grow to hate it soon enough.

"It's going to be a full moon tonight."

I knew. I could feel it already in my bones. It was the first full moon since my final shift to a werewolf and a familiar anxiety had set in as memories of the months leading up to my shift surfaced: bones cracking, sweat dripping down my neck, and vomit creeping up my throat.

Taking a sip of coffee, I tried to shove those away. But I felt like I could almost hear the moon calling to me, creating an itch to shift and run out into Her light. I knew my body wouldn't break tonight, but with my new relationship with this "beast" in me, I wasn't sure if something else would.

"What do we do?"

"Come in early. You're not going out during it."

"Why not?"

He took another sip of coffee. "When you're fully in control of her, you can. That, and you haven't been integrated with the pack. It's too dangerous."

"But you're here," I pointed out.

"This isn't a discussion."

"I feel like you don't do many discussions?" I found myself saying.

There was still so much I didn't know about the loner man who'd saved me. My wolf whined in the back of my mind. All I could do was pick at my Pop-Tart. Levi finished his cup of coffee then had another before dragging me outside, where he proceeded to have me chop down dead trees instead of wood.

I was worn out by the time the day was waning, which I assumed was his intention, but it didn't stop this feeling in my soul—this need that had me constantly on the edge of shifting all day.

After I showered, Levi and I reheated some of Derek's lasagna. When the timer in the shape of a melting egg went off, I set my glass of wine down and reached for the oven mitts, only to catch something out the widow from the corner of my eye. Levi was standing outside near a column, almost red in the face, yelling at someone on the other side of it.

I felt the hair on my neck rise. The beast in me felt like she was pushing closer, trying to also get a view of what had him so worked up. I tried to peer through the trees, thinking at first I may spot his brother, Lander, but the moment I approached the window, Levi snapped his head toward me. I jumped and turned for the lasagna, trying to shake off the wild look in his glowing silver eyes.

He said nothing when he stormed inside. He silently poured himself bourbon on the rocks then marched to his room, slamming the door.

By the time I was on my second helping, Levi came out. There was a vibrancy pulsing off him, almost like an electric wave that rolled through the cabin. Something in me crackled.

"I put the lasagna back in the oven to keep it warm for you."

Silence stilled my heart before the sound of clanking dishes started it back up again. "I see you took a corner piece."

"Should have gotten here earlier."

He snorted a laugh and the tension I'd felt myself holding rolled off me. "Fair enough."

I poked around at what was left of my second helping, but I couldn't stop my eyes from drifting outside. The moon was hidden behind wispy clouds. I found myself hating them, as did my beast. She was pacing back and forth, begging to be let out. But I knew Levi was right: I had no idea what would happen if I went outside, and the last thing I wanted was to lose control of myself and hurt someone.

Levi took a seat in his recliner. Through the window dusted with snow, I could see the moon's light pooling over the ground. My feet made the decision for me, and carried me to the window. My mouth dropped and my breath escaped me the moment the clouds parted so Her fullness could shine.

Nothing was more beautiful than that sight. Electricity rolled through me, igniting parts that I didn't know existed.

It felt like my mother calling my name after a long day of playing outside, or the way my own joy would dance when I was witness to a rare moment of my father laughing. I so badly wanted to hear him laugh; I so badly wanted to hear her call my name just one more time, just like I so badly wanted to walk outside and let the light embrace me.

My beast wailed in the echo chambers of my mind as howls in the distance sang into the darkness. I found myself wanting to let out a call of my own, my lips quivering until I threw a hand over my mouth to stop one from sounding.

My beast snapped at me, angry that I had her contained. I could feel her pulsing under my skin. My nails started to elongate to claws as I panted hotly.

"Charlotte."

I turned my head to see glowing silver eyes. Levi checked the moon, a curse hissing under his breath. "Come sit down."

"Please," I all but gasped.

"You know you can't. You won't be in control of yourself."

That was the last thing I wanted. I didn't want to walk into danger right after I had fought so hard to free myself from it.

But my beast was relentless, snarling in the back of my mind. Howls sounded from the woods again. My toes curled as the fangs in my mouth grew long and sharp.

"Charlotte."

A growl vibrated off my chest. Levi put his plate down.

"Charlie girl, either you come sit down or I will drag your ass over here."

"Will it always be like this?" I asked through clenched

teeth that were set on stopping the noise desperately trying to escape my mouth.

He shook his head. "You get better."

"I don't—" I bit back another howl. "I don't know if I can hold her back."

"Look at me." I forced my eyes to meet his. He cocked his head. "You can. You're going to feel it more than others because you're moon-blooded. But because you're moon-blooded, you have to be stronger—you have to have a grip on her. We have a movie to watch. Come here and turn it on."

I blinked hard, my anger for him reaching a new level. "How is this so easy for you?"

He cast me a long look. "Years of practice. Close the curtains and turn the movie on."

My beast whined again, a sound that almost had me in tears even as I reached for the curtain cord with trembling fingers. My teeth sank hard into my lip until I tasted blood.

Levi arched a brow at me as I took a seat on the sofa closest to his recliner. I snatched the remote and turned on *The Godfather*. He offered me his drink, which I ended up finishing.

"Christ, Charlotte," he grumbled, going to the kitchen to fetch another glass and the bottle.

He took his seat again and poured me a glass before pouring himself one. My fingers dug into the cushion, claws sinking into the cloth while my beast raged.

Levi grabbed the remote and turned the volume up. "I'd appreciate it if you didn't ruin my couch."

"You're such an asshole," I hissed. "Has anyone ever told you that?"

"It is Lander's nickname for me," he pointed out, a smug smile tugging on his lips.

I rubbed my temple. "What if we stayed in the yard?"

"Why? We're watching a perfectly good movie."

I leaned my head back, trying to focus on anything but the torment raging inside me. "Can we play the question game?"

"No." He snorted, clinking the ice in his glass. "Watch the movie."

I blinked my eyes open to see the horse head bleeding on the bed. The sight of it made my mouth water. My legs itched to run—to hunt—and let the predator in me out.

Levi sighed, swirling his glass next to me. He turned the volume down, then ran his hand over his scruffy face. "I wish you'd let me smoke again."

"It's not good for you."

He shrugged.

"Why—why does this happen?" I asked.

"Why does what happen?"

"The moon? All of this bullshit?"

He leaned back in his chair and laced his fingers behind his head. "Well, She made us."

"Tell me about it." *Distract me. Keep my mind on anything but the need to lose it the minute I step past the rose bushes.*

He rolled his eyes. "*The Godfather* is on and you want to hear that bedtime story?"

"Please?"

Levi held my gaze before nodding. "All right," he agreed. He took another long drink then turned the volume down on the television until it was almost mute.

He leaned forward, resting his forearms on his knees. Lacing his fingers together, he turned to me with glowing eyes. "A long time ago, a very long time ago, the world was wild," he said, his voice hushed as the fire crackled in the background. Instantly, I felt her still in my mind. "Beasts and creatures of all kinds roamed the earth with man. But it was a dangerous, brutal place, because not all of them were friendly to humans. And there, in this savage world, was a human family. There were two brothers, twins who hated each other. Their mother was the only child of the moon. But her husband died, and it shattered her heart into a thousand pieces. It's said not long after she also died."

"How?"

Levi looked at his drink, eyes distant like he was watching a memory. "Broken heart." He let out a breath through his nose, breaking the trance. "The children were left alone, completely broken. It's said that the moon cried tears of blood that day because the cries of Her grandchildren were too tormenting to hear."

"The Blood Moon."

He nodded with a hum. "Supposed to be the moon's way of remembering Her daughter's heartbreak."

"Is it bad that I turned on one then?"

He shrugged. "Who knows." He took another drink. "Anyhow, to compensate Her grandchildren for the loss, the moon granted them one wish, hoping it would help them as they faced the world alone. So the elder twin, Hagan, went to Her one night when She was full and asked to be king of all the beasts on land. Not knowing what he was really asking for, She turned him into a werewolf right there.

"Seeing this, his twin brother, Hektor, was insanely jealous. The next full moon he went to Her and asked to be made superior to his brother. So She turned him right there into a vampire. Able to walk among men and beasts but never truly living, always dependent on the life of others."

"How is that superior?"

"Hell if I know."

"So that's how we happened?"

"I'm not having that conversation with you."

My chest vibrated with a growl. Levi chuckled into his glass and nodded to me. "Yes, at least that's how the story goes."

"But after that? What happened after?"

He shook his head. "Chaos broke out. After Hagan turned into a werewolf, it's said he went mad because he couldn't control his beast. On the flip side, it's said Hektor was equally as bad, because he couldn't contain the blood-lust. It was the beginning of the conflict between our kinds that has gone on for generation after generation.

"The twins lived in a small town. After they both turned, their friends tried to help them but then ended up being turned by the twins. They each bit six men, creating the first vampire and werewolf lines. After that, more or less, peace was a crapshoot. There was a lot of bloodshed between them all."

"And Leo is one of them?"

He tilted his head. "Supposedly. There's only him and one other vampire left that are rumored to be the first of the line. Seems to be working out for them. Their world treats them like fucking royalty."

"What about you? And your family?"

He nodded. "Long line in our family. We've been here, at Thunderhead, as long as anyone can remember. Some of the older packs trace back to those lines, but some of the lines have died out." He leaned back against the seat.

"Why *Thunderhead*? Why not name it after the family? I don't know, it seems like that has happened in the past with human dynasties?"

He hummed in agreement. "Well, we have to stay hidden. That creek you love to swim in?" As in the creek that I fucking hated. "It's the Thunderhead Creek. Packs across the globe pick a landmark close to their borders as a way to stay under the radar with humans but also signal to other packs where they are located. For example, Talia down south is the Timber Pack because the Timber Falls borders her territory. If you're around humans, you can easily say 'I live by Thunderhead' and they won't know a damn difference."

"You know I hate that creek, right?"

He snickered and took a sip of his drink.

"What happened to them? The twins?"

Low gunshots popped in the background as the movie kept playing. "It's said they tried to come together for peace, but Hagan was uncontrollable. He ended up murdering his twin. So the others ended him. After that, the wolves and vampires split up, all settling in different places. A few came here and made deals with the locals so they could stay hidden from humans. They had enough on their hands with all the chaos and wars, the last thing they needed was for humans to get involved in their mess. Wasn't until the last few hundred years we've had peace with the vampires because of the treaty we somehow got signed, which for our kind is a miracle. My father was a stubborn man, and he got it done."

"What happened to your father?"

He leaned back in his chair. "My mother got ripped apart by a mountain lion. She was older, both of them over two hundred. Her body was more or less done fighting. When she died, Dad didn't go nuts or lose his mind. I remember that evening, he was the calmest I ever saw him when he turned in for the night. I found him the next morning in bed. He had passed in his sleep." He paused, eyes pulsing with a glow. "Claire said he had the moon's favor, being able to join my mother so peacefully."

I didn't say anything because I could see the bitterness in his eyes, the hardness growing. The fairness of it all didn't make sense to me, but then again, fairness in life didn't make sense in the human world either.

"He sounds like he was a great man," I quietly offered.

Levi took a sip from his glass. "He was."

I leaned my head back against the couch as cries rang in the distance, igniting the embers in me yearning to join them. To know them. I was never good at making friends, but I couldn't deny this feeling.

"How long until I can go out there with them?"

"When you're ready," he told me.

I turned to him. The glow of my eyes reflected off the edge of his glass. My beast was standing now in the back of my mind, pawing at me to keep going—temporarily disregarding her plight to see the moon.

"I want to be part of the pack."

"First you have to pick a job for the pack."

I swallowed before saying words that I'd found myself wanting more and more with each day that had passed since the night I'd sat with Elliot on the porch.

"A tracker."

Levi didn't move. He didn't even turn to look at me.

"Elliot said he thinks I have a knack for it."

"He says a lot of things."

I swallowed. "Well, it's what I want."

"Is that right?" He set his glass down. "It's dangerous, Charlotte. It's one of the more dangerous things you could do."

"So is being human and getting bitten by a bunch of rogue wolves," I countered.

"People have died in the Hunt."

Without a second thought I said, "People have died trying to transform into a werewolf too."

The glow from my eyes increased, and this time I wasn't stopping it. Because even though I wasn't sure if it was a good idea, I still wanted to try. I owed it to myself to fucking try to do something that made my heart feel like it was flying.

"No."

"This isn't your decision." My voice was firm.

Levi leaned back in his chair, watching me like he wasn't sure if I was going to start shifting again.

I leaned forward and dipped my head so I could see the glow of my eyes reflected in his. "This is my choice."

He arched a brow. "You want to do it? Bring me a deer."

"What?"

"You heard me," he clipped. The current that was rolling from him earlier picked up again. "Bring me a deer, then we'll talk."

The beast in me sat back in the back of my mind, like she was pleased with this accord we had come to. I kept my face neutral because it wasn't going to take Levi more than two seconds to realize I hadn't killed anything in my life.

But this beast in me was calm, pleased.

I leaned back into the couch. "Fine," I said, reaching for the remote and turning the volume up.

CHAPTER
THREE

The forest held its breath around me. It was early, dawn barely broken. Snow was falling like powdered sugar, sprinkled over everything in sight, including the little squirrels scampering about. A few birds chirped, as if they were having a morning chat while they wound through the trees going about their tasks.

The beast in me paced. She was ready to dart through the trees and let the snow dust her fur. My naked toes squirmed in the snow. I tugged at my fitted tank and long yoga pants, shifters that Claire, Lander's mate, had gifted me. The cold nipped at the bare skin of my arms while snow kissed my cheeks; I should have been shaking, but my heart was fluttering in my chest like the wings of the little birds above me.

I was hunting this morning. At least, that's what I'd announced to Levi when I'd left the house earlier, set on bringing him back something with horns that he could shove up his ass.

Yet with each step I took into the woods that I ran through day after day, I felt like I was swimming farther and farther into uncharted waters. Because I had never been hunting in my fucking life.

Part of me wondered if I should have actually paid more attention to some of those dumb survival competition shows that Nate used to love. They were always trying to track something and find the signs the animals had left around them. Although another part of me remembered that those people usually tapped out of the competition because they were starving to death.

My wolf pawed at the back of my mind. I wasn't sure about letting her run wild, but this was her domain, after all, and I wasn't going home empty-handed. Licking my lips, I ran a few feet and lunged into the shift. My joints cracked painfully as they broke through the stiffness caused by the cold. My beast whined as her paws stumbled to the ground, but soon the pain was forgotten, because the feeling of cool air snaking through my fur was invigorating.

I let the beast have more control while she pushed harder, her senses like live wires waiting patiently to be set off. Turning a corner, we combed through familiar trees that I knew were near an area of the forest that bordered Levi's glacial lookout point.

My wolf curled around a boulder then slid to a halt. Her nose went to the ground as something musky snaked into our nostrils. Looking up, I could see them—the tracks that made a stark outline in the snow. I wasn't sure if this was good, but my beast seemed to think it was because she set off like a ballerina, prancing quietly over the snow as she followed the trail with her nose.

Soon the prints faded, but the scent was still thick. My beast licked her lips, springing forward with stealth that took my breath away, because I had no idea that we could be this graceful, this fluid in this domain. We ran until we arrived at thick evergreen trees, then she slowed and fell to her belly, squirming through the white powder until she could dip her head under a branch.

At a little pond created from a small vein of the creek that wasn't frozen over, a deer was drinking from a tiny pool of running water. He had a crown of antlers on his head, seven, with the innermost one broken in half. He looked tired, almost like he was half asleep, but the sight of his ears flicking in every direction said otherwise.

The most unsettling thing was how naturally my instincts took over—how my wolf's paws ghosted forward, not making a single sound as she drifted closer and closer to our prey. We could smell the musk rolling off his coat. See the pulse in his neck that said he was very much alive. My beast licked her lips, taking another step, when the deer looked up and caught us in the spotlight of his eyes.

In that moment, I found myself frozen to the ground. The beast wanted to move but my hesitation made us lunge too late, missing the deer by a breath. Grinding her teeth, my beast stumbled after him, but in a blink he was gone into the forest, vanishing as if he had never been there in the first place.

My wolf wanted to chase after him, but I knew that we needed to not venture farther than where Levi had told us to go. She tried to run, tried to kick me to the back of this body we were sharing, so I reached for my skin, through her snarls and snaps, until I was sitting next to the pond where the deer had once been. I wiped my hands on my shifters while cursing myself inwardly.

Levi was in the greenhouse when I got back home. He walked out of the makeshift plastic door and crossed his arms, smirking at the sight of me: barefoot, with tiny icicles hanging from my hair.

"Guess we're having pasta for dinner again?"

"Piss off," I grumbled.

"You have to work together," he told me.

The beast snapped in the back of my mind, vexed. I tightened my jaw, not looking at him as I walked into the house.

The next morning, I went out again and found myself lucky, because the deer was back at the small pond. I decided to call him Ned. He was eating the grass on the bank. Levi had told me that animals would dig near running water for any grass or food hiding under the blanket of snow.

I felt the beast stir. After yesterday, I'd decided to take more control today, only letting her toss in her thoughts when it seemed appropriate. It had gotten us this far, and Ned seemed to be completely unaware of us in our hiding spot under the tree. However, the moment I decided to charge him, I realized how very aware of me he was.

Because he turned and, instead of bolting, took a swipe at me with his sharp antlers. I blinked and he was once again disappearing into the safety of the trees, while I stained the snow red. The beast in me growled, snarled, and gnashed her teeth like she had been cursed with the daftest human alive. She didn't even fight me when I shifted back to my skin.

I brushed my fingers over my side, testing to see how deep the wound was.

"I just got my ass handed to me by a fucking reindeer," I groaned.

It was so cold that my blood was almost frozen by the time I got home. Levi was sitting on the front porch with a beer in his hand. His eyes locked on my side before he tipped his head back in a deep laugh, his chest shaking.

I dug my numb toes into the snow while I held my torn side. He stood and nudged his chin at the house, a smug smile plastered on his lips. "Good thing we're not relying on you for food."

The beast in me was quiet, as if she was sitting there with her paws crossed and lips pursed, saying *I told you so.*

"Bitch," I muttered under my breath before stumbling into the house.

Levi tossed a blanket over my shoulders then had me sit close to the fire. After a few minutes, the heat had melted the frozen lumps out of my hair. Something wet slid down my rib cage.

Levi walked over and set down a tackle box crammed with first aid supplies. He pulled open the side of the blanket to look at where Ned had sliced a solid six inches along my ribs.

He reached forward and tested the skin next to the cut. "It'll be fine tomorrow."

I looked at him, brows knit. "That's pretty deep? There's—"

"You're a werewolf, remember? You're not human anymore."

I pressed my lips tight together. He sat back on his heels and quietly went to work wiping the cut clean while I fell lost into the pit that was my own thoughts.

"Do you want to know what happened?" I found myself asking.

He snorted. "I already do."

I snapped my gaze to his. He shook his head. "You can't keep fighting her."

I blew out a breath. "You told me I have to control her?"

He nodded in concession. "You don't want someone to control you all the time, do you?"

"No . . ."

"You can't let her run wild, but you need to learn to work together. You're a team now, whether you want to be or not. She's half of you and she's going to share half of everything you are from now on. Which means you have to learn to trust her and she has to learn to trust you. That and a little discipline isn't going to hurt either of you."

"The hell is that supposed to mean?"

He stood up and tossed the dirty gauze into the fire. "How does it go? 'Know your enemy and know yourself'?"

I gaped at him. "*The Art of War*? Really?"

He shrugged. "Isn't that what you're doing?"

The fire crackled. I bit my lip. "What should I do then?"

"You learn to shift until you can do it in your sleep," he said simply. "And you learn to wait, watch, and to be patient.

Opportunities will come to you, not the other way around. You do that and then you'll be ready."

"Ready for what?"

"Blood."

That night I found myself flipping through the photos in the box again while the wind screeched outside. There was one of a young Lucas holding up a badger, a giant smile on his face. I felt the beast stir within me, creeping closer as my thumb swept over the photo. I set the photo next to my lamp. Lucas had been born into this life; I hadn't, which meant that I was going to have to work twice as hard to have it.

And I would. I promised myself I would.

The next morning, instead of finding Ned, I ran my normal route around the house, forcing myself to shift between wolf and human form over and over. Each time, it was still ugly. There was no denying what it was. I would fall, flop, and even hop into the alternate form, but I was making progress. I was hitting the ground less and landing on my feet more, even if it was the most ungraceful thing in the world.

Levi didn't have to spur me on. He sat on a log by the trail and gave me pointers on different approaches to take.

In the mornings for the next week, this became my new routine. I would shift and shift and shift until my legs felt like they would fall off. In the afternoons, I would stalk Ned. The beast hated it. She hated smelling him so close to us without being able to react, but I refused to let her act on her impulses. We weren't wild animals, and just because we could do something, it didn't mean we were going to.

Instead, through my stalking, I found that Ned liked to lie under a thick evergreen after eating so he could digest. He also had choice trees he would scratch his antlers on when he seemed bored. In my mind, Ned and I had full-length fictional conversations. Our topics ranged from how the grass was to whether or not we thought Queen was a better band than the Beatles. We always agreed on the Beatles, although Ned had a soft spot for Queen.

I liked to think that Ned wouldn't mind me, but that was fooling myself because I was the thing his legs were built to run from. Levi reminded me of that daily. Ned hadn't survived as long as he had by being ignorant. He had been put through the trials of this wilderness, and that alone made this task a tricky one.

Today, however, instead of stalking Ned, I was determined to lunge into my shift without falling. I was tired of feeling like a Claymation character tumbling down a hill. Because each time I shifted, I found myself on the ground with traces of dirt, snow, spit, and my own blood trailing behind me.

My beast shook out her fur, irritation running across her spine. She ran, charging down our familiar path. With a whine, she picked up the pace, begrudgingly jumping as I reached for my skin.

By the time the air hit my face, I could taste blood in my mouth and pain shot across the leg I'd fallen on.

"Fuck this," I snapped, jumping to my feet. "What is your problem?!"

The beast in me stilled. I paced, feeling something familiar crackle over me as my temper sparked to life.

"Well?" I blinked hard and looked up at the snow starting to fall again. "We can't keep doing this, we're going to get hurt," I found myself murmuring.

It was her turn to pace. I could feel her annoyance as she moved back and forth in the back of my mind.

"It can't just be always you or always me," I pointed out. "What if something happens to you and I have to take care of us? Or vice versa?"

She snapped at me like I was being idiotic. And maybe I was? I probably already looked like a lunatic talking to nothing but the fucking trees out in the forest.

"Listen to me!" I barked.

She instantly stilled and waited, like she was holding her breath.

"I can't lose myself again." I felt my throat tighten. A moment passed—a moment where memories flooded with a version of me I didn't recognize. Because that person wasn't living for herself; she was living for someone else's fucked-up delusion.

"And I want to learn," I admitted. "And I want to trust you. I'm just fucking scared, okay? I'm just—I can't let this not work. I don't have the option to go back anymore . . ."

My eyes were watering. She was quiet for a beat, then moved like she was taking careful steps closer in the back of my mind. I felt her nudge me. I looked down at my arm, which slightly rippled as she pressed closer, yet it didn't feel like she was trying to rip out of me. Instead, it felt like she was trying to show me that she was there.

"Okay, well, I can't cry in the forest. Levi already thinks I'm nuts." I bit my lip, nodding to myself before saying, "Let's try this again."

My legs pounded the ground as my arms pumped. She was close, waiting and watching patiently for me to near the log that we had used plenty of times today. A few more steps and I leaped for the log, using it as a springboard into the air. The beast rolled forward as I dove toward the ground. Joints cracked and bones realigned in a perfect symphony that ended with four paws landing easily.

But we weren't done. Because if you could do something well once, it was luck. Do it twice, and it's skill.

My beast charged forward, rounding a bend until she hit a straightaway in the trail. She took two large strides before plowing into the air, letting me reach for my skin, which came as easily as putting on a jacket.

I landed on my feet with a smile and jogged around a corner to find Levi rising from his seat and brushing the snow off his jeans. I had half a mind to snatch one of his beers and celebrate. Instead, he told me, "Let's go."

"Where?"

"You want that deer or not?"

I nodded.

He jerked his chin toward the forest. "Well, go on, lead the way."

Wordlessly, I turned and headed to the pond where I knew we would find Ned.

Ned was in his usual spot, facing away from us and munching on the mangled grass at the edge of the water.

Levi lay next to me, snow dampening his inky fur, which had a tint of blue in the shadows. One of his paws moved forward, disturbing a pile of snow that shifted like sand as it slid down the small hill of snowdrift in front of us. Ned looked up. His ears twitched for a few seconds before he went back to his meal.

"Seriously?" I said into the shared link with Levi.

He slid back. My beast cocked her head. *"Go."*

"What?"

"Watch the antlers this time," he told me.

Something stilled in me as I looked back at Ned.

I shouldn't have named the damned thing.

"This is what you are now, Charlotte."

My beast was quiet. I knew that. This was the whole point of everything I had been doing, but still, I'd named him Ned.

I felt her press forward, almost as if she was asking to lead. I let out a quiet breath through my nose, and slid back slightly so her instincts could drive us.

She crawled so quietly that it almost sounded like snow falling. The deer couldn't have heard us even if he'd wanted to. Instead of stopping her, I was observing, trying to learn, trying to pay attention as adrenaline coursed through me. Ned dipped his head down to the pond to take another drink.

He shouldn't have done that. He shouldn't have taken his eyes away from the forest. But he wasn't that stupid; Ned was smarter than being ambushed.

Slowly, he raised his head, tilting it to the side as water dripped down his chin. I froze—my nostrils flared as I took in the smell that called to me while the droplets falling from his chin pinged into the water.

In a blink, he bolted away. But my beast wasn't stopping. She tore after him, not caring a second about the extra snow he was trying to kick up with his back feet. The scent of him made our mouth water, and the fire burning in us was something I realized I never wanted to let go of. It was as though she had played this game thousands of times.

He dropped his shoulder, turning with his antlers pointed in our direction. But my wolf wasn't fazed. She leaned out of the way and dashed around him, confusing his footing. He slid on the slick ground and my beast used that as an opportunity to lunge for his neck.

Claws sank into his shoulders while our teeth quickly ripped into his jugular. By the time he hit the ground, his life had already left him.

I couldn't help but stare in stunned silence at the crimson streams carving their way through snow. Cold air nipped at my skin as I shifted back to two legs.

"Fuck, I killed Ned," I panted.

I tried to catch my breath but the adrenaline pounding through me made it feel as if I should still be running. My mind reeled. I had done something that'd felt like learning to ride a bike again, and I wasn't sure how I felt about it. Dread sank in, but my beast snapped at me. She was proud, and part of me was, too, but the blood on the ground made my stomach curl.

"You did well."

Over my shoulder I could see Levi reaching into a hole in a tree marked with silver paint. He pulled on a pair of navy sweatpants and a gray sweatshirt then reached back into the burrow for a small leather pouch. "Burrows are always marked with silver, remember that." He knelt down by me. "Lander will shit himself when he sees this."

"Lander?"

"We're taking it to the pack."

"Yeah?" I breathed.

His eyes glowed like he and the devil and been exchanging inside jokes. "It's not going to be easy, if being a tracker is what you really want to do," he said in almost a question.

This was my decision to make. Mine to own. Mine to choose. I had already come this far and I knew what my gut, my beast, were urging me to do.

"It is," I answered.

"All right. We should dress it then take it to the pack house. You want the antlers?"

"I can keep them?"

"It's up to you."

I felt a nudge from my beast, an instigation to do something brash. I bit my lip then shook my head. "Send it all to the pack."

He chuckled darkly. "As you wish, Charlie girl. Go to the house and get that small sled next to the woodpile. Bring it here and we'll use it to take the kill to the pack. You're going to learn to do this so you can do it next time."

"All right," I said, as the reality of what we were going to do set in.

It felt like my beast was smiling along with me in satisfaction. We practically sprinted to the house to get the sled. When I got back, Levi had a set of knives laid out neatly on the leather pouch next to him. I knelt down next to Levi while he started to dress the deer, and tried to keep mental notes of everything he did.

After he was done, he asked again if I was sure. I picked up the deer and put it onto the sled. "Show me the way."

CHAPTER
FOUR

A strange red carpet trailed behind me, creating a path I'd never intended to make.

The pack house was more like a large log cabin. Thick wooden beams made up the outer walls of the two-story structure; at the top, two stone chimneys steadily streamed smoke. Large wood doors were carved with images of wolves dancing under a full moon.

The snow turned to mud closer to the front steps, where paw prints marred the ground. Dozens of scents scattered about, but there was no distracting from the task that made the hair on my arms rise.

There were a few faces behind the foggy windows, and the outlines of wolves in the proud barrier of the forest. My beast stepped closer, something in me rushing forward, crackling, while I moved my feet purposefully one after the other. I pulled the buck off the sled and dragged it to the base of the steps. With a shaky breath, I ascended the stairs, then placed the deer in front of the large wooden doors.

Turning, I willed myself to only look at the crimson lane I'd created, because I could feel eyes on me, gazes raking up my form as whispers followed me all the way back to the edge of the forest where Levi waited.

He gave the pack house one glance before he turned to me. "Let's go. The weather is going to get bad later."

We worked the rest of the afternoon to get things tied down before the storm blew in. By the time I was done with my part, I could barely see my own hand in front of me from the swarming snow.

To my surprise, Levi had a glass of wine for me on the counter and chili simmering on the stove. I arched a brow while I wiped my boots off on the doormat.

He rolled his eyes. "Keep the commentary to yourself."

"I wasn't going to say anything." I tried to hide a laugh as I shrugged my jacket off. My body temperature may run warmer than it used to when I was a human, but that didn't mean that temperatures this cold couldn't chill you to the bone.

Levi pulled the lid off the pot and gave the chili a stir. "The pack council has to approve it. Should know before the holidays."

I grabbed my wine and took a long sip, the beast in me purring at the taste. Slipping onto a barstool, I asked, "Do you think they will?"

"They won't have much choice."

I cocked my head, watching him for a moment. "Why's that?"

"Because I can still override them," he replied simply. "Go get those corn chips, will ya?"

I slid out of my seat and worked my way around to the cabinets. I pulled out the jumbo bag of chips then fished some cheese out of the refrigerator while Levi retrieved some bowls for us.

At the table, I layered cheese and chips at the bottom of my bowl. Levi brought the pot over. "You're going to have to work hard for this." He took a seat while I ladled some chili into each of our bowls. "You can't just walk into a pack, not with what you are."

I leaned back, spoon up in defense. "What's that supposed to mean?"

"You're a fucking unicorn, do you realize that?"

I said nothing. Because what should I say? I knew this wasn't normal, but it wasn't like there was a manual for me to follow.

Levi leaned forward, resting his forearms on the table. "You're a moon-blooded former human. Nothing like you has ever happened before from what I know. No one is truly going to believe that you are what you are until they smell you. Even with natural-born moon blood wolves, fuck, they always want a piece of you. They always want to see if the moon blood truly makes you special. Lander got into so many fights growing up. I was no different."

"But I'm not a violent person, Levi."

"You're in a violent world, Charlie," he stated. My tongue

Z.W. TAYLOR

felt thick in my mouth, my appetite suddenly gone. "It's our way. Half of you is something that doesn't want to mediate, it wants blood and it wants flesh. Sometimes we talk things out because we're not feral animals, but sometimes it's our animals that need to settle things."

"That's so . . . brutal." I shook my head.

"How? Your world has a brutality of its own. The only difference is we call it what it is, whereas humans call it entertainment to mask the truth. Better to have it out in the open than behind a curtain." He reached for his glass and took a long sip. "Besides, you don't just have other wolves to worry about. There's what's out there too—other predators in the wild."

A shiver ran down my spine. "What do you mean?"

"Those woods, this land, any land—we're not the only thing with teeth out there, and if you want to be a tracker you're going to have to be able to fight off any threats you come across. Shit, Lander killed a fucking mountain lion on his eighteenth birthday. Eighteen. I thought he was dead. He was on a hunt on his own and ran into one. I got to him so late. He was covered in blood, so much of it his own, but smiling like he'd won the fucking lottery. He's fearless—he always has been. After that, no one from this pack, or really any other, ever thought to screw with him."

"And you?" I said it before I could take it back.

Levi chuckled. "Grizzly. Made a blanket out of it. It's in the attic, I think?" He paused, letting out a long sigh. "It was just me on the pack line."

"How old were you?"

"Sixteen."

My breath caught. "You were a child."

"I was way past being a child. Same age as Lucas when he killed a bear."

"You're kidding?"

He shook his head as a soft smile pulled his lips. "My nephews Ethan and Eli—Eve's brother's kids—were staying with us a few days. He and Eli were always getting into something, always bringing Ethan with them. Well, one of those nights, Lucas had a shift on our patrols, which meant that the other two boys would sneak out with some of my damn beer.

"Usually it was a pretty quiet area, but that night a bear showed up. Eli said Lucas went after it with no questions asked. Wouldn't even let the other boys help. By the time I found them, they were laughing their asses off, covered in blood, still drinking my beer."

I opened and closed my mouth as dread filled me. This wasn't going to be a fun scavenger hunt through the woods. It was me versus the wild, and I wasn't sure if my own claws were sharp enough for that yet.

"Maybe I should have stuck to gardening?" I offered with a small laugh.

"We both know that's not what you want."

"I mean, will I have to kill a bear? I'm not ready for that." I wasn't sure if I would ever be ready for that.

He tilted his head, his eyes slightly pulsing with a glow. "When I'm done with you, you will be. There's no *maybe* anymore, Charlotte, there's just doing. Somehow, you are moon-blooded, and a former human, which is going to make this world all the more dangerous for you. But if you make it through this—through the Trapper's Forest—then none of them will blink twice at you. You'll more than earn your place." He paused, picking his spoon up. "And I think Elliot's right. I think you have a knack for it."

"Really?" I breathed a laugh.

"You've got a good nose on you," he said before he took a bite of his chili. "Just focus on not freezing your ass off for now—it's going to be a hard winter."

"Hard" was a hellish understatement.

I never thought that it could get that cold—the kind of cold that takes your breath away, and not the kind of breathlessness that an orgasm leaves you with; the kind that comes from your lungs freezing in shock as the cold turns them to constricting concrete in your chest.

It was excruciating.

But it was even more unbearable inside. I had books to read, but as the days went by both Levi and I started to go a little stir-crazy together in a cabin that felt like it was shrinking, much like the hours of sunlight.

Thanksgiving came and neither Levi nor I cooked a big meal. Instead, we heated a pan of lasagna that Derek froze for us before he left and had it along with two coffee mugs of whiskey in the living room while a movie played in the background. Luckily for us, the snow calmed down a little around the holidays. The house had no decorations. I thought I'd seen some ornaments in the attic but I didn't want to stir up any ghosts by bringing them down. Instead, I asked Levi if we could at least have a tree. First, he looked at me with a furious gaze that he carried outside with him. The next thing I knew, I was being dragged out to the middle of the woods, where he had me chop down a tree and haul it all the way back to the house.

The sap was the worst part. By the time the tree was in the house, I had little green barbs all over my skin. Levi took one look at me and laughed. The man actually laughed, then told me to shower off. It took me at least two shampoos to get the sap out of my hair, and even after the shower I could still feel some of it on my skin.

He already had the tree lights out and was making mulled wine when I strode back into the living room. The whole cabin smelled like a holiday from my childhood, when I didn't hate the winter so much.

"Here," Levi said as he put a bowl of popcorn next to me. He then set a spool of fishing line and a thick curved needle next to me too. "Knock yourself out. Want a drink?"

"You're such a Betty Crocker since Derek has been gone," I teased.

He rolled his eyes, stealing a little bit of popcorn. "It isn't hard, it's my uncle's recipe. He used to make it every year," he said, his eyes finding where I was trying to flick off popcorn that was sticking to my fingers. He laughed and poured two big mugs for each of us. "It will come off eventually."

"This is so annoying."

"Try this."

I took the mug from him and carefully took a sip. My beast came closer to smell it as the sweet warm liquid danced down to my belly. "This is really good," I said. "Thank you."

"It's not hard. If my uncle Laurent could make it, a squirrel could."

My fingers drummed along the edge of the cup. "Was he your only uncle?"

He set his mug down and picked up the lights. "Yes," he answered. "My father's brother. My mother was an only child."

"Did he have kids?"

"No," Levi said as he shook the lights out. "He died before he could have children."

I bit my lip, pausing a moment before carefully saying, "Elliot told me about him. What happened to him . . . in there?"

He shook out the lights, shaking his head. "He was helping my father canvas an area where people had reported seeing a bunch of traps. He was always so careful—but he got caught in one. Shot silver dust into his face. Slowly destroyed his lungs. It took hours for my father to get him out of the forest. By the time he did, there was nothing that could be done. Dad ended it quickly for him."

I felt my gut lurch. "I didn't mean to—"

His eyes hardened as he held my gaze. "Let it be a good lesson to you. The traps are meant to keep you in your fur, alive, until the trapper can come collect you. Well, most of them anyways."

I could hear the beast in the back of my mind whining. The image of that dark forest burned into my brain—the unsung song of it calling me to it, ringing in my ears.

"Did he have a mate?"

"Dead," Levi answered. He took a long drink. "She tossed herself onto his funeral pyre."

The breath in my lungs left. I opened my mouth then closed it when I heard Levi curse under his breath. He set the tree lights down as the wind howled outside.

Levi blinked. "Lander said your offering was accepted."

"Really?"

Levi nodded with a hum. "He also invited us over, but I don't think anyone is getting out in this. It's supposed to do this for days." The snow was relentless outside, and the last thing I wanted was to get lost in the vortex of it. "Said the other pack leads were excited to meet you."

"Yeah?"

He offered me a one-shouldered shrug, taking a sip from his mug.

"Is that a good thing?"

"Well, it's not a bad thing." I flattened my mouth in response. Levi rolled his eyes. "You'll like them. Bowie especially."

I laced another popcorn kernel on the thread, my heart pacing a bit faster. I had wanted to get out and meet more people, but knowing I would now have to do it flared my anxiety. I took another long drink, hoping the wine would calm me down.

"Is that all?"

"Other than some meddling bullshit from him, yes." I glanced at Levi, arching a brow. "Let's finish this up," he said, nudging his chin to the tree.

He picked up his task with the lights while I kept trying to string the popcorn on the fishing line, but my beast wouldn't stop pacing. I set the popcorn down and picked up my mug, the mulled wine in it dwindling. He eyed it. "You shouldn't pick up all my bad habits, Charlie girl."

"My uncle Benji always said that everyone needs the right amount of corruption in their life."

Levi breathed a laugh. "Fine then." He took my mug with his to the kitchen and refilled them, returning to me with the steamy deep-red liquid.

I took a long sip, staring at the swirling liquid. The warmth of it spread over me like a hug, tempting me with the thousands of questions I had stored up.

"Why did Laurent's wife throw herself on his pyre?" I asked.

"She was his true mate," he answered quietly. "It was like half her soul had been ripped from her. She said it was too excruciating to be without him—her mind was . . . it was something they did more often back then. Now it's different, but the madness is still unbearable."

"Do you have a choice?" I asked, shaken by the idea of anyone ever having that kind of control over me. "Your true mate—don't you have a choice?"

He shook his head. "There's always a choice, but you don't want to deny this one." He raised his mug to his lips.

"What about bondmates?" I'd heard about mates that people choose. The ones they had a spark of a connection with that they flamed into a fire to burn together.

"It's not the same. Your true mate, they're made for you. You couldn't fight it even if you wanted to, and you won't want to, because it's the best fucking thing that's ever going to happen to your ass," he said so quietly that I wasn't sure if he was even talking to me.

"And you?" I found myself murmuring.

He took another drink. "She smelled like red wine and

roses. If I could have drowned in her scent, I would have. If I could have followed her to the other side, I would have."

Tears gathered in my eyes, but the wine had made me bold. "Do you ever wonder what happened to them?" I asked, immediately regretting it once the words slipped out.

"It won't bring them back." He turned his gaze to me. "Do you ever wonder about him?"

I took a sip of wine. "Not intentionally," I admitted.

"That's good, you're getting better."

"Am I?"

He shrugged and took a sip from his mug, watching the snow pummeling the ground through the window. "It's going to get bad." And it did.

There would no traveling to Lander's. We spent the majority of the morning shoveling around the house and stacking logs near the door. Levi was meticulous with the fire all day, which became my new place of residence when I wasn't dashing outside for wood.

He made another batch of mulled wine and I tried to make cookies with holiday-themed cookie cutters that I had dug out of the back of a cabinet. Levi inspected one. "The fuck is that?"

"It's supposed to be a reindeer?"

"Looks like an amoeba."

He wasn't wrong. The cookies had all lost their shapes and the mess of sprinkles didn't help my case. I took a bite. "Doesn't taste like one."

"You're drunk."

"I wish." I laughed.

Lightning cracked outside. He wiped a hand over his tired face and snatched a cookie before settling in his chair. I carried a plate over with the rest of the cookies and set it on top of the small coffee table. "Do you think we should save some for Lander?"

He shook his head. "We'll all be snowed in for a few days."

I finished my cookie and ended up watching the window where the wind wailed outside, like a mother crying in mourning. It pounded against the house as the booming thunder shook the walls around us.

Lightning cracked and the lights flickered. I blinked as darkness swallowed us.

"Charlotte . . ." I heard my name whispered through another clash of thunder.

I whipped my head around to Levi as the lights flickered on. "What?"

He furrowed his brows.

I tilted my head to the side and quickly scanned the room. "Did you say something?"

He shook his head. "No."

I bit the inside of my cheek. "Must be the storm," I mumbled, leaning back against the couch. "When will it settle?"

"I don't know."

CHAPTER FIVE

"Well, how is it?" Derek asked.

I checked for signs of Levi. He had been out all morning even though the weather had been brutal. Spring was coming in with a vengeance of its own, and the snow was merciless, as if it had something to prove when recently its perfect white flakes started turning into vicious pelts of ice.

Levi told me that we would be in the melt-off soon, and on days like today, when the sun was finally peeking through the clouds, I believed him.

"I thought you were just staying for the holidays?" I replied into the phone, fingers toying with the edge of my coffee cup.

"I've been away from my duties here for too long," Derek

said reluctantly. "It won't be for much longer. Besides, it's impossible for anyone to get into pack lands right now with the roads in the state they are."

I took a sip of the coffee that was almost too cold for my taste. "And Elliot? How is he?"

"Oh, he's fine, stuck mostly in the office or the library. He's been busy with teaching his classes online and the two papers he's trying to get published. He sends his love, of course. So tell me, anything exciting happen?"

"Nothing really," I said.

"Nothing? I heard that you got yourself a nice juicy stag."

A smile tugged at my lips. "I did."

"Next thing you know, you'll be hustling through tracker camp."

"Derek—" The hair on the back of my neck stood up as a familiar scent curled into my nostrils. Lander stepped out of the forest and into the front yard, bare-chested even in the uncomfortably nippy weather. "Lander's here."

"Keep an eye on Levi," Derek told me, his voice holding a serious note. "We'll be home before you know it."

"All right."

"Bye, Charlotte," he chimed, ending the call.

I slid off the stool and padded to the door. Lander jogged up the steps. Carefully, I opened the door and the screen door. "Morning," he said, his hand scratching at a half-moon-shaped scar on his chest.

"Morning," I replied. "He's not here."

"I know," he huffed, steam coming out of his mouth. He rubbed his hands together and looked over his shoulder. "He's almost here. Mind if I come in?"

The wolf in me crept closer. She cocked her head as she looked Lander over. "What are you here for?" I asked, feeling her pulse under my skin.

Lander chuckled. "For you, of course," he answered, eyes glowing. "Don't worry, Levi knows. You're coming with me for the day."

"Why?"

"Do you want to be holed up here forever?"

It felt like a subtle dig, and neither I nor this beast in me liked that. I moved to the side and let him step into the house.

"There's coffee."

"Thanks." He helped himself to a cup, fumbling about the kitchen as if this was his home too.

I turned my head the minute I heard the crunching. The scent of Levi was like the light from a lighthouse through the fog. He shifted from his fur to his skin, then jogged up the stairs, eyes slightly glowing and hair disheveled. His gaze shot to Lander as his feet carried him steadily to the kitchen.

The skin on Lander's back twitched. He turned, slowly stirring his drink. "How was it out there?"

"Get me a coffee," Levi said in a tone that held no room for argument. He took a seat on a stool before arching a brow at Lander. Lander cocked his head but kept his mouth shut and reached into the cabinet for a new mug. "The far side of the forest looks stable. I didn't see anything."

"What forest?" I slid onto a stool next to him.

Levi leaned his forearms on the counter. "The Trapper's Forest. Some of the trackers thought they heard something over there. It's probably an old trap malfunctioning. The wind probably knocked a few around."

"The wind dies in the Trapper's Forest," Lander stated, sliding the coffee over to Levi. "That's what Dad always said."

Levi held Lander's gaze as he took a sip. "There wasn't anything."

I tilted my head. "I thought we weren't supposed to go in there alone?"

"Sometimes we have to," he replied quietly. "Go get dressed. You're going with Lander today."

"Claire is going to give you a tour of the pack," Lander added with an easy smile. "She's been excited to finally meet you and show you around." Lander tilted his chin to the window. "The weather is calm today, it will be a nice day to get out."

My heart fluttered as the anxiety butterflies started to bat their wings. "Okay."

Lander leaned on the opposite end of the counter. His eyes grew firm with determination. To Levi he said, "David said he was ready today if you were."

Levi took a sip of his coffee, as if Lander was rattling off the latest local news to him. "Where?"

"Hopper's Patch." Lander's eyes darted to me then back to Levi.

Levi was quiet for a moment. I could feel something pulse off him. My beast pressed forward, wanting to match the pulse—meet it with her own.

Levi chuckled under his breath. "You're going to have to learn how to control that or you're going to have this pack in a fit." He straightened. "And you?"

Lander matched his height, hands tight on his coffee mug. "We're not putting this off anymore. We're going to the patch."

"What's there?" I asked.

Levi cast me a side-glance. "We handle things our way. We talked about this."

My heartbeat picked up. Settling things "their way," with teeth and claws, made my stomach curl. "Levi—"

"No," he told me, his eyes pulsing a glow. "He's right. It's time." He nudged his chin to Lander. "Drop her with Claire, I'll meet you." He held Lander's eyes for a moment in which I was sure more was being said for only them to hear, before he looked back at me. "Go get dressed. We don't have time to waste."

Reluctantly, I handed my coffee to Lander, who dumped the remaining contents in the sink. Levi was still calmly sipping his when I walked out of my room with my warmer pair of shifters on, long yoga pants and a fitted base-layer top.

Pausing at the table, I opened my mouth a few times before closing it. Levi set his cup down. "Go on, Lander's not going to wait forever." He paused, watching me for a moment before he said, "I owe this to him at least."

"For what?"

"For being a royal piece of shit. It's well past time. Now go," he told me, words that felt like they stuck to my skin.

I met Lander outside and we walked in stride across the lawn and into the woods.

"Are you going to tell me what this patch business is about?"

Lander turned, watching me carefully. His eyes were heavy with exhaustion, although I had never noticed how tired his eyes always were. "It's a place my father used to take Levi and me. Where we could sort things out."

"What does he need to sort out?"

He was quiet, his lips in a firm line.

My jaw ticked. "Either you tell me, or I will eventually figure it out," I promised him.

He shook his head. "He's right about you."

"What do you mean?"

"You have a good nose on you," he quipped. "Levi took David's eye. Well, he didn't mean to. David tried to stop him from hurting anyone when he lost his mind after he found Eve and Lucas. David lost his eye, and I lost my brother," he explained, as if he was talking about how to put a shelf together.

"He's not lost," I found myself saying.

Lander arched a brow. "No, he's not, but we're wolves, Charlotte," he reminded me. "Sometimes blood is the only answer," he added before he clapped his hands. "All right, let's link up."

I didn't like how fast he shifted the conversation, but he was done with the topic. The glow in his eyes said as much. I nodded to him as something pressed into my head. I grabbed onto the line, letting it sizzle through to connection.

"We good?" he asked.

I nodded. *"Loud and clear."*

"Perfect, now follow me," he said, stepping into the forest. *"Claire's waiting at the pack house."*

I took one more look behind me then trotted after

Lander. Quickly, I picked up my pace and used a stump to spring into the shift that was starting to feel as natural as diving into water. Bones cracked and the familiar feeling of prickling came as fur covered my body, finishing right as my four paws hit the ground.

Lander was waiting for me close to a clearing. We ran until we hit a shoveled path that smelled of other wolves. My beast lowered her nose to the ground, trying to store the scents into memory while Lander ran next to us; his wolf had black fur and blazing silver eyes, but his body was sleek and leaner than Levi's. He also had a spot of white on his ear.

He curved around the path until it spat us out in front of the pack house. The trail of red I'd left was long gone, and only the paws prints of other wolves marred the snow.

He shifted to his skin and grabbed the door handle, opening it for me. I jumped up a step then let my skin come forward, hurrying into the lodge, where the warmth of the common room's roaring fire combed over me.

Lander waved me toward the grand wooden staircase at the center of the room. "Welcome to the pack house," he practically sang, arms waving at the log cabin–style building.

"This is really beautiful," I said, eyeing the Douglas fir beams lining the ceiling.

We jogged up the stairs in sync. My beast was so close I thought she would break out of my skin; she was so curious, so eager to take everything in. I was, too, but my nerves were eating at me. "This was originally built by my great-grandfather then renovated by my grandfather. Dad did some work too. Originally, my great-grandfather lived here with his family, but my grandfather Leonias hated all the commotion and wanted something quieter. So he changed it to be more for community use and moved the family to a smaller cabin," Lander noted.

"How long ago was that?"

He stepped onto the second floor, landing with a cheeky smile. "Very long ago. Dad renovated some about seventy years ago." My breath caught. It was hard to forget with his youthfulness how old he and Levi really were. "We age slow, Charlotte. Besides, I think Claire and I are doing pretty damn good for our nineties."

"Is it the Botox?" I teased.

He tipped his head back in laughter. "Liam thinks I'm a dinosaur. Although, when you're twenty-one, anyone over thirty is, I guess."

We turned down a hall that was lined with framed photos. There were pictures of people holding up fish they'd caught, children lined up for the curtain call of plays, and shots of the family throughout the years. One caught my attention, smaller and hung lower, of Levi and Eve in an office. She was sitting on his lap, pressing her lips to his cheek while he beamed at the camera. Something twisted in me. The beast in the back of my mind held back a whimper.

A door flew open at the end of the hall. A young boy who couldn't be older than twelve barreled out, dark hair flopping around his ears. "Dad!"

"Lyle!"

"Dad!"

"Lyle!"

"Dad!" He panted, stopping in front of us with an electric smile and bright, blazing silver eyes. "Can I take the snowmobile to school?"

Lander's brows went high. "Did you fall on your head?"

"Come on!"

"Absolutely not." He chuckled. "Lyle, this is Charlotte. Use your manners."

The boy turned his gaze to me. He pushed his dark hair out of his eyes. "Liam told me about you."

"Did he?" I asked, praying my cheeks didn't give away my inner embarrassment.

Lyle shrugged before slowly grinning, dimples just like Liam's showing. He turned to Lander. "Can *she* take me on the snowmobile?"

Lander pinched the bridge of his nose. "Is Mom still on her conference call?"

"Yeah, but she's finishing up. She said she left Charlotte clothes in the bathroom to change into."

Lander tossed his hands to his sides. "Why did we not start with this?"

"I have priorities, Dad."

"Right." Lander shook his head. "Better get downstairs and get a snack before school."

"No snowmobile?"

"What do you think?"

Lyle stepped around us, pausing with a sly smile. "I'll ask David," he said before tearing off for the stairs.

"And that's my youngest, Lyle." Lander laughed. He pointed to a wood door a few feet away. "There's a bathroom there. You might as well change first. Claire's office is there," he said, pointing to another door with hand-drawn pictures taped on it.

"Thank you," I replied, before stepping into the bathroom, where a set of joggers, a sweatshirt, and boots were laid neatly on a chair. Reaching for them, I tried to make quick work of throwing them on, but the anxiety adding a shake to my hands made the whole ordeal slower than I'd intended.

My beast nudged me, giving me the comfort I needed to still my hands. I let out a long breath and stepped out of the bathroom, and when I did, a door across from me opened.

The smell of spring and the feeling of a fire crackling to life rushed over me. My wolf came closer, scanning Liam, who had his hand frozen on the door handle. He was all lean muscle, golden hair still damp from a shower, and skin smelling of some kind of soap that sent a flush to my cheeks.

I brushed my hair out of my face and found myself pulling at my sweater.

We both stood there awkwardly, like two kids at their first middle-school dance.

"So." The door shut behind him. His silver eyes pulsed in a slight glow. "What brings you here?"

We both held our breaths before laughing quietly in the hallway. I blinked and the next thing I knew, he was hugging me. "Sorry I've been such a ghost," he told me, taking a step away. "Mom's had us on lockdown with the weather. I should have made a link with you before."

"It's fine," I said, trying not to stutter like it was my first time talking to someone of the opposite sex.

He touched his temple. "Ready?"

I nodded as something tapped on my mind. Quickly, I felt myself snatch it, like I was grabbing the line of a kite and reeling it in from the sky.

Liam smiled, dimples showing. *"Nice, now I can pester you even when it's a blizzard."*

"Lucky me," I offered with a tiny smile.

"Come on," he said out loud. "I'll take you to Mom's office."

Butterflies were taking flight in my stomach. I shook them away. The feeling was overwhelming and the last thing I needed was to be overtaken by it. But dammit if it didn't feel good to catch him glancing at me with a soft smile and warm eyes.

We had just turned to take a step when his hand shot out in front of me. He held a finger to his lips.

"I don't know why Ethan is being so damn stubborn about it," a woman hissed.

"Tell him he's coming when the snow melts or I will drag his and Evan's asses here," a frustrated voice I recognized as Lander's groused in reply.

"You tell him." The woman's voice was clipped. "I'm done being the peacekeeper."

Liam and I tilted our heads as we tried to listen. *"What's that about?"* I found myself asking.

"Levi," Liam told me.

My head whipped around to look at him. *"What about?"*

"Coming back—mending things isn't always pretty." He licked his lips. *"They know we're here. I'll tell you later. I promise."*

He reached for my hand, pulling me forward a step as

the door opened and a woman stepped out. Liam walked past me and bent to give the woman a quick kiss on the cheek before disappearing through the doorway.

"There she is," she greeted with a smile as warm as a sunrise. She gestured me forward. "Come on, Charlotte, I won't bite."

She had long milk-chocolate-colored hair, eyes a dark shade of brown that looked like candy, and full lips that plenty of women I'd known before would kill for. Nothing about her was fake—not the flawless complexion of her warm-brown skin, the fresh love bite on her neck, or the fullness of her brows.

When she smiled at me, I was ready for it. When you're a woman, you have to always be ready for it—for meeting another woman. Because you can't just meet another woman, oh no. You're meeting another red-blooded, kale-eating, moisturizer-loving female ready to rival any of your good hair days and outsquat you at the gym.

You're meeting your new friend-petition.

The girl you take to drinks with you because she's good-looking enough to attract the right kind of desired attention and makes you up your game when you're getting ready so you don't end up as her "cute" friend for the rest of the night. She's fun and kind, your friend-petition. You like her instantly and hate her for that. But you can't have her realizing that you're onto her in the same way that she never gives you the actual name of the foundation she uses because she doesn't want to give you an edge.

You're friends, but put into a ring, the two of you would go head-to-head until every bit of your bodies were past a makeup tutorial's ability to fix. It's the game. You can't hate the player in it, you can't hate her hustle—you want her hustle, and you recognize it instantly from the first moment you lock eyes.

I was looking for that recognition, that silent acknowledgment of duty when my eyes met hers. But it wasn't there. There wasn't an ulterior motive behind her kind eyes—there was just a welcoming smile and a beast who looked at me like she was smiling too.

"Well, I hope you're Charlotte, otherwise Levi has much more explaining to do," she said with a mischief that reminded me of Lander. "I'm Claire."

The tension in me deflated. "Hi," I replied.

Her nostrils flared, eyes growing a hair wider. "Lander was right—you smell like the moon," she said wistfully. She held her arms open for me, a silver crescent scar on her wrist flickering in the light. "He has so much explaining to do." She laughed as I stepped in to let her quickly hug me. "I'm glad you're here." When I pulled away, I could see in her eyes that she meant it.

"Me too," I answered with a soft smile of my own. "Oh! Thank you for the shifters, and the books. It's so kind."

"They fit fine?"

"Yes, they're really great. You really didn't have to do all that."

"We'll have to get you some stuff of your own when we go into town. I have some hair ties that are magicked, too, so you can shift with them—lifesavers. I'll get you some," she told me. "I can send you home with more books too. Although, I will warn you, I only have dirty romances left."

I bit my lip, trying to contain my laughter. She ushered me into her office, where Liam was lounging in an old chaise longue with teal cushions while Lander leaned next to the window. "We're off," she told them. She pointed at Liam. "Don't forget to get your brother today."

He rolled his eyes. "I thought about drop-kicking him off one of the cliffs with Rem."

Lander snickered while Claire waved him off. "Then you're scraping his ass off the bottom." She offered Lander a small smile. "Be safe," she told him with a quick dip of her head.

We made our way downstairs, then past a large living room with a roaring fire in a large stone fireplace; around a corner there was a large dark-wooded kitchen that smelled lemon clean. "The kitchen, as you can see," she said with a wave of her hands. "The pack has some meals together on holidays and during parties," she told me. She opened a cabinet and fetched two paper to-go coffee cups. "We try to do a monthly pack meal, if the weather holds. It's optional, but usually everyone comes. For morning and evening shifts for any job we always have breakfast and dinner provided. We also have tons of snacks in here for anyone who wants them, so help yourself whenever you want."

"Where is everyone?"

"Pack house is a little dead in the winter, but today it's nice, so I'm sure it will get busier later," she explained as we walked to the back doors. "In the winter, the shifts get skimmed down. It can be dangerous traveling around, but there is still plenty to do." She turned and backtracked like she was a tour guide at a museum. "This is more or less our common room. If there's a meeting for the entire pack, which we do around once a month, you'll come here. If it's nice, we'll hold them outside then cook out after, which is a lot of fun. You'll see."

We stepped outside to the backyard covered in a thick blanket of snow. A path wound through the trees to where a playground with a swing set rested, along with a large boulder, in the middle of the yard. We walked around it, curving with the path as the sun held its position in the sky, which was starting to cloud.

Claire led us down the path until we came up to a row of large silos, from which I could smell various grains as well as the scent of herbs. "We keep wheat and corn stored here for either our own use or for trade. Before the summer season, or the growing season, we have to have the growing plan ready along with all the projections for the pack council to go over. David oversees it along with pack security, so he wears two hats. For our agriculture, he's got a few wolves under him as well who help him manage everything."

"That sounds like a lot."

Claire nodded. "His job is essential for our survival. He and Bowie carry a hefty burden. Part of her responsibility is keeping tabs on all the game around here and in the region. She manages relations with the park rangers—"

"Do they know?"

She wiggled her head. "Yes and no. There are actually quite a few wolves that are rangers, her mate is one of them actually. Most of the human rangers are clueless but the ones that suspect something know enough to keep their mouths shut. Some humans are trustworthy, but it's best to not say a word. If that ever happens, don't panic. Call Levi or me or Lander and we'll get Derek or Elliot to handle it."

"Do you ever feel bad about that?"

"About what?"

"It's their memories, their minds." I ran my hand through my short hair. "I don't know, it seems . . ." *unsettling*, is what I wanted to say. Instead I told her, ". . . unfair."

She blew out a breath. "We have to protect ourselves. It's bad enough with the status quo. There's plenty of wannabe werewolf hunters who would love to lay their hands on one of us," she answered before taking a sip from her coffee. "Anyway, Bowie also is in charge of managing all the game harvest, so she is who you would get your hunting tags from."

"Tags?"

"Mhmm," she hummed. "We can't just go and take whatever we want, even though this is technically private property. Taking too much would be bad for the ecosystem around us, so it's her job to determine how much of what each wolf here can harvest and what percentage has to go to the pack for community storage. We also have to be careful. Humans will eventually notice if the game numbers are down on their land. We can't take chances."

I bit my lip, thinking of my buck.

Claire seemed to catch on. "Don't worry, Levi put that buck on one of his tags."

I let out a sigh of relief. "Sorry, I feel like an idiot."

She squeezed my shoulder. "Don't, you had no idea."

"So, what if you're low on supplies?"

"That's why everyone has to pitch in. We have the

reserves to supply everyone in case of a down season. Part of my job is that. If we're lacking then we seek out trades from other packs or tribes who know about us, which are few. If we have excess of anything, we store it, sell it, or trade it."

"You sound busy." In the moment of learning the weight she carried, my respect for her grew.

"I enjoy it," she admitted before pointing ahead of us to three large Plexiglas structures. "And these are the greenhouses. We have certain crops we stick to, and if someone wants something different, then they're on their own."

"What do you grow then?"

A wicked smile curled her lips. "Weed mostly, but don't tell Lander, he hates when I taste like it." My head snapped around to look at her before laughter rolled off her lips.

"Now, when you meet other wolves, it's like in the human world, make sure you greet them. A nice nod is always fine, but the animals in us will get their fur ruffled if you don't acknowledge them."

"Got it," I replied.

"Now, with the pack leads, you always address them by their title first unless you have special privileges. For example, you'll notice once you're around more wolves that people will address Levi as 'My First' and Lander as 'My Second.'"

"What about David and Bowie?"

"They both hate it, but when you meet other packs, it's good to always address the ranked wolves by their proper titles unless you're told otherwise. Now, with other packs, like Timber down south, you would address their pack lead, Talia, as 'Her First' and the second as 'Her Second.' More or less, they have sworn an oath to the moon to serve their packs, so when you say 'Her' you're referring to the moon itself."

I held my hands out. "So normal people, normal greeting."

She chuckled. "Exactly. Don't worry. You'll get the hang of things fast." She pulled the door open for me. "Go on, see for yourself."

Three females who were pulling up carrots raised their gazes to us. I felt my heartbeat pick up.

"I haven't brought any liquor if that's what you're wondering," Claire told them, breaking the tension that had me holding my breath.

The women laughed before they all nodded to Claire, and I didn't miss the respect they showed her. I felt her hand on my shoulder. "This is Charlotte, I'm showing her around today."

An older woman with long white hair held back by a crocheted headband stepped up. She had a crescent moon tattoo cupping the side of one of her eyes and what looked like stars on her fingers.

Her dark eyes looked me over before her wrinkled lips turned into a smile. "They were not lying, you do smell like the moon, child." My breath caught as she took my chin in her hand, tilting it around, methodically inspecting me. My beast walked forward, creeping closer to watch her. "Levi's doing well with you," she mused before taking me into her frail arms and hugging me to her. "I'm Signey, Tia's gran. Everyone just calls me Gran."

The other women all waved with bright smiles,

murmuring their names to me, which I promised myself I wouldn't forget.

Claire eyed the carrots. Her lips fell into a glum frown. "We have so many."

"It's good for you. Good for fertility," Gran teased.

Claire rolled her eyes. "Come on, Charlotte," she said.

"Don't be a stranger!" Gran called, waving good-bye.

"I'll try not to!" I called back, murmurs sounding again until the closed door silenced them.

Claire gave my arm a reassuring squeeze. "We haven't had a new wolf in a while."

She turned us down another path, the trees starting to thin and the ground curving down. I could smell animals on the breeze rolling off the hill, hear the murmurs of the sheep that made my wolf lick her lips. I reminded her that these were pack sheep, animals we were to care for and not hunt. She sighed and settled down, still licking her lips in her own form of rebellion.

We made it over the hill to see a few wolves were down at the bottom, while a flock of sheep gathered together in the sun.

"This is part of the herd," Claire explained. "There's another pasture where we have more of them. The barn is closer to that pasture—it's just beyond that tree line." I followed where her hand was pointing, west where trees waved in the breeze. "The barn is where the dairy cows are, and we have the chickens there too. We had some at our place but I made Lander move them. God love them, but they smelled awful and the rooster kept attacking Lyle."

"They're not scared of you?"

"No, most of them were born here and raised by wolves. If anything, I think some of them prefer our fur to our skin to be honest," she replied as we approached two dark, furry blankets covering bundles on the snow.

A hand lifted the edge of one blanket, and a face stared at me with sharp lavender eyes. A woman emerged from under the second blanket. Her long black hair waved in the wind like a flag, and from where I was standing, I could see that at least half her body was covered in tattoos.

"That's Bowie, she doesn't bite . . . hard, at least," Claire teased.

"Nice walk in the snow?" Bowie asked as a boy with lavender eyes climbed out of the first bundle. He was in his early twenties from the look of him, lanky, with dark hair tied up in a small bun and almost as many tattoos as the woman.

"It's not bad," Claire told her.

Bowie stepped to me, her unnerving violet eyes studying me. She had a scar that ran over her eyebrow and a gap between her front teeth that showed when she smiled. "So, you're Charlotte."

"I am," I told her.

She huffed a laugh under her breath. "You do smell like the moon," she observed. "It's good to finally meet you. Claire told us a lot about you already."

"All good?" I asked, rocking back on my heels.

"Mostly." She chuckled with a wink. "I saw the deer at the pack house."

Before I could think twice, I found myself saying, "I thought I would be a tracker. I mean, I would like to try."

Claire's mouth parted while I shut mine and half hoped

the snow would swallow me. Bowie tilted her head, eyes twinkling. "I think that's a very good idea." Her smile deepened into a full grin before she looked over her shoulder. "Remington, come here."

The boy walked cautiously over, looking me up and down. I felt the beast in me push closer, almost as if she wanted to banish any feelings of discomfort from my body by providing a curtain of her own.

"This is my son, Remi," Bowie said.

He held out his hand. Forcing a polite smile, I took it gingerly, never letting my gaze leave his strange lavender one. His nostrils flared as he shook my hand, letting it go quickly.

Claire squeezed my arm. "I'll be right back," she told me, then gestured to Bowie and they walked silently away.

"Probably just business," Remi explained with a bored tone. "They're always up to something. So, what do you think of all of this?"

"It's a lot to take in."

He nodded, kicking the snow in front of him. "So you're going to come track with us?"

I swallowed. "I want to do it. Elliot thinks I have a nose for it."

"You killed that big-ass buck in the middle of winter, I would say you probably have more than a nose for it." His tone was clipped. "Have you been to the Trapper's Forest yet?"

"Levi wouldn't let me go in."

He tilted his head. "It's just a forest."

"No, it's not," I replied, saying it more to myself.

"Elliot tell you that?"

"He didn't have to." Because unless you were a rock, you could discern the foulness in that forest.

Remi smirked. "I miss Elliot. He used to come into the forest with me all the time. We've never had a human in tracker training before."

I felt the hair on my arms rise as something simmered through me. "I'm not a human anymore."

Remi closed his mouth, saying nothing as his mother returned with Claire.

"Sorry," Claire said. "We should get moving."

Bowie's hair fluttered behind her, almost as if it was dancing. "I have a good feeling about you—I'll more than enjoy having you at training."

"Looking forward to it," I replied politely, although I was pretty confident that I was not going to enjoy choking this decision down and forcing myself to swallow it whole.

Remi nodded to me then followed his mother back to their blankets in the field. "Come on." Claire gently tugged my arm forward. We walked back to the pack house. The sky was still sunny but if I had learned anything, it was that the weather here could change in a blink. "Bowie is a wonderful wolf," Claire commented. "You can learn a lot from her."

A few wolves yipped playfully at us as they ran past us in their fur. Claire nodded and I waved, a smile on my lips. The beast in the back of my mind yipped in reply, taking in everything like a sponge yearning to soak up more.

She liked this feeling of belonging somewhere.

And I did too.

Claire took me on a different path than the one we had

come from, and we climbed up to where a set of rocks sat alongside a foot trail.

Next to her, I could see the entire valley. Mountains slept quietly in the background while a blanket of dark trees covered the base. The trees curled around and eventually grew thicker as they reached the edge of the valley, where they lined the pasture like soldiers. Behind the wall they created was a darkness that seemed as if it was sucking out the light around it.

"That's the Trapper's Forest."

"It is," Claire acknowledged. She paused, her gaze turning to me. "Never go in there alone. It's very dangerous, Charlotte. There's days I wish I could burn that forest down."

"Why don't you?" I asked.

She turned away from the forest. "Some things are better left undisturbed."

CHAPTER SIX

Snow started to fall on our way back to the pack house. At first it was a few delicate flakes, enough to seem magical. But by the time we got to the pack house, it was falling thick, like giant cotton balls being hurled down at us by angry cherubs.

I could smell him before I saw him outside. Liam was waiting impatiently, shifting back and forth on his feet.

"Dad said to take her back on the snowmobile," he told us.

Claire nodded. "Be careful. Link me when you're on your way back."

She pulled me into a tight hug. "May Her light shine on you. I'm so very glad you're here, don't hesitate to ask for anything." She pulled away then tapped on her temple.

I nodded to her as something delicate tapped on my mind, as if it was a fairy knocking on the door of a tiny home. Carefully, I let myself grasp the connection that fizzled to life like a streamer in the wind.

"Anything you need," her warm voice told me.

"I will. I promise," I said out loud, hugging her again.

I offered her one last smile before letting Liam pull me into the blizzard, which was roaring as it approached. In the distance I could see the front, pushing the clouds that rolled with lightning like electric eels getting caught up in a swirling current. Liam and I ran hard to a shed that was set alongside the pack house. I helped him pull open a door, which he dashed through so he could tear the cover off a snowmobile. "Ever ride on one of these?!" he yelled over the wind.

"No!" I shook my head as he started it, the sound of the engine blending in with the storm.

"Get on and hold on! We gotta move!" he shouted. Wordlessly, I climbed onto the vehicle behind him. He backed the snowmobile up then hit the gas, jerking us forward. I tried to hold on to the strap on the backseat to begin with, but after hitting a few rough patches of snow, I ended up with my arms around his waist.

The feeling of it was too good—too dangerous, and too addicting. It made my skin buzz, like I had drunk too much champagne without becoming drunk; my lips tingled and my skin was covered in goose bumps from the delicious chill running over me.

I didn't need whatever this thing was between us. I couldn't trust myself. How could I, after Nate? I barely knew

Liam. I barely knew anything about him. Bad people come from good families all the time.

Liam pulled up right next to one of the stone columns near the cabin, not daring to let the machine cross past them. He killed the engine; the snow was letting up slightly but the thunder in the dark clouds in the distance promised more was coming.

I jumped off and started to walk away, but he grabbed the arm of my coat, stopping me. I turned to him in question. He looked at his hand and let go of my jacket, something sad hanging over him. "Be careful."

Thunder cracked overhead as the wind bullwhipped around us. It was getting too dangerous to be outside. Soon the snow would make it impossible to see anything.

"Come inside! It's about to get bad!" I shouted. His eyes had been on the cabin, like they were looking at a memory he wanted to run to and run away from all in the same breath. "Liam?"

His silver eyes snapped to me, and in that moment it felt like it was the middle of a scorching summer in the desert. "I'll be fine! Don't be a stranger, yeah?"

He leaned back in his seat on the snowmobile as the wind violently whipped through his hair. "Liam, don't be stupid! It's bad—"

"I'll be fine! Get inside before it gets worse!"

I looked back at the house. Levi wasn't there but I could smell him close by.

I turned to Liam. "He's not the boogeyman, you know?"

"Oh, I know!" He half laughed, a sardonic tone that didn't sit well with me. He turned the snowmobile on and started to back it away. "He's worse!" He grinned, trying to make his words a joke. They weren't, and I noticed. So did the beast in the back of my mind, which hummed a low growl in displeasure at his tone.

I bounded up the steps and into the cottage. Inside, Levi was cooking chili. The smell of it felt like him, and the sight of a whiskey bottle on the counter took the storm away from me.

"Thought something spicy would be good today," he said without looking up.

"You thought right," I agreed breathlessly, shrugging my jacket off as the snow pounded harder outside. "Do we need to tie anything up outside?"

"No, I got it."

The fire was starting to dwindle. Without asking, I walked over and tossed two more logs on it before slipping my shoes off and putting my feet up to its warmth.

"It's going to get worse between you and him if you feed it," Levi said plainly.

"It's nothing."

"It's not nothing."

I sighed, my warring thoughts flooding back.

"Don't feed it," he repeated. "It's only going to get worse if you do."

"Is that such a bad thing?"

I hadn't realized that I'd said the question out loud until the stretch of silence stifling the cabin said otherwise.

Levi finally said, "One day, you'll have more than just this flimsy thing. You don't want to tarnish that if you can help it."

I was already tarnished.

My beast disagreed, but I knew that anywhere I went all my skeletons would be trailing behind me. The scars on my flesh were proof enough of the misfortune that followed me, the damage that had already been done. I may not be the girl who hid in the bathroom to get away anymore, but she still stained every fiber of me.

"You better decide now, though," he said.

"Decide what?"

"If you're going to let this shit eat you up, spit you out. You think this is bad? Meeting your true mate is going to knock you on your ass only to pull you up by your toes so it can beat your ass again."

"I know," I groaned into my hands; it's not like that scene wasn't vivid in my nightmares already.

"No, you don't."

"Levi, I—"

"You don't."

I jumped at the sound of his voice. The growl rolled off him, feeding the crackling feeling around me as the air was sucked out of the room. Something pulsed in me, meeting the challenge that I felt brewing. My beast ran forward, shaking her fur out before pacing in the back of my mind.

Something was wrong.

Turning, I looked over his form. A stain of blood was growing on his back, deep claw marks raked up his forearms, and his cheekbone was sporting an angry bruise.

"Oh my god." I sucked in a breath. "Levi, what have you done?"

I ignored his growl as I shot into Derek's bathroom for

the first aid supplies. Levi's shirt was ruined with his blood. He probably needed fucking stitches. How had I not smelled that?

God, I was so stupid. Too consumed with something else, with my head up my own ass, to notice.

I ran back to the kitchen. Before he could argue, I took the bottle of whiskey from the counter and walked it back to the kitchen table. It looked like Levi had made a dent in it already, but he wasn't taking another sip without complying.

"I'm fine."

"Bullshit."

"It's not bad."

"So your shirt was half red this morning?" He growled at me but I only growled back harder, my fangs showing in my mouth. "I'll even let you have your whiskey. Come on, you probably need stitches."

"And you know how to do that how?"

"Derek," I answered. Although I wasn't that sure, I knew I was the best Levi had at the moment. I would make it work. "Seriously, you can't just let that go."

"We heal fast. I'm fine, Charlie girl."

"No, you're not."

"Char—"

"You're not." I bit out the words with a snarl of my own chasing them. "Pull that shit with someone who isn't as fucked-up as you are and maybe they'll believe you."

He sighed, setting the wooden spoon down on a plate next to the pot before covering it with a lid. "Fine."

I laid out the supplies on the table while he pulled his shirt off. It took everything I had not to gasp at the mangled skin that was his back—the place where teeth had ripped through his flesh. Maybe he was right? Maybe we did heal fast, but I didn't care. I wasn't going to let him walk around like this.

He pulled up a chair and sat backward in it. I took a long sip from the whiskey bottle before handing it to him. "Jesus Christ, Levi." He had another set of claw marks raking across his ribs that were angry and red; even angrier bruises would come in the morning. "I think—" I paused. "Levi, this looks like it was to the bone?" Fuck. I was so sure I could see his fucking bones through the mangled flesh.

"Not that," he said, nodding to his ribs. "But you better remember one thing: when you go after someone, you don't quit until it's to the bone."

My fingers curled away from his skin. "Levi?"

"To the goddamn bone, Charlotte." I felt like holding my breath because the pulse coming off him was so overpowering that it almost knocked me over. I felt my own skin start to sizzle, like electricity was dancing up from my fingertips until it licked the hills of my shoulders.

I cocked my head. I was not a violent person. I detested how *Nate* used it. How he threw me around as if I was a rag doll. But I also knew I was never going to let someone like Nate have his way with me again.

Levi turned around, his eyes glowing as they met mine. "Charlotte, you do not let go until you feel their fucking bones. Do you understand?"

I felt my beast settle down. I nodded, because in that moment, I more than understood. "Yes."

He turned forward, leaving me with his shredded back. I

looked at his shoulder, which was hardly intact. "We should call the pack doctor." He had mentioned that they had one, they had to have one . . .

"Just stitch me up, I've had worse." He took a long sip of whiskey. "It's just chipped. It will heal itself."

I rubbed my face then walked to the sink and washed my hands. Before I walked back, I grabbed a bottle of vodka, because we were out of disinfectant. I wasn't sure if it was good to use, but they used it in some of the doctor shows, so it seemed safe. "Do you want to divulge?"

"Not really." Levi took another swig of the whiskey then nodded to the bottle of vodka I was holding. "That will work."

I didn't ask. I poured a bunch on some cotton balls and cleaned the wounds as best I could. He didn't even flinch.

And I hated it.

I could handle rage-filled Levi. I could handle annoyed, pissed-off, grumpy, assholish, eager-to-watch-me-run-a-sled-of-shit-around-the-house Levi, and even chain-smoking self-depreciating Levi. But there was something about sad Levi that was different.

He looked like he'd swallowed a bottle of one-hundred-proof heartbreak. The kind of heartbreak that's slow, that rusts at the edges and grows like a sickness so it can continue to slowly eat away at you until you're ready to rip your own chest open.

The whole concept of a mate shook me, but even I couldn't deny how the idea of losing one made me feel. It scared the living shit out of me. The idea of having your soul torn in two was unfathomable—a sentiment the wolf in the back in my mind agreed with, as she howled low and sad, like a tragic songbird.

I tossed the dirty cotton balls and swabs away then threaded a needle, careful to follow the stitching pattern that Derek had taught me before he left. "How did the other guy look?" I asked, needle piercing skin that only twitched like a fly had landed on it.

"I used to ask my son that."

I kept back the heavy breath that wanted to escape. "I only got in one fight my whole life."

"How'd that work out?"

"I was in first grade. Some boy ripped all the hair out of my best friend's doll, so during recess, I told him to apologize. He told me to eat shit. He was just a bully, so mean to everyone. He told me that the reason my dad died was because I had cooties and brought them home to him."

"Shit kids."

"Yeah," I agreed. "Anyhow, I was so mad. He picked on everyone. My friend had a stutter and he used to make her cry all the time. I had no idea what I was doing, but I ended up knocking his front teeth out. I didn't even realize what I'd done until I saw his teeth at my feet."

"And?"

"He got up and I hit him again. I guess I broke his nose? There was so much blood. It was all over the white shirt that my mom had ironed forever that morning. I was more worried about her being mad that I'd ruined my shirt. She'd spent so much time on it.

"He didn't get up. He just lay there and cried. My friend pulled me away and the next thing I knew I was in the principal's office. They called my mom, who took me home early. I was so scared of what she thought. Whitney Houston was playing on the radio. I remember because I loved her but I couldn't enjoy her song because I was so worried.

"My mom"—I paused as a smile broke over my lips—"she finally asked me, 'Well, how did the other guy look?' I told her. She told me that next time I should try to use my words, gave me a long lecture over dinner about it, but for a few moments she seemed proud of me."

I pierced Levi's skin with the needle again, the last time before I would tie off the stitch. Fixing him up was more painful for me to see than it was for him to endure, it seemed.

"They'll think twice before they get on their high horse again," Levi said.

"Who?"

"The other guys."

"And you?"

He took a long sip of whiskey. "Be better about watching my hackles."

"Who were the other guys, Levi?"

Silence greeted me before he tilted his head to me. "I have a few other guys to deal with."

I paused, trying to keep my own anger from boiling over. "Was it David?"

He nodded. "Sure was."

"Levi, why?"

He snickered. "An eye for an eye, I suppose."

I bit my lip, knowing the answer even before I asked the question. "And the other?"

"Lander."

My hands stilled. "He's your brother," I hissed, tying off the thread.

"This is our world, Charlie. It's how we work things out."

"Wolves—or you?"

"Us, wolves, both? Hell if I know. It's how my brother and I work things out."

I paused, leaning on the table as anger raged within me. Levi chuckled into the bottle. "I know what you're thinking. There's no need."

"You sure?"

"You think *I* look bad?" He took another drink before a dark smile spread over his mouth like a disease. "He knows who's still in charge of this fucking pack now."

"Only a few more," I told him as I tied off the thread.

The bottle was almost gone with his next swig. "Get to it, then, we've got plenty of bottles."

"The chili smells good."

"I'm a shit cook. You're lucky it was frozen."

"You're not that bad."

"I'm the worst, Charlie girl."

"I know."

He glanced at me over his shoulder, his eyes almost black with something creeping, the beast in him begging to be let out. Like he was just trying to survive—like for a moment he didn't trust his other half.

"You're not the only one hanging out at the bottom of the barrel," I told him.

"Self-deprecation doesn't suit you."

"And it suits you?"

"You should have let me keep smoking."

I started to sew up the next area, this time moving faster in the comfort of doing something that now felt familiar. "You can't die on me. I need you."

He grunted in agreement. "Why didn't I kill you again?" he asked, his mood slightly lightening.

I let out a laugh of my own. "I honestly have no fucking idea."

He took a sip of whiskey, almost choking on it before he was laughing with me. The two of us, broken in our own ways but putting each other back together through the sounds of buzzed laughter and the glue of our shared misery.

"Really, though." I laughed. "Why didn't you kill me?"

He was quiet. Too quiet. My hands kept steady but for a moment I thought I'd stepped into dangerous territory again.

"Because I made a promise," he finally said.

My mind flickered back to the two silver bullets that he had left in my room the morning after I had made it through my first full moon. Sealing a deal he had made with me—because he'd promised me he would help me if I didn't die on him that night.

"You did," I murmured back. "You can't quit on me."

"My beast damned well wouldn't let me anyway," he said, and chased his words with whiskey.

He must have been drinking long before I showed up. I hadn't seen Levi truly inebriated before and I wasn't sure if I wanted to. If this was what it looked like when he was a calm drunk, I wasn't sure I wanted to see the other emotions when he was in this state.

"And I tried, oh, I fucking tried. Nothing worked. He

always fucking stopped me," he drawled out, my heartbeat picking up with each sip he took. "I couldn't understand why he didn't want to be with them again." He looked at me, and I saw it—the red in his eyes. It was so faint that it looked like he'd just been scratching at them, but the coloring and haziness was so familiar—the rogues that'd bit me had the same haze in their eyes. I couldn't mistake it even if I wanted to. "I could never pull the fucking trigger. He wouldn't let me get near a damn knife—he took over. I would wake up days later fed and watered. Couldn't even succeed in starving myself."

The thought of Levi trying to hurt himself made my throat clench. The idea of losing him—I'd never really thought about it. I never really thought that Levi could actually be gone, but I'd hated the prospect. It terrified me. The thought that he was so close to losing it made the air leave my lungs. My beast wanted to rip the idea apart.

"I'm almost done." I tied off the thread then taped a bandage over the area. Before he could take another sip I held my hand out. "Let me have some?"

He handed the bottle to me, not questioning my ask. I took a swig then carried it with me to the kitchen, tucking it away in a cabinet before checking the chili. I hadn't realized that my hands were shaking until the wooden spoon rattled against the pot. I paused and tried to calm myself, tried to pass it off as nothing. "The chili is almost ready."

His eyes were like theirs had been—I couldn't lose him to that.

"Charlotte."

"Mmm?"

"Charlie, look at me."

I stopped and looked over at him, his eyes turning more human as the beast in him seemed to settle. The red was gone and I prayed I would never see it again in his silver eyes. "I'm not going anywhere."

"Do you swear? Swear on the moon?"

"Fuck the moon," he answered with a tired laugh.

I sighed, relief flooding as his normal mood of cranky seeped back in. "Do you promise me?"

He looked me right in the eyes, chin tucked into hands folded together before he nodded slowly to me. "I already did."

My fingers drummed on the counter. "They miss you, Levi."

He hummed. "I miss them."

"If I got into that forest, it only seems fair that you come out of this one."

He grunted. "You should have let me keep smoking."

"You hated smoking."

He looked back at me. "I did."

CHAPTER
SEVEN

The winter felt like it would never end—even when spring
won the battle of seasons with a few sunny days, somehow
snow would plummet again from the sky as icy temperatures
whipped around us. But eventually it did relent, and spring
set in. Levi said the melt-off had begun and from the looks
of it he was right, since we were constantly walking around
in a sludgy mess. But I didn't care; I was thrilled to have
more bright days than gray ones.

The sun was already out, the snow in the middle of the
yard almost gone, and Bowie was walking across our lawn
with a smile on her face and a spring in her step. She didn't
give two shits about whose land she was walking on. She
walked over like it was Sunday morning and there was a stack

of pancakes waiting for her. She jogged right up the steps, her eyes meeting mine through the window. She winked at me before knocking on the front door like she was the most well-mannered thing this pack had ever seen.

I opened the door, leaving the screen one between us. "Teeth are only sharp if they catch you," she whispered.

Levi hissed curses under his breath as he stepped around me. He opened the screen door, not moving a muscle for the lanky female in front of him.

"Good morning, My First," she greeted Levi with a respectful nod. She turned her playful gaze to me. "Morning, Charlotte."

I closed my mouth and offered her a small wave. Levi was watching her like he was trying to decide whether to skin her eyelids off or invite her in.

"Typically, you reply with 'Good morning, Bowie,' before you offer me coffee. We have to work on your manners, My First." She cocked her head, eyes slightly dilating as she and Levi fell into a trancelike state. "Oh Levi, you'd have to catch me first. I told you I was coming for her today. The snow's breaking, which means we start tracker training. Now, are you going to invite me in for coffee or not?"

Levi let out a long breath, eyeing me before he looked back at her. I arched a brow at him. "Go get dressed."

I nodded and ran back to my room to throw on a pair of shifters. When I came out, Bowie was still waiting at the front door.

"Mind your hide," he told me. He shook his head, laughing under his breath while Bowie watched us curiously. "I forgot, do you want some coffee?"

She snorted a laugh. "Some of us have work to do," she teased. "Seems like you do too."

Levi smiled, all his teeth showing. "Lander and I have business to attend to today."

Bowie leaned back, nodding in approval. "She'll be back before dark."

Levi said nothing; instead he dipped back into the house, blending in with the shadows.

Bowie smiled like she had won fifty bucks on a scratch ticket. "Come on." She waved me forward, purple eyes glittering in the sun.

Jogging forward, I fell in step with her. The silence was too much for me. "So? Training, then?"

She chuckled under her breath, cutting her eyes to me. "The minute the snow melts it means it's time. So, yes, it's time for tracker training."

I scratched the back of my neck. "I am going to apologize in advance for the burden."

She laughed. Loudly. So loudly the birds in the trees flew away while I cocked my head. My beast was nudging my brain, almost as if she wasn't sure if we should run or keep walking.

"Oh Charlotte, training you is no burden at all. It's going to be my absolute pleasure."

"Uh-huh." I looked around the forest, my beast stepping closer. "Why is that?"

She smirked. "I know when a rock moves on this land." Her eyes glimmered, and for a second, they looked closer to those of her wolf than a human's. She looked at me with what seemed like hope, but I was too startled to be sure. "Levi's barely left that house. I would know. We've all been having to come to him, which I don't mind, but being cooped up for that long isn't good for anyone. So, my moon-blooded one, it seems to me that if you get better, he gets better, which is better in all ways, right?"

"I—" I froze in place. It was at that moment I realized I would be meeting more people—people I would have to work with. It was one thing to do it with Claire by my side, another to do it on my own.

Bowie gave my arm a light squeeze. "It's time for you to get out of that cabin too."

"You're right," I agreed, on the edge of a shaky breath.

Her long, elegant fingers, which were decorated with inky swirls of tattoos, tapped her temple. Immediately it felt like a hummingbird fluttering close to my brain. I closed my eyes and let myself grasp the line that raced in like a dragon-fly sailing across a lake.

She winked. "*Keep up,*" she said into our link, before shifting into her fur without warning.

She was so fast that before my paws could even hit the ground out of my shift, she was out of sight. My beast pressed forward, her nose in the air, sniffing out the trail that was as clear as day to us. We charged ahead, following the scent down a hill and around a few boulders, where Bowie was waiting for us. She yipped at me as the wind combed through inky fur that had patches of brown scattered through it, like a watercolor painting that had bled together. She was lanky, her lean legs clearly built for running.

We ran through the forest and past the pack house until the land sloped upward. We were closer to the mountains, where boulders and trees stood taller and the land curved in nonsensical ways. It made following her even harder as I tried to keep my footing on the tricky terrain. Eventually she led us through the forest to a clearing.

About a dozen people were gathered in the sunlight. Liam slid off the boulder he was perched on, strolling over casually, while Remi's calculating lavender gaze held mine as he stood. Bowie shifted into her skin and I followed; cold air hit my arms the second Liam reached me.

"I wasn't sure if he was actually going to let you come, but I'm glad he did."

"Why wouldn't he?" I asked.

Liam opened and closed his mouth a few times before rubbing the back of his neck. "Dad was just surprised, that's all."

"Right," I huffed. "So, what do you know about this?" I whispered.

"You don't need to whisper, remember?" he teased with a wink that made my cheeks flush more than it should have. *"And you'll see."*

Bowie walked over to another male, who was lurking off to one side, older, with an eye patch. He had a military-style haircut, with scars littering his cool, umber-brown skin. There were gashes along his bare torso, deep and angry wounds that came from claws. His shoulder had a nasty bite mark that looked like it was slow to heal; it would leave more scars to match the others on his body.

My eyes reached his face to find his one green eye locked on me. I looked down at my toes.

"Who is that? With the eye patch?" I asked Liam.

"*David,*" he answered.

I could hear Levi's words echoing in my mind. *An eye for an eye, I suppose.*

Carefully, I looked up again. In my gut, I knew who'd torn his skin and whose bite marks were on his shoulder. I found myself without an ounce of pity.

Bowie murmured a few things to David before she waved her hands at everyone, gesturing us forward. I pushed my hair behind my ears. It was still too short to reach my shoulders, but finally long enough to have what passed for a workable ponytail. Remi walked up to stand next to his mom.

"Remi," she said, a look in her eyes that made him stand a little taller.

"Right." He half yawned. "So, this is tracker training—" He paused, smirking as he looked over the group. "In case you maybe found yourself lost this morning."

The group laughed together except for me. Because for a moment, I wondered if I was in fact lost. If this was something that I could do—or if I had made the worst mistake.

"*Are these people all pack?*" I asked Liam.

"*Some are from other packs coming to train, others are pack and now old enough to officially apply.*"

"*But Remi is already one?*"

Liam snorted. "*He has like two years on me, but he was the youngest to ever do it. His own mother couldn't keep him out of the forest.*"

"Okay," Bowie said with a clap. "Some of you know me, others are new, but regardless, we're excited to have all of you this year. Before I put you into groups, a reminder of our schedule: we will have you training for eight weeks. At the end of the eight weeks is the final challenge in the Trapper's Forest. The forest is absolutely not to be ventured into by any of you alone until you are a tracker. And even then, many parts of it need my specific approval. This is dangerous. We have lost wolves during this training, good wolves, so if for any reason you want to stand aside, there is no shame at all."

It felt like all eyes were on me, combing over me like a thousand cuts to any confidence I had. The beast in me snapped her teeth, pushing closer because she was the only one of us that had an inkling of boldness to her. For a moment I felt like raising my hand. Stepping back. Standing down.

But that moment was gone the second Bowie spoke again. "Good, welcome. Now, to be a tracker, you must finish the final challenge with your team, the Hunt. We will be putting you in those teams today," she explained as David pulled a small cloth bag from a knapsack on the ground and held it up for everyone to see. "You'll draw a stone from this bag. The stone has a color painted on it—red, blue, orange, or black. You will be in the group with the same color. Very complex, I know," she added with a chuckle. "You will absolutely not be allowed to change groups once you are placed in yours. No exceptions."

"Fantastic," I murmured to myself.

I felt Liam's shoulder bump mine. *"Don't worry, I'll try to manifest us being in the same group."*

I bit back a smile. *"I don't think that's how it works."*

"You never know," he added with a soft tone that chased my anxiety away.

David circulated with the bag. He held it open for each

person, nodding to them one by one as they each drew a stone, slowly making his way toward us.

My heart kicked to life. Liam tipped his chin at David. "What's up, big D?"

David cracked a smile. "Don't worry, I saved a good one for you."

Liam stuck his hand into the bag and pulled out a blue stone. "My favorite, how did you know?"

David snorted a laugh then stepped to me. His smile died as his single ivy-green eye looked me up and down. "There's one left, but you still have to draw."

I bit my lip and reached into the bag like a snake was about to bite me, pulling out a smooth white stone stained with red paint. My eyes darted to Liam's blue stone, while dread bubbled in my gut.

David nodded to me, his nostrils flaring. "You smell like the moon."

I snapped my gaze back to David's. "Thanks?" What the fuck was I supposed to start saying to that anyway? Like, *Oh! How lovely, I used this new perfume, it's called getting bit by a fucking werewolf.*

"Damn, looks like we're on opposite teams."

"Yeah." My fingers rubbed over the red paint. "We are."

"All right, get into your groups and we'll get moving," Bowie called.

Liam gave my wrist a gentle squeeze. *"You'll be fine. If you need something you can just link me. I can take you home later if you want?"*

"Sounds good," I answered, probably less enthusiastically than he would have liked.

Looking around at the various groups, I found two people standing close to the tree line with red-painted rocks in their hands. My stomach slightly turned because the one female in the group was not like Claire. No smiles here, just amber eyes carefully looking me over as if they were going to dissect me later.

She looked younger than me, but dark, inquisitive eyes framed by full brows made her seem so much older. She pushed a handful of icy silver locks that were a stark contrast to the rest of her long black mane behind her ears. "I'm Christina, but everyone calls me Tia." Her nostrils flared. "You're the human, aren't you?"

"I'm not a human anymore," I quickly corrected her.

"No you're not," the male next to me said. He tipped his square chin to me, arms crossed over a thick chest that he seemed to slightly puff out for show. "I'm Jake."

"Just Jake," Tia teased.

Jake cracked a smile at her, his fit arms relaxing. He was plenty taller than me, but a hair shorter than Tia, who was willowy. He looked scrappy, like he was the kind of kid who was always underestimated in a playground fight. He scratched the side of his head, sandy hair in a buzz cut like David's.

His brown eyes locked on me as my beast came closer, as if she was sliding on her belly through the paths of my brain—closer and closer to my skin. "So, you really live with Levi?"

I cocked my head. "Yeah. I'm Charlotte."

Tia coughed in her hand then looked at Jake expectantly. She turned back to me with a tight smile. "I'm from the States but my aunt Talia leads a pack down South. I'm taking a gap year before I go to college and wanted a job I could take to any pack so I had more options for school."

"School," Jake teased. "Baby Tia is growing up."

She rolled her eyes at him. "All right, old man."

"Bro, I am so not old." He paused, and eyed me. "We're probably the same age."

"I think I have a few years on you," I replied dryly. What the hell? I turned back to Tia. "Are you staying here?"

She nodded. "Yeah, with my gran. She's pack here." She paused, looking at Jake again then rolling her eyes. "Jake is from next door."

He scoffed. "The pack over."

"Which one?" I asked.

"The only one next door," he replied matter-of-factly.

I crossed my arms. "This pack is surrounded by other packs. Lotta neighbors."

"She's right, Jake," Tia agreed.

He let out a breath through his nose. "Hemlock Pack."

"And did you want to be a tracker there?"

"No," he scoffed. "But I do want to be our Head of Security after our current one retires. He won't let me be officially considered until I do this. So here I fucking am."

"He's staying with David," Tia told me.

Jake kicked a rock. "Yeah, who was a real fucking joy this morning." He shot his eyes to me, both of us knowing exactly what he meant. "Seems like his shoulder is still bothering him."

I felt my beast press forward but I pushed her back. We weren't taking the bait. I had been baited too many times and was done walking right into petty little traps.

"So you've been here a while, though, right? We haven't seen you on the full moon runs," Tia asked.

"Just a pup." Jake chortled, casting me a side-glance. "Can't handle herself yet."

I stared at the rocks on the ground, trying to ignore the way his words twisted in my gut.

"You good?" I heard Liam say.

My eyes flickered over to his. He was standing next to a male with shaggy brown hair who looked around his age, and a younger woman with two long black braids down her back. My lips turned to a small smile. *"Yeah,"* I answered, but I felt like I was starting to understand why Levi liked his isolation.

"Let's get started," Bowie said. "We'll spend half our time training in the forest and the other half on training courses. Today, however, we want to get a gauge of your skills, so we'll be doing a hunt. You and your team will track down two doves that we killed earlier and hid somewhere in the forest. We've painted them with your team's color. Now, during the final challenge the entire Trapper's Forest is fair game, however, today you'll find a border that is marked by white chalk. That is the border between the training forest and the Trapper's Forest. Do not cross it. Track the birds down and bring them back. You must do this as a team. I will know if you did not."

Tia raised her hand. "How long do we have?"

"Sundown," Bowie answered.

She looked at each of us, as if to confirm that we understood, before nodding to Remi. "Some of the other trackers are already in the forest, there to keep an eye on you in case you need assistance. If you ever want practice outside of this exercise then I suggest you bribe one of them—and bribe them well, they're not cheap dates."

Remi snickered before backtracking to the trees. "Can we head out?"

Bowie nodded with a smile. "Run fast."

He winked at her. "Like the wind," he said before he tore off with David and a few other men and women on his heels.

She looked back at us with a crooked half smile. "You'll notice that I haven't told you the sex of the birds, where you are, or really anything useful—welcome to being a tracker. We're sometimes given very little and are expected to perform regardless. Does anyone have any more questions before I release you?"

Everyone shook their heads.

"Happy hunting then," she said. She jogged into the forest, easily blending in with the trees until she was out of sight.

Tia crossed her arms over her chest. "All right, so how do we want to do this?"

Jake eyed me. "What did you do before this, again?"

"I worked in a law firm, mostly administrative."

He let out a long whistle. "Okay, Tia, what do you think?"

She wiggled her head. "We have no idea how big this area is, but it's obviously limited before the chalk cuts us off from the Trapper's Forest."

"This isn't it?"

Tia shook her head. "No, this forest turns into it, though, eventually, once you get deeper into it." She paused and eyed the trees. "I say we head north, put our noses to the ground, and start there. See if we can find something."

"Sounds good," Jake said with a confident nod. "Let's link up then. I say we run together but fan out a little to cover more ground at first, at least until we get a trail."

"Yeah, I love that idea," Tia added with a bright smile. "I'll take Charlotte," she added, like she was now my new babysitter.

I bit back my frustration. "Don't worry about me, I'll keep up."

Jake rolled his eyes. "Look, desk jockey—"

The beast in me charged forward, pressing closer while electricity curled deliciously around my arms and down to my fingers. Tia's jaw snapped shut, while Jake cocked his head. I bit the inside of my cheek, gently pulling my beast back, settling her down.

"I'll be fine," I answered, although I wasn't even convinced myself.

"I'll make the link," Jake said slowly, his gaze still fixed on me.

I could feel a pressure at my temple. My beast was so close now, almost like I could feel her under my skin. I had let so many people into my head. I hated knowing that they were only a breath away from the nightmares—the night terrors that still kept me up. Levi told me that the links were just for communication, not mind reading, but it felt like too much at times. Like I was giving up too much of my own privacy.

Jake arched a brow. "Levi explained this to you, right?"

I smiled politely, and snatched at the pressure that was still knocking at the door of my brain. Carefully, I grasped the pressure, letting it into my mind like a jet of cold air.

Jake tipped his chin to Tia. "We ready?"

Tia nodded before her eyes caught me from the side. "So, how's your nose?"

I frowned pensively, although something gave me a spark of hope. "Pretty good, I think," I slowly answered. "Levi thinks so."

"Well, let's see it then?"

There was a challenge in her voice and I didn't have to look at Jake to see his suspicion. I felt the beast in me start to pace, ready to break out. Wind combed over my shoulders as I took a long breath and jumped, sailing through the air in a symphony of crackling as fur combed over my skin and claws replaced my fingernails.

A set of sandy paws landed next to me, carrying with them a thick body that surged forward. There was a slice in Jake's ear that mirrored the same slice he had on his ear when he was in his skin.

Another set of paws trotted up—a sleek silver-coated body with bright-amber eyes that glowed in the darkness of the forest. She had four black paws, and the tip of her left ear looked like someone had dumped an inkwell of onyx on it.

Tia cocked her head at me expectantly. I put my nose to the ground and let my beast fully take over. The birds we were looking for were dead. Hopefully they hadn't broken the birds' necks; hopefully there was blood, because that would be the easiest thing to pick up.

I sat back and let my beast drive a little more. She looked around to take everything in—every tree, every shrub, every rock, as if it was the most natural thing ever. My beast scooted her nose along the ground, sucking in scent until we found ourselves near a bush. Looking up, we spotted crimson drops of blood decorating the edge of a leaf.

"Here, there's blood," I said.

Tia slid in next to me, shifting quickly to her skin. Her fingers lifted the leaf up to the sky before she put her nose to it. "It's a bird. I can't tell which kind."

"So which way then, blood pup?"

Ignoring Jake, I walked around the bush, nose still in the air. There were trails of so many things in so many directions.

"It smells like iron this way," I told Tia, nudging my chin to the east.

Her bones cracked quickly as she sifted back into her fur. She tipped her nose to the sky and yipped. *"It's blood. Fresh. Similar to what's on the bush."* She paused, her amber eyes twinkling at me. *"Maybe Levi is right about you after all."*

We ran through the trees, silently following a trail that grew fainter with every step we took into the darkness of the forest. After a few hours of searching, we curled around a boulder and it hit me: a putrid smell that made my legs lock to a halt. I turned on my heel and chased after the scent that felt out of place, as if it was screaming to be found.

Shifting to my skin, I walked over to a shrub, a broken limb catching my eye. A broken limb that had a few faint red marks on it. Quickly, I lifted it to my nose, the smell of paint immediately making its putrid self known.

Tia nudged my arm with her snout. *"What? What is it?"*

"Paint," I said with a smile. "They had to have carried it through here."

Jake paused and looked at the branch. *"Well, fuck me, you got lucky."*

"The paint had to be wet when they hid them," I mused.

Jake nudged my arm. I lowered the branch to his snout, letting him smell it again.

"I'm going to see if I can't catch a trail off this."

It didn't take him five minutes before he looked up and dashed forward. I followed and shifted to my fur again, my beast happy to be out and in an element that felt closer to home than my home ever really was. We ran in focused silence except when we found more fragments of red paint. Jake ended up tasting a chip off a leaf and insisted it was different than the others, that there were other birds with different paint on them to confuse us, which I thought was ridiculous. Bowie seemed like she had a few tricks up her sleeve, but that sounded way too involved, even for her.

We ended up continuing on the trail, but eventually the paint trail faded. Eventually we were just running through a forest aimlessly, but something in me told me to keep going. Something in me was itching to just push through a few more trees.

Jake skidded to a stop next to a small pond and took a long sip of water before shifting to his skin. I half dunked my head into the water, letting my beast drink before shifting, too, then looked up at the sky where the sun was threatening to fade.

"We should head back—it's getting late and we've run into a dead trail," Tia said.

"I don't think it's dead."

"There's nothing, there's been nothing," Jake clipped.

"I've done this before, that's dead. We should have split up earlier." His eyes cut to me.

Tia caught his gaze then shook her head slowly. "You know that's a bad idea."

I let out a long breath and looked at the sky. "There's plenty of daylight left. And we're not near the Trapper's Forest," I found myself saying.

Both of them stilled, looking at me. "How would you know that?" Tia asked.

How did I know that? I shook my head, splashing water against my face. It was like I could scent out the dark in it—the smell of the foul magic.

"I just know."

"But we have to run back, and it's going to take forever to get through this forest," Jake grumbled.

Tia cocked her head at me. "What? You want to stay? On your own? Are you crazy?"

Probably. If they only knew the half of it.

"I don't think another hour or so will hurt."

"Crazy-ass human," she hissed under her breath. "We really should think about heading back, Charlotte. I mean, next time we can hit it hard with a fresh head, yeah?"

I shoved off the tree I'd been leaning on and walked toward the forest, pausing to look back at them. "Go on, I can't make you stay."

Jake pointed to me. "If something happens to her . . ."

"He sent her out here, he knows."

"I can handle myself," I said. "Besides, someone's always been watching us."

I knew that there was someone else in the woods with

us. I could hear them—smell them. I thought Jake and Tia passed it off as other trainees, not that someone was on our trail. Half of me wondered if they had been leading us in circles or if they were just following pack rules—that we really couldn't be left alone.

"If she wants to stay, she can stay. She's not my problem," he said, walking away the way we came.

Tia paused. "You don't know what's out here, Charlotte."

"Can't be any worse than what I've been living with," I answered. "Go, Tia. I can find my way home." I shifted to my fur, my beast taking over and carrying me away.

But now I was all the more aware of another presence nearby. I didn't mind it. It was maybe Tia, who was probably annoyed that she had to chase after me, but I had to see if my gut was right. I kept running, my nose picking up faint scents that wound me around the forest until it spit me out into a clearing with tall grass swaying around boulders. A few big rocks jutted out of the ground up the hill above me and smaller boulders littered the ground around me. I ran past them, into another set of trees where leaves covered the ground, leaves that were speckled with red as if crimson snowflakes had kissed them.

The air wasn't moving. It smelled slimy, like sugar that had burned and crusted over on a rusty stove, clinging to everything around it. My beast skidded to a stop. Carefully, I shifted to my skin and picked up a leaf, holding it to my nose in the faint thread of sunlight that made it through the canopy of limbs.

Blood.

I dropped the leaf as I caught the sight in front of me.

My stomach plummeted as a sick feeling crept up my throat. Another breeze picked up, this one heavy enough to shake the branches.

I was in the Trapper's Forest. Alone. Standing on a carpet of dried blood that led in every direction, as if it was trying to escape itself. My feet started to move on their own, the beast in me urging me to run.

My nose caught wind of it before my eyes could lock onto it. And when I saw it, I was already in front of it. With one step, there was only air in front of and beneath me—air that I fell through before crashing into the hard ground below.

There was the sizzling song of silver, a now-familiar sound, like mosquitoes buzzing. The smell of rot forced its way into my nostrils. I scrambled up. What was left of a dried-out, decayed arm was lodged on a silver spike in the ground in front of me. The pit was filled with spikes like the open jaw of a shark. Bones carpeted the ground. I frantically scrambled away until I was pressed tight against the wall.

I'd almost fallen on those fucking silver spikes.

I covered my mouth with my hand as a whimper threatened to escape. I had to get out of here. I tried to climb out but the walls were steep, without any nooks to use for leverage. It was as if someone had lined them with a layer of smooth mud for just this reason. They were high enough so one wrong slip would land you on a spike but low enough that someone desperate enough would risk it.

"Fuck, fuck, fuck."

I heard the breeze pick up above me as the treetops waved like they were laughing at me. Somehow, the breeze curled down into the pit, tickling the backs of my ankles before curling around my calves. It felt like someone was breathing on me, whispering against my skin as it danced up to my neck. My wolf howled in the back of my mind, stirring me to move.

My breath caught. I should call for help.

I should call Levi.

I should have never left my group.

Cracking sounded above me. I felt my beast press forward against my skin. My nails elongated to claws as I carefully pressed myself into the wall, hiding. A trick that I knew worked because it had saved me from Nate so many times before.

Another cracking sounded. I wanted to call for help, but I had no idea who this was. If they were friend or someone with reddened, hazy eyes—a rogue.

"You know, I am not even surprised." Remi was standing at the edge of the pit. He pushed his moppy black hair back, lavender eyes glowing in the darkness of the forest that he looked almost at home in. "How the fuck did you get down there?"

"I didn't realize how far I'd gone."

Remi tilted his head. "And your group?"

"I'm too human for them, apparently," I heard myself say.

He scoffed. "Do you even know where you are?"

I nodded. "I do." My eyes flickered to the arm across from me.

He followed my gaze, clicking his tongue. "The spikes aren't just silver. They're laced with blood magic that keeps a wolf in their fur until a trapper can find them so they can harvest it." He turned to look at me. "And somehow, you missed them. You either have some wild luck or the moon fucking loves you."

I felt my breakfast threatening to spill out onto my feet. I pushed my hair back. "Can you please get me out of here?"

He squatted and sat at the edge, letting his feet hang off like he was sitting on the edge of a dock about to dip his toes in the cool water. "You're not supposed to be here. Not alone. And especially not so close to night."

"It's just a forest," I tried to offer, trying not to let my voice show how quickly my resolve was fading.

He laughed, all his teeth showing. "You're an idiot if you believe that."

"I don't," I muttered. "Have you been following me this whole time?"

"I've been following you for a while," he said, his lavender eyes holding a wicked gleam. My breath caught. "It's easy to pick off the weak pups when they're separated from the pack."

My beast was pawing at my mind now. I pushed her back. We had to play nice with him, otherwise we were going to have to get really creative with our new friend, bones and company.

"How did you miss the white chalk?"

How did I miss it? I hadn't even realized I had stepped foot in this god-awful place until it was too late.

I shook my head. "I don't know. Are you going to help me out or not?"

"I ought to make your dumb ass sleep here," he blandly retorted. "You do understand you almost died?"

I could hear the silver singing behind me, smell both the rot around me and the faint odor of decaying magic in the air. My heart was racing, my mind picturing my own body lodged in the pit with only the ghouls of the forest and the trees to bear witness. My beast cringed at the idea, the sound of the silver like sharp nails running over glass.

"Yes."

He rolled to lie on his stomach, then reached an arm down. My gaze landed on his hand—it would still require a decent jump to reach. "Well?" Remi cocked his head. "You don't trust me?" I swallowed. It wasn't that I didn't trust him, but one wrong move and I wouldn't make it out of this pit. "Do you trust anyone?"

Something sour twisted in me. I clenched my jaw. I squatted then launched myself upward, frantically reaching for his hand, which easily caught mine.

He pulled me up, leaning back before grabbing my other hand with his; I pushed against the wall with my legs while he yanked me backward until I was lying on a blanket of bloodstained leaves. The sunlight was quickly fading from the small bits of sky that I could see.

I pushed myself to sitting with a groan. I passed a hand over the stained leaves around us. "Why is it still red? Shouldn't it have faded?"

"Blood magic takes a long time to fade," Remi replied. "This has been this way since before I was born, and I would be willing to bet it stays this way for a long time."

"Thank you." I was still heaving deep breaths.

He hummed back with a dip of his chin.

"What now?" I asked.

Remi was already standing. "You found your way this far." He laughed. "Shouldn't be too hard to find your way home. Just don't step on a trap. I won't be there to save you again."

With a blink, he was gone, leaving me utterly alone in the forest.

I ran until I found the clearing again. I looked up at the moon, which was starting to fade into the sky.

"Shit," I hissed to myself while the dark forest stared at me. The resonating feeling of being alone settled in—almost suffocating me. I took a deep breath and ran hard to beat the darkness that I knew would not be far behind me.

Thankfully, my beast remembered the way, remembered the scents that led back to the training ground where there was, in fact, white chalk marking the ground and the trees before the entrance of the forest. I shook my head. I had too many questions, but the need to get far away from that place won over my curiosity.

It took me longer than I'd expected at a steady run to get back, and it was dark by the time I found Lander and Bowie waiting for me. Lander let out a mutter of curses, rubbing his hand over a face that was sporting a black eye, the rest of him looking much worse for wear.

Bowie let out a long breath, her shoulders relaxing. "I told you she would find it."

Lander glared at her before he eyed me over. His frown softened. "You okay?"

I shifted to my skin, my legs wobbly. "I'm fine," I answered, with a weak nod.

Bowie's grasped my arm, her violet eyes watching me closely, almost pleading. "What did you find out there?"

Lander cut his eyes to me.

I pushed some loose hair behind my ears. "Just the trap I fell into and what was in it."

"What was in it?" Bowie said sharply.

"Bones," I replied, with a shiver.

She tilted her head. "Nothing else?"

"Should there have been?"

She held my gaze before releasing my arm. "You don't leave your team again."

"I'm sorry," I stammered. "I didn't mean to—"

"Neither did the wolves that died," Lander said, his voice firm and unrelenting, like the ground on the floor of the pit. "Come on, let's get you home."

CHAPTER
EIGHT

I could spot the smoke rolling out of the familiar chimney above the tips of the trees. My stomach was twisted in knots. Lander was silent walking next to me, his footsteps steady, which was a miracle considering the bite mark along his calf.

"Charlotte." I froze in place, and he walked around me, his eyes hard. "I don't want to lecture you."

"I didn't ask for a professor."

He scoffed with a shake of his head. "You're too smart to do something that stupid. Do you realize what could have happened?"

Swallowing, I dipped my head in a small nod. In my dreams later I knew I would be haunted by that pit. I more than knew what could have happened.

"Yes."

"I'm not talking about you," he snapped, taking a step closer. "You think your death only affects you? Do you realize how it would affect the people here? Derek? Elliot? My brother?"

My mouth parted as I tilted my head back to look him in his icy eyes. "He wouldn't—he wouldn't lose it again."

"No, he won't; at least, not because of your stupidity. You have to be smarter. The minute you think you want to walk into the darkness, you better remember everyone you're leaving behind to do so."

He turned on his heel and stormed forward, leaving me to walk alone in his wake. Levi was waiting on the porch when we walked past the columns. Lander stood at the edge of the lawn, staring at Levi, but Levi's eyes never left mine. He stepped aside when I jogged up the stairs.

"In the house." It was a tone I hated. The tone of an order. The kind that reminded me of days when all I was supposed to do was smile and nod.

For a few moments I avoided him and opted to shower instead of receiving the tongue-lashing I was expecting. I found myself scrubbing and scrubbing, desperate to get the feeling of the dark breath of that forest off me. Even after drying off and putting on a fresh set of sweats, I could still hear the shrill soprano voice of the silver spikes playing over and over in my mind.

When I walked back to the kitchen Levi was at the bar with a glass of whiskey in his hand.

Carefully, I walked over to a barstool and hopped up. My legs burned from running so much today. Levi rose and pulled some steaks from the refrigerator and turned on the burner under a cast-iron skillet.

He was quiet. Too quiet. I was ready for my lecture, but this was even worse. I found myself squirming in my seat, almost sweating because I knew I'd screwed up.

"Okay, listen, I—" The look in his glowing eyes made me close my mouth quickly.

"I told you not to go into that fucking forest by yourself."

"I didn't even realize I was there until I was standing on the red leaves . . ." My beast whined at the memory that made my stomach curl. How red it was. How it didn't look old. How it smelled foul—rotten. Like candy well past its best-before date.

"You can't go off by yourself like that."

"I thought . . . I can handle myself. I mean—"

"Handle yourself? Against what? A squirrel? You ended up in a fucking *trap*, Charlotte."

A growl ripped through my chest but he gave me another look that made my beast quiet; he continued with rubbing the steaks with seasoning.

"It was stupid." My voice sounded small, and I hated it.

"No shit," he agreed, tossing the steaks onto the skillet. They crackled, the sound not quite enough to ease the tension between us. "What if your team had followed you out there? What if one of them had fallen in and hadn't gotten as lucky as your ass? Being in this pack means thinking about more than yourself."

"I get it!" I tossed my hands up. "I fucking get it, okay?"

"Do you?" His voice was even, like the glassy water of a lake first thing in the morning.

I wrapped my arms around my torso, avoiding his eye because in my mind I saw what could have happened. I saw not only my body, but Tia's and Jake's lodged in that pit. I saw their blood spill. I saw good people take a fall for my mistake. My throat clenched. I didn't want someone dying because of me. I could never forgive myself if that happened.

"Charlie?"

"If you want to keep on, go on," I said, my voice tight.

The steaks sizzled in the background. I heard something crack while steam rose over them.

"They say that moon-blooded wolves are different from others because we have the blood of the moon Herself in our veins. It's like pure whiskey, what the original werewolves had, the best kind you could drink. Over time, things dilute, but some families back then tried to pair people up to keep the bloodlines pure.

"The myth is always bigger than the reality of it. Moon-blooded wolves are supposed to be stronger than normal wolves. For the most part they are. Those of us who are feel it in our veins. The road for us is harder because of what we are and what the world will throw at us. People are going to challenge you at every step, and you can't let your own selfish pride get in the way, otherwise, in this world, you'll end up dead."

He flipped the steaks, his hand steady. I let my hands run through the locks of my short hair before tugging on the ends of it. "They hardly recognize me as anything more than human."

"Then prove to them that you're not," he contended. "Prejudice isn't just a human problem. You want them to listen to you? Trust you? Listen to them. Trust them. The pack survives because we rely on each other. You won't make it without your pack out here."

"I've made it this far."

"This is what you wanted, remember?"

"It's not that simple," I countered quietly.

Listening was easier said than done. All I ever did was listen for so long. Listen and sit quietly. Speak only when spoken to. Say the right things at the right time, and *Listen, Charlotte, goddammit, don't you ever listen?!* I could see Nate's mother shaking her head at me. Telling me that I never thought about things before I did them—never listened. Never paid attention—*I mean, my god, Charlotte, are you really that dumb?!* I doubted I would ever get that woman's shrill voice out of my mind.

I took a long drink from my cup, my appetite slowly diminishing. The unsettling feeling of butterflies fluttering in my stomach made the steaks look as appealing as dirt.

Levi tilted his head, his eyes pulsing with a slight glow. "What else did you see?"

"I didn't see anything else."

"But?"

"I thought I was going to hear something." His lips sealed in a tight line. I pushed off the stool. "I don't think I'm hungry anymore."

"Charlie . . ." he called after me, but I was long gone to the quiet of my room.

The wood split under the weight of my axe. A familiar feeling, a familiar task that I was good at. That I could do without thought, which was what my weary mind needed. Last night I dreamed that my mattress turned into leaves stained with red. They curled around me like fingers, imprisoning me in an iron grasp I couldn't escape.

"Psst!" My axe froze midair. Turning, I spotted Liam at the edge of the lawn. He winked at me, his lips tugging into a soft smile.

I looked at my toes but quickly lifted my chin to face him as a flush warmed my cheeks. "Hi."

He looked both ways like he was about to cross a road, then took a step past the columns. "Hi, yourself," he replied, strolling across the grass.

For such a bold move, he still appeared to be on edge; walking lightly enough on his feet that he could turn and dash at a moment's notice. His silver eyes gave away nothing. A smile was on his lips but it didn't reach his eyes. No, his eyes were holding mine like a lifeline.

"What are you doing here?"

He offered me a one-shouldered shrug. "Well, you have a rotation today and we've come to take you to the greenhouse. Derek told Dad before he left that you helped him in the greenhouse here. Didn't Levi tell you?"

No, because I wanted some fucking space after getting a lecture from your father and from Levi in the same night. "We?"

Liam stopped a few feet away from me. He looked over his shoulder. "You coming?"

Remi stepped from the forest that he blended so well

into and strode right past the columns and over to the woodpile.

I leaned the axe against the stump, glancing at Liam, who didn't dare move. Remi rolled his eyes. "He'd have to catch me. He won't fucking catch me."

"He's not the boogeyman," I chided them both.

Remi's amethyst-hued eyes locked with mine. "I know."

"Do you want to come inside?"

Liam looked at the house then smiled politely at me, like I had seen his father do so many times before. "We should get going."

The screen door slapped against the frame. "Why? There's fresh coffee." Levi was rolling his sleeves up, jogging casually down the steps. He eyed me then looked at the two boys. "Liam."

"Uncle," Liam replied with a nod.

Before Liam could open his mouth, Levi held a hand up. "I know." He turned, facing Remi. "Your mom is taking you to a few areas on the line that need looking at. The far east corner."

"My First," he replied, dipping his head. "We were there a few days ago."

"You're going again." Levi paused as recognition flooded Remi's eyes. "You better get going, it's going to take you two a solid day's run to get there."

"Why are we going there?"

"Because your job is to fucking find things and there's things that need to be found out. You mom has instructions."

Remi held Levi's gaze before nodding slowly to him.

Levi paused by me, his eyes holding a warning in them.

"Get home before dark, it's a full moon out." Like I needed a reminder. He held my gaze a moment before walking back to the house. "And, Remi," he called over his shoulder. "There's only one wolf who can outrun me, and it's your fucking mother. Remember that." And he strode into the house with a calmness that sucked the air out of my lungs.

Remi's eyes went wide, showing everything that his firm stance didn't want to give away. Liam slapped his arm on Remi's shoulder. "Let's go. You've got a long run, Rem."

I fell into step with them along the small foot trail that was developing over the new, budding grass in the direction of the pack house. Remi brushed past me. I jogged a few steps to catch up with him. "What's there to find out there?"

He eyed Liam for a moment. "Not sure, to be honest. Something is off, though, in the forest."

"What do you mean?"

He rubbed his jaw. The constellation tattooed on his neck rolled with his skin as he leaned his head to the side to crack his neck. "That's the problem. It smells the same. Looks the same. But something feels off. We've been tearing through it."

"The forest is always weird though, right?" Conceding, he nodded silently to me. "So is this not just another weird forest thing?"

"Did it feel like any weird forest to you yesterday?"

"Considering this is the first magic forest I've ever been in, I wouldn't know," I quipped. Remi cracked a smirk in reply. "But it felt bad."

"Bad?" Remi stepped closer to me.

"It just felt foul—smelled rotten. It was so quiet where you found me. It just—it felt really bad."

He looked at me like he had heard this story a thousand times. "You're lucky I found you." With that, he darted off, shifting quickly and disappearing through the trees.

Liam bumped my chin with the back of his fingers. "Don't worry, Remi has been in that forest almost as much as Levi and Dad. You okay?"

"Yeah," I replied.

He grasped my wrist gently. "Char, are you okay? I wish you would have called me. I would have come to help yesterday."

My cheeks flooded as shame rolled through me. "I feel so stupid."

"Hey," he said, carefully pulling me to a stop, his words forcing me to meet his soft silver gaze. "Don't be so hard on yourself. You're new to this. It's going to take time and it's not going to do you any good to keep beating yourself up. Unless you want someone to lick your wounds for you," he added with a cheeky grin.

"Wow." I rolled my eyes and walked down the trail. "Does that work on girls around here?"

He laughed while he jogged to catch up to me. "You would be surprised."

I tossed my hands up. "I don't want know."

His chest shook with laughter before he took off ahead of me, shifting quickly into his fur. I followed, along the familiar path to the pack house. He showed me where all the rotation schedules for the different jobs were posted on a bulletin board in the kitchen before grabbing us both coffees.

Together, we walked quietly to the greenhouse, my mind starting to drift far from the day before because it was easy when I was with him. Liam could somehow make the ghosts vanish and put a smile on my face.

He guided me around another corner. A crowd was gathered around a set of three pits. In each wide hole, a pair of wolves clashed with each other like two bolts of lightning. A small group was gathered around the left pit, where one of the wolves shifted back into its skin. Jake stood up, blood running from his laughing mouth.

I moved my hand over my lips, blinking to see another set of wolves roll on the ground. Snarls and snaps of jaws sounded through the air and cut like knives at my resolve. I stepped closer to Liam, who had paused to watch the commotion. A few wolves were refereeing at each pit, but it hardly looked like they were doing anything but cheering on the violence.

"She want in?"

I was snapped out of my daze by Tia's voice. She tipped her chin to us as she walked over from her perch on a boulder. She had a shiner on her cheek and a nasty bite on her torso.

I couldn't look at it. The sight of it, the sound of the fighting, brought back memories I wanted buried in the ground a thousand feet deep.

Liam shook his head. "No, she's got a shift at the greenhouse. I just wanted to swing by and see how it was going."

"Boring." Tia sniggered. "Come on, human, let's see how good that moon blood is."

Other people were turning to watch the conversation

while Levi's words played in the back of my mind. I forced a tight smile on my lips. "I don't want to be late."

"I need out of here," I told Liam.

His hand came to rest on the small of my back, pushing me forward. "Another time."

Tia rolled her eyes before walking away without a word, and I was glad. I didn't want to open my mouth. I wanted to get the hell out of there. I knew that I would have to defend myself at some point, but goddammit, I didn't want to be a monster. I didn't want to turn into the one I'd run from.

"Charlotte—"

"It's okay." It wasn't, but it was not a topic we were going to visit.

Liam took the hint and let the sound of thunder cover my silence. Storm clouds were gathering overhead, causing all the wind chimes hung up around the barn-sized greenhouse to sing.

Liam walked me inside, where hundreds of herbs were growing in neat rows. I was staring at the largest set of basil plants I had ever seen when David walked out of a closet. His green T-shirt was tight across his chest and his jeans struggled to keep up with muscles that flexed with every step he took in our direction.

He held his fist out and Liam reached forward and lightly tapped it with his own.

"Looks like you're with me today," he said, his single eye watching me.

Liam stepped around David before looking at me, eyes heavy with worry and an apology that he never needed to give. *"You good?"*

With a quiet nod I answered, *"Yeah, see you later."*

David nudged his chin at a side plot where a small girl was yanking up fistfuls of weeds. "Well, it's very simple. We're pulling weeds. They get in here even though I feel like we've wiped them out time and time again."

"I think I can handle pulling weeds," I replied, with a light laugh, praying it hid the skittish jump in my voice.

David chuckled. "You may not think that after a few hours, although I do find it relaxing. The plants don't talk back," he said. "I have gloves?"

He was kind, and I hadn't expected that. I was living with the man who'd taken his eye, and he was looking at me with the kind of mischief that friends held in their eyes for each other. I found my own lips curling in a smile, and replied with a small nod.

He grabbed a pair of gloves off a table and tossed them at me. "Penny, say hello to Charlotte."

Penny looked up at me with bright-green eyes that she must have inherited from her father. Her dark hair, in French-braided pigtails, had traces of mud in it. She took my hand in her small soil-covered one and quickly shook it. "It's nice to meet you," she said before going back to destroying the weeds in front of her.

David pointed to a large basket that she was tossing weeds into. "Toss everything in there. We'll burn them. The ash is good for the soil."

"Really?"

"Mhmm," he hummed as he slipped some gloves on. "Good for other things too—you can mix it with mud and other things to cover up your scent."

"Why would you want to do that?"

"Hunting, tracking, sometimes we have to be covert about things," he explained, eyeing Penny, who let out an exasperated huff.

"It was one time, Dad!"

He rolled his eye and looked at me. "Penny and Lyle covered themselves in mud and ash a few years back so they could steal the absurd amount of candy Lander keeps in his office."

I bit back a laugh mostly because Penny's gaze looked fierce enough to cut anyone. She went back to her weeds. "It would have worked," she grumbled.

"If you wouldn't have tracked mud everywhere." David laughed. I pulled on the gloves then made quick fists with both my hands to test them. "Now, this is the part where I get to grill you."

I whipped my head around to stare at him. He tilted his head back in a deep laugh. "I didn't realize you'd be so jumpy. We're going to have to work on that."

"I just—" I paused, unsure of how to proceed, so I opted to pull out a weed in front of me instead. "Sorry, what the hell?"

He waved me off with a laugh. "Lander told me you were sharp."

"Lander says a lot of things," I muttered out loud before I could even realize what I was saying.

David arched a brow before nodding. "He frets like a hen sometimes. I told him he was spending too much time with his chickens."

I snorted, falling into laughter with him.

"But Lander is Levi's second for a reason. He's tactful and always tries to protect everyone. Sometimes he goes too far, but it's his job."

David had a look that said he knew about my misadventure in the woods during tracker training. My shoulders tensed while I prepared for my third lecture. David tossed some dirt at me with a smirk.

"Anyone can see that you're punishing yourself enough over yesterday, there's no reason to add onto that."

"Thank you." I licked my lips.

He hummed next to me before looking over his shoulder, spotting a man waving at him from the door. "I'll be back."

He got up and walked over to the man, leaving room for Penny to quickly scoot next to me, as if she had been planning to do this the whole time.

"So," Penny said before wiping her brow, smearing mud across her face. "I'm eleven," she stated. "I hate weeds."

"I think everyone does," I agreed.

She nodded and looked at the mess in front of us that was going to take hours to get through. "I don't know how they get in here or get to this . . ."

I tried not to laugh. "Let's make it a game, yeah?"

"What do I get if I win?"

"Who says you'll win?"

She arched one brow. "What's the game?"

"We could see who can pull the most the fastest?"

She thought for a minute then jogged over to David, whispering something that made him roll his eye. He reached into his pocket and handed her an iPhone that she quickly snatched and unlocked.

She jogged back and put the phone down in a smooth patch of dirt.

"Okay, how long?"

"Ten minutes?"

"Okay." She eyed me. I nodded and her finger punched the screen before her hands went to work in a fury.

We ended up playing the game a few times before she decided that we needed a snack break. Levi hadn't thought to send me with snacks, so Penny shared her jerky and fruit snacks with me. Her gaze locked on my shoulder, the burn scars in clear view because my hair was half up. I hadn't thought to cover them and had already forgotten that I had a tank on today. Her fingers innocently reached to touch them.

"Is that from silver?!"

I paused and looked at where her eyes were lingering. "This?"

"Yeah—are they? My dad has a few of those. They're so cool!"

"Cool?" What the actual hell? Shaking my head, I tugged my tank strap over my scars and started to wish I had a T-shirt on instead.

"Penelope," David said as he walked back to us. "Mind helping some of the others down there?"

I offered her a shrug. "They obviously need to learn how inferior they are at pulling weeds."

She thought for a moment. "You're right," she agreed, before running over to a group of elderly women who playfully tossed a few pulled weeds at her.

David sighed and knelt in the space where she'd been. "She's always been so inquisitive."

"She's fine, she's a really sweet girl."

"If it makes you feel any better, she thought you were some kind of Amazon because of your scars. She saw you, I think, walking around the pack with Claire and could not stop talking about them when she got home. I had to tell her that Amazons were reserved for Greek mythology."

I snorted a laugh because I was the furthest thing from them. "That's amazing. Levi will get a kick out of that."

David nodded with a smile. "Thank you again. She can be a handful. She's at the age where she has more questions than I have answers. Most are smarter than I'm capable of answering at this point."

"She's really no trouble at all." I paused. "Seems like you and her mother have your hands full, though."

His smile was bitter. "Just me and Pen," he shared. "Her mother left us for her true mate years ago."

My tongue felt thick in my mouth. I brushed my hair back. "I'm sorry, I didn't—"

He lifted a hand. "Don't be hard on yourself, you didn't know."

I wiped my hands on my shifter shorts. "If you need help with her, I mean, I wouldn't mind."

"I think she'd like that. She seems to have taken a liking to you," he answered, just as Liam stepped back into the greenhouse. "It seems your escort is here."

I rolled my eyes. "So it would seem."

He laughed through his nose, stepping away from me. "Sharpen your claws, blood pup. You'll need them soon enough. Oh, and tell that jackass you're living with that I want my eye back, yeah?"

My mouth went dry. David bellowed in dark laughter as he walked away from me, the echoes sending haunting vibrations through me. A hand grabbed my shoulder.

"Let's go, Levi wants you back," Liam said.

CHAPTER NINE

When I got home Levi was jogging down the steps in long black shifters, which were starting to develop holes.

"Let's go," he said.

"Where?"

"Going for a hike," he answered, on his way to the trees.

I swallowed the anxiety then darted after him. He didn't wait for me, but ran straight into the woods, jumping into the shift and leaving me with the bushes rustling from his departure.

My beast darted through the forest, following his scent like it was breadcrumbs laid out for us. Eventually we caught up enough that we could see him in the distance, running at a steady pace and aiming for an area that smelled like water. The creek was nearby—we were close to the tree. The one with the initials carved into it. The one that the pack leads at Thunderhead would all carve their initials into when they swore allegiance to the moon. The one that still had Levi's initials etched deep into the bark.

Levi shifted to his skin and strode into a grassy meadow between the trees. He waved me forward.

"Come on, shift back."

I let my bones crack over my body until I was standing in my skin, grateful I had on a long pair of yoga pants and a tank top, as it was cooler here by the water.

"What are we doing?"

He eyed the trees that circled us and looked back at me, his eyes glowing as a sly smile pulled at his mouth. "I figured now was as good a time as ever to continue teaching you how not to punch like a human."

I put my hands on my hips. "Levi . . ."

"Charlotte, this is the world you're in now. You're going to have to learn to defend yourself against other wolves or whatever is out in the wild waiting for you. Wolves will care that you're moon-blooded, all the more so because you were a human, but bears won't give a shit. Which is why you have to learn to become one with that beast of yours. Work together."

My breath caught. "Right . . . bears . . ."

Levi leaned against a stump. "That's the predator you'll most likely see out on the Hunt or along our lines. Badgers are also an issue, and moose—"

I frowned. "Moose?"

Levi snickered, cracking his knuckles. "Aggressive

motherfuckers." He walked lazily toward me, with a smile that made me wonder if he wasn't entirely through trying to kill me. "You're going to have to defend yourself, whether it's a bear, a bobcat, or another wolf. You live in this world now."

Wordlessly, I tied my hair up. Snow was still hanging on to the corners of the shadowy ground around us. It crunched under Levi's bare feet.

"First lesson: when you bite something, you never stop biting until it's to the bone."

My heart started to race while the beast in me paced back and forth. "You've said that before."

"You need to feel it crunch, hear it. To the bone. Understand?"

I bit my lip, eyes on my toes.

"Charlotte, tell me you understand."

I dug my toes into the mud, trying to keep steady. I blew out a breath. "I understand."

"Any predator, bear or wolf, will go for this first," he explained, pointing to his stomach. "They'll try to either rip your intestines out or rip your throat out because both places are the most vulnerable on the body."

My hands moved to cover my own stomach. I could feel his eyes on me as he walked around me. The hair on the back of my neck stood. "With bears, or any larger animal, you have to always keep moving. You're smaller, more agile than they will be. With wolves, every inch of movement has to be calculated, because one wrong move and you could be a fucking mess of intestines on the ground."

"What about a mountain lion?"

"Run," he told me. "They're fast and their claws will

rip you to shreds. Don't ever take one on by yourself. Not everyone is as lucky as Lander. Just get the hell out of there. There's nothing wrong with that."

Rocking on my heels, I answered, "All right."

The beast in me crept closer, instincts kicking in. But in that moment, Levi felt like he was everywhere at once. I turned to face him but only found a blank forest ahead of me. His low chuckle sounded from behind me; slowly, I turned to see him standing there with a fangy smile looking back at me.

"You're going to have to do better than that."

I rolled my eyes and walked toward him, the beast in me coming forward. "Now what?"

"Now?" His smile turned dark. The beast pushed me forward as Levi squared up to face me. "Hit me."

Something cracked in me like a set of fireworks going off. My fist sailed through the air before I realized what was happening. He easily caught my wrist and froze me in place.

"Now, see, here, this isn't good for you. I could either do this"—he yanked me forward and moved his fist to rest against my ribs—"or I could do this." He whipped me around and with his other hand yanked my ponytail so my neck was bared in the air. My beast was howling now, fury growing in her. The feeling of our neck so exposed was sending her into a frenzy. "In this scenario, you would be dead."

He shoved me away, eliciting a growl from me.

"Anticipate. Always think three steps ahead."

He circled me, and I found myself mirroring his steps. Silver eyes watched my feet mimicking his movements. "Good," he said. "But don't rely on following your opponent, because when they decide to do something unexpected, well, then you're shit out of luck." He barely finished speaking before he was over to me in a blink.

I tried to dodge, but in a breath, I was in the dirt. Levi easily strode back to the little circle our footprints had made. I could feel her pace back and forth and back and forth in my mind. I could see his smile, which only infuriated me more—infuriated her more.

Something cracked in me as she pushed closer to the surface. I felt my feet carry us over to him. He dodged a fist I sent as a fake so my other hand could nail his side. It didn't faze him. He just dropped a shoulder and nailed me in my chin, sending me flying back on my ass.

I was once again in the snow, fury fueling the blood flowing in me. She was snapping in my mind now, begging to be let out, but I was still trying to wrap my mind around what I had just done. I was trying to shake off this feeling of seeing stars. The last time I saw stars was the night I stopped being fully human.

"Get up, Charlotte."

I pushed myself up, standing tall as his eyes pulsed with a glow.

He cracked his neck and stalked toward me. "I won't lie, I am a little impressed," he said before he took a shot at me.

I dodged out of the way but his other arm shot out like a guardrail that froze me in place. "Good, but you're going to have to learn how to take a hit. Sometimes avoidance is a trap."

"I know how to take a hit, Levi," I found myself hissing.

He let me stumble back. "Is that right?"

She snapped again, my instincts fading fully into hers, actions being driven by the desire of her teeth. I felt my skin become fur before I even knew what was happening, and when my paws hit the ground, the only thing I could feel was the rage coursing through my veins.

Levi just chuckled as she snapped her jaws at him. "You can't rely on your fists and teeth all the time, you're going to have to learn to dance with those demons that keep you screaming your head off at night."

I lunged at him. He dodged and jumped into the air, shifting into his fur. When he turned, I was already after him. He dodged and knocked us over. We jumped up, then stalked him. Electricity swarmed over me like a wildfire.

Levi's low growl was enough to scare the rest of the creatures safely nested in the trees. My beast snapped her jaws back and let out a growl of her own. We blinked, and he was in front of us.

Claws and jaws met skin and bone. I heard cracking, growling, and snarling as we became a blur of our own pent-up anger. I thought I might have bitten his flank but I definitely felt teeth sink into my rib cage. In another moment my beast was rolling on top of him to go for his other shoulder.

I thought I could hear Nate laughing at me.

Baby, it's easy if you don't fight it, Nate's voice whispered to me from the depths of my mind where I had buried him. Nothing buried can stay away for that long. It always claws itself out of the grave.

The distraction was enough for Levi to get the better of me. I flew through the air until I hit a tree; the snow caught me at the bottom but the laughter, Nate's laughter, in my brain wouldn't cease.

"Get up, Charlotte. You lie there you're as good as dead."

We surged toward where Levi stood in his skin. We lunged but he somehow used the momentum of my movements to send me flying into another tree. I opened my eyes and I was back in the house in California, picking myself up off those perfectly hand-scraped wooden floors that Nate demanded we have. "Get up, Charlotte, you're making a mess of the floor," Nate said as he walked toward me over the snow.

My beast lunged again and this time he didn't catch me. I sank my teeth into his leg but he yanked my muzzle away then tossed me a few feet outside the circle. All I felt was a Pandora's box of rage being unleashed within me. I stood up and felt my fur ripple back into my skin. Levi wiped some blood off his leg while I walked toward him with my fists clenched. "What the hell are you still so afraid of?"

"And what the hell about you?!" I snapped as hot anger licked along my skin. My heart was pounding now, my canines descending again, ready to sink back into his skin. "You want to talk about my problems?! What about you and your shit?!"

"That's none of your concern," he said, glowing eyes telling me I was treading too far.

"You fucking hypocrite," I spat.

"Really?" he asked darkly. "You think I don't see it? Your damn melodramatic ass with insecurities from here to the fucking moon? I swear you wallow in more self-pity—"

I lunged at him again, fur quickly taking over, and my claws sank into his sides. A growl shook the forest as hands grabbed the scruff of my neck and threw me back into the grass.

He squared off in front of me. "You want them to take you seriously? Then you need to take yourself seriously and come to terms with your reality. You were a human. You were a human who almost fucking died. Do you not realize how close you were to death at each full? You are now a moon-blooded wolf, but that won't mean shit if you can't accept your own shit, deal with it, and let it go, because you've got a lot of work to do before you're anywhere near ready to live up to that name."

My beast snapped at him as fur rippled to skin. I shoved myself up, not minding the feeling of blood running down my arms. "I didn't ask to live up to that name! I just wanted to live a normal fucking life—or as normal as I can in this world. I didn't fucking ask for this!"

"None of us did. No one asks to be born into what they are, but it happens. You have to accept that you're not just a human anymore, you are a monster now, Charlotte."

"Well, that makes two of us." The words tasted sour as tears prickled at my eyes. I shoved off the tree and stormed into the forest.

I didn't eat dinner that night. I took a long shower then curled up in my bed and prayed that I could sleep through the full moon. And I did, until my sleep turned to dreams where I found myself following Eve through the forest. She kept running farther and farther into trees that started to move, as if their roots were walking. I blinked and it was my mother smiling at me before she faded into the darkness where hazy reddened eyes waited for her. Eyes that quickly tore her limb from limb in front of me while darkness wrapped its fingers around my ankles and pulled me away from her.

I woke up in what felt like a pool of my own sweat and tears, fur piercing my skin. The moon was full, Her light trying to shine through my curtains. I didn't dare look at it. I didn't dare look at Her. I didn't want to lose it in front of something so beautiful.

My wolf moaned to be with Her as the ugly tears came. My insecurities poured out and my fear spilled down my cheeks. I took deep breaths and tried to calm myself but I felt like I could barely breathe. It felt like my throat was closing. I gulped into the blackness of my room, but the constriction in my chest forced a cry out of my mouth.

I didn't hear him or sense him come in, but suddenly arms were wrapped around me. Hands pushed the wet hair out of my face as I tried to control my breathing.

"You can breathe. You can breathe—in and out, in and out," Levi said, holding my shoulders as my mind came back from the place between asleep and awake.

I was trying, but failing miserably, and he seemed to sense it. I was still angry with him, royally pissed off, but right now he was the only thing that could convince my lungs that they could still function. I took another breath, my lungs burning less until I was breathing normally again.

Levi didn't say anything else. He walked out of the room and flicked on a light in the kitchen. I wanted to follow him but my whole body felt like it had been dug out of the grave, battered from our fight today. He returned and scooped me up without a word. I was going to protest but the minute he picked me up, pain shot through my body. He carried me into the kitchen then placed me on a barstool in front of the counter.

He eyed the blood seeping through part of my shirt and sighed, although he didn't look much better. "Let's get some food in you before we fix you up."

"Can I have a drink?" I rasped.

"Absolutely."

He reached into the cabinet and pulled out a bottle of gin. I smirked. "Want to join the misery?"

"It does love company."

He fetched two glasses and poured two shots in each of them. I quickly threw mine back, praying that something would dull this pain. Take away the feeling of rot brewing inside me.

I snaked shaking fingers through my hair. "I just want to move on. I just want to fucking sleep for once. Why can't I just sleep?"

"You won't," he answered with a breathy, bitter laugh. "People say they 'move on' but they're full of shit." He rubbed his face. "You're never going to be able to erase it. It's a part of you. It's there. It happened."

"What did you do?"

"Doubt I'm the best example."

"You do have good taste in liquor," I pointed out.

He breathed a laugh and opened a bag of chips for me. "There's just your way, and you have to find it," he said tiredly. "No one else can do it for you. It can be at the bottom of a whiskey bottle, crying your eyes out, or screaming at the moon—doesn't matter. It's your way, and if someone tells you different, then you can beat their ass because they probably don't have to sleep with the same shit running through their brain at night as you do."

We fell to quiet while he made a peanut butter and jelly sandwich. Howls sounded in the night around us. The beast in me pawed at my mind, but instead of trying to do a mental gymnastics routine with her, I tried asking. Pleading. To just let me be. Because I didn't have it in me to fight her tonight.

She stilled.

I could feel his eyes on me as he slid the sandwich over.

"I'm sorry," I said. "Earlier, I was mad—I'm sorry. I was an ass."

"I was too," he admitted. He was quiet while he made another sandwich for himself. "Next time, you don't stop until you can feel the bones breaking." I scrunched my nose while he took a sloppy bite of his sandwich. He wiped his mouth. "Why did you stop before?"

"What?"

"Before, when you had your teeth in me. Why did you stop?"

I leaned back. "I, uh—" I paused and tried to remember the moment I let the monster too far out. "I felt the skin—I felt it tear." I hated admitting it. The words themselves sent goose bumps over my skin.

He nodded as if this was a decently acceptable answer. "Next time, you don't stop until you hear cracking."

"Are you insane?"

He chuckled to himself. "Plenty would say that." He took another bite of his sandwich. "They're going to underestimate you. You know that by now. We're not heathens, but we are wolves, and plenty of those wolves will try to dick you around because of what you were, and what you are."

"So what do I do?"

"You make them regret it," he said darkly. "The only thing that is going to defeat the monster is another bigger, badder monster. You be ruthless, Charlie girl. You never regret putting some asshole where he belongs when it's necessary. It's what's going to keep you alive against both predators out there in the wild and other wolves."

I ran my hands over my face before taking another bite of my sandwich. The peanut butter stuck to the roof of my mouth, but I couldn't get enough of it. There was another cry from the wolves outside. I started to glance at the window, but forced myself to toss back the rest of the gin instead.

"You're getting better and she's listening to you," he observed in a gentle tone that I had noticed growing in his voice with time. "She's your responsibility now, do you understand?"

"Yes," I answered. I felt my beast and this bond we shared. I felt her need to protect me and her ever-growing love for me. I felt the inner unrestrained being of her nature—something I was growing to love and fear all the same.

The wind howled outside as we ate quietly. "I pulled weeds with David today. What happened between the two of you? I know you said you took his eye."

He sighed. "I tried to kill him." The air around me grew

thick. I licked my lips then drank some liquid courage. Before I could speak, Levi held his fingers up to stop me. My mouth closed. He rested his forearms on the counter. "He came to find me. He and Lander did. When I found . . . them. When I saw what had been done to Eve and Lucas, I lost my fucking mind, as anyone would. I don't even remember doing it." He poured more gin into his glass.

"But he didn't die."

He shook his head.

"He told me he wanted his eye back."

He breathed a laugh. "He must like you. He has a twisted sense of humor."

"And he's fine . . . with it?"

"I told you, we have our way of working things out. We worked it out," he said matter-of-factly.

I took another sip of the gin. The howls in the background were starting to sound like white noise. "He's in charge of all the agriculture and security?"

Levi nodded. "He teaches combat and defense in tracker training too." I felt the hair on my neck rise at the thought. "You're going to have to learn to defend yourself. There's no way around it. Either accept it or don't, but if you don't, then don't expect me to stitch your ass up."

"Why would I let you do that? We both know you're shit at sewing."

Levi cracked a laugh, which made me laugh alongside him, allowing me to evade his comment. The beast in me stirred. I needed to get a grip. He was right. He was always right. I didn't love the idea of fighting. The sound of flesh tearing made me want to puke. But he was right.

I was a monster now. There was no way around that. And I sure as shit wasn't going to be a doormat.

More eerie howls echoed in the night, this time closer to the house. My beast was quiet, like she was watching for my lead. I didn't dare look outside. I took another drink.

Levi leaned against the counter. "She's getting better."

"We are," I acknowledged. "So what about you?"

"What about me?"

"It's not good for two monsters to be cooped up in the same house." I paused a beat. "And this is your pack, Levi."

He watched me a moment before digging his hand into the bag of chips. "It is mine," he stated, turning to look out the window. "Eat up."

Ignoring the howls, I downed the sandwich in front of me and then devoured another. The beast was calm in me. She ached for the moon, a feeling I knew, but both of us knew we could wait. I thought about her and the way she fought for us today. A smile pulled at my lips.

Because we were a team. She was going to always be in my corner and I hers. And I was going to make this fucking work.

CHAPTER
TEN

Tia looked at the basket in my hand like I had rattlesnakes stored under the cloth covering it. She blew the strands of silver hanging in her face away. Jake shifted his weight on his feet. Their faces were a firm wall that I wasn't sure would ever come tumbling down.

I dug into the handle of the wicker basket with one hand while my other hand carefully pulled back the cloth, revealing a fresh batch of blueberry muffins. Derek's recipe—which I had tried four times until I got it right, or at least until Levi stopped complaining that they tasted like I had put sawdust in them. My mother used to tell me that the answer to any quarrel with anyone was food.

Tia's nostrils flared, then slowly, her lips twitched into a smile. "You made these?"

I rocked forward onto my toes. "Yeah."

Jake flicked the back of his ear with the cut on it. "You trying to poison us?" He sounded serious, but the twitch in the corner of his lip told me it was a tease.

Relief flooded my chest. "I thought five blueberries might be enough to knock you out, but I could be wrong. Worth trying, though?"

Jake snickered and snatched a muffin from the basket. He tossed it in his hand. "Going to take a hellava lot more than blueberries for that."

The beast in me stirred. It felt like she was shaking her fur off, licking her teeth in anticipation. I felt something crackle through me, something that tasted almost as addicting as adrenaline.

"Charlotte?"

Forcing a smile, I looked back at Tia. Carefully, she took a muffin. The hair raised on her arms gave away what was pulsing beneath her. I forced the beast back. We were going to settle things without our teeth today.

"I shouldn't have run off," I told them. "I just—" I hated how hard this was. When you're a kid, making friends, and even saying *I'm sorry* is the easiest thing in the world. Because as a child, you're quick to believe the good in people. You haven't been hurt by the sharp claws of the world. You haven't held open your soul, baring every beautifully flawed detail of it, only to have someone light it on fire and watch it burn.

I turned to Jake, who took a large bite out of his muffin. "You're right, I did work at a desk for a long time. I know I have a lot to learn. I'm trying. I want to try."

"Why?" he asked.

"Because I never want to go back to that fucking life again," I found myself saying in a tone that was hotter than I'd intended.

Jake's eyes changed to something that looked almost like respect. "Good," he stated, softness lacing the edge of his voice.

"I just need help, mostly patience. I'm bad at making friends," I admitted, laughing wryly to myself. "And I've never really—team sports weren't something I did before."

"We were shitheads too," Tia conceded.

Jake took a larger bite out of his muffin. Tia elbowed him in the rib cage.

"Shit!" He swallowed his bite and wiped some crumbs off his mouth. "Yeah, we were shitheads."

I bit back a smile. Tia took another muffin and handed it to Jake. She clasped her hands in front of her. "Well, I think that should be our team name."

Jake grimaced. "Muffins?"

Tia smiled, her fangs showing. "No, the shitheads, dumbass."

Jake gave her a side-glance. "Whatever, it's better than 'muffins.' Are we going to do this today or what?"

Today was an obstacle course. The goal was to run through a marked trail without being snatched by any of the traps that Bowie had laid out. None of them, she assured us, would kill us, but they were similar snares and triggers to what we would find in the Trapper's Forest. We had to follow the trail to the end, capture our flag, and come back with all our team members.

"So—plan?" Tia dropped to a crouch and drew a rectangle in the dirt. "To be fair, Charlotte does have a great nose—"

"Yeah, but I'm not as observant as you," I pointed out, dropping to a crouch next to her.

"That's okay, you'll learn," Tia said easily.

Jake dropped to face both of us. We both watched as Tia marked an X at the top of the box. "Your senses are already good. You just have to work on the other things, which is okay. We all have things to work on. That's why we practice," she explained, no annoyance or patronization in her voice. The sincerity of it caught me off guard. "The goal is to just get the flag. It's not timed. We go slow. That way Charlotte can get practice and I can work on studying the traps. Out on the real hunt, the more I know, the better I'll be at getting us out of them or keeping us away from them. I know they're not the real traps that are out in the Trapper's Forest, but Bowie mimicked a lot of the setup so the training grounds are as real as possible."

"So what am I? Good looks?"

Tia chucked some dirt at Jake. "Everyone needs muscle."

"I mean, is protein powder all you eat?" I jested.

Jake smirked. "Anytime you wanna see the gun show, all you have to do is ask."

Tia giggled. "Anyway, Jake, you're going to have to help us do any heavy lifting during the Hunt. I think you and Char will be able to tag team well. What if today you two run together ahead of me? I'll go on foot so I can bring my bag and take notes."

Jake nodded and turned to me. "I'll take the left, you take

the right. If I stop, you stop. If I shift to my skin, you shift to yours. I'll try not to get you too beat up," he remarked, a hint of mischief in his eyes.

"Levi would have your ass," Tia warned him.

I rolled my eyes. "He's not like that."

Jake didn't say anything. He finished his muffin then wiped his hands on his long bicycle short shifters. "You ready?"

I nodded. Tia took the basket and set it next to the pile where we had left our things. She tucked a few muffins into her bag, then jogged back to where Jake and I were standing.

The forest was alive today. I felt the beast in me dancing with delight, pulsing through my veins. I closed my eyes and let the feeling run over me, washing down my spine like the fingers of a lover in the early morning.

Turning to Tia, I caught her glowing eyes. Behind them, it was like I could see her beast pacing. "You really are moon-blooded," she said.

"I am," I affirmed, because even if I didn't fully understand it, I could feel it every time this cool electric pulse shot through me.

"You smell like it," Jake observed. His nostrils flared. The hair on his neck was raised, shoulders stiff. "Fuck, that's trippy."

I cocked my head. "Is—I mean, Liam is too? I'm sure there's a lot of others out there?"

"Yeah." Jake scratched his head. "Maybe it was because you were a human before? No offense."

Tia gave my arm a light punch. "Come on, let's get to it."

I was stepping forward to fall in line with her when

Jake caught my arm, holding me back as Tia walked a little ahead.

"What did you see?"

I arched a brow. *"What do you mean?"*

"Before," he asked. *"When you were in the Trapper's Forest?"*

"I fell into a pit lined with silver stakes. Only bones left behind. Remi helped me out."

The breeze picked up, tickling my arms. The beast was pawing at me now. I felt my canines elongate while my nail beds started to itch.

"That's it?" He gave nothing away, but his tone said what it needed to.

I eyed Tia, who was jotting something down in her notepad. I looked back at Jake.

"I didn't see really anything else. I don't know how to describe it other than it felt bad."

"Why do you say that?"

"I don't know, it just did."

Jake rubbed his face then nodded. "Let's go, stay with me on my right."

"Okay," I answered.

The two of us jogged around Tia. I ran until I found a fallen log. The beast was rushing forward. I jumped onto the log, using it to springboard us forward in a drumline of cracking. Fur combed over me as the electric feeling ran all the way down to my toes.

I sat back and let my beast push forward. She yipped at Jake before darting into the trees with him.

It took longer than any of us would have liked to find the

flag, but we did find it. We dodged plenty of the traps, but a few ended up catching us. Luckily, we could get out of them unharmed. Unluckily, Tia always wanted to draw a detailed description of them, which meant we had to stay trapped while she took notes. Jake or I had to hang upside down, flailing about like a fish, while she scribbled on her notepad more times than either of us would have preferred.

Jake was a good teacher, whether he wanted to admit it or not. Throughout the day he showed me how to spot certain things, like whether a fallen limb was natural or a setup for a trap. He stopped a few times to walk me over to a snare that he would set off just so I could see how it worked, although it didn't stop one from snapping me up by my ankle. However, instead of being angry, both he and Tia found it hysterical.

After we turned our flag in, they offered to run home with me. But before we could head out together, Liam spotted me at the entrance of camp and quickly took my hand, leading me into the forest. "Let's get out of here."

Awkwardly, I waved good-bye to my team. Tia's eyes were wide while Jake shook his head with a laugh.

"Where are we going?" I asked.

Liam's eyes twinkled with delight. "Follow me?"

I should say no. I should just go home. But instead, I found myself saying, "Okay."

So I followed him.

Back through the pack compound and up windy slopes until we reached a small party of boulders nestled on top of a hill where the signs of spring were in full bloom. A golden field of flowers surrounded them along with tall grass waving like streamers in the breeze. Liam hopped through it like a rabbit and I couldn't help but shake my head at him. I hadn't met anyone so comfortable with losing themselves in the joy of a moment in so long.

I chased him, following his steps as he shifted to his skin, the wind combing through his hair like gentle fingers. Heat rolled over me at the sight of his naked torso. I shook it off. Tried to bat it back. The last thing I needed was to let that feeling control me, to lose myself again without thinking. I didn't think last time. Last time I followed a pair of hazel eyes all too easily.

"Are you coming?" he asked, striding toward the boulders at the peak.

I shifted into my skin and tried to carefully climb up the slick rocks, but ended up misstepping a few times too many.

Liam shook his head with a warm laugh.

"Where are we?" I asked.

"It's one of my spots." He held out his hand for me.

I took it, and let him help me up next to him on the rock. Carefully, we climbed a few feet until I was able to stand on a semiflat surface.

The land before us was rolling with hills and green grass that seemed to stretch out like a hand; at the palm of the hand was a large log cabin with wolves running around it. The land was surrounded by an ocean of forest, and beyond the forest was mountains with snow still on their caps.

We sat next to each other. He let his legs hang off while I crossed mine.

"It's beautiful, isn't it? I come here a lot. It's quiet," he said, scratching the back of his head.

I brought my knees up to my chest. "I could get used to this." My voice was quiet, almost a murmur.

He leaned back on his elbows, humming in agreement. "Lucas showed me this spot, actually. He used to let me ride on his back when I was a kid. He carried me out here all the time."

Shifting toward him, I watched him watch the view in front of us. "What was he like? Lucas?"

"He was just like Levi. Always followed him around. But Levi was much different back then. Lucas was always pranking him. He was menace," he said with a smirk. "But he had every right to be. He was so strong—so fast. Fearless. Lucas was not fucking scared of a thing. I wanted to be just like him."

"I'm sorry." The wind picked up, dancing around us. The smell of him breezed past me, a scent that made my skin heat.

"I'm sorry too," he replied.

"For?"

"I'm sorry about what happened to you. My dad told me a little," he mumbled. He looked over at me and opened his mouth but closed it quickly.

I felt my heart twist a bit. I pulled my knees closer and tried to shield the scars from his view. "Thank you." I paused, hoping to change the conversation. "Well, I don't think Tia and Jake hate me anymore."

Liam rolled his eyes. A grin formed that showed his dimples. "They never did. Your past is your business. You did nothing wrong. It's just going to take time. I also threatened Jake, so, you're welcome?"

"Liam," I groaned, shoving his shoulder as his warm laughter sounded around us. "You're right, though, there is a lot to learn."

"I can't imagine. Being born this way is hard enough."

I looked over and gave him a small smile. "Seems like you're not doing too bad."

He chuckled. His well-defined torso was on full display and I couldn't help but stare in appreciation. "According to who? You or my uncle?"

I quickly snapped my sight away and tried to hide my blush.

"Levi cares about you."

Liam was quiet before turning forward again. "I missed him too. I used to sneak out and go to his house. Always staying far from the columns. That was the rule for so long for the whole pack. Never go past them. I always wanted to go to him, but either Derek or Elliot would catch me and shoo me away. Up until recently I think that was totally fair to do. They stopped doing it a while ago. A few times I've run into him."

"And?"

Liam laughed through his nose. "Every time we talked about the weather before one of us would walk away. It was almost a running joke between us, or I liked to think it was."

I licked my lips. "After so much time, people become strangers to each other. It's hard when people expect you to act like someone you can't be again."

His smile fell a hair. He looked forward. "Maybe you're right."

I shrugged. Silence encompassed us. I felt a humming.

It was like there was a tiny force dancing between us. I loved and hated it at the same time. I tried to shake it off. I couldn't let it influence me. I had enough to worry about.

"What about you, though?" he asked.

"What about me?"

Liam leaned on his side. "I mean, how are you doing with all of this?" When I couldn't answer him, he reached over to my knee, giving me a reassuring squeeze. "Hey, you don't have to talk about it if you don't want to."

I brushed his hand away. "I'm sorry, I just—" I exhaled. "I'm not good at this, at being friends. I hadn't really had any until I came here and met Derek and your uncle." Pausing, I looked back at the mountains. "It just all baffles me. I mean, some days I feel like I can handle everything, then other days I remember that the life I am now living was once make-believe to me and I feel like I'm about to lose it."

"Blows," Liam said, shaking his head. "I think you're doing badass to be honest. I mean, you made it. Which, like, never happens. And you're a moon blood, which is sick. I knew you'd make it, though."

I smiled. "Well, the rabbits' feet helped. Which Levi totally knows about. You're lucky he didn't have your ass."

He arched a brow. "Thinking about my ass?" My cheeks heated. Liam laughed, giving my knee a gentle shove. "Kidding. Besides, Levi has already threatened me if I so much as look at you wrong. I would prefer to keep my balls intact."

I bit back a smile and nodded. "So, friends then?"

"Is that what you want?"

It felt like he was asking something else—asking for

permission for more. Something I couldn't give him. At least not now. Slowly, I nodded.

His smile deepened. "Friends, then."

I turned forward and pointed at the mountains. "What's out there? Just the range?"

Liam shook his head. "No, this actually faces west. Hemlock Pack is on the other side of the forest, facing the mountains. Farther down the pack line the forest breaks and it's just hills between the two packs." He watched me a moment. "Hemlock was Eve's home pack. It's where it happened, the attack."

I swallowed. What was I to say to that? It was insane to think about how close yet how far away the next pack over was—and how so many rogues were able to overcome them.

"And it was this pack and Hemlock that were attacked?"

Liam nodded. "And Switchback. They're on the other side of Hemlock. They face the mountains too," he said, pointing farther west. "We have a border that we share with them. Their territory looks like a boot, kicking the bottom half or our land, with the top half bordering Hemlock."

The sun rolled over his skin as he stood, highlighting his abs in a way that made my skin heat. Immediately, I lowered my eyes. I felt the beast in me prodding, trying to get a peek, and I could not blame her, but now was certainly not the time for that.

"Come on, Char, if I don't get you back soon, I'm pretty sure Levi is going to skin me alive."

I gave the mountains one more look before quickly shifting and chasing after Liam.

When I got home Levi was drinking on the porch. He

nodded to Liam, who didn't step past the columns today. I waved to him before watching him dip into the forest, like a rock falling below the surface of the water.

"He going to be putting any more shit on the window-sills?" Levi snickered and stood up before walking inside.

Striding across the yard, I was careful not to step on the baby blades of grass I could see sticking up from the dirt.

Levi came back outside with a bottle of beer. He uncapped it with a bottle opener screwed onto the outside wall of the house, then handed it to me.

"I've never been a beer girl."

Levi sat back in his chair. "Today you are." I took a drink, trying to hide the small cringe. My eyes darted to the bottle opener. "Lucas put that damn thing there," he said.

Levi leaned back in his seat and closed his eyes, letting what was left of the sun warm his face. I sat in the chair next to him, taking another pull.

"How was your day?" I asked.

"I checked some borders with Lander."

My heartbeat picked up. "Why? Is there something wrong?"

Levi opened his eyes, holding my gaze for a breath. "There are no rogues, if that's what you're asking."

I shook my head. "Then what's out there?"

He wiped his face. "I don't know." He took a drink from his beer. "How was the team?"

"Well, they thought the muffins were really good."

Levi snorted. "They have no taste." My jaw dropped. He tipped his head back with a laugh. "Well, they weren't as bad as that cardboard you made earlier."

"Wow." I took a pull from my beer. "Love the encouragement."

"I'll get you an apron."

"Fuck off."

He chuckled quietly. I traced the condensation on the bottle with my thumbs. Levi leaned forward. "You remember what we talked about? With bondmates and true mates?"

"Bondmates you can have a bond with, and true mates are what we should hope I don't find for a while. Do I get a gold star?"

He rolled his eyes. "Just be careful. Little embers can become full fires faster than you think."

I pushed a hand through my hair. "What would we do? If they showed up here? What if they're from the other side of the planet?"

"Then I hope they get real used to Thunderhead," he answered with a laugh. Relief flooded me, the beast in me pleased with this answer. "In our world, the woman doesn't always have to follow the man, but mates do stay together. Hell, Bowie's mate is from Japan. Point is, it's not unheard of."

"He's a park ranger, right?"

Levi hummed in confirmation.

"Where is he now?"

"He's visiting his family. He doesn't go back often, so he's going to be there for a few months to catch up," he explained. "Point is, you have a choice."

"But what if that happens?"

"Then it happens. Cross that bridge when it comes. There's nothing more you can do but that."

"So, you think I'll have one of these mate things?"

He rolled his eyes. "You're a real piece of work, you know that?"

I lifted my beer to him. "Learning from the best." I tipped the top of my bottle at a column. "Why do you still keep them up?"

He was quiet a moment before saying, "I don't know." He took one last pull then stood. "My two cents? Don't feed it."

Stepping around me, he walked inside the house. The screen door banged shut behind him. Suddenly, this pull I'd felt with Liam felt like one of the weeds I had been ripping up with Penny, and I wasn't entirely sure if I wanted to rip it out.

CHAPTER ELEVEN

"We should take the Jeep," Liam groaned from behind the open hood of a beat-up white F-150. Even parked, it looked ready to give out.

"White Lightning is as good as gold. Nothing wrong with it," Lander countered.

I was sitting on the ledge of the truck bed, next to Lyle, who was eating a bag of Goldfish crackers. He nudged me with his arm, offering me the bag.

"I'm good," I told him.

He shrugged. "Suit yourself." Tossing another cracker into his mouth, he spotted Penny talking with Tia. He shoved the bag into my hands. "Hold this."

Jumping down, the boy darted after Penny, who lunged

out of his grasp. The two of them laughed as they chased each other around the truck, and the Suburban parked next to it.

Bowie had showed up on our front porch this morning. She'd told Levi that she and Lander needed to make some trades with Talia's pack, and I was going with them. After a heated argument, thankfully Bowie somehow won. I was looking forward to venturing out. The idea of seeing what else was around pleased the beast in me, although I could not deny a small sense of anxiety.

Before I'd left, I'd dug out some of the cash that I had stowed away from when I first ran out of my duffel. It was so foreign to look at. I hadn't had to use money since I came to the pack, but Levi had told me a while back that everyone should have cash stored in case shit ever hit the fan. So I kept it in the back corner of my closet along with an old Chanel bag and some jewelry that I could pawn just in case.

Penny screamed again, laughing as Lyle tickled her side.

Tia came to lean against the truck. "They've been inseparable since they could walk."

"Do you think they're mates?" I asked, surprising myself with my question.

It didn't seem to faze Tia. "You can't find your mate until after you shift and get through puberty. Which is different for everyone."

Remi jogged up with Claire on his heels.

"Morning, you," Claire said, hugging me to her. "I'm so glad you're coming along. You'll love Talia."

"It will be good to get out," I agreed.

Claire winked at me then eyed Lander. He stiffened,

silver eyes darting to hers in a heated look, before he shut the hood. "Play nice," he told her with a sly smile.

She licked her lips. "Absolutely not."

I looked away, blushing.

"Let's get a move on." Claire turned to Tia. "Bowie forget something?"

Just then, Bowie jogged out of the trees with a brown bag in her hand. "Left my purse."

Liam came around to the back of the truck. His hair smelled like fresh shampoo and was still damp. My fingers itched to run through it. Immediately, I felt exposed for having that thought.

"You're with me and Rem," he told me.

"She is not," Bowie interjected. "You and Remi are with your dad and Lyle."

"And Pen!" Lyle added.

Bowie rolled her eyes. "Fine, little Thorne." She turned her violet gaze to me. "You're with the girls."

Liam didn't argue. Instead, he gave my fingers a squeeze before tapping his temple. I nodded to him, avoiding the question in Tia's eyes as I followed Bowie and Claire to the Suburban.

We pulled out behind the truck and drove together for almost half an hour down a small path that curled around the trees until we hit a dirt road. I looked back at the path. "Has that always been there?"

Tia laughed. "Yeah, but humans think that path is just trees." She rolled her window down. "Smell it?"

The scent of burning sugar floated into the cabin. My breath hitched. Claire's eyes caught mine in the rearview mirror. "It's why you only saw trees before. Although some areas are starting to fade. We're about due for the witches to come in and spruce them up."

"How does that work?"

"It's dictated through our council. Like humans, we have plenty of bureaucracy," she explained. "For the witches, someone from our regional council brokers a deal with a coven that the rest of the council will vote on. Our region has worked with the same coven for years. They're good at what they do, discrete, and not overpriced. As far as the magic? It depends. Some areas require more tune-ups because it takes more magic, and some don't. For our region they usually send someone to come check the borders around once a year. If they need reinforcements, they'll schedule a time later to bring in more of their coven to help."

"It's pretty corporate," I observed.

Claire laughed. "You'd be surprised. They keep to themselves, but money is money. For most of them, if you want anything, you just have to know their price."

I leaned back in my seat. Tia rolled the window up while Bowie turned the dial on the radio until an oldies rock station came on. The cabin tossed with every pothole that we hit, the road bumpy due to the storms we'd had.

"So," Tia whispered into my mind. "*You and Liam?*"

I picked at my sweatshirt. "*He's just a friend.*"

Tia rolled her head to look at me, her brows arching. "*Does he know that?*"

I shrugged. "*It's nothing. It's the last thing I need right now.*"

She waved me off. "*What's a little fun going to hurt? It's not like your true mate is here. You'd know by now. Oh! What if you meet them at Talia's? How wild would that be?"*

A cold sweat broke out on the back of my neck. I had to bite my lip so a whimper wouldn't sound.

The light of excitement died in Tia's eyes. She cocked her head. *"It would be a good thing—one of the biggest blessings the Moon Goddess could ever grant."* She licked her lips. *"It's supposed to be a feeling that no one can truly explain. I can't imagine what it would be like to have a mark that never fades."*

"What are—what's a mark?"

Her eyes went wide and her cheeks flushed. Her eyes darted forward, her chin tilting toward Claire. *"The scar on Claire's wrist. The silver one. That's where Lander marked her."* Vomit crept up my throat. *"Lander's is on his chest,"* she noted. My mind flickered back to the silver scar right above his left pectoral. The half-moon one that I always assumed was from silver or something odd because it looked almost elegant compared to the other scars he sported. *"Marks from true mates never fade. If you only have a bondmate they do, and you have to—"*

"I don't want know." My tone was colder, harsher than it should be.

Tia frowned, her eyes filling with worry. *"Charlotte, it's common knowledge you should know. It's how mates bind their souls together. It's beautiful."*

In that moment, eating my own vomit sounded more beautiful than that. Tia bit her lip, holding her words for a moment. *"Look, you could always have Levi send out a worn item of clothing of yours to the other packs around. That way you could know."*

I shook my head as fear wrapped around my chest. *"I don't want to know."*

My beast whined in the back of my mind but I swatted her away. Tia tilted her head. *"But it would be a blessing . . ."*

"But you're stuck with them—trapped," I found myself answering. *"What if you want to get away? Why don't we have a choice? Why is it so fucking hard to be able to have that? I just—"* I stopped the words that were pouring out of my thoughts. Rambling was a habit I didn't know if I would ever break.

She plucked at her seat belt. *"I never thought about it differently. It's how we all grew up,"* she conceded. *"I'm sorry."*

"For?"

"Whoever hurt you."

I turned and looked out the window. *"He's long in the past. He can't touch me anymore."*

"I didn't know." She was quiet for a beat. *"What would do if you saw him again?"*

I shook my head, realizing more and more that what Nate had done was more than physical. Bitterness was not something I wanted to make my best friend, but I wasn't sure how to shake it. I felt the electricity gently pulse through my veins, like a blanket wrapping itself gently around me.

Tia's hand reached for mine. *"You don't realize it, do you?"*

I turned back to her, my brows furrowed. *"Realize what?"*

She offered me a small smile. *"Your blood sizzles like you're always on guard. It's like a constant low simmer. You don't have to be."*

"Habit, I guess."

Her smile faltered slightly.

"Stop gossiping without us," Claire teased us from the front seat.

Bowie smirked. "In this car, you have to spill the dirty deets."

I rolled my eyes. "What is Talia's pack like?" I asked, desperate to change the conversation.

Claire turned to face us. "It's by the ocean. They've been there for a long time, but she's always loved the water. We used to joke when we were girls that she was really a mermaid."

Bowie chuckled along with us.

I leaned forward in my seat. "How did you meet her, Bowie?"

"My father and hers were quite close, so we spent a lot of time together growing up. Thick as thieves. I would spend many weekends with her. She would always come visit too. We practically had dual membership to each other's packs." She tilted her head up and looked at Tia in the rearview mirror. "Practically had to help her chase that one around when she was a pup."

Tia rolled her eyes. "I wasn't that bad."

Bowie nodded with a soft smile. "You weren't. Anyhow, Talia is practically family."

A smile pulled on my lips. Claire leaned the side of her head against the headrest so she could face us. "Bowie, tell them about how you had a crush on Talia's mate before she met him."

Bowie scoffed. "I did not. He does have a nice ass, though."

Tia and I broke into giggles, as if we were schoolgirls. Claire gave Bowie's shoulder a playful push. "Talia is a good friend. We were both there when she beat her father and took over the pack."

I looked back at Tia, then at Claire. "What do you mean?"

Claire leaned an arm on the console. "Every pack has their way for how leadership succession is done. Talia's pack is like ours. There is a vote by the council that has to be unanimous, and the new pack lead has to defeat the old one in a challenge."

"Do they die?"

"Sometimes," Claire acknowledged. "It depends on a lot of factors. Like, if there's bad blood between old and new—think of it like a hostile takeover. But typically, in a case like Talia's, the goal is to fight until one submits. Her father was more than happy to turn the reins over to her."

"Did Levi have to do that?"

Claire's eyes pulsed. There was something that moved behind them. "He did. It was a very happy day."

"But his father . . ." Bowie laughed darkly. "Luca Thorne was a stubborn man. Lander was half convinced he would kill Levi." Her eyes caught mine in the mirror. "He loved his son, but he wasn't going to hand over the keys to the kingdom easily." She paused, looking forward at the road. "It was a happy day."

We turned off the highway close to Anchorage, following the pickup truck down a dirt track with more puddles than road. Tia smiled as she rolled down the window. The smell of salt hit my nose. She stuck her head out and took in a deep inhale. "We're almost there."

Bowie rolled down her window as well, and we all tightened our seat belts after one pothole had us all flying a foot up out of our seats. She groaned. "Max needs to re-gravel these damn roads."

After a solid forty-five minutes of feeling like my brain was ice in a cocktail shaker, we leveled out and pulled down a path where the trees started to disappear. We drove next to a cliff with the ocean licking the sides of it. I took in the view eagerly; I hadn't been able to enjoy the sights on my drive into Alaska before.

We followed a hill down to a large three-story cabin that faced the water. The front of it was all windows with what looked like hundreds of wind chimes hanging from each floor. A woman walked out the front door. Her long silver hair danced in the wind, and her green eyes smiled at us.

Bowie stopped the car, and Tia was already running toward the woman by the time I got out. She caught Tia in her arms and swung her around. "My little lightning bug," she cooed.

Butterflies filled my stomach. I tugged at my collar while I trailed behind Bowie. She held an arm out and pulled me close to her. "Come."

The woman looked up as Claire approached. Tia stepped behind her as the woman opened her arms for Claire. "Her First," Claire said with a dip of her chin before they both broke into laugher. The woman muttered something to Claire before they laughed again, embracing each other in a tight hug.

Talia leaned back to look at Bowie. A delicate brow arched. "Well, it took you long enough."

"Lander drives like your father used to. Ten miles below the speed limit." Bowie dipped her chin. "Should I call you Her First too?"

"Bitch." Talia laughed before she hugged Bowie close to her. "Should have passed him, then."

Lander stepped next to Claire, sliding his arm around her waist. He held his other hand out and grasped Talia's. "It's five miles below, I'll have you know." He dipped his head to Talia. "Her First, good to see you."

Talia rolled her eyes. "Her Second—honestly these formalities are exhausting. You're going to make poor Charlotte think that we're some dysfunctional antiquated dynasty."

Lander barked a laugh as she released his hand. She stepped around him, waving her hand forward to me. "Charlotte, I've heard so much about you."

I felt like I was naked as I walked to her. She looked ethereal, with high cheekbones decorated with freckles that many would pay to have tattooed as perfectly as hers. The beast in me pressed forward, making herself known to let me know that I wasn't alone. The tips of my fingers tingled.

I held Talia's gaze, never letting my eyes drop. The beast in me stepped closer, pushing me to hold fast, banishing my insecurities to a part of my brain where they'd be locked away.

Pausing, I darted my eyes to Bowie's then back to Talia. "I'm sorry, I'm—" *Suddenly so aware of everyone looking at me and unable to form complete sentences.*

She shook her head at Lander. "See, I told you." She

opened her arms, carefully pulling me to her in a warm hug. "Talia is fine. You're most welcome here."

My arms acted on their own, hugging her back. "Thank you."

She pulled away from me with a warm smile then leaned around me. "And you two, well, you're not going to say hello?"

Liam and Remi groaned. Talia tapped her cheek as Remi walked to her. He lazily rolled his eyes, then pressed his lips quickly to her cheek. "Hey, Auntie Ti."

She playfully shoved him away before hugging Liam. He stepped away and strode over to stand with me. His fingers gave mine a reassuring squeeze.

Talia waved us all forward. "Now, come on, I bet you're hungry." Penny practically launched herself at Talia, who easily picked her up with a laugh. She set the girl down and took her hand. "Max is grilling for you all," she said.

"Thank god. I am fucking hungry," Remi said.

"Remington!" Bowie snapped.

Talia snickered then looked at Lander. "Let's you and me handle business first. If you behave, I'll let you have a beer."

We followed her around to the back of the pack house, where a tall man with a bright-red man bun was flipping burgers on a long black grill. A few wolves were running around in the giant yard with picnic tables set up around it. Liam ran forward to hug one of the younger men, Remi on his heels.

"Come on, Char," Claire called to me from over her shoulder. The wolf in me was pacing. I jogged to Claire and Tia, who were following Bowie over to the man at the grill.

She muttered something to him, and he grunted a laugh. Claire put her hand on my shoulder. "Charlotte, this is Max, Talia's mate."

I held my hand out. "It's nice to meet you. Thank you for this."

He held my gaze for a moment before taking my hand in his large one, which was covered in tattoos, like the rest of him. "Levi's pup?"

"She is," Bowie answered for me.

A soft smile tugged on lips almost camouflaged by a beard that was braided a foot below his chin. "Eat," he told me, handing me a plate.

Tia took my hand and pulled me in line behind the boys, who had already each piled three burgers on top of their plates. I was reaching for a smaller patty with the tongs when Max stopped my arm. He shook his head, taking the tongs from me and plating one of the larger ones for me. "You need to eat more."

"Thanks?" I replied, stumbling after Tia.

She eyed me. "He likes you."

"He only said like four words to me?"

Tia chuckled. "Max has never been much of a talker. For years I thought he could only grunt."

Turning, I checked him out again. "Well, Bowie's right. He does have a nice ass."

Tia laughed, her body shaking. The sound of it was contagious, spreading to me. We stopped in front of the tables, looking for an open seat. I scanned the area and found a woman sitting on her own. Long chestnut hair flowed in the wind behind her.

"Who's that?" I asked, watching the woman, who refused to look around her. She chewed methodically, almost like she was asleep. It was a hollowness I recognized all too well.

Tia stepped closer to me. *"That's Andrea. She—well, her partner found his true mate recently. Auntie Ti said it's been horrible for her."*

I felt my own heart squeeze for her. *"He just left her?"*

"Auntie Ti said that he told her he loved her, but the mate pull was too strong. He left with his new mate before winter to go back to the mainland."

"Tia!" a voice called. A group of young people were waving at her.

She nudged her head at them. "Come on."

I shook my head. "You go on."

She looked back at Andrea. *"Be careful. Heartbreak makes people dangerous."*

Oh, I knew that. I was living with the most heartbroken man in the world. Heartbreak was familiar, almost comfortable at this point.

"I'll be fine," I assured her.

Walking around a table, I stopped next to a cooler and picked up two bottles of beer, then continued until I was standing in front of Andrea.

Her skin was flawlessly tan and her long legs stretched out to the side of the table. She looked tired. The kind of tired you become after seeing too much—from existing through things that rob you of too much sleep.

Her nostrils flared. "What are you doing?" she drawled.

"Well, clearly I would like to sit and eat. I brought beer." She looked up, her twenty-four carat golden eyes blazing at me as if they were molten. My toes twisted in my shoes. "Also trying to break this awkward silence. This is fucking uncomfortable. Do you mind?"

Her pouty mouth twitched, body held stiff. But I didn't miss the way her eyes pulsed slightly in surprise. There was a glow that started to form around her eyes, as if the beast in her was as curious about mine as mine was about hers.

Suddenly, she leaned back, tipped her chin and laughed. I could feel the gazes from the people around us beaming into my back. Licking my lips, I looked back at her.

She snatched one of the beers and nodded to the bench across from her. "Go on, then."

I set my plate down and slid onto the seat. She took my beer and twisted the cap off, then passed to back to me. "Thanks?"

She raised her beer to me. "Don't mention it," she replied, before drinking about a third of the beer.

I tossed back a big sip of mine before taking a large bite from my burger.

Andrea wiped a few loose drops from her lips. "So, you're Levi's new charge."

I swallowed, shrugging. "More like his pain in the ass."

She angled her head to the side, the sun catching her high cheekbones. "My dad said he heard good things from David about you."

I sat forward, tossing a chip in my mouth. "Yeah?"

She pressed the bottle to her lips, chugging another sip. "He's Head of Security at the Hemlock Pack. He and David are best friends."

"That is kind of David to say."

My eyes flickered down, locking onto her hand snatching a chip from my plate. Her lips twitched before curling into a smirk. Then she stole another one.

I shoved the plate toward her. "By all means."

She laughed before we fell into a comfortable quiet. She stole my chips while I ate my burger. I ended up fetching us more beers and another plate of chips. Silently, she opened the bottles both for us, then took a handful of chips and tossed them into her mouth.

She wiped her hands on her jeans. "I don't want to talk about it. If that's why they sent you over."

"No one sent me. Sometimes it's good to not be alone. Friend or not." I paused, because I knew what I was saying wasn't coming out as eloquently as I had hoped. "I'm bad at this."

"At what?" she asked.

"Being friends, making friends. Being fucking friendly."

Andrea breathed a laugh. "I think you're a lot better at it than you think."

I offered her a tired smile. "I still dream about him—my ex. Even after everything. Even after all that he did to me. I can't imagine what you're going through. I'm sorry," I told her, my voice growing to almost a whisper at the end.

She leaned forward, a pressure pressing into my mind. The beast in me crept closer. My elbows rested on the table. I leaned my head to the side, holding her liquid golden gaze as I let in the intruder. A line sizzled through my brain, electricity sparking like gunfire.

"*What was he like?*" she asked.

I set my beer down and carefully tugged the collar of my shirt aside at the shoulder to show her the burn marks. *"A monster,"* I said. *"He's why I'm here. How I got bit. I was running from him."*

"I was with him for twenty years. It was like it didn't matter." My brows rose while I studied a face that didn't look a day over thirty. She laughed bitterly under her breath. *"Forty."*

"I wasn't going to—"

"I know. Slow aging and good genes," she muttered before taking a long pull from her beer. Her fingers doodled along the condensation of the bottle. *"Did you kill him?"*

I breathed a laugh through my nose. *"Death would be too kind for him."*

A slow smile crept on her lips, her canines showing. *"And Levi?"*

"He's good." I rubbed the edge of the bottle with my thumb, chasing a drop of water. *"He saved my life, helped me start this one."*

"Maybe that's what I need," she commented, looking off to the distance.

"What's that?"

"A new life," she replied. *"It's hard when everything around here reminds me of him."*

I shrugged. *"Maybe a change of scenery would be good, then?"*

"Maybe," she agreed with a nod. *"Dad said David and Levi finally sorted things out. That Levi was starting to take on more of his duties again and getting out of his hole."*

Grimacing, I took a sip of my beer. I didn't want to

remember that awful night when I stitched Levi up. "He's not a monster," I said out loud.

"No, he's not," she agreed. "He never was. After what happened, how could anyone blame him?"

"And they never found anything?" I needed to ask.

Andrea shrugged. *"Only dead ends."*

I shook my head. *"That just seems nuts. An attack that big? And nothing."*

She let out a long breath. *"It is nuts. What they found didn't lead to anything. Dead ends, like I said."* She leaned back. "Dad heard you're going through tracker training?"

"Your dad seems to hear a lot."

Andrea snickered. "He and David have always been like two gossiping hens."

"Well, it's true. Levi said I had a knack for it."

"What do you think?"

I took a sip of beer. "Let's hope Levi's right. What about you?"

She cracked a smile. "A guard. Daddy's girl. Anyhow, you didn't answer my question."

I paused a beat. "I think I have a good nose."

She hummed as if this pleased her. "You're right, sometimes it's good to drink with someone else." She drummed her fingers on the table. "I'll have to put my money on your team."

"For?"

"The Hunt," she remarked.

I grabbed my beer and leaned back in my seat. "So are we friends or what?"

Andrea cracked a lazy smile. "Yeah, we're friends." She

finished her beer then leaned forward. *"You know how to find me,"* she added, squeezing my hand before she stood up.

The wind blew, as if it was pushing her away from me. In a few seconds, she was gone, with only the memory of her long chestnut hair waving in her wake. I ate another chip, my eyes drifting to her empty beer bottle when I heard, *"Thanks,"* murmured across our new link.

CHAPTER TWELVE

Lander and Talia didn't take long to settle business. Claire said it would be an easy trade—we were bringing them new seeds to plant during the growing season as well as some fresh crops, and in return Talia was going to ship us fresh fish that we could smoke and store before next winter.

Claire took the initiative to introduce me to more members of Talia's pack, all of whom seemed to watch her with admiration—and how could one not admire her? When she smiled it was contagious, so much so I found myself always smiling around her.

When it came time to leave I helped pack up the trucks. When we said our good-byes, I looked for Andrea, but only spotted a golden wolf watching me from a distant hill. In my gut I knew it was her. I raised my hand, waving, before she disappeared to the other side.

A hand touched my shoulder. I turned to face Talia. A few wisps of silver hair floated in the wind, her eyes glowing almost a neon green. "Thank you."

I tilted my head. "For what?"

She nudged her chin toward the hill. "She's been far away from us since everything happened. I was afraid she would retreat into herself. I haven't seen her laugh in a long time."

I put my own hand over hers, holding it. "It's nothing. It's easier to sit in the dark when you've done it before."

Her eyes went soft as she pulled me in for a warm hug. "You are always welcome here." She leaned toward my ear, whispering, "And if you ever need somewhere to go, just remember to follow the Thunderhead Creek until you start to smell the ocean. Remember, we're the Timber Pack, the Timber Falls border my land."

It was a kindness, I knew. A kindness that she did not have to offer, because I had a home. A good one, and I wasn't about to leave it.

"I won't leave him," I asserted.

She hesitated. "It is not him of whom I speak, for I know he would no sooner harm you than he would his own pup."

"Wha—"

"Char!" Remi called from the SUV, waving at me. "Let's roll!"

Talia hugged me tight to her, like she was trying to feel if I was real or not. "May the moon's light shine upon you," she murmured before backing away.

Scratching the back of my neck, I backpedaled to Claire, who closed Penny into the SUV with Liam and Tia. She smiled at me. "You're with me and Bowie. Did you have fun?"

"Talia is lovely," I told her. "It's beautiful here."

Claire looked around with an easy smile. "Next time we'll plan to stay longer. It's fun in the summer. She has a few beaches that are the best."

"Is the water even warm?"

She waved me off, her silver scar gleaming in the sunlight on her wrist. "We're there to tan our cheeks."

Laughing together, we walked to the truck where Bowie was sliding into the driver's seat. I opened the door and found Lyle looking up from his tablet. I narrowed my gaze at him. "You don't snore, do you?"

He tossed a goldfish at me, which I caught in my mouth. Laughing, I slid in next to him and buckled my seat belt, the sound of his video game covering the silence as we drove. But the silence only allowed more questions to marinate in my brain.

When we hit the highway, I slid forward and rested my arms on the center console. Bowie flickered her gaze at me. Claire turned to face me. "Well, do you want fries with that?"

I laughed quietly before looking at Claire, letting this beast in me carefully walk forward, because it was now as much her right to hear things as it was mine. "I have questions," I told them. "I would like answers."

Claire's face held no panic but her eyes grew a hair wider. She opened her mouth but Bowie waved her off. "Claire, enough. Look at her, she's one of us. She's a grown woman."

Claire closed her mouth, holding Bowie's gaze before she eyed behind me. She dipped her chin to me, then tapped her temples.

"*His hearing is too good, even with headphones,*" Claire said.

I rolled my eyes. "*Probably because he puts them in and turns the sound down. Classic trick.*"

"*You have to get with the times, Claire,*" Bowie teased.

Claire looked over my shoulder again, her eyes growing wistful as she watched Lyle. "*I wish I could keep him like this forever. Away from the bullshit.*"

I rested my chin in my palm. "*He's smart. He's probably more exposed than you think.*"

"*I suppose,*" she agreed.

My wolf nudged me, spurring me forward. "*Are there any pack leads that are not moon-blooded?*"

Claire nodded. "*Many are, but you don't have to be. It's not different from a lot of how humans work. The strongest isn't always the best to lead. Intelligence gets you a lot further. There are also plenty of moon-blooded wolves that choose to go into ordinary positions. Just because you have it, it doesn't mean you're some golden child. Neither David nor Bowie are.*"

"*And Talia is not?*" I asked, guessing because I never sensed from her the same feeling of pure electric power I did when I was around Levi or Lander.

Bowie's eyes caught mine. "*No, her bloodline is older, but unlike Levi and Lander, she is not. It's not uncommon— there are plenty of pack leads and their councils here and in the mainland that are not moon-blooded. You don't have to be moon-blooded to be ranked. When it comes to leading*" *a pack, there's a lot more to a person that matters besides what's running in their veins."*

"She told me how to find her pack if something happens." Bowie and Claire stilled ever so slightly in their seats. They looked at each other in a silent conversation, like they were debating which storyline to tell. "I used to work for attorneys. Believe me when I say that I'm pretty good at knowing when someone is lying. So, why would Talia tell me that?"

Bowie laughed under her breath. "I told you, she has a good nose." I arched a brow. "Trackers are observant, Charlotte. That doesn't just mean finding tracks in the woods."

Claire let out a long breath, settling back in her seat. "Many people think there's still danger in our woods, and rightfully so. We looked for so long for anything that could help us catch the right people after the attack. Stop it from happening again, but it was dead ends. Whoever attacked was working with powerful witches—the magic they used was advanced, untraceable.

"After years, the leadership in the region agreed that we would close the case. We needed to move on, heal. Obviously, you can understand how that would upset a lot of people. Levi was beside himself. He had been holding it together better than I thought because of the investigation but when it ended, he lost it again. A lot of people did."

I couldn't imagine. It had to have been like watching the lifeline of hope disappearing. "So," I began, "some people think there is still danger?"

"Yes," Bowie answered. "Talia was one of the ones who adamantly wanted to keep looking. She thought it was foolish to stop."

"*And you?*"

She drummed her fingers on the steering wheel. "*I agreed.*"

Claire ran a hand through her hair. "*I had to help Lander, you have to understand. Levi and Eve ran the pack together. Levi was the pack lead but Eve was like an extension of him. Lander and I supported them, and not just because Lander's his second or his brother, but it was how we did things and it worked really well . . . but then it was just the two of us. We had David and Bowie but it was a lot. And with the kids, it was—*"

"*It's okay, Claire,*" I told her. She didn't need to make an excuse, apologize for something that she shouldn't feel sorry about.

"*Talia is just—well, she's cautious. That was very kind of her to offer you that,*" Claire acknowledged.

I turned to Bowie. "*So what's in the forest?*"

Her eyes darted to me. "*So far, nothing, which is what scares me the most.*"

The sound of the video game murmured behind us, the muted music ascending over and over—Lyle must have hit a string of high scores. Biting my lip, I felt my wolf nudge me again. "*But you think there's something there?*"

She was quiet for a moment before she looked at me, her eyes holding a soft glow. "*I do.*"

I leaned back against my seat, thinking back to the forest, to the silence of it—suffocating darkness that seemed to lurk at its edge.

"*I found them,*" Bowie whispered into my mind.

Furrowing my brows, I felt around the link. It was just

the two of us. Just her and me. My eyes slowly rose to meet hers in the rearview mirror.

"I was the first one to make it to Hemlock. I knew something was wrong—very wrong. But we couldn't link that day, something stopped us. I knew I could get there first. I'd already locked Remi in the basement with Gran and my mate. He'd been attacked by a rogue, and his injuries were too severe for him to come with me. When I knew they were safe, I ran and ran and ran. I've never run so hard before."

Her fingers tightened on the steering wheel. Claire was looking out the window, her shoulder to us. *"There was so much blood. Everything was red. I won't ever forget what I saw. I can't. Walking into that pack was like walking into a war zone. It was littered with bodies. So many of the bodies had their fangs pulled."* She moved the truck into the right-hand lane, a long breath escaping her lips. *"The bodies of the guards who stood by Chris, Hemlock's pack lead, that day were hanged from the trees near where the murders took place. I found one of my best friends there—Cash, their Head Tracker, hanging from the trees. They'd cut his feet off.*

"And then I found them. Eve and Lucas. They were executed together with Chris, his mate, and his oldest son, Eli. It was like the stories of fur traders that my own father used to tell me. They were all lying face down in a giant pool of blood, the skin on their backs gone. Chris's mate was half-shifted."

I covered my mouth. Bile crept up my throat. She nodded. *"They took their pelts, and fangs, and claws. Which is a vile thing to do. Taking the fangs from a wolf is what old clans used to do to the enemies they defeated. Skinning them? It's a desecration—spitting in the moon's eye."*

Lyle was still glued to his game, which was a good thing because I felt my throat constrict at the thought of what had happened. Bowie hit the blinker to switch lanes and pass a slower, beat-up silver car.

"It's the screaming I can't forget. Ethan was somehow still alive. He was covered in Eli's blood, holding on to him, howling—I'll never forget that sound," she added, her voice trembling. *"I tried to pull him away, practically had to fight him, but Levi showed up with Lander and David. More guards were finally coming in from other packs. We had killed most of the rogues by then. It smelled like bad magic there. Foul magic."*

I didn't want to know, but I had to. I had to know now. My eyes were wet. I could feel the tears wanting to fall. *"What happened to him? Levi?"*

She shook her head, her own eyes starting to water. *"Ethan ran to him. Levi forced him away. We could all see him about to lose it. I could never blame him, I almost lost it. Eve was my friend. . . . She didn't even look like herself, and Lucas . . . I grabbed Ethan and had our guards get him out of there. Levi—he took one look at Eve and Lucas and it was all a blur. He was fighting all of us. He almost killed David. We only got him back to our pack because I was able to get him to chase me."*

"You weren't scared?"

She shook her head. *"He'd never be able to catch me."* She paused, her eyes finding mine again. *"We all felt his pain that day. It was our pain. The first year after it was a haze. We all took turns watching him."*

"Where?"

"At home," she answered. "We never locked him up because we knew he'd break out—it's why we built the columns. They were a warning to the pack to stay away. A border for them, if you will. But even when Levi got out, he always ended up back in the yard. I spent so many nights herding him back to his home when he lost himself to the sadness."

"I'm so sorry." I wiped my cheeks.

There was a sad smile on her lips. She wiped away a tear of her own. "People started to create ghost stories about him after a while. The stories became so far from the truth, because he was never a monster. He was broken in a way I wouldn't wish on anyone. The real monsters are the ones that took them from us."

I licked my lips. "Ethan and the other kids are Levi's nephews?"

"That's right. Chris, their pack lead who was murdered, was Eve's brother. Three of his children are left. Ethan, Evan, and Evangeline."

"What happened to them? What happened to that pack?"

"Well, Thomas took over. He was Chris's second, and made it, by the grace of the moon. He was more or less on life support for weeks and weeks. They'd hung him up with the other guards—we all thought he was dead. They tortured him. Ripped his fangs out."

"Oh my god . . ."

She nodded. "Ethan is Thomas's second now. Evan and Evangeline still live there. We don't see them often, not unless it's for business. The pack mostly keeps to itself."

I sat there, shaking my head slowly. "No suspects at all?"

"Nothing that panned out to anything. All we know is that they were working with a powerful clan of witches, using *vile blood magic no one had ever heard of or seen before, and creating rogues. A lot of them. Many thought it was a rogue experiment gone wrong, some blamed it on rebel groups, but we never could find anything concrete.*

"That doesn't make any sense."

Her eyes lifted, meeting mine in a gaze that sent a chill down my spine. *"I know."*

We pulled into a place called The Hole that had a faded Piggly Wiggly sign on the far left. The doorway was painted yellow, and a few cars littered the parking lot.

Lyle looked up. His eyes spotted the sign. "Mom!" He bolted forward. "Mom, can I get—"

"Limit the candy to two bags," Claire told him. "We just need to get gas and pick up a few more things."

"I need to stretch my legs," Bowie said, cracking her neck to the side. She looked cramped in the cabin, as if she wanted to run. I did too. The sadness riding as another passenger with us was suffocating.

She parked the car close to the doors. Claire looked at me over her shoulder. "We won't be long."

"I think I may just take a hot lap and stretch my legs."

"They have some good snacks," she remarked, but I didn't have an appetite.

I jumped out of the car and caught smiling silver eyes. Relief poured over me as Liam approached. "Come on, let's walk around," he said, taking my hand.

I shouldn't have let him hold my hand, but it was nice to

have someone leading me forward while my mind felt like a despondent mire after the earlier conversation in the car. He led me through the sliding glass doors to what seemed like a normal grocer. Aisles lined up in neat rows, carrying standards like rice, condiments, and toilet paper. In the far corner the groceries ended and retail began with clothing, camping gear, and what looked like an auto section.

"Cupcakes or camping?"

I didn't have the appetite for anything with pink frosting at the moment. "Camping."

Liam pulled me along with him, passing the meat market where a man was slicing ham for a woman with two small children. A smile tugged on my lips at the sight of the baby, who was babbling nonsense like it was the most important thing in the world.

We turned a corner and walked through men's clothing. Liam paused and picked up a pair of wool socks. "Want some?"

I swatted them away. "I think I'm good."

He put them back. "You sure? No one likes cold feet."

"Maybe they do?"

He arched a brow. "Well, let me rephrase, no one likes cold corpse feet touching them."

My cheeks heated. "Liam," I groaned. He laughed under his breath, his eyes darting to me again in a look that set the butterflies to flight in my stomach.

We found an area with tents. Many were on display in a setting that was made to look like a campsite. Some of the tents were huge—I was convinced you could put a whole army in there—while others were tiny, only made for one person.

"Are you okay?"

"Yeah."

"You're not." He stepped closer, his brows furrowing in concern. "Char?"

"Bowie told me about that day—about what happened," I whispered.

He let out a long breath, tightening his grip on my hand. "Yeah." The sadness in his eyes grew. He brushed some hair behind my ears. "It's not your pain to carry."

"It is now," I answered. "It has been." Because living with Levi meant living through the sadness that was still left. Carrying the burden when he was in a mood. It was never not going to be my burden, but now, I would be more than happy to carry it for him. It was the least I could do.

Liam pulled me toward one of the tents, a mischievous grin on his lips. "Camp much?"

I shook my head. "Only blanket forts."

Liam chuckled while testing one of the structures. "Sounds like my mom, she loves a good blanket fort."

"My uncle Benji would always make a giant blanket fort and my mother would help me roast marshmallows in our fireplace. He always convinced my mom to let me stay up late so we could watch movies." As an adult, I realized he'd been trying to give my mother some space so she didn't have to pretend to be so strong all the time after my father died.

"That sounds fun."

"It was."

I pointed to the tent he was standing in front of. "So, what about this tent? Proper for camping?"

Liam shook his head a bit, tossing the idea back and forth in his brain. "It's too small. You're going to be cramped in there with a sleeping bag. I think this one would be better," he said, pointing to a purple tent.

I peered inside while Liam did a large circle around it. I crawled into it to see if I would be comfy. It was big enough for only one person, maybe two. I sat down, oddly enjoying how snug it was.

"On the Hunt we'll probably be out there overnight, but we don't get tents. We'll sleep in our fur." Liam looked through the entrance and smiled deviously before tossing himself inside, practically knocking the tent over. He laughed and leaned on his elbows as he sat back. "I like it in here, it's cozy."

I rolled my eyes and shoved him away. "So no tents?"

He shook his head, his smile showing the dimples in his cheeks. "No tents."

"Levi said there are maybe bears out there? Mountain lions?"

Liam sat up and pushed his white-blond hair back. I so wanted to run my fingers through it in that moment, but I clenched them into a fist to keep them from doing what I knew I should not.

He wiggled his head back and forth. "Maybe? You never know. Some people have finished the Hunt and not seen anything but their team and the buck. Others have run into trouble. It just depends."

"Lucas killed a bear, though?"

"Lucas was a fucking nightmare. I don't know if anyone could live up to him." Liam smiled, eyes growing heavy with something I didn't dare acknowledge. He pushed a dark lock of my hair back. "You know, Dad wasn't sure what Levi would do for so long after they died. He was just . . . existing. But you seem to have given him something to live for."

"Do you think we'll run into trouble?"

"The only trouble I hope to run into out there is you," he said teasingly.

My cheeks heated up. Goose bumps broke out over my skin. My heart fluttered and I knew that I should stop it— walk away. But I couldn't deny how good it felt.

I felt fingers on my cheek. Cool fingers that left spurts of electricity as they traced my cheekbone. I sighed and leaned into it. I couldn't help it. The feeling was so enticing, so deliciously magnetic.

"I think we're bad at being friends," he whispered to me.

His lips drew near mine. His breath was hot, like a warm wind against my skin. It was spicy and sweet, his scent mixed with the smell of desire quickly filling the small space.

I felt his lips graze mine, testing the waters to see if they would invite him in. I wanted to invite him in. I knew better. I so knew better.

But in that moment, I just wanted to enjoy feeling desired by someone whose agenda wasn't to use me and toss me away. After so long, it was almost foreign to be kissed by someone who wanted to make me smile just because they could. But the newness of it was easily cast away, because the little flames of fire sparking where his lips touched mine were enough to make me want to drown myself in his kiss.

Then it hit me. The stench.

Rotten and sickly.

Liam snapped his head away from mine and looked out the tent flap, where the scent was flowing in. His silver eyes glowed as he pulled me close to his side. He closed his mouth and inhaled then let out a low growl that he immediately tried to suppress.

I knew before he even said it.

"Rogues."

He moved to the flap, cracking it to look around. His shoulders tensed as the encroaching scent of the rogue wolves grew thicker.

The beast in me was pulsing now, a pulse that I could feel rolling off Liam in waves. She was licking her lips, eager to charge out at the threat. I yanked her back. We had to be smart right now. This time, instead of fighting me, she listened, and settled until I could feel her comfortably waiting on my next move.

Liam took my hand and pulled me close to him. His raised his finger to his lips. *"Stay right next to me and act natural. We are going straight to the car. There are humans here, remember that."*

Before I could answer, he planted a chaste kiss on my lips, taking the breath out of me. He started to pull me out of the tent when panic hit me. My feet froze in place. *"Lyle and Penny?!"*

"With my mom, in the car."

He held me tight against him as we walked briskly out of the camping section. Remi sailed around a corner, falling in step next to me. His eyes were a storm, his jaw tight.

"They're in the back right. Just keep walking."

"How many?" Liam asked.

"Three," Remi answered. "Follow me."

He turned us down an aisle with cat litter and food, all of us walking silently on our toes. Remi stopped at the front of the aisle, then held a hand up. He pressed his back against the wall, holding a finger to his mouth. Liam plastered me next to him, my other shoulder digging into Remi's side.

I put a hand over my mouth, holding my breath as the stench combed over my face. Remi stilled as footsteps approached. There was a squeaking sound, the rubber of a sneaker catching the clean tiles.

Two men walked past us. Two men who didn't look as distraught as the kind of rogues that had been described to me. Two men who looked like the ones I had seen before. They were calm, almost in a trance, wearing worn clothing that looked like it hadn't been washed in weeks. One man had a nasty bruise on his bald head, but he seemed to only be concerned with the Twinkie he was shoving into his mouth.

"I thought you said there were three?" I asked Remi.

The steps grew faint and the smell thinned. He looked at Liam and me. *"The doors are less than fifty feet away. Keep walking. Your dad wants everyone out before he comes in."*

Remi tipped his nose to the air, his nostrils flaring again. He looked at Liam then nodded. We darted from our hiding place toward the doors that were opening and closing lazily as customers walked in and out. We took another step then the scent hit me like a punch.

I felt the hair on the back of my neck rise as fur started to poke through. Liam's fingers dug into my ribs. We kept walking even though my wolf wanted me to turn around.

Remi reached for my shoulder, but the beast in me wanted blood.

I looked over my shoulder and met the hazy red eyes of a male who licked his lips like I was his next meal at the sight of me. Liam cursed under his breath then came to stand next to me. "I suggest you two turn and go back where you came from."

One of the men, tall and gangly with buzz-cut white hair, chuckled darkly. "Not with that pretty thing on your arm, nope. She is a fine-smelling little thing."

I bit back a snarl. Remi stepped alongside us, starting to circle the men like prey. "She isn't any of your concern," he sneered.

The shorter man tipped his nose into the air, his nostrils flaring. His hand reached for his low stringy ponytail, curling it around his fingers in a way that made it look like a rat's tail.

"I don't see your mark on her, son. And she does smell awfully rich."

The beast in me snapped her teeth. Electricity pulsed over me while my feet took two steps forward. Rage was fueling me now as memories flooded me.

"Why don't we all go outside and I'll show you boys a good time," I said sweetly, letting my fangs show with a smile that seemed to scare theirs off.

The tall man stepped forward but the short one caught his arm. His eyes met mine before he shook his head at the man. The tall man stilled. I shifted my weight to the balls of my feet. The ding of a cash registered sounded. A baby's laughter rang through the air. I could hear the sound of change falling into someone's palm. Time seemed to slow, until a hand gently wrapped around my arm.

"Let's go," Liam urged me. I tore my gaze away and met his silver eyes, pulsing in a steady glow. "Let's go."

Wordlessly, I conceded, and let him pull me quickly to the doors, Remi behind us, none of us looking back.

The moment we stepped outside Lander walked inside like a calm, icy storm. My breath hitched. His eyes were set straight ahead of him, looking like cold moonlight as something rolled off him. Every step he took was deliberate and firm, his palms clenched into fists to hide the claws on his fingers.

In that moment I saw the beast that Lander could become—the nightmare that could temper even Levi.

The next thing I knew, Claire was yanking us into the SUV. Bowie was fanning around the side of the building with Remi jetting to the opposite side. Claire watched Bowie and Remi disappear, her face white and hands frozen on the steering wheel.

Lyle turned to her in the front passenger seat, and put a hand on her arm. "Let's go, Mom."

Liam reached for the door handle. "I'm going with Dad—"

"You're not," Claire snarled. She shifted the car into Drive. She looked at him in the rearview mirror, her eyes heavy with a plea. "Please?"

Liam slowly retracted his hand before grasping Lyle's shoulder. "You good?"

"Yeah, let's get the hell out of here," Lyle answered, leaning back in his seat.

Penny was shaking where she sat. I slid over and put an arm around her small shoulders. "It's okay," I told her. She squeezed my free hand. She said nothing, but her grip said everything.

"Is Lander not coming?" I asked.

"They'll bring the truck back," Claire answered, not finishing with what we both knew would happen. That the trailer would have new cargo inside it.

Liam's gaze was still fixed on his mother's face. "What were they doing here?"

Claire shook her head as she peeled out of the parking lot. "I don't know."

"They weren't sick, Mom," Liam pointed out.

Claire shuddered. "Yes, they were, Liam." She wasn't wrong. These were sick, vile creatures ready to commit vile acts.

"*They were like the ones that attacked me,*" I told her.

"*I know,*" she answered before wiping a palm over her face. "We'll be home soon."

Liam was quiet next to me, his eyes fixed forward in a look I had come to recognize when wolves were linking each other.

I played idly with Penny's hair. "Do you think Bowie is okay?" she whispered, her voice tiny.

"Of course," I reassured her, offering her a small smile. "She's the fastest, right? No one can catch her."

She nodded weakly then leaned her head against my shoulder. Liam's silver eyes caught mine in the rearview mirror; they were filled with so many emotions that it almost took my breath away. His hand reached for mine, lacing our fingers together. Both of us were a mess of fear and lust; however, there was one emotion holding his whole expression together: hope. It was that emotion that sent chills down my spine.

CHAPTER THIRTEEN

Levi was sitting on the corner of the porch with a bottle of whiskey in his hand. David was sitting on the bottom step. He smiled at me but it didn't reach his eye. Liam reached out an arm to stop me from stepping forward, his eyes on Levi.

"Enough," I hissed, shoving past him and past the columns.

I hated those columns.

I hated all of this.

As I approached, David whispered something over his shoulder to Levi. David looked at me as if to tell me to wait, but I didn't care. My beast and I calmly strode forward, finding the whiskey bottle with only two shots left.

Something fizzed in me, something that made David sit

a little straighter. I carefully picked up the whiskey bottle. "I think you're done with this."

Levi was quiet. So quiet that I wasn't sure if he was going to burst out of his skin. He blinked, looking at me like he thought I wasn't really there. Before I knew what was happening, he was hugging me.

"I'm okay," I assured him.

He pulled away. "Did you have fun at Talia's?"

I nodded slowly. "I made a friend—Andrea. Talia's very lovely."

He put his hand on my shoulder. "Are you hungry?"

I shook my head, my eyes never leaving his. "I could eat. Max told me I needed to eat more," I said, laughing a little to break the awkwardness.

He nodded, squeezing my shoulder, his eyes not leaving mine, like he was pleading for me to both run and stay. I didn't know what to do, because his eyes weren't just silver.

If you looked close enough, there were fuzzy, thin red veins around his pupils. At first it looked like he had been just scratching his eyes, but after seeing the red in his eyes before, and seeing it in the eyes of those who bit me so many nights ago, I knew better.

He turned his gaze to Liam. "Go home. Now. Your mother's worried."

"Uncle—"

"Now."

Liam gave me one quick glance before turning toward the foot trail.

"And, Liam," Levi added, stilling Liam's steps. "I better not smell you around here tonight."

Liam swallowed before darting into the forest. David stood to face Levi, his green eye focused.

"Call the council. We're meeting today." Levi's voice was so calm, so cool. My spine straightened at the sound of it.

"When?" David said.

"Tonight. Here."

"I have some calls to our neighbors to make," David told him. "Hopefully I'll have intel before then."

"If you're hungry, there's plenty for you and Penny," I offered.

David's smile finally reached his eye. "That's very kind, but I need to check on her at Lander's first, then handle this. I'll be back," he promised Levi before walking off the steps and into the forest.

A quiet settled between us. Levi stepped around me toward the house. Silently, I followed him in. The beast in me paced back in forth as anxiety ate at both of us. I couldn't lose him—the madness for him had to be unbearable, but I knew that being in this pack would be impossible without him.

"Levi."

He looked at me, his eyes calming. The red was slowly starting to recede, familiar silver shining brighter. "It doesn't go away, Charlotte. It's always there."

My heart clenched. Thinking of what Bowie had told me—of what had happened—I clenched my fists, trying to snap the fear out of me. Levi went to the refrigerator and pulled condiments out while I sat at the bar.

"Do you want help?"

He shook his head. "No, you sit."

"You don't need to make a lot."

"Max is right, you do need to eat more." And right now, I wasn't about to question him.

He stopped his task and pulled out a coffee mug, then uncorked a bottle of wine we had opened the previous night, pouring a healthy amount into the cup decorated with blue-birds. He slid the cup across the counter to me then reached for the whiskey bottle he had been drinking out of. "Are you all right?"

"Yes," I answered honestly. "They never touched me."

He arched a brow. "Did they try to?"

I shook my head. "No." I paused, watching the liquid swirl in my glass. "You know, they seemed almost as surprised to run into us as we were to see them."

Levi took a sip from the bottle. "What did they look like?"

"Like the ones that attacked me," I stated. "I know that rogues are sick, but these didn't look how it sounds they're supposed to. They weren't decomposing. They seemed unhinged but not totally lost."

"Tell me everything, now."

And I did, sparing no detail other than the moments Liam and I had shared in the tent—telling Levi about that felt like it would be more dangerous than telling him about the rogues. The whole time Levi listened while making sandwiches for us.

When I was done, he took a long sip from his bottle. I had already finished my mug of wine, which had done little to calm my nerves.

"This isn't normal." It was a statement that we both knew

was true. I may have been new to this world, but this much I knew in my gut.

Levi nodded. "No, it's not normal."

"But why are they here?" I asked, my mind wandering to that dark night many months ago. A night when I met real monsters. I traced the scar on my leg. "Are they after me?"

He reached behind him for the wine, pouring more into my mug. "No. They would have tried to come after you. If you were a target, they would have recognized you." Before I could open my mouth, he caught my gaze. "Some people just want to destroy purely for the sake of destruction."

"Even destruction has a purpose," I found myself whispering back.

"Maybe so," he mused. "Regardless, we've had two of these encounters in less than a year. It's not normal at all. Usually when wolves go rogue, the packs around keep a log of them. It's shared with the other packs so we can all keep an eye on them. We try to keep them away from people if they're unstable, help them. These weren't on any logs."

I stared at the sandwich in front of me, taking another long sip of wine while Levi took up his post outside again. I finished the sandwich but it felt like a rock in my stomach that was twisted with fear that followed me all the way to bed. I stared at the ceiling for hours, my mind spinning in dizzy circles until something pulled at a link in my brain. I cocked a brow.

"Charlotte?"

"Andrea?"

"Hey."

I swallowed. *"Hey."*

"I heard about the rogues. Are you okay?"

I rubbed my face. *"Yeah, I'm fine . . . it's just unsettling. I can't sleep."*

She hummed. *"Yeah, it's pretty wild. I cased out the area with Max. We didn't find anything, if it makes you feel better."*

"It doesn't." I chuckled.

She laughed back. *"I'd probably feel the same way."*

We were both quiet a moment. *"Do you think there's more?"* I asked.

"Do you want to sleep tonight?"

"I'm already awake."

"True," she agreed. *"My dad said that rogues like these are like rats. When there's one, there's more."*

"Yeah, that will not help me sleep."

She snorted. *"You asked."*

"Also true."

"Try to sleep," she told me. *"You're deep in pack land now, and they've only been spotted on roads."*

"What do you mean?"

"Well, the ones that attacked you were spotted first at the diner, then on the dirt road up there. These were at The Hole, which is right off the highway. They've been sticking to highways."

"That's true." While it didn't make me feel better, I somehow found this information enough to quiet my racing mind. *"Thanks."*

"Don't mention it. Link if you need anything," she finished, letting me drift off.

I couldn't have been asleep for more than a few hours when I woke to the sound of arguing, voices that weren't trying to be kept down. Groggily, I walked out of my room, rubbing the sleep out of my eyes. Lander was here, and I could smell Bowie and David. I stilled when I saw them outside, all crouched around a map that was laid out on the floor of the porch.

Levi was pointing to the map, his eyes blazing silver. Lander shook his head, his hand moving in sharp lines across the map. A growl vibrated off David. I felt myself take a step backward, pressing myself against the wall.

Bowie ran her hands though her ponytail. Her arms were covered in blood. Blood that stained Lander's shirt and hands. Blood that Levi had up to his elbows.

A hand went over my mouth as Bowie spoke. She was talking so low, so quietly that I could only catch pieces of her words. Levi snapped his gaze to meet hers. I didn't know if anyone else could see it, but there was fear in his eyes. Fear that horrified me, because Levi was the most terrifying thing that I knew.

David put his hands out, almost as if to calm everyone. He pointed a finger to somewhere on the map, talking as if he was trying to barter for a compromise with them. Levi shook his head, holding David's single glowing green eye.

Lander snarled, leaning forward toward his brother in a strange, bitter challenge. He hotly whispered something to Levi that caused the veins in Levi's neck to pulse. Something crackled, something so strong it sucked the breath out of the room.

"He's right, Lander," David said, calm and resolute. "Enough. He is Our First. He is right."

Lander tossed his bloody hands up. "We can't reopen it.

That would get every fucking pack in the region involved. And with what we have, we won't be able to convince them of anything."

Bowie clicked her tongue. "That's not a bad thing." The three men turned their heads to her. "Right now, all they think was that we spotted rogues. Nothing else? Right?"

David hummed in agreement. "Nothing else. I told Ethan they were strays, which isn't untrue, but Talia has been hounding me. They both want a meet. If we lie to them and this is bigger than it is . . ."

She rubbed her chin, not caring that blood stained her face. "They don't need to know everything. We don't know everything. We don't know if this is bigger than it is. So we let them know what's pertinent to them now."

Lander watched her for a moment. "What do you propose, Mistress of our Forest?"

I'd never thought that woman could get angry—violent— but she snarled at Lander with a warning that promised pain later. I felt my own beast retreating to a corner of my mind. Bowie turned her head to Levi. "Let me do what I do best. Let me hunt them."

Levi leaned back on his heels, turning to Lander. "What do you think?"

"We should hunt," Lander conceded. "You're right," he said, looking back to Bowie. "But we can't cause a panic. News of what we're doing will get out if we're not quiet, not only here but to other packs. If we turn up nothing, then we caused panic for no reason."

"So we compromise," Levi stated. He looked back at Bowie. "Keep it small. Only the wolves you trust most."

"It will just be me and Rem," she confirmed to him. "I trust no one else to keep quiet yet."

Levi turned to David. "Tell the other packs only what they need to know and get them off our ass. We need a cover if she's going to be combing through the woods again."

"Consider it done," David answered with a firm nod. "I'll double the watch. We can tell the neighbors it's to keep an eye out for bears coming out of hibernation. It's that time of year anyway. They'll have plenty of cover."

Lander rocked back on his heels. "Hemlock is going to suspect more is going on. Thomas and Ethan are going to have questions."

Levi laughed lowly. "Let them ask them. If they want to meet, then they know the way here."

Bowie smirked before standing. She wiped her hands on her shifters. "What do you want us to do with the rogues?"

Without skipping a beat, Levi said, "Get rid of them."

David stood, nodding to Levi before following Bowie into the night. I wanted to move but my feet felt glued to the floor. I watched Lander finally disappear into the night, leaving Levi outside, but I didn't dare walk out to meet him.

He turned and paused at the door, glowing eyes locking on me. He didn't even look surprised to see me awake. He dipped his gaze, eyes glowing like the moon. "Not a word."

In the morning, Levi woke me before the sun was even up. He said nothing but "Get dressed." I wanted to ask why, but after last night, I felt like it was better to comply for now.

He was waiting outside, where dew was on the grass and sleepy clouds floated in the fading night sky. "Let's go," he said, taking a step toward the forest and already running in his fur before I could shift. It was always hard to keep up with him. For as much whiskey as he drank, he could still outrun me through the maze of trees that I felt like I would never get used to.

He led me to the cliff. The glacier was quiet this morning, the lake below it like glass. I shifted to my skin as a warm breeze danced over my shoulders. Following him forward, I reached out my fingers to brush across the stump that always put a smile on my face. He paused, eyes staring at the water like he was watching a familiar ghost.

The darkness was fading faster now. We were facing east. The sun would soon shine the hope of a new day over the glacier.

"What are we doing here?" I heard myself whisper in an attempt to not disturb the peacefulness around us.

"Do you remember the night I found you?"

"Unfortunately." I took a seat on the stump, the beast in me pacing back and forth. "What are we doing here, Levi?"

"I'm very bad at this." He leaned his weight on one leg. "In a week, it will be nine years to the date—"

My stomach dropped. "I'm so sorry, Levi."

"I never thought I would be the kind of scared I was, or close to it, ever again. Then yesterday when Lander told me that rogues were at the fucking Hole—" He paused, licking his lips before he looked back at me. "I have no idea what's going to happen to you or where you're going to go. I have no idea what you'll do or become."

My heartbeat picked up as the beast in me paced faster.

"Nothing happened."

"Not this time," he countered. He walked to the ledge and sat down. I found myself following him and taking a seat next to him. Sunlight was starting to peek over the glacier, shooting forward in bursts.

"Should I be worried?" I asked.

"No, but there was a time when I wasn't cautious enough, and I won't make that mistake again."

I shook my head. "You couldn't have known."

He hummed. "Maybe." The glacier groaned in front of us, almost as if it was yawning awake as the sun continued to gently pour over it. "I know I'm not always going to be with you. It's why you have to be able to protect yourself, you understand?"

"What are you saying?" I asked, trying to hide the tremble in my voice.

Levi shrugged. "Life is life, Charlie. It may take you across the world. It may take me to walk across the moon to Eve." I bit my lip because the latter tasted sour in my mouth. "So I'll do what I can so I know that I gave you the best chance you're ever going to have in this world."

The glacier groaned again. The sky was turning orange as streams of yellow danced through it. The light looked almost purple, dancing on top of the glacier, reaching across the pond almost to the shore.

"You've done so much, Levi, plenty—"

"True," he admitted with a laugh. "However, you are the unluckiest person I have ever met, and are probably going to give me more gray hairs in the next few years than the last hundred have. If anything, you're going to do this more for my own sanity than for yours."

"Do what exactly?"

"You're not technically pack yet. Rules are rules. But even being protected by a pack has its limits." He reached into his back pocket and pulled out a pocketknife.

"Do what exactly?"

"I am claiming you as one of mine so any wolf—or vampire for that matter—will think twice before fucking with a pack lead's kin." My mouth parted. He opened the knife. "I'm not making the same mistake twice."

I didn't know what to say. My beast pawed at me. I had a family, before; I knew that. But I also knew that my family was what I chose, and right now I knew this was more for him than it was for me. After everything, I more than owed him this. "Okay."

A look of mild relief flooded his face. "You'll smell like one of mine, and that alone should keep you safe if I can't."

"Do other people do this?"

He shrugged as he pulled the knife across his skin. "Sometimes when someone's parents die, people will so they have legal rights over them in our world." Blood pooled in the center of his hand. He turned the knife around, offering me the handle. "Your turn."

"Right."

My heart raced as I sliced the knife across my palm. The skin broke and a trail of blood followed the blade. I hissed and stopped when I felt like I had cut enough. I handed the knife back to Levi as the blood began to pool in the middle of my hand.

He scooted closer to me then narrowed his eyes. "Now you'll feel it. Like you did when you first learned to link. You need to accept it or I swear to god, Charlotte—"

"I get it!" I found myself laughing as he muttered curses under his breath. "Christ, Levi, it's not like I've done this before."

He rubbed his face with his clean hand. "Jesus Christ, Charlotte." He eyed the blood pooling in his hand. "Are you ready or—"

"Yes," I replied before blowing out a breath, and repeating with a confidence that surprised even me, "yes."

Levi took my bloody palm in his. It was like a lightning bolt running through me. He whispered some words as he clenched my palm but I didn't hear them. I felt so many things. I felt his blood running through my veins like small fireworks whizzing into the sky, the bond reaching out like a wildfire in the wind.

I took it.

My wolf and I grasped it as Levi said something else and squeezed my hand hard. The moon blood danced in me, crackling like a sparkler dancing in the night. I saw so many colors as my veins came alive with this bond; it poured through me and wrapped itself around my heart, like a hug from an old friend.

I blinked, sucking in a sharp breath when Levi released my hand.

The feeling fizzled again before it slowly fell to a simmer.

Levi was looking at the cut in his hand, his brows knitting. He tilted his head and watched me, like he was waiting for me to pass out. "Charlotte?"

"I'm good?" I nodded to myself. "I'm totally good."

"You're not very convincing."

"I know." My hand stung from the knife and part of me wondered if there had been silver in it.

"Did it work?"

He rolled his eyes. "Yeah, it fucking worked."

I shook my head with a laugh. "Well, then, what now?"

Sunlight poured over the glacier, the sunrise in its full glory as the morning breeze danced through the trees.

Levi grinned. "You haven't been swimming in a while."

My smile dropped.

I was frozen to the bone when we finished my torment in the creek. Levi told me he would fix dinner while I thawed out in Derek's bathtub. He was still looking at his hand when I left him for the bathroom. I found myself looking at mine; the cut was starting to seal, the bond still pulsing steadily.

As I changed clothes, I found myself staring at the photo of Eve and Lucas I had set against my lamp. Biting my lip, I reached for the box I had stored, the beast nudging me to do so. Before I could second-guess, I tucked the photo into the box then walked into the kitchen.

Levi was eating a pint of ice cream, watching the soup simmer, when I stepped up to the counter. I slid the box over to him. "You should have this."

He set his carton down and reached for the box like it was a grenade. As he opened it, his mouth curved into a tired smile. He picked up the picture I had tucked in last, the one of Eve and Lucas.

"She was so beautiful," I said, my voice quiet so as not disturb his thoughts.

He hummed in agreement, his thumb rubbing over the photo. He looked past it into the box, carefully setting it down before reaching for the other photos. "Jesus," he said with a breathy laugh.

I leaned across the counter to see what picture he was looking at. "It was in the dresser."

He never looked up from the photo, setting it down and moving to the next one, leaning toward me so I could see the photo of him and Lucas, both smiling next to the woodpile. "Lander used to say he was my twin. He was always following me around. He and his cousins were always getting into trouble."

He flipped to the next photo, laughing at a picture of Lucas covered in mud, missing a few teeth. "Shadows. That's what Chris called him and Eli. Our shadows."

He reached for a trinket in the box, an embroidered key chain that read "Lucas Kicks Ass." Shaking his head, he tucked it back into the box. "We had a lot of good years. For that I'm blessed."

He looked at another picture of Eve. She was in a garden full of roses, smiling almost as if she was a blooming flower herself, red hair like fire falling in perfect curls around her and green eyes shining like two emeralds. Her skin was adorned with dozens of freckles; she had been kissed by angels.

It was Eve I dreamed about that night. We were in the

garden together. She was calling me with a smile that was undeniably contagious.

I chased after her, through the sunflowers that grew taller and taller until the flowers became trees, blocking the light of the sun.

Eve stared at me as she backed into the darkness, the silence of the forest around us all too familiar to me. The trees felt like they were drawing closer to us, the ground like ice under my toes. Weeds shot up from the ground. Thorns laced what looked like roses, but they were rotten, ashy, falling apart before they could even bloom.

"We shouldn't be here," I told her.

She laughed, her eyes dancing with delight. "Yes, you should, Charlotte."

I was clutching my chest when I woke with a gasp. Sweat was running down my spine. I wiped my brow and lay back on my pillow, willing my heart to calm so I could try to drift back to a dreamless sleep.

My eyes grew heavier as my heartbeat steadied. Sleep was calling me back into its embrace again.

"Charlotte."

I shot up in my bed.

It was a whisper, so faint, so delicate, that I almost didn't hear it. My eyes darted around. The beast was awake now, pressing closer while I studied every corner of my room.

But there was nothing, only a peaceful darkness around me. My eyes darted to the clock on my dresser. It was the early hours of morning; the sun would be rising soon and I knew I wasn't going to be catching any more sleep.

I strode into the kitchen, at first with the intention of

grabbing a snack, but then I spotted the stone pillars in the yard through the window. Something pulsed through me.

I had no idea what came over me, but I was tired of them. Tired of looking at those fucking columns.

I grabbed the sledgehammer that rested against the house next to the axe, and marched toward one of the columns. I had no idea what I was doing other than destroying them.

Maybe I was going mad? Maybe the madness was spreading from him to me? I couldn't be sure except that with every blow to the column I made, it felt like I was freeing something.

"Charlotte?" Lander called tentatively. I hadn't even heard him coming. I didn't really care.

"Yeah?" I went to work on the second column, the first a pile of rubble ready to be carried away and dumped into the stream, as was my plan. He stepped around one, eyeing me as I pounded at the stones with the hammer.

"What the hell are you doing?"

I paused and looked over my shoulder. "Renovating."

"Ah," he said with a nod, scratching the back of his neck. "And you decided this was a good idea, because?"

I shrugged. "Because it's time."

Something flashed in his silver eyes. He smiled to himself then looked at me with a soft smile. "He's going to be pissed about the mess in the yard."

"Okay?"

He laughed under his breath and walked to the steps to take a seat. His eyes grew soft. "You smell like us."

"Yeah?"

He nodded with a soft smile. "Want me to start the coffee?"

"Please!"

He chuckled. "I'll help you clean up when you're done."

"Fantastic," I said, smiling, all my teeth showing.

He laughed again, his belly shaking as I took another swing, my hammer meeting the stone, smashing what should have been destroyed a long time ago.

CHAPTER
FOURTEEN

Lander made good on his promise and helped me clean up by the time Levi was awake. When I went in, I found Levi sipping a cup of coffee, leaning on the counter with his hair tied back in a neat ponytail. The neatness was slightly jarring.

"You were busy this morning," he said flatly.

"I couldn't sleep."

"I can see that." He snorted, tipping his mug to the front lawn. "Looks better, actually."

Walking to the table, I leaned on the back of a chair. "Really?"

"Really, really."

I arched a brow. "Someone has a little pep in their step this morning."

"Today is going to be a good day, Charlie girl."

I drummed my fingers on the back of the chair. "How's that?"

"Training with David today." He took one last sip of his coffee then told me, "Get dressed. We need to get moving."

"You're coming?"

"Yes."

"What's today?"

"A fun time," he chimed, walking outside.

My stomach twisted into tiny knots. I very much doubted there would be anything fun about today. I changed into a pair of shifters, my favorite yoga pants, and a sports bra that was practically a tank top. It covered my skin and provided a feeling of security I felt I was going to more than need today.

Levi was waiting on the steps for me when I jogged outside. Wordlessly, I followed him across the pack land, past dozens of wolves who all paused to look at us. We ran past the entrance for the training forest and kept going until we approached three familiar dirt pits. My gut curled as we approached the group of people gathered around David and Lander.

Levi shifted to his skin without a care for the whispers and stares following him. He strode over to David, who dipped his chin in a respectful nod. I quickly shifted to my skin and tried to avoid the feeling of eyes combing over me.

My gaze swept the area. Tia tipped her chin to me. I walked over to where she was standing next to Jake and Liam. Jake didn't tear his eyes away from Levi, but Liam could look only at me.

"Hey," he said.

"Hey, back." I sighed. His nostrils flared, lips curling in a knowing smile. He opened his mouth to say something, but my nerves demanded answers. "What are we doing?"

"It's David's turn," Jake answered.

"For?"

"The fun part," he said, his words clipped. His nostrils flared before he slowly shook his head. "You smell like him."

"Okay?"

"All right!" David hollered. "Let's get today going!"

He looked around the group as another set of four wolves approached, bulkier men and fit women, all of them wearing gray T-shirts with matching designs on them that read "Thunderhead Guard," with two axes pictured below the name. They all turned to Levi and Lander, who were sitting together on a fallen tree, nodding to them, before walking to stand with David.

"As you have noticed, Bowie is not here. Which means it's my turn with you all." A dark smile tugged on David's lips as snickers and laughter murmured through the group. "Out there, whether you're on the Hunt or out in the world, there's always a potential for danger. We've had some wolves go through the Hunt and run into bears, others have not seen anything but their deer. You have to always be ready, and my job is to get you all ready.

"So twice a week we'll have a group workout in the morning before you head out for training with Bowie. One day out of the other three a week, you'll spend the day with me. On all of those days, we meet here. Understand?"

The crowd murmured back to him in an agreement that seemed to appease him. "Today, we need to gauge where you're at and what we're working with. I have some familiar faces from the pack guard here to help me. We'll be splitting you off into four groups. We'll work two pits. My people here will direct you on which pit and which side to stand on.

"You will spar with your opponent until one of you submits. You will not shift into your fur until one of the people reffing your pit says so. We want clean spars today. Don't insult me by letting me catch you doing anything dirty, otherwise we'll have fun together later," he added, a dark delight in his tone. "Now." He waved his hands to the guards next to him. "Get in a line. We're going to sort you out into groups."

I felt frozen as dread concreted my feet in place. Liam tugged my arm. "Let's go."

All I had to do was make it through today. I could do that.

The beast in me stirred, a calmness about her. She pressed against my skin, almost as if she was trying to comfort me, but one look at the pits and I wanted to evaporate.

We lined up in front of a female guard who was giving people numbers then directing them to a pit. Liam was sorted into group three. I turned to the woman who had kind dark eyes. "Group four," she told me. "Pit two. You'll be great," she added with a bright smile that I could not even force myself to return.

Tia nudged me with her shoulder. "You good?"

Was she fucking serious? "Yeah." I was great. Peachy. Looking forward to publicly getting laid out in front of everyone. Fucking fantastic.

I was walking to where a guard was holding two fingers up in front of a pit when a voice stopped me. "Charlotte."

Levi's eyes were calm, and that seemed to still the kick drum beating in my chest. I heard voices around us, murmurs that felt like they were sniffing my skin for any sign of weakness. He stopped in front of me and dipped his head.

"Do you remember what I told you?"

"When?"

"You remember when."

"To the bone?"

He nodded. "I don't care who it is. You don't stop until it's to the bones—"

"Levi, I—"

"You be vicious," he whispered to me. "Make them pay for underestimating you." He leaned back as the wolf paced in the back of my mind. "It doesn't make you a monster, it makes you what you are now—you've got moon blood, it's time to use it."

I let out a heavy breath then nodded to him. He walked back to Lander while I willed myself to tread to the guard at pit two. On either side wolves were standing in a line that curled around the circle. The guard directed me to stand next to Jake. Liam looked at me from across the ring, offering me a small smile. I looked down at my feet, praying that this would go fast. It doesn't hurt as bad if it goes fast.

The girl who had sorted us jogged to the center of the pit, her short black ponytail bouncing with every step. "All right! I'm Alison, or Ali for short, for those who don't know, and I am going to be your ref today!" she said, as if she was going to be our cheer coach too. "Let's get this show on the road. Remember, no fur until either myself or David say—you got that, Anamaria?" she added, turning over her shoulder to look at a girl I recognized as one of Liam's teammates.

Anamaria tossed her long braid over her shoulder, the muscles in her quads flexing as she shifted her weight to the other side. "Yeah, sis." She mocked Ali with a sly smile.

Alison rolled her eyes and backpedaled to the middle of the ring. She waved her hands up to either side, calling forward the dueling opponents. I stepped closer to Jake. "Who is that?"

"Ali," Jake answered. "Total sweetheart you don't want to fuck with."

Inching closer, I whispered into our link, *"Jake?"*

He shot me a side-glance. His arms were crossed across his chest. *"Yeah?"*

"I've only done this with Levi."

He watched me for a moment but didn't push. *"Watch them. The goal is to pin them down and get your teeth around their neck. Have them submit to you."*

"What about skin? Like if you break the flesh?"

He snorted. *"If anything you'll get bonus points for that shit."*

Two young male wolves approached the middle of the ring with bloodthirsty grins. They gave each other a fist bump, then backed up a few paces.

Alison stepped away and pulled a whistle out that had been hiding under her shirt.

The whistle blew. The sounds of flesh hitting flesh drew sweat across my skin. The two men rolled on the ground before one kneed the other in the stomach. They jumped to their feet as the crowd cheered them on.

"But he had him on his back?"

Jake snickered. *"And end it so soon? What's the fun*

in that? Remember, it's until someone submits. He didn't submit."

I swallowed as the two men threw punches at each other. The beast in me nudged my skin again; I felt her start to pace. She was calm, quiet, and I was glad to have something that felt like a life raft in the middle of this ocean of anxiety.

"Shift!" Ali called.

Fur and teeth snapped into the air like two swords hitting together. Snarls and growls echoed around the ring, where the crowd's cheers blurred in a bloody song. The two wolves rolled on the ground, biting into each other without relent. Blood flowed across the dirt.

"They're not going to stop it . . ."

Jake arched a brow. *"Do we need to go over this again?"*

I blinked and one wolf was on top of the other, his long teeth around the other's neck, frozen in what could be a deadly bite. Ali blew her whistle. "Nice work, you two."

The two wolves separated and shifted to their skins, each of them toothlessly smiling back at each other. They laughed, fist bumping again before limping out of the ring.

My breath hitched. "This is savage."

"The fuck you think the UFC is?" Jake quipped. I closed my mouth. He had a point.

The line shifted forward; another pair entered the ring.

"You good?"

No, I wanted to scream my fucking head off and fall back into the forest where I could disappear.

"You're not good."

I picked at the edges of my yoga pants. *"I hate that everyone's watching."*

He stared at me for a moment as snarls sounded over the crowd. *"People have always been watching, you just didn't see them before."*

I stilled and looked back at the ring. Over and over I watched as pair after pair tried to tear each other apart. When it was Jake's turn, I offered him a "Good luck."

He feigned a scoff. "Like I need it," he teased.

And he didn't. He beat his opponent faster than any of the other pairs, moving with a precision that showed how disciplined he was. After Jake won, he walked back to me, pausing next to my shoulder. "I'll be here," he told me quietly. "We're a team, remember?"

"Thanks." I exhaled and stepped forward to the edge. Levi and Lander both walked to stand next to David, the three of them murmuring into each other's ears.

"All right!" Ali waved her toned arms forward, startling me to almost jump. "Let's go!"

I blew out a breath, praying inwardly that this would be like ripping off a bandage. That it would be over and I could move the fuck on from it. But when I looked across the ring to see who I was facing, all I saw were Liam's wide eyes. He looked at his father, who shook his head in a firm no.

My breath caught. Hushed voices picked up around me, making my toes squirm in the soft dirt. I felt the beast pulse through me, the electric feeling running to my fingertips. I hated the voices. I hated the whispers that felt as sharp as small knives across my skin.

Liam took cautious steps forward, meeting me in the center of the ring. He turned his gaze back to his father, who shook his head at him again.

"Fuck," he hissed out loud before whispering into our link, *"I'm sorry."*

I could hear Ali's feet crunching over the dirt as she moved away from us. My gaze flickered over to Levi, who raised his brows in a challenge of his own. The murmurs picked up, now a steady engine around me.

Liam scowled at the ground. *"I really don't want to do this."*

"Me neither," I murmured back as Ali's whistle screamed through the air like an alarm.

My eyes shifted forward while I focused inwardly on my wolf. On her instincts and on the hum that was crackling in me. In that moment we both agreed that it was going to take the two of us leading, dancing in a careful tango as a team.

Liam cracked his neck then backpedaled away from me. I held my position as he stalked around me. My beast crept closer, the two of us watching him closely. He tilted his head forward, brows raising in an expectant gaze that was quickly turning to confusion.

"Stay patient," I heard Jake say to me. *"Remember, he has to submit. Get your teeth around his neck."*

Small drops of mist started to descend from the sky. The sound of them hitting the ground was almost tranquil. I focused on that for a moment, using it to help me keep Liam from linking me. I couldn't talk to him—hear his voice—when I knew I was about to draw his blood, otherwise I wouldn't be able to go through with it.

He pressed again against my mind, but I pushed back twice as hard before shaking my head in a warning to him.

Liam tilted his head in surprise. "Goddammit, Char," he

hissed so quietly that I was sure no one else could hear it. "Fine, then," he snapped before he lunged for me.

He was bigger than me and less flexible. I used his size to my advantage and easily dodged out of the way. I blocked two of his blows before my movements allowed me to step away from him while he stumbled. The beast in me surged with pride, the feeling of her like rock candy crackling through my veins.

Liam swung and I blocked it then sent a calculated blow to his rib cage. There was another fist coming but I ducked then socked him in the sternum, sending him back a few feet.

He caught his footing and strode forward with blazing silver eyes. There was no more "going easy."

I blinked and Nate was walking to me with a smile. A growl ripped through my chest as I instantly marched forward. I blinked again and one of Liam's fists hit my side, a grunt of pain finding its way out of my lips. He tried to use his weight to crush me to the ground but I kicked up and kneed him hard in the gut before slamming a fist into his chin.

My beast growled as he reached for me and yanked me down. I looked up, and Nate was standing over me with a bored smile. "Get up, Charlotte," he told me.

The crowd was now roaring around us. I felt the beast in me pulse again, sending a galvanizing current through me that almost took my breath away. Blinking, I scrambled to my feet.

"Shift!" I heard Ali yell.

Liam jumped into his shift and prowled forward like a

hungry lion. I took a step then let the shift come to me like rain.

Sitting back to let the beast have a little more control, I felt Liam's claws rake down our back while we sank our teeth into his shoulder. My beast ground her jaw until we heard crunching, then released the flesh and jumped away.

There was bloodlust in Liam's eyes, and blood running down my muzzle. He snarled, but my beast snapped back with a bone-chilling clink. Stalking each other for a moment, it was Liam who made the first move. He charged us, but my beast dodged him and rolled to jump onto his back. She sank her teeth back into the shoulder where we had previously bitten, sawing her jaw until it hit something that crunched.

But Liam just rolled us over, crushing us under his weight. I blinked and pain shot through my flank. The memory of golden eyes yanking my leg around like a chew toy again cackled at me, along with Nate roaring with twisted laughter of his own. A terrible cry came out of my mouth. My leg was on fire, but I wasn't about to quit—I wasn't about to let him win. My beast lifted her paws and raked both of her claws down Liam's head. He let go of our leg and stumbled back, shaking his head as if bees were swarming it.

Something crackled over us. I wasn't sure if I was on fire or if my veins were about to burst from the heat, but the consuming feeling was one that shot new energy through us. My beast rushed him and nailed him to the ground. He snapped his teeth at us but we dodged them as skin rippled over us. My fist sailed down at his muzzle, easily crushing into him. The shock on his face was priceless. I did it again and again, until he reached up to me with his hands to stop me.

Nate was looking up at me in horror, but I wanted him to feel every inch of pain that he had inflicted on me. I wanted him to know what it was like to carry his demons with me. My fist flew again until someone yanked me back. I struggled in their iron arms, desperately trying to claw my way free.

My ass hit the dirt and I tried to jump up until Levi shoved me back. "Calm down—you don't want to do this with me."

Nate's laughter grew louder in the back of my mind. My beast snapped at him while Levi held on to my shoulders. "Easy, Charlie," he said to me, his silver eyes steadying me. He looked over his shoulder and called, "Lander, you owe me fifty bucks!"

Liam's eyes found mine, then my gaze drifted to the missing chunks of skin on his shoulder and the mess of blood in the circle. Horror wrapped his sickly fingers around me. I started to shake. Jake stepped into my view, eyes wide, staring at me as if he wasn't sure if he was going to have to stop me too.

My chest was still heaving. Pain raced through me, lacing up my leg like a dagger digging into my skin.

The crowed had quieted. The whispers had stopped.

Jake dipped his chin to me, his eyes heavy with determination. *"Don't let them see you limp."*

I swallowed the taste of blood in my mouth, fighting back the hot tears I could feel building. Levi turned, pulling me forward with him. "Let's go."

231

Every fiber of my body hurt, but Jake was right. I wasn't about to let anyone see me limp—see me do anything but walk out with whatever dignity I had left.

David arched a brow at Levi, who paused and looked back at the group. "Unless any of you all want a go with her?"

People quickly shook their heads while others looked away from me. Dread sank in my belly.

David snickered, nudging Levi's shoulder with his fist. "Bunch of fucking chickens."

Levi smiled with a dark chuckle. "You owe me seventy-five bucks. Don't forget."

He quietly led me away until we were in the clearing. Each step I took felt like I was walking on knives that screamed through my muscles. I gripped my side, where blood rolled down my skin. The pain grew to a familiar hum that greeted me like a long-lost friend. "Levi . . ."

He wrapped an arm around my shoulder. "Let's get you home."

We walked until my legs felt like they would give out. Then Levi picked me up and carried me. He said we couldn't shift because it was dangerous. He told me what happens to one, happens to both. If you shifted while seriously injured, all the bones moving around could make things gravely worse.

When we reached the house, he walked inside and sat me down in a chair at the kitchen table. My blood was staining the floor but he didn't say anything. Instead, he poured me a glass of brown liquor.

"Well, you took a nice chunk out of Liam's arrogance."

It felt like a dam was breaking in me as tears and angry

cries poured out of me. In a second he was in front of me, hugging me while I tried to hide the shame that came out in torrents of sobs. I couldn't believe I had been so monstrous.

"I'm sorry," I croaked.

"Why?"

"What do you mean, 'why'?! You know why—I fucking lost it! I was a fucking monster—oh god!"

He pushed me back, tilting his head to the side. "Why do you think that?"

"I just"—my breath caught in my throat—"I snapped and it was like Nate was there instead. I just . . . I wanted him to hurt so bad. I just . . . and Liam—" A cry tore through my lips, stopping the waterfall of words.

He released a long breath and stepped over to the counter to grab a clean dishrag, which he pressed against the gash on my leg. "First of all, you did exactly what I told you to do for once," he pointed out. "He's going to think twice before his wolf thinks he can cross yours. All of those wolves today will. And that's a good thing."

"I was so scared. I felt like Nate was there." I sucked in a harsh breath. Levi eyed me expectantly, patiently waiting for the truth that was burning behind my lips to get out. "I didn't want to be helpless again. I just wanted him to hurt as bad as I did. What's wrong with me?" My voice sounded so small and fragile, like china put back together with craft tape.

"You fighting for you, protecting yourself, is one of the most human things you can do. There's nothing wrong with what you did. We're wolves, Charlie. When we fight, there's blood. And when you fight, now others will know that there will be blood. You did more today to protect yourself than you realize."

"It doesn't feel that way."

"Your ex? What he did to you was monstrous. If anyone should feel ashamed, it's him. Don't ever feel bad about fighting for yourself—if you have to fight like hell to keep your ass safe, then so be it."

I wiped away the wetness on my cheeks. "She just—she was so vicious."

"She was protecting you, someone she loves. We're all monsters when it comes to protecting the ones we love, and there's nothing wrong with that." He added, "I should have let you have a few more minutes with him."

He stepped back and grabbed another clean dishrag, handing it to me. I wiped my eyes with it. "Is he okay?"

"He grew up with this, Charlotte. This is more than normal for him. His pride is shot to shit, but he'll be fine."

I took a long sip of the liquor, the liquid bringing a welcome sting down my throat.

"Charlotte, look at me." I set the glass down and let my watery gaze meet his tired silver eyes. "You're not a monster. Not even close."

I sniffled. "I bit to the bone."

He huffed a laugh. "I know. I could hear it."

"Lander's not mad?"

Levi shook his head. "Not at all. If anything, he told me he was proud of you."

I leaned my head back. "This world is backward. I almost tore his kid to shreds."

"No one was going to let that happen," Levi assured me,

his fingers inspecting the flesh of my shoulder. "I mean, I thought about it."

I was about to retort when I saw his lips pull into a devious smile. "You're an ass."

He chuckled and leaned back on his heels. "We're going to have to get these clean then stitch you up."

I took another long sip from the cup. Levi poured more liquor into it before walking to the sink. He put a bowl in the bottom of it and turned the nozzle on to fill it with water.

"Was David betting that I'd lose?"

He shook his head with an easy laugh. "No, he said you would win in twenty minutes. I told him it would be less than ten," he answered, turning the tap off. "Drink up. This isn't going to be fun and we need to get it done soon. It's another full moon tonight."

I tossed the liquor back. "I don't care." I didn't. Neither did my wolf. Both of us were exhausted, even though we could feel the full moon coming as if it was breathing down our neck.

But for once, I wanted nothing to do with the howling wolves. Levi stopped in front of me and laid out some supplies on a towel. He pulled a lighter from his pocket and handed it to me along with a curved needle.

He cleaned the area around my leg while I flicked the lighter on, letting the fire flutter over the metal of the needle to clean it.

CHAPTER FIFTEEN

I spent two days limping around the house, but by the third day after the spar I was walking normally again. My skin was starting to heal; in some places the stitches were already beginning to itch. Levi told me to leave them alone. They dissolved, which I was more than grateful for, because as much as I hated the process of having them put in, cutting them out didn't sound any better. Five days after the spar I was shocked to see that they had mostly disappeared, with scabs taking their place.

I hadn't heard from Liam. Nothing linked. No rabbits' feet. Nothing. The absence of his presence was a whispering voice that ran around my brain every night.

My fingers kept reaching to scratch my leg before I

willed them to stop and reached for my bacon. Levi laughed under his breath while he sipped his coffee.

Then his skin twitched and he set his mug down. I spotted Claire walking across the lawn. She lifted her chin high, trying to show a confidence that never reached her eyes.

Levi stared off to the side before snorting. "Go get dressed. She wants to run with you to tracker training." At least I was well enough to shift again.

Carefully, I put on a softer pair of shifters that Claire had gifted me: bicycle shorts and a fitted sports tank. Levi wasn't in the kitchen when I reached the front door. I tugged at the shorts as I stepped outside, offering Claire a polite smile. A smile that tried to hide my fear—because if I was her, I don't know if I could ever forgive someone like me.

Her eyes found my shoulder before looking to my stomach, a long sigh falling out of her lips. "Levi was never good at stitches—you should have called."

"Claire, I—"

She held a hand up then pulled me to her, wrapping her arms around me in a hug. I clutched her back, holding on because for a moment I was so afraid that she would disappear. That the relationship I had come to love would vanish.

"I can't imagine how hard that was," she said, her voice soft.

"Claire, Liam . . ."

She cracked a smile. "Is fine." She paused and pushed me back to look me in the eye. "Charlotte, this is how Liam grew up, this is how most wolves grow up. Lander and Levi would have never let you two seriously hurt each other, and besides, after everything you've been through, how can I be upset about someone I care for finally learning to throw a punch back?"

I did cry then. I felt it bubble up from my throat and run out in an ugly sob. Claire wiped my tears then pulled me back into a hug. "None of that," she cooed. "None of that."

Her eyes in that moment were the kindest I had ever seen. I think that's what made it all so painful—I was used to seeing judgment. Cruelty. Vindictiveness. I wasn't used to the kindness, even when I fucked up.

"I feel like I lost it," I admitted.

She turned, and linked her arm through mine as we crossed the yard.

"You did," she carefully stated, before laughing. "But sometimes it's good to lose it. Sometimes you need to." Maybe she was right? Maybe it was good that I got a little crazy—got out the things I had been working so hard to keep locked down.

"Anyway, I wanted to check on you." She tightened her ponytail. "How are things with your team?"

I shrugged. "They're not bad. Sometimes—I just—I feel like—" I stopped, avoiding her eyes. "I just really want to make this work."

"You will. Remember, you've already survived living with my brother-in-law," she pointed out.

I laughed. "True." When we got to the training entrance, only Jake would speak to me. Tia lowered her gaze before walking to a group of girls to chat with them. Jake didn't pay her any mind. He eyed my shoulder and asked, "You going to be good today?"

"Yeah, it just itches."

He grunted. "Yeah, it's a bitch when it does." He kicked a stone away. "You did good, though."

I tugged my hair. "Yeah?"

He scoffed a laugh. "Fuck, yeah. I already told the guys back home that you almost castrated Liam."

"Jake!" I hissed.

He shrugged lazily. "Embrace it."

I nudged my chin to Tia. "What's her deal?"

He waved her off. "Don't worry about it. I think she's a little pissed she was wrong about you."

"What do you mean?"

He chuckled. "I don't think anyone expected that match to go the way it did."

"And you?"

He turned his gaze to me. "You may be a pain in the ass, but I know a fighter when I see one."

From the corner of my eye I caught sight of Liam. What had probably been a black eye had faded to a sickly yellow, and the angry bite mark on his chest was a little puffy but mostly healed. When he walked toward Remi, he still limped slightly, and hid a wince that felt like it was screaming at me.

Bowie gave us our day's challenge: we were hunting for a set of white rabbits painted with our team colors. Tia was adamant about stopping to document all the traps, but Jake and I wanted to keep following the scent before the trail died. While Tia won the argument, we lost the trail and our rabbits to a burrow as the sun started to slowly lower to the west, and came back empty-handed.

Liam's team had caught their rabbits before lunch.

The next day was no better for team shitheads.

We were running through the obstacle course, trying to avoid the lines that were so cleverly laid under fallen limbs or leaves. I was faster than Jake and Tia, easily able to swerve between the trees and cut around corners. There was a dead squirrel painted with our team color at the end of the course, and I would be damned if we had to wander around all day to find the fucking thing.

Instead of creeping through the forest, we ran hard, setting off traps that we sprinted hard through to avoid. A few times one would nick us, or a set of small boulders would swing from the trees and knock us off our asses. One finally hit me square in the gut, sending me flying back about ten feet before the unforgiving dirt drew violent raspberries on my legs.

"Shit!" Tia ran to me.

I waved her off. "I'm fine, let's keep going."

She narrowed her gaze on me before pointing at my side—at the old gash that was starting to bleed. "You sure?"

Jumping up, I bit back the pain and dusted my legs off. "I've had worse."

She pressed her lips together, eyeing it again. "We should stop for a bit."

"I don't need to stop," I snapped, stepping around her.

Jake was standing a few feet ahead. He looked at my leg then back at me. "Those lines are hidden in the leaves, remember?"

I nodded, wiping some sweat off my brow. "Yeah, sorry—"

"I don't want to be fucking impaled because of a dumb mistake."

I tried not to roll my eyes. "I said I'm sorry, what else do you want?" I snapped. He held my gaze, eyes showing nothing, but I could see the contempt brewing. "Do you want to keep standing here, or what?"

He flicked his gaze to Tia before looking at me. "I'm leading this time."

Tia tossed an arm up. "Jake—"

"She's right, Tia. We need to move," he told her, voice so firm it felt like cold concrete. "And besides, you have a fucking notebook full of shit from here. What else do you want?"

"For us to not die out there!"

Jake waved her off. "Then stay here and take your fucking notes. I want to actually have lunch today," he finished, before storming ahead.

I tightened my ponytail, looking back at Tia with an apologetic smile. "Let's go. We can always come back if you want?" I offered.

She rolled her eyes. "Just try not to get me caught in a trap."

Well, fuck you, too, then.

Wordlessly, I turned and lunged forward, letting the shift roll over me so I could sprint to catch up with Jake.

The link was quiet between the three of us. The only thing I could feel was the exhilaration my beast felt from running between the trees. The feeling of wind combing through my fur was almost addicting in itself.

Jake and I approached a corner, the scent of the squirrel getting stronger. I spotted a fishing line hidden in the grass. I quickly jumped over it, avoiding a trap, earning me a nod from Jake.

Carefully, I followed him, diligent about stepping where he was stepping while also looking for things on the horizon. We turned another corner and when we did, both of us skidded to a stop right before our paws hit another line.

I took a few steps backward with him and shifted to my skin. Carefully, I knelt down and looked at the line—the first line of dozens that were laid out in a chaotic crisscross pattern, almost like one giant spiderweb. At the end, nailed by its fluffy brown tail to a tree, was our red-painted squirrel. On the other side was another route laid out like ours, and a squirrel painted blue for Liam's team.

Tia pointed at the trees. "Look."

Jake and I tipped our heads up to where numerous logs and boulders were waiting to swing down. Jake rubbed his face. "Great."

I jogged a few steps backward and scanned the rows laid out like swim lanes next to each other. Our team was locked in. The teams on the ends were locked in by boulders.

I pointed to the other lanes. "This is the only way, we can't go around."

Tia pulled her notebook out. "I can try to disable them?"

Jake scoffed. "There's gotta be at least fifty. That will take hours."

The lines were close together but it wouldn't be impossible to get through. I eyed my feet then lifted my head, studying the space between the lines. "I can do it."

"Charlotte—"

I whipped around to face them. "My feet are small. I can do this in my skin."

Tia crossed her arms. "And if you get knocked down by one? How are we going to help you?"

"I won't." My beast stirred in me with confidence. If anything, I knew I would be faster than the two of them. There was no way we would get all three of us through it.

Tia's brows furrowed. "Charlotte, be realistic."

"Do you want the fucking squirrel or not?" I insisted.

Tia slowly raised her brows. I could see the hair on her neck rise. The beast in me paced, digging her paw at the ground floor of my brain, where we had already worked out how to get through the web of traplines.

I nudged my chin at our target. "What if I set them off as I go? That way one of you can follow me without getting hurt."

Jake barked a laugh. "Are you high?"

In that moment I wished I was. "All right, what are the other options? We let Tia disable them? It's going to take all day." Jake closed his mouth. What could he say? We were both right. "I can run through it and come back with the squirrel, but neither of you seem a fan of that, so the other option is that I set them off as I go and outrun them."

Jake eyed Tia before looking back at me. "Fine, set them off. I'll follow you."

"Jake—"

"She's not wrong, Ti," he cut in, his eyes hard. "If you want to stay, by all means. I am not scraping your ass off a boulder."

She rolled her eyes then stomped back to her saddlebag. Ignoring her, I turned to Jake. "I'm going to run a few feet then set them off. I don't want you to get hit by anything in the front of them. They look like they all swing, so you'll just need to let them fall."

Jake shook his arms out. "Let's do it then."

Tia walked around with her notepad in hand. She had it tight against her chest, the end of her pen in her mouth.

My beast nudged me carefully, close enough to help without ripping out of my skin. Taking a few steps backward, I let out a long breath, then ran.

Sailing over the first few feet was easy. It was like doing knee-highs in elementary school. I could have done this all day, but god forbid I leave the team behind.

"You gonna set them off or what?!"

I clenched my jaw and looked up, eyeing what lay overhead before looking at the closest line, prepping myself to run faster.

"Screw it," I muttered to myself.

My toe caught a line. Something snapped over my head that echoed down the lane. I picked up the pace as a series of cracks and the groaning of trees echoed through the forest behind me. I could hear both Jake and Tia yelling for me, but I blocked them out and kept moving. If I stopped I would be on my back, and I wasn't about to be on my back again.

I stepped on another line and a log hurled down for me. Ducking, I avoided it then leaned out of the way as three rocks the size of bowling balls swung toward me like I was the unlucky last pin. My legs worked hard, the feeling of the beast pulsing within me, propelling me forward until I was only a few feet away from the squirrel.

After two more strides, I latched my hand around the squirrel, yanking it off the tree. Smiling, I took a careful step back.

"Charlotte!"

Rope whined behind me while something whistled through the air until the sound turned to a scream as someone howled in pain.

I whipped my head around, my stomach dropping.

A little stream of blood seeped past where Jake lay between a set of trees. A boulder was swinging slowly by him, stained in crimson. Tia was jumping frantically, waving to me. She eyed the traps that were slowly stopping their swinging before taking off.

"Shit," I hissed, darting around a swinging log and avoiding some rocks that were still spinning fast enough to be dangerous.

Tia reached Jake first. She whipped a rag out of her bag. I skidded to a stop next to her, my stomach curling. He had been hit alongside the head, his skin slapped with the angriest raspberries I had ever seen. Blood ran out of his deformed nose and from his scalp.

"Did you not hear us?!"

My eyes snapped to hers. "What?"

"They were swinging too fast," she said, pressing the rag to his head.

He groaned, his eyes glassy.

"He has a concussion," I said. I had seen it before in the mirror.

"No shit!" she spat. "Jake? Can you hear me?"

I knelt down and pulled out another rag, wiping away the blood from his nose. "I thought he was right behind me."

Her eyes pulsed with an angry glow. "He was! How did you not hear us! You should have stopped."

"Tia, I—"

"We need help," she cut in. "We need to get him back."

I shook my head. I knew I couldn't have stopped running because I would have gotten hurt, but after one look at Jake, my gut clenched.

"Jake, can you stand?"

One of his hands came to take the rag from me and hold it to his nose. "Yeah," he groaned.

"Okay," she said with a nod before looking at me. "Let's stand him up."

Tia put her hand behind his head and the other around his back, carefully lifting him up. My arm shot around his back to steady him.

We each put one of his arms around our shoulders then silently walked back through the forest. At one point, Tia and I agreed to carry Jake a little of the way together when he was too tired to walk. We didn't make it back until it was well into the afternoon. Liam was waiting at the entrance, his eyes going wide when he saw us stumble out of the trees with Jake.

One of the trackers ran to us, Bowie next to them. Wordlessly, she took the squirrel from me. I stepped away and let another tracker take my place holding Jake up.

Liam ran to me. "Are you okay? What happened?"

I shook my head. I got my fucking teammate hurt was what happened.

"I can stay with him," I offered.

Tia's eyes cut to me. "We're good," she said, her words clipped, before walking with the trackers to a Gator, in which they placed Jake in the back.

Liam's hand gently grasped mine. I slipped out of his grip. "I'm going home."

CHAPTER SIXTEEN

Levi didn't say anything when I got home. He watched me for a moment, silver eyes studying my face before he said, "I'm thawing steaks."

"I'll change."

He hummed something while I went back to my room. I reached for my phone and dialed Derek's number. The ringing eventually went to voice mail, like it had most of the previous times I had tried to call him recently.

I shot him a text. *Miss you. Call when you can.*

Levi and I ate our steaks in a comfortable quiet we had fallen routine to. He was looking at a map during dinner, making notes in certain areas.

I noticed an area where he was drawing neat lines with

a yellow highlighter. "The rogues," I asked. "Any news?"

"You're safe," he told me, his eyes not leaving the map.

I started to slice another piece of steak. "That's not what I'm asking."

He lifted his eyes to mine. "No, no news."

Sometimes, no news was good news. However, in this case, I didn't get the feeling that was true at all. If anything, it ate at my lurking insecurities, which were now companions with the guilt I was still harboring from today. Fear of what could happen on the Hunt followed me to bed. My mind kept wandering to images of the Trapper's Forest eating my team, trapping us in pits of silver teeth that swallowed us whole.

I was half asleep when something outside tapped on my window. Rubbing my eyes awake, I sat up to see the dark trees and soft grass in the moonlight.

Then a pebble hit the window.

I jumped back and caught silver eyes that made my heart flip.

"What are you doing?" I hissed to Liam.

"Come on, there's a bonfire!"

"Liam . . ."

"Come on. Seriously, you gotta get out more, Char."

I bit my lip as he stepped out of the darkness, the moon making his hair seem almost white and his eyes hypnotic. I sucked in a breath and looked away, my thoughts a war between logic and emotion that didn't want to dance together.

"You can't hide out here forever."

"Fine." A smile tugged at my lips. *"Give me a second to change."*

He dipped back into the forest while I threw on shifters. Before I could think twice about it, I carefully tiptoed through the kitchen, prying open the doors and shutting them with a featherlight touch.

The night was warm with the promise of summer. Liam was waiting, leaning against a tree. He snatched my hand and pulled me into a light jog. "Hurry, before Levi skins our asses." The way his fingers laced through mine was too much.

"Liam, wait." I pulled his hand back, stopping us. "The other day, the spar—I felt horrible. I should have said something sooner, I'm sorry."

"Stop," he told me, his voice dropping to a deepness that sent delicious goose bumps over my skin. His thumb brushed the back of my hand. "You have nothing to be sorry about. I wasn't mad at all, honestly, I was giving you space because I thought I fucked up."

"Liam, I hurt you."

He pushed some hair behind my ears. "Who could blame you? Better me than someone else who doesn't know why."

Liam was too good of a person for his own good. The feelings I had for him and him for me were starting to cloud what was wrong and what was right.

He squeezed my hand with a teasing smile. "Next time I'll let Mom patch us up together." He eyed me from the side as we continued to walk hand in hand. "You were something else, though. I thought Lucas was ruthless—you were like a wicked storm."

I wasn't sure how much I liked that, but the compliment

drew another feeling in me. One that I found myself liking. Pride.

"Today was the shittiest day," I found myself telling him.

A heavy breath poured from his nostrils. "I heard. You'll all work it out."

I shook my head. "You know, even though I'm older than all of you by a respectable amount, they think they need to constantly babysit me."

"A couple of years is not that much," he answered with an eye-roll. "They don't trust you, you're right. But you don't trust them either. And don't lie and say it's not true," he pointed out with a smile. "You're smart. You'll figure it out."

"I don't want to die in the Hunt," I found myself saying. "Or get one of them killed."

He was opening his mouth to respond when someone coughed near us. I froze in my tracks. Liam groaned.

"Jesus, both of you are like friggin' elephants," Remi huffed, sliding out from behind a tree like a shadow.

I waved at him. "Hey."

Remi tipped his chin. "You good?"

"I guess," I mumbled.

Remi fell in line beside me. "At least you found the squirrel. That's a bitch of a course. I was impressed," he offered. I bit the inside of my cheek. Liam looked at Remi, a warning in his eyes. Remi laughed under his breath, jogging ahead of us so he could turn to walk backward in front of us. "Come on, man, it's not like anyone died. And besides, I saw you run through the first half of it—that was sick."

I blinked. "You saw all that?"

Remi raised his eyebrows. "Someone has to help keep an eye on all you pups running around."

"Piss off," I groaned. "So why didn't you do anything?"

He gave me a one-shouldered shrug. "I can't do anything for you in the Hunt. No point in being a crutch now."

"Fair," I agreed.

"Look." He held his palms out by his sides. "Tia is, well, Tia. And Jake is Jake—thickheaded. Give them a few days for it to blow over then talk to them."

"He's okay, right? Jake?"

Remi scoffed. "He has a concussion. He's fucking fine," he answered, turning to fall in line with me. "He's probably already convinced someone to come lick his wounds for him," he added, wiggling his brows.

Liam shook his head. "Let's get going."

Liam shifted into his fur, all black like his father with two white paws in the front, followed by Remi, who darted forward with a sleek brown body with patches of caramel and honey, like his mother's.

Together we ran through the woods in our fur, shifting back as we reached the edge of the forest.

"Just stay by me," Liam whispered next to my ear.

I was glad it was dark enough that he wouldn't be able to see my cheeks flush—at least, I hoped it was. Remi turned. "So, how drunk can we get her tonight?"

Liam gave him a long look. "Rem—"

Remi waved a hand. "Whatever, you're taking a shot, Char."

Liam intervened. "Dude, it's what she wants to do."

Remi's eyes sparkled with mischief. "One shot. Come on."

I tilted my head, walking across the cool grass with him. "And what do I get out of this?"

Remi rubbed his chin. "Inside deets on the Hunt."

It was my turn to laugh. "I could get Levi to tell me—or Elliot—and you know it."

Remi narrowed his gaze before nodding in agreement. "Fine," he answered before holding his pinkie finger out. "You need more friends. So friends?"

I eyed his pinkie then looped mine around it. "Fine. Friends."

Remi snickered, letting my pinkie go. "Besties forever. We're doing tequila shots."

"You should have asked for deets," Liam groaned. "Bowie never makes anything easy."

"Yeah, fuck that noise, nothing is 'simple' with Ma." Remi laughed.

In the field there was a roaring bonfire in the middle of a group of wolves who were spread out on blankets, drinking and chatting. Laughter twirled in the air like the flames of the fire. My lips curled into a smile. It felt like magic was laced around us.

We walked toward a boulder where a group of people were talking next to a big red cooler. A few large plastic tables were set out close to smaller fires that had been turned into barbecue pits. The smell of meat cooking made my mouth water.

As Remi darted off to one of the coolers an "Oh, hell yeah!" cut through the air.

Ali squealed as she slid off the boulder, tossing herself at Liam, who caught her with a laugh. She hugged him then took a step back, a smile in her eyes, which felt like they carried the sweetness of the world in them. "Oh my god, you got her to come!" Her arms snatched me for a tight hug. "I didn't get to really say hi the other day at the pits."

I stepped back with wide eyes to look at the female with a high black ponytail. "Right, I'm Charlotte."

She put her hand to her chest. "I'm so rude. Well, I'm Alison or Ali, I'm one of the guards. I am so glad I got to ref your fight. You did so good!" she said, her palms face down in front of her. "So impressed!"

"You're hurting my pride, Ali," Liam teased with a smile that could melt a hundred women in place.

Ali waved him off before turning to me. "Seriously, I'm so happy you're here. I have been meaning to ask you to hang out."

I pushed some hair behind my ears, unable to hold back a smile. "Um, that would be great."

She beamed at me. Remi ran back to us and handed us each a red Solo cup. "You're doing this, too, Ali." He clinked his cup against mine. "Bottoms up, bestie."

I rolled my eyes and tossed the tequila back, the burn of it making my lips curl before I coughed. "We better be besties after that," I choked out. "That tasted like piss."

"Fuck me," Liam grumbled. "I need a beer. Char, beer?"

I shook my head. "What else is there?"

"Oh, I made sangria!" Ali grasped my arm. "It turned out so good! Get some!"

Liam marched to the cooler. He tossed Remi a beer before grabbing himself one. Ali smiled back at me. "Anyhow, our little girls club in the guard and trackers wanted to do something. Maybe after the Hunt?"

Remi tossed an arm over my shoulder. "You're not taking my new bestie away."

Ali gave him a playful shove. "Fuck off."

"You wanna go?" he asked, tilting his head.

Ali smiled, all her teeth showing. "We've got a pit running. I think my sister is over there."

"Oh, hell yeah, has Ani been there long?" Remi asked.

She narrowed her gaze. "Yeah, have fun trying, dipshit."

Remi shrugged with a tiny innocent smile that promised nothing innocent at all. "Hey, I gotta shoot my shot, Ali."

A cup was shoved into my hand. Liam winked at me before taking a long sip of his beer. He took my hand in his. "Let's walk around."

Ali spotted where our fingers met before looking at me with a coy smile. "Come out more, we'd love to show you around," she added.

I smiled back, for once finding the invitation easy to accept. "I would love that."

"Good." She clapped her hands, taking a step back to the boulder. "Hey, Li, don't let Anamaria wear his ass out too much. Yeah?"

Liam snorted then pulled me forward. Remi fell in beside me as we followed a footpath toward a group of people sitting around a firepit. Someone took a hit from a joint and passed it to Tia. She put it to her lips as her eyes flickered to mine, hardening quickly. Her lips thinned before turning to the person next to her. I looked away, and instead took a long sip of the sangria in my cup, hoping it would wash away the feeling of their stares.

Liam walked us next to a giant dirt circle where a crowd had formed around the edges. Remi pushed past some of the wolves until we broke through to see a lanky male sparring with a female who had long inky pigtails braided down to her waist.

I shook my head slowly. "And you do this for fun too?"

Remi rolled his eyes. "Humans have fucking bare-knuckle. How is this worse?"

He wasn't wrong. For a species that was about peace, we did enjoy violent pastimes.

Liam leaned his lips close to my ear. "That's Anamaria, or Ani, Ali's little sister."

"I remember her from the other day," I said. "She's on your team, right?"

Liam nodded. "Yeah, she is. She's a sweetheart, like Ali. You'd really like her."

The man was bleeding from his mouth. Ani had a few claw marks on her ribs. She socked him right in the nose but he didn't budge; instead he kneed her in the stomach. I thought she was done until she jumped back and kicked him right in the chest, knocking the air out of him on his way to the ground.

Remi grinned, eyes sparkling in delight. "Ten bucks says Ani TKOs him in about a minute."

The group of people around the circle were cheering into the night, all the more ravenous with every hit taken. Ani may have been small, but she was so much faster than her opponent. She spun and kicked him again, sending him flying back and onto the ground with a loud thud. Remi took a sip of his beer. "Told you, man, she'll wear your ass out."

"You know from?" Liam asked with a coy smile.

Remi lifted his hand in a wave to her. Her eyes lit up, a smile glowing on her face as she jogged over. She looked me over before she nudged her chin to Liam. "You want in?"

He shook his head. "I don't feel like a beating tonight, Ani."

"What about her?" she asked, her fangs slightly showing.

I felt my beast come forward, too excited for my comfort. I shoved her back then smiled politely. "I'm good, uh, thanks?"

"You're Charlotte, right?"

"Yeah, that's right."

"Sick. Sis has told me about you." Her eyes pulsed with a glow. "She said we should hang soon."

"Yeah, she told me," I replied with a smile. "After the Hunt, we'll probably need something to wind down."

"Oh, no doubt," she agreed. "Glad you're here, though—you sure you don't want in?"

I tipped my cup to her. "I'm good. Promise."

She clicked her tongue. "Damn." Her lips twitched, and she tilted her head at Remi. "Well?"

Remi held her gaze, the two of them quiet in a silent conversation. She snickered under her breath and walked back to the center of the ring. Liam arched a brow as Remi pulled his shirt off.

He tossed his hands up with a grin. "I don't think I'm going to mind her wearing my ass out."

"You're fucking sick." Liam laughed. Just to me, he said, "That's not going to last as long as he thinks it will."

"Is she wanting to be a tracker?"

"No, a guard like Ali. David makes the guards do the Hunt too," Liam said as we headed for the big bonfire. The crowd around it had dwindled but the crowd of stars above it had swarmed.

Liam pulled me around the fire until we reached a long log, which he sat on. He patted the seat next to him, which I collapsed onto.

For a few moments we were quiet. The sound of the fire licking away at the wood piled in its center was the only music we needed. Liam took a sip of his beer and I couldn't help but look at the sky and wonder how so many stars could be in it—how they could seem so close, within reaching distance.

I turned slightly toward him. "So, can I ask you—"

"A question? Well, yeah."

I bit my lip with a grin.

He bumped his shoulder against mine. "Go on."

"So people date? I understand the concepts in this world, but Remi and Ani . . ."

He breathed a laugh through his nose. "Remi does not date, if that's what you're asking."

I found myself laughing alongside him. "I figured as much, but it made me curious."

"Yeah?" He scratched the back of his head. "I mean, I never thought about it differently? I guess it's similar to humans in some regards. Most people date around and try to find a bondmate when they're ready. True mates are hard to find. Some people want to wait for them to properly fornicate—"

"Oh my god, Liam," I said into my cup, almost choking on my drink from the laughter.

He grinned. "But some people never find them. So I guess, yes? People date around and look for a bondmate, which I guess isn't far off from humans? You date around until you find someone you like enough to be with, right?"

"Well, yeah, that's usually the gist."

"Yeah, it's kind of the same."

I frowned. "I don't think so." I laughed.

"Well," he conceded, "maybe not? Anyhow, there's plenty like Remi who want to—what am I trying to say?" He lifted his beer and swirled it around in the air.

"Go taste testing before he buys a whole cake?"

He turned to me with wide eyes. "I'm using that." He snorted. "Yeah, that's Rem for you. But he's my best friend." He twisted around and threw a leg over the other side of the log to straddle it. "So, why are you asking? Who are you trying to sink your claws into?"

I snorted. "Don't be ridiculous, I'm just curious. And last time I checked, I sank my claws into you. But do not get any ideas."

He put a hand to his chest. "Why? Am I not pretty enough for you?"

"You're absurd."

He feigned a pout. "Charlotte, what? Do you hate blonds?"

Laughter tore out of my mouth. Playfully, I shoved his chest. "Clever."

He chuckled and pushed the hair falling into my face behind my ear. "Obviously."

I swatted his hand away. "Maybe I do hate blonds."

It was his turn to bark a laugh. "You're so bad at lying."

My cheeks heated. His eyes flickered to my lips. I couldn't help but look at his. The light of the fire dancing around his face only made the curl of his smile that much more beautiful.

He rubbed his thumb against my lips, the feeling like electricity running through me. "Is this okay?" he murmured to me.

It felt more than okay. People who say you should know better should watch their tongues, because they should know what moments like this feel like.

When it feels like the world is just the two of you. When the heat of their gaze makes you feel like the most beautiful thing in the world, and the gentleness of their touch shows you how precious they really think you are. When the thumping in your chest becomes a kick drum in a moment that sounds like a serenade you want to drown in.

But it's moments like these that become dangerous. Because reason dies. Logic dies. Your inner voice telling you to run is drowned out by one simple touch.

I should know better. But when his lips brushed against mine, all I wanted to do was fall into the feeling.

"Liam," someone said.

I yanked away from him and turned to see David a few paces away. Liam stood up and scratched the back of his neck. "Hey, big D."

I stood and took a step away from them. "I'll go check on Remi."

"Stay with me." David's words stilled my feet as cold prickles ran down my arms where Liam was once caressing.

He pointed back toward the pits and said to Liam, "Remi just got knocked out. Go get him up."

Liam nodded to David, wordlessly leaving.

David pulled a beer from his pocket and uncapped it with his palm. I stared as he took a long sip. "You going to sit or stare?"

I knew better than to back down—to run. I wasn't running. Not anymore.

I looked at my drink, which was almost gone. "You didn't bring another?"

He grinned before reaching into his other pocket. He pulled another beer out and uncapped it then handed it to me. "But don't waste that sangria. Ali spent a lot of time on it."

I sat again on the log. David sat next to me then turned so he could slightly face me.

"It's really good," I agreed before finishing it off. "She's really great."

"She is," he murmured back. "One of the good ones."

The light of the fire danced over his face, making him look dangerous. Almost as if he was the shadow of the flames themselves.

David watched me for a moment before looking into the fire. "Why do you want to be in this pack?"

So we were having this talk. "It's a community—"

"Bullshit." He laughed. "Try again."

It was my turn to watch him as he watched me, his eye giving away nothing, but the way he studied me gave away the suspicion that I supposed he was right to carry.

"Why do you want to be in this pack?" he asked again.

He was right. While friends were something I did need, saying it was a community was the fluffy answer that was easy to hide behind. There was no room for fluff in this world, no room for a facade.

"You'll think I'm nuts."

"You've been living with Levi for a while now—I already do," he countered.

I took a pull from the beer. "Fair." I caught his gaze, not daring to let it go. "I can't explain it, but it's a feeling I've had since I shifted. It feels like home here, and I haven't felt like I was home in a long goddamn time." I paused, shaking my head. "The forest feels like home. The cliff feels like home, being at his house—this is my home now."

"Much better," he replied with a pleased smile. "You're not what I expected, but you got him out of his own self-imposed prison." He tipped his beer back as the fire crackled around us.

"You don't hate him for your eye?" I found myself asking.

David shook his head. "He had his soul torn in two and then some. I think if it was me, if that happened to my Penny—I can't blame him for my eye. I'm thankful it was just my eye and no one else got hurt."

"You're not what I expected either," I replied, offering him a smile of my own.

David laughed under his breath. "The other day in the pits, that was something. But I would expect no less from Levi."

"I lost it," I admitted. He tilted his head to look at me. "The past showed up when I thought I was done with it."

He held my gaze for a moment before nodding slowly in

understanding. "It does that," he acknowledged. "It's hard. No one is going to know how hard but you. We've never had a human before, not like you. You survived the shift, which is impressive enough. Whose idea was the Hunt?"

"Mine." My voice was firm, unyielding.

He smile slowly curled on his lips. "Good." He took a sip of his beer. "We'll start working the new trackers in on routes along the borders to do patrols after the Hunt. You'll come with me first."

"Well, I'll warn you, I bore easily."

David cracked a cheeky grin. "I'll bring cards. Someone needs to teach you how to swindle Levi."

I leaned an arm on my leg, watching the liquid in my bottle. "Any advice for the Hunt?"

David turned to face the fire, his gaze far away. "If something feels wrong, that's because it is. When you feel that, run."

"The rogues." He cut his eye to me. "He said that I shouldn't worry."

"Then you shouldn't."

"They were like the ones that attacked me."

"I know." He tossed his empty bottle into the fire. "Like I said, if something feels wrong, run."

CHAPTER
SEVENTEEN

Over the past week Levi had been taking trackers out into the Trapper's Forest, not returning until well past dark. Other than the days I trained with David, Levi was always there. Always watching, always talking with David on the sidelines, like they were inspecting the new lot.

Today was no different when he'd followed me to the pits where David had us sparring again. One by one the pairs fought, the sound of the crowd roaring through the trees like church bells ringing in a strange song that almost felt like a hymn.

I stepped up next, watching Tia spar with Ali. David had us sparring with the guards, not each other. It made me nervous, because these people were trained for this—were much more collected and strategic.

Within a few minutes, Ali had her jaws around Tia's neck. She stepped away as Tia scrambled up, shifting to her skin. Tia wiped some blood from her mouth then marched to the sideline.

Ali tipped her bloody chin to me with a winded smile. "You ready?"

I bounced on the balls of my feet. "Fuck it."

Ali laughed. "Fuck it," she echoed before she winked at me. "Hit me with your best shot, babe." Her laughter died away as the sound of people around me faded. "Whenever you're ready."

I glanced at Levi, whose lips curled into the tiniest of smirks. The beast in me was licking her lips, running forward like a wave hurtling toward the shore.

I cracked my neck, nodding to Ali. "Green light?"

Ali nodded back, then started to circle me, her steps heavy, loud even among the roaring. I let out a long breath and let her come closer, let my beast's instincts wash over me so I could hear how heavily she was breathing. How she cracked her knuckles while slightly dragging her feet. I could smell the blood dripping off her chin and hear how the air around her almost whistled when she lunged forward.

Today, I never saw Nate. Today it was just my beast and me doing a dangerous tango that left Ali with a cracked rib and a solid bite into her ass. We hadn't shifted into our fur but for a few moments before I had my teeth around her neck. No one was more shocked than me, but no one was more pleased than Ali. When we shifted back, she smiled at me with a bloody laugh. I reached my hand down and pulled her up.

"You know, I usually last longer," she teased, spitting blood to the side.

Snickering, I replied, "Well, that sounds like a personal problem."

Ali barked in laughter and walked out of the ring next to me, limping slightly. She slapped her hand in another male guard's, who jogged to the center of the ring.

David nudged his chin to me. "Charlotte, you've got laps. Take the green route today."

"Okay," I replied, then turned to Ali. "Do you need help or anything?"

She waved me off with a wink. "Just a flesh wound. I'm definitely going to find someone to lick my wounds later, though," she added with a saucy smile.

David narrowed his gaze, shaking his head at her. She murmured a laugh then gave my arm a squeeze. "You did good."

"Thanks," I told her, returning her smile.

She waved good-bye to me as I darted toward a tree that had three arrows nailed to it, all pointing in different directions. I took a left, following the green arrow.

I wove around trees, which started to smell like the holidays as the evergreens grew thicker. A smile pulled on my lips as the wind blew, the cool breeze sounding like a song.

Shifting, I let the beast run, falling into a familiar motion that we'd both grown to love. She yipped at the bluebirds in the sky above, jumping toward them playfully as we powered down the trail. We kept running until the icy fingers of another breeze combed through our fur. Breathlessly, I shifted to my skin. My feet moved on their own, carrying me off the path and down a small foot trail, where it felt like the breeze had originated, but all I saw were more evergreens. They started to grow closer together. I was shoving through them when another cold breath hit me.

I paused for a moment, considering turning around, but something pushed me to keep going. Something drew me through the thinning spruce trees until I was facing a wall of taller trees. They cast a dark shadow over the evergreens, which felt as though they were quivering behind me.

It was quiet.

There were no birds chirping. No squirrels scampering. There wasn't even a buzz of flies.

The breeze was gone; no cold wind flowed to me.

My gut dropped. The beast pawed at me as we looked straight into what I knew was the Trapper's Forest.

Suddenly, the grass quietly rippled around me, like tiny ballet dancers twirling across a dance floor. A breeze rolled past me as a whisper of wind picked up. A whisper that I couldn't place, because it sounded like hundreds of them at once, until they settled when the breeze did.

I took a step back.

"Charlotte," a whisper called from deep in the darkness.

I froze. The beast in me snarled. I felt my fangs elongate, nails turn to claws.

The current picked up again. I took another step back, because the darkness felt like it was reaching for me with claws of its own. Cold whipped around me and the trees in the forest shook.

My breath hitched. "What the hell?"

Stepping back, my eyes cut to my right where Tia was

standing on the edge of the forest, staring into it as if she was stuck in some sort of trance.

How did I not smell her?

Her foot lifted to step forward, her gaze steady ahead. My beast howled in desperate alarm inside my head as the wind whipped around us again. My legs moved on their own, my heart racing as the cold felt like it was slithering behind me.

Tia reached forward like she was about to take someone's hand.

"Tia!" I cried, snatching her arm and yanking her back to me.

She blinked as if she wasn't sure if this was a dream or not. She looked over my shoulder as the trees shook behind us.

"We're leaving. Now," I told her without turning back to the darkness, pulling her with me through the thick evergreens and back onto the trail.

She stumbled a few steps, her trembling hand still holding mine. "Are you okay?" I asked her.

She turned to face me. "I don't understand."

"What happened?" I asked.

She shook her head slowly. "I thought I heard something, and then I—you're going to think I sound crazy . . ."

The corner of my mouth lifted into a half smile. "Try me."

She blew out a breath. "I couldn't stop looking at it, the darkness. It was like it wanted me to follow it."

I couldn't let her see me shudder. The beast in me paced in the back of my mind, snapping her teeth in frustration. A sentiment I agreed with—because I was starting to get good and annoyed by the damn darkness in that forest.

"It's done that to me too," I admitted to Tia. "It's not just a forest, we can't forget that."

She released my hand and wrapped hers around her stomach. "We're going to have to be in there," she murmured, looking back at the trees from which we had come.

"And we're going to come home," I assured her, drawing her amber eyes back to mine. "We're coming home." Turning, I nudged my chin forward. "Come on, let's walk together."

She nodded quickly and fell in step beside me. After a few moments she finally said, "Thank you."

"We're a team," I answered with a shrug.

"Look," she said quietly after a few quiet paces. "I'm—I've been a bitch and I'm sorry."

"It's all right." Because we all were assholes from time to time. "I was pretty bitchy too."

She offered me a small smile. "Well, I am sorry."

"It's all right," I replied with a smile of my own. "Look, that forest—well, it really fucking sucks."

"You're telling me," she groaned.

"We're only going to make it through the Hunt if we work together, that's the only way," I told her as we turned a corner. "Why don't you and Jake come over? I can make dinner. We can hash it out and put things to rest."

"You want us to come over?" I couldn't miss how her voice rose an octave.

I tugged the end of my ponytail. "Yeah, I mean, I just thought—"

"No." She held a hand up. "No, we can do that. We'll do that," she said, more like she was convincing herself than me.

We walked a few more paces, my mind reverting back to the woods. "Was there anything special about that entrance of the forest?"

Tia bit the side of her lip. "Honestly, not really from what I know. I mean, farther in is the border between us and Hemlock. Other than that, nothing that I can think of. I mean, Gran always said it was haunted in there. Why?"

I looked over my shoulder, scanning the proud ever-greens that lined the path. Turning to her, I shrugged. "Maybe your grandma is right? Maybe it's haunted."

That evening I attempted to make a recipe of Derek's. I tried to FaceTime him but he texted me back saying he would call in the morning. In the end, I fucked up the pasta dish, so Levi offered to make steaks. He found the whole thing amusing.

Levi got a bottle of bourbon out while I assembled a salad. He poured himself a glass. "You know, you could always just toss your teammates around the yard."

I turned to check on the baked potatoes. "We're using our words for this."

He leaned against the counter. "Well, at least we know you can't poison them."

I chucked a dishrag at him. From the corner of my eye I could see movement in the trees, and stepped onto the porch to see Tia and Jake emerge then stop at the edge of the yard. Tia searched for the columns before her eyes widened with the realization that they were gone.

Jake's brows rose high while he kept searching the yard for the columns that were long gone.

"He promised not to kill you until after dinner!" I yelled across the lawn. Levi bellowed a laugh from inside the house.

Jake's brows knitted. "Screw it," he grumbled, marching forward. Tia watched him for a minute before jogging after him.

I leaned against a post as Jake skeptically approached the steps. "You can come in," I told him, trying to hide my laugh. "We made steaks. And we have booze."

Jake considered this for a moment before shrugging, jogging up the steps, and entering the house. Tia stopped next to me, her fingers tugging her long ponytail, the silver streak catching in the light. I took her hand in mine and tugged her forward. "Come on, I'm not going to let him skin you alive until you're good and drunk anyway."

"That is not funny," she replied, stumbling behind me into the kitchen.

I had to bite the inside of my cheek to keep from laughing. "It's fucking hysterical."

Tia cleared her throat. "Her First," she said with a dip of her head to Levi. "Thanks for having us."

Levi casually sipped his bourbon. "Better stick to hard liquor tonight, Charlie girl." He looked at Jake, who looked like he had forgotten how to form complete sentences. "The hell is wrong with you?"

"I—" Jake began.

"Sit your ass down," Levi ordered him. Jake took a seat

on a barstool, sitting as still as a corpse. Levi slid a glass of bourbon over to him. "Drink, it helps."

"What do you want?" I asked Tia. She looked at me, her mouth opening and closing. I rolled my eyes. "Never mind. You're having wine. Don't argue. Sit."

Levi snickered as I reached for a bottle. He leaned on the counter, close to Jake, who had almost finished half his glass. "Charlotte, did you tell them what we did to the others?"

"Levi . . ."

Jake crossed his arms. "If you make me into taxidermy, it better be fucking good. Her First," he finished with a quick dip of his chin.

Levi cracked a smile. "Well, do you want to be hung in the living room or the bedroom?"

Jake scoffed. "Full standing mount in the doorway."

Levi shook his head as his chest shook in laughter. He poured more bourbon into Jake's glass. "See, it helps."

I handed Tia a glass of wine. She took it with a small smile. "Thanks."

"The potatoes are almost done, and then we just have to set the table," I said, taking a long sip of wine from my mug.

Jake arched a brow. "Are you having coffee?"

Levi snorted. "No, she has a sippy cup so she won't break another glass."

Jake burst into laughter. Tia shoved his shoulder before saying, "She can drink out of whatever she wants."

I found myself laughing with them.

Levi stepped around me. "I'll get the steaks. They need to rest anyway."

Nodding, I waited until he went outside. Jake's laughter

died. Tia looked at me, giving me an encouraging smile. "All right, look," I started. "We are not the best team, we're kinda the fucking worst. I don't want to die in that forest, and I don't want to come back empty-handed."

Pausing, I turned to Jake, who was rolling the liquid around in his cup. "I'm sorry you got a concussion. I know I can be a pain in the ass, okay? I more than know. We have to trust each other, which I know is hard, but if we don't, this is going to be the worst camping trip ever."

Jake leaned back in his chair. "I wasn't ever mad about the concussion. I mean, I've had plenty before. I was fucking furious because you actually got the stupid squirrel. I don't know how you dodged all those traps." He finished his drink. "Look, I'm a dick, okay? I know. And I'm sorry." He stopped and turned to Tia. "Sorry I was a dick. I'm glad you're taking notes." I grabbed the bottle and refilled his glass. "We should have trusted you more. You do have a good nose."

Tia slid up in her seat. "I'm sorry, too, I was a—"

Jake's lips split into a sly smile. "Big-girl words, Ti."

She narrowed her gaze at him. "I was an ass, too, okay? He's right, and you're not a human anymore. I'm sorry for saying that. It was a really shitty thing to say."

"So, we're going to agree to not be dicks?" Jake asked, looking at each of us.

A smile formed on my lips. I nodded to them. "Agreed. No dicks."

"No dicks," Tia echoed.

"Only my dick, but no others." Jake snorted before tossing his hands up. "No dicks."

"Back to team shitheads." I breathed out, relief washing

over me. "Good. I was thinking we can eat then talk about strategy?"

"Please," Tia answered, as Levi walked back in with the steaks.

He slid them onto the counter before saying to Jake, "If you're going to drink my liquor and eat my food, then you're going to set the table."

Jake gave him a mock salute. "Show me the good china, Her First."

Levi muttered curses under his breath. He opened the cabinet where the plates were stacked in neat columns.

"Can I help?" Tia asked.

Levi grabbed his glass and tipped it toward Tia. "Absolutely you can."

"You're a dick." Jake chortled.

Levi smiled smugly at him. "You have no idea."

"Ti, want to help me with the sides?" I asked.

"Sure," she answered before sliding off the barstool.

All the steaks were gone and the sides as well by the time we were done. Levi offered to thaw a cow out for Jake, which Tia found hysterical enough to burst into a laugh that made us all stare. At first, the other two were unsure of what to do at a table with Levi, but after a few bites and a few more drinks, laughter had flowed as easily as conversation.

The boogeyman was forgotten, as he should be.

After dinner, I made brownies out of a box mix because Levi said they would be "fuckup-proof" for me. I was pulling them out of the oven as Jake laid out a map on the living room coffee table, setting our salt and pepper shakers on the corners of the paper to keep it from curling.

I set the brownies on the counter. "These need to cool."

Jake waved us over. "Come see. Billy gave me this before I came over."

Tia looked relieved. "This is so great." She leaned over the map that highlighted the areas of the pack land that were in the Trapper's Forest.

Jake nodded. "We've only got a week, but that should be plenty of time. Typically Bowie starts everyone here," he said, pointing to the far southeast end of the forest. "Because then the whole forest is truly game."

"How long does the Hunt typically take people?" I asked.

"Almost a week," Levi answered from the corner. "Some teams have done it in two days. Bowie did it in one day."

I caught Levi's eye. "How long did it take you?"

He ran a hand over his tired face. "Two days. Took Lander four. Bowie never let either of us live it down." He came over and sat where he could see the map. "You're chasing an animal, a deer. It's a prey animal. It's built to run from you and *wants* to run from you."

"They're going to want water, though," Tia pointed out. "Are the deer from the forest?"

Levi arched a brow. "Smart question." He leaned back. "Bowie catches them where she catches them. Probably good to figure out soon."

"Why?" I asked.

Tia leaned her elbow on the coffee table. "Gran said the animals in the forest are wild. Almost like rogue wolves."

My gaze traveled to Levi while my heart started to flutter. "Is that true?"

When he looked at me, I knew it was. He took a long

sip of his drink. "What's been done in that forest is beyond unspeakable. It's evil. And evil corrupts everything around it. The blood magic, it's a dark and foul magic that is like a sickness in there," he told us, his voice distant. "You all better pray it's not a deer that's from that forest. Otherwise there's no telling what it will do if its mind is lost to chaos and its instincts set on pure violence."

"But it's just a deer . . ."

Levi shook his head. "And is that just a forest?"

"No," I answered quietly.

"Regardless," Tia said, "wild or not, it will want water. If it's not from there it's going to look for an escape or for water."

"And we'll need to make sure we find water too," Jake pointed out. "Unless we're done in a day, but that seems unlikely."

We hummed in agreement. I looked up at Levi. "How much of the forest have you been in?"

He stared at the maps. "There are plenty of areas that I've never been to. We did the last big sweep to clean out traps when my father was still alive. Now we do it as we find them, but it's a giant forest. Impossible to stop them all.

"The areas that are the most quiet, the silent ones, stay away from them. There's bad blood magic there. I would stake around the area if you think a deer is in there and wait for it to come out. It will come out."

"What kind of blood magic is in there?" Jake asked.

"The kind that would keep your team from hearing you scream," he answered somberly. "Where did you say Billy got this map?"

Jake shrugged. "He didn't say. He just said he had it."

Levi hummed, nodding as he looked at the map. "I need to talk to Lander. Stay out of trouble," he told me. Then he went out the front door.

Jake watched Levi through the window as he disappeared into the trees before turning back to us. "We can't go slow. We're going to have to work fast. Look, Billy told me stories about that forest. I don't want to be in there longer than I have to."

"Remi's not scared of it," I countered.

Jake snorted. "Remi and Ethan are the only people I've seen wandering around in there on their own. They're freaks. Levi is right about the fact that the forest fucks up what's in it, and I don't want that to be us."

I looked back at the vast swath of forest on the map. "So we work fast. You're right," I told him. "That place feels wrong."

"It does," he said under his breath.

Tia tapped her lip. "We're going to get through traps. Char is the fastest and her nose is probably the best on the team. We can let her lead and have you watch her hide," she told Jake. "We're going to need to find our way back. My gran said something about that place, that scent dies. That people get lost in there all the time."

I frowned pensively. "But we're wolves, we can smell a trail?"

She nodded, her eyes growing heavy with worry. "I know, but Gran said that when she was young someone got lost in there for so long that it drove them almost mad."

"Jesus," Jake muttered next to me. "Yeah, Billy mentioned

something similar to me about wolves who got lost in there and went nuts."

"So we need to leave a very visible trail just in case. Bowie said we can take things with us. She's going to inspect all of them, but we should think about taking something that we can mark a tree with," I thought out loud.

"What about a knife?" Tia said. "We can mark the way into the trees. It would also be good to have something that we can use as a tool in case we do get into a trap."

"I like that." Jake rubbed his hands together. "So, Tia, you get us home. You also have all the trap notes. If you want Char and me to lead, we should start studying those so we can recognize them fast."

I looked at Jake. "We can quiz each other."

"We don't have practice with David this week," Jake told us. "He said he was going to announce it tomorrow. He's giving us time to rest up, but I say we use that time to practice in the training grounds."

"Agreed," Tia chimed in. "And we can study the traps and the map. It will be good if someone other than you knew this map, Jake."

Jake quickly shook his head. "I don't know that map. Billy just gave it to me."

She groaned, eyeing me. "We can study the map."

I drummed my fingers on the table. "What if we run into trouble?"

Jake tilted his head. "Like?"

"Someone falls into a trap? Or we meet a bear?"

"Well, Bowie is going to give us all emergency flares," Tia reminded us. "Bears—"

"We fucking kill them," Jake said, his tone clipped. "We're not coming out of that forest without that deer."

"And each other," I added.

"And each other," he agreed.

"You can come over to my place tomorrow," Tia offered. "Gran's been wanting to have you both over."

"Let's do it," I told her, smiling. Jake started to fold the map up but I stopped him. "Let me see if I can get Levi to tell me more."

Jake laid the map back out. "Oh, please and thank you, ma'am. Brownies now?"

We all sat on the porch, sharing the brownies right out of the pan along with what was left of the bourbon. Tia hugged me before they left. Jake waved, which in his terms felt as good as a hug.

When Levi returned, I was cleaning up the kitchen. He slid onto the barstool, rubbing his hands over his face. His eyes were tired, but I felt like they were growing more and more tired each day.

"Everything okay?"

"Yeah," his gravelly voice answered. "That was a good thing you did."

"What?"

"Those pups. You should be proud of yourself."

I set the plate I was drying aside and leaned against the counter, my eyes trailing back to the map, still open on the coffee table. "What else is in there, Levi?"

He let out a long breath, sliding off the stool and walking over to the map. I followed, standing next to him as his fingers ran across the boundary line of the forest. "I've never seen a map of it like this. I've seen all my father's maps, but this is much more detailed."

His fingers trailed back to the northeast part of the forest. "There are places like this up here you never need to enter. The fur trade would camp out here. It's one of the worst areas for wolves. My father called it the Silver Mines because of how much silver to trap wolves was found there."

"But what if the deer goes in there?"

"Wait for it to come out. It's not worth your life."

I nodded and pointed to the northwest edge, where a thick dotted line cut through the middle of the forest, running along the middle until it curled to the edge of the forest that eventually disappeared. "What about up here? What does this line mean?"

"That's the border for the Hemlock Pack. Their border cuts through the forest before it eventually edges it. I'd be amazed if anyone made it that far. You'll know it's a border because their colors will be marked on things—rocks or trees."

"And don't cross it, I'm guessing?"

"We're not as friendly as we used to be with them," he admitted, his voice dropping a hair. "You won't need to worry about it. Like I said, it would be a miracle if you made it all the way over there."

"Thank you," I told him. "Do you think we'll see mountain lions or bears in there?"

"Knowing that forest, there's no telling what you'll fucking see."

CHAPTER
EIGHTEEN

The rest of the week we trained hard, and studied the traps and lures that Tia had drawn for us on flash cards. We had them spread out over the carpet at Tia's grandmother's house. We came over for lunch and spent the afternoon reviewing maps and the flash cards, and organizing our packing lists. Before we left, Gran's frail hand caught mine and stopped me from stepping out of her house. She told me again that I smelled of the moon. I smiled, thanking her politely, when she stopped me, her wise eyes glowing as they looked me over. "No, you smell like the moon, child."

I watched her for a moment before quietly thanking her again. Part of me wanted to ask what she meant, but with everything else going on, I also didn't want to find out. Not yet, anyhow.

When we left Gran's, Liam was waiting for me outside. Jake let out a long whistle, snickering playfully before trotting away. Liam scratched the back of his neck. "I thought I would run home with you?"

"I can find my way," I told him, my voice dropping into a dry tease.

Liam shrugged. "I want to run home with you. Can we do that?"

It was hard to tell him no when he was looking at me like all he wanted to do was hold me before he let his hands find out what my curves really felt like. A shiver ran over my skin. I hadn't thought I would have these kinds of feelings again.

I nodded, walking next to him as his eyes trailed over my face. It was in that moment that I realized that he made me feel beautiful—the foreign concept of being admired was something I'd forgotten I could experience. Forgotten that I could like.

"We should take the long way," he suggested.

"The long way?"

"No one likes anything short and fast," he quipped, eyes darkening as he looked at me. My cheeks heated. He laughed before jogging ahead to shift into his fur.

Shaking off the feeling, I shifted quickly and ran after him. He led me down a new trail that coiled through tall grass waving like an orchestra the wind was conducting. The trail curled around until it straightened out alongside a smaller cliff that looked over a creek. Liam trotted off the trail a few yards then shifted back to his skin.

I followed suit, letting the wind rake over my skin. The golden hues of the sunset danced with passionate pinks and cast a light on the grass that made me wonder if we were still on Earth or if we had ventured to another planet.

Liam took my hand and pulled me to sit next to him, wrapping his arm around my shoulders. I hadn't felt this close, this intimate, with anyone other than Nate—and Nate had only used those sweet moments to his own advantage.

But one look from Liam and I knew that he could never harm a hair on my head. He pressed his lips to my temple, lingering. My breath hitched. I knew I should think about what I wanted with him. I knew I should decide before things got carried away.

There was a bond between us. I could feel it growing every time I was around him. It was foolish to deny the feelings between us, the sweet chemistry that took my breath and the heat that tingled along my skin.

We didn't say anything. He didn't move his face; he just inhaled the scent pouring off my neck, which drew vibrations from his chest—vibrations that were traitorously tantalizing across my skin. The bond had never felt this strong before, this dangerous.

His lips grazed the edge of my jaw and I knew that I shouldn't let it go on. I should stop it. But I couldn't, because when he kissed me I felt for a moment like I was the most lovely thing he had ever beheld.

He nipped at my bottom lip and I let out a soft moan. He growled into his next kiss and pulled my body closer to him—closer so his hands could roam places they shouldn't.

I kissed him back and poured all my pent-up desire into

him. He sucked on my bottom lip then trailed it with his tongue; his tongue that was begging to invade my mouth and claim it as its own.

I wanted it to go on. I wanted to forget the world and just stay here with him.

But the tiny voice inside my head was growing louder.

I knew I clearly had feelings for him—but a relationship? So soon after everything? The thought of that had me pushing him away.

"Liam, we can't."

He was panting hard and his eyes glowed. I shook my head and tried to rein myself in. I hated that I had to do this to him.

He let out a sharp, hot breath. He didn't move, only stared at me.

"I'm sorry." I sucked in a breath, then let it out slowly. "I don't know what I'm doing, I'm sorry."

His thumb wiped across my cheek. "It's okay," he murmured. "We don't have to do anything."

"I just—this is a lot. I'm sorry, this isn't fair to you."

He smiled slowly, his dimples showing. "I'm patient, I don't mind waiting."

"Liam." I shook my head, looking back at the valley. "What if your true mate shows up?" I asked, trying to find an excuse that could sound stronger than my own wavering resolve.

He looked around, arching a brow. "You see them anywhere around here?" He brushed the hair that had fallen out of my ponytail behind my ear. "Why would I look around me when I have all I need in front of me?"

Christ, he wasn't going to make any of this easy. "Liam, you barely know me—"

"Charlotte." He laughed under his breath, turning toward the valley. "Let's watch the sunset, yeah?"

But we weren't just watching the sunset. We were sitting there like two wound-up explosions with nothing but heat rolling off us.

Once the orange sun had slipped below the horizon, Liam agreed to take me home. He was pressing a good-bye kiss to my cheek in the woods at the edge of the lawn when shouting stilled us. I raised a finger to my lips and crept closer to the tree line as the shouting grew louder.

Lander's voice boomed across the yard. "Is this not enough?!"

"Go home," I murmured to Liam.

"Char—"

The beast in me surged, a hum running over my skin. "Go home now." I wasn't in the mood to argue, or to let him walk into something he would eventually wish that he could forget.

"Charlotte . . ."

"Trust me?" I dipped my head. "Go home."

Liam hissed a curse under his breath then fell back into the forest. Turning, I walked with steady steps across the lawn. As I got closer, the voices stilled.

A wave of suffocating electricity hit me as I stepped through the door. The beast in the back of my mind snarled, pushing closer. Her readiness kept the waves rolling off them from sweeping me up in their angry tides.

Lander's hands were making indents on the back of the

wooden chair. Levi's eyes were glowing bright, his fingers tapping on the other side of the table, claws clicking instead of nails.

"Well, hello," I said, taking careful steps.

"Go wash up." Levi's voice was a low hiss that cut like a cold knife through the room.

I shook my head. "No."

His gaze snapped to mine. On the table a series of maps were laid out, including the one of the forest I had from Jake, which was buried under the others. Dozens of sticky notes littered them along with markings from pens, Sharpies, and highlighters.

Lander tilted his head at me. "We can get dinner started."

A low laugh found its way out of my lips. I shook my head again. "No."

Stopping at the table, I leaned my arms on the back of a chair. "I already know you're hunting them." Lander opened his mouth but I raised my fingers off the chair. "I won't say anything. Tell me."

Lander turned his hard gaze to his brother. "Levi—"

Levi's eyes turned to mine, softening slightly. "She's not a pup. She's going to find out, and I'd rather it be from me."

Lander's jaw ticked before he pushed off the chair. "Fine," he grumbled. He walked to the kitchen and opened a cupboard.

"What's wrong?" I asked Levi.

As Levi stood, his claws were replaced by fingernails. "They caught traces of rogues close to Talia's. Some of her guards found a camp where it looks like two of them were. The physical description she gave and how they behaved sounds exactly like the ones you saw at The Hole."

"And from when I was attacked," I tacked on.

Levi nodded in concession. "Yes, and those."

"What are you going to do?"

Levi crossed his arms, turning a feverish glare at Lander. "I think it would be wise to assist Talia and question them."

Lander uncapped the whiskey and took a long drink from the bottle. "The packs in the South already are. We should keep our focus here."

"Why not go?" I found myself asking.

"Yes, why not?" Levi sneered, taunting his brother.

Lander shook his head. "We shouldn't even be discussing this with her."

"Well, if you two weren't as loud as a pack of hyenas, you probably would have heard me walking up," I pointed out. "So?"

"Christ," Lander hissed. "Because, we need to be careful. We cannot be the pack that cried wolf. We were that for so long. If we want anyone to take these claims, this threat, seriously, we have to have independent instances that we can tie together." He took another long sip before looking at me. "It will be a better case to the regional council if we can say—"

"That you all saw the same thing on your own," I finished. "Because if you're at every interrogation, then they'll think you're planting a seed."

Lander's brows rose. "Well, shit. Yeah, that's right."

I stood a little straighter. "I worked at a law firm for a while, remember? I can help."

"No," Levi said, his voice unforgiving.

I crossed my arms over my chest. "Well, if it helps,

whether you want my opinion or not, Lander is right." Lander's head whipped around to look at me. "Look, in court, that is what will win. And if your council is anything like how humans do things, he's right. You trust Talia?"

"Of course I fucking trust Talia," Levi grumbled.

Lander held his hands up. "If we want this to be taken seriously, we have to be tactful, especially if you think that it's worth eventually bringing to the regional council."

"What's the benefit to having the regional council open a case for this?" I asked. "I'm assuming if it's like how humans do things, you'd get more resources and manpower?"

Lander nodded. "That's right. A full-blown team, and not our little makeshift band here. It also goes on record, which in itself is a powerful thing to have. They don't open full cases for just anything though, it has to have substance to warrant the resources that will be used. The council won't agree to open the case if we don't have a solid one to present to them."

Quietly I asked Levi, "And you think they should open a case?"

Levi rubbed the back of his neck. "Like I said before, we should be more careful. Rogues, the sightings on their own, aren't full-blown fires, but something is off, and we'd be foolish to sleep on it."

"Then Lander is right," I pressed.

Levi turned to me, the weight of the last nine years showing in every ounce of desperation he was trying to hide. "Will you go shower now?"

I dipped my head in a short nod. "What's for dinner?"

"Fuck if I know. Lander's cooking."

Lander watched Levi for a moment before turning to me. "Hope you like breakfast for dinner, because that's all I'm good at."

I walked to him and gave his arm a squeeze. "As long as you make the bacon extra crispy."

Lander made us eggs, bacon, and some biscuits from a can for dinner. The two men were quiet the rest of the night, and I opted to leave them to their thoughts and silent links. Although, it was in the silence that I found my mind drifting to memories of golden eyes defiled with a red haze holding only foul intentions. I traced the scar on my leg from that night.

Lander paused next to Levi, who was drawing on the map. "We need to talk to Hemlock."

Levi looked up, eyes starting to glow. "I thought we agreed to keep everyone on a need-to-know basis for now?"

"We did," he agreed. "But if we're right, we will need them and their support, especially with the council, and we need to repair what's been damaged between you and them."

Levi set his highlighter down. "The Hunt is in two days."

"I know," Lander replied. "They agreed to meet halfway on the line. We won't tell them yet, not until we have a better grip on what we're dealing with. It's just an initial conversation, nothing more."

Levi tossed his drink back, finishing it. "Good."

Before Lander left, he hugged me. I watched him disappear into the night and lingered well after he was gone as the crickets in the trees sang their nightly song. Levi followed me outside, bringing his drink with him. He sat on the steps, looking at the waning moon. I sat next to him, lifting my eyes to look at Her as well.

"Are we safe?"

"Yes," he told me.

I turned to look at him. "You're sure?"

He took a drink. "Yes."

"I didn't mean to pry before."

He smirked. "It's in your nature. But you're right."

I rested my forearms on the tops of my legs. "Do you think it's connected?"

"I don't know," he answered. "But I know that last time we should've been more mindful. More proactive. We won't make that mistake again."

Reaching for his glass, I pried it out of his fingers then took a long sip for myself. "I won't say anything."

"I know."

He was the most relaxed I had seen him in weeks. Closing his eyes, he leaned back, letting the moonlight rake over his face. I took another sip then passed the glass back to him.

"Who are you meeting next door?"

One eye cracked open to look at me. He closed his eyes again and let out a long breath. "My nephews," he replied, confirming the hunch I already had.

"There's two and your niece, right?" I asked.

"Mhmm," he hummed.

"I'm sure they want to see you," I offered.

Levi scoffed. "I don't think they have a lot of cozy feelings toward me. Which isn't their fault. I can't blame them, I am a piece of shit."

"It's hard, when you fall away from people you become strangers again. People that you used to know. Meeting again, it's never the same. The expectation is things will be like they were, but they never are." He lifted an inquisitive gaze back to me. I licked my lips. "I haven't talked to my uncle Benji in years. I don't know what I would even say to him. We just fell apart, you know? He hated Nate and I was insistent back then. Suddenly we were always too busy to see each other. Neither of us has tried, but maybe we should? But you're trying, and considering everything, that should count for something."

"They're my family still," he murmured into his glass. "She would have wanted me to look after them. I failed her in that."

"People always want something to point their finger at," I countered. "Even when no one is right or wrong."

He hummed. "Maybe so."

"Have you seen them since it happened?"

He shook his head. "Ethan tried to see me shortly after the attack. I don't even remember it, but apparently he does. He never came back." His words felt like a ghoul screaming around us. He took a long drink from his glass. "I should have gone over there before."

"They also know the way here."

He swirled the ice in his glass. "You may have a point, but they are our neighbors and both of the boys help run the pack over there. They're going to have to deal with me now whether they want to or not."

"You'll be back for the Hunt, though?"

"'Course," he said, his voice firm. "We used to have more of them in the Hunt. I'm glad they let Jake come."

"Me too," I agreed.

He watched me for a moment as the moon's rays rolled over my skin. It felt like sunlight on a summer day, brightening my soul. "You need to be careful around Liam."

"It's nothing."

"Bullshit." He chortled. "I could smell him all over you when you came in."

I tugged my ponytail. "I know, I know."

"You need to figure out what you want to do before you get both of you hurt."

I hated how right he was. How much I knew that in my bones. Because what Liam wanted was something I wasn't sure I wanted, and it wasn't fair for me to lead him on until I had a sense of direction.

"It was nice," I admitted.

"You have to remember our world—your world now. Humans think they have it hard, but look at Andrea. Billy's kid got the shit end of the stick when her bondmate's true mate showed up. Same with David. Those marks fade but the pain does not."

My gut clenched. I wasn't sure I could handle another heartbreak, not now and potentially not ever, after everything. But I certainly wouldn't want to put Liam through the kind of pain that lurked behind Andrea's eyes, and which still sent chills down my spine just thinking of it.

"Marks fade?" I found myself asking.

He nodded. "Marks from bondmates are temporary.

They fade, so the couple has to do it again regularly. They're not your other half, your true mate."

"And those are forever?"

He shook his head. He pulled his collar aside to expose the clean skin at the base of his neck. "They are until they die. Eve's was there." My breath caught. Levi handed me the glass. "I would think about what you really want. He's a good young man, and you're both adults. If that's what you want, then that's what you want." He sighed. "Eve used to say that lust was like sand, easily swept away in the wind."

"I think I would have liked her."

"I do too," he agreed. "Derek and Elliot are coming back. Elliot wants to make it in time for the Hunt. He usually helps Bowie with them."

"It wasn't so bad without them."

Levi was quiet, the song the crickets were singing picking up. "No, it wasn't."

CHAPTER
NINETEEN

There was a knock on my door the morning of the eve of the Hunt. I groaned and pulled my comforter over my head. My door creaked open. Before I could turn over, two bodies yanked me out of bed. One crushed me into a chest, while another pressed his lips to my cheek.

Derek hugged me tight to him. "Oh, we missed you!"

I squealed. "I missed you guys so much."

Elliot stepped back and looked me over. "Winter wasn't too bad?"

"No," I answered, smiling into his sparkling green eyes.

Derek looked exhausted. There were bags under his eyes and his skin was ashy. His palm cupped my cheek. "I'm so happy you're well."

"Are you all right?" I asked him.

He waved me off. "Just need to feed. We've been traveling nonstop to get back."

Elliot's lips thinned as he forced a smile back to me, quickly pressing another kiss to my temple. "And the good news is we made it in time for the Hunt. Levi said your team looks good?"

"What else has he told you?" I asked, almost in a whisper.

Derek stood up, his legs like two pieces of stiff metal being forced into position. "Enough." I couldn't help but notice how fidgety he was—how he felt like a firecracker about to ignite.

I squeezed Elliot's hand. "You guys look hungry. I think there's blood in the freezer I can thaw out?"

"I look hungry because I am," Derek said, his voice almost a hiss.

"Derek," Elliot said, his tone dropping a hair. "Go drink. Now, before you go with Levi."

"Where are you going?"

Derek blinked hard, his eyes softening as he looked at me. "To the pack border. We'll be back by afternoon."

Elliot put a hand on my shoulder. "I thought I could help you get packed up and ready?"

"Well, it's a date then," I replied, still watching Derek, who almost seemed as if he was going to fade away.

It wasn't long before it was just Elliot and me in the house. He fixed breakfast while I poured some blood into his coffee. The smell of cinnamon and vanilla coming from the oven made my stomach growl. He leaned against the counter. "I'm so proud of you. You've grown so much. I can tell."

"Where were you guys?" I asked. "I tried calling so many times."

He put his mug down, offering me an apologetic smile. "I know, I'm sorry. It's hard when we're with Leo." He tapped the edge of his cup. "I can't tell you where we were the whole time, so please don't ask me again."

Leaning back, I slowly nodded. "Okay," I agreed.

"Coffee?"

"No blood."

Elliot was quick to pour me a cup before adding some creamer to it, fixing it just the way I liked it. He'd remembered. Although, I figured Elliot was one to never forget a damn thing.

Taking it from him, I pulled the mug between my hands. "Is Derek okay?"

Elliot sighed. "He will be," he said, almost as if he was telling himself rather than me. "It can be very taxing for him when he's there. We hate the bloody politics." He huffed a wry laugh. "There's good people in our coven. Many you would absolutely adore. But a lot of our business there is draining for him. He wasn't meant for that life."

I reached for his hand, squeezing it. "I'm glad he's back home then."

Elliot took my hand and pressed his lips to it, a bright smile rising on his face. "Me too. Now, let's eat and get organized. Is your team coming by?"

"Yeah, we're going to pack up together."

He nudged his chin to the yard outside. "And I do love the renovations you did to the yard. Long overdue."

Laughing, I took a sip of my coffee. "They were," I agreed.

Elliot and I finished eating and saved another pan of rolls for the team. Tia apparently knew Elliot, and threw herself into his warm hug. Jake, on the other hand, was slightly apprehensive. He later admitted to me that he had never actually met a vampire before, which I found strange considering everything. But Jake immediately fell into an easy banter with Elliot, who was more than happy to help us prepare. We had all our supplies laid out alongside three saddlebags in the living room.

Tia took the map and set it on the coffee table. I sat next to her as she began to add more notes on it while Jake leaned on the arm of the sofa, sharpening his knives as he watched.

"We can't take the map," I told her.

She exhaled a shaky breath. "I know, but writing it out helps me remember."

"We'll be fine, Ti," Jake's steady voice assured her. "We get in, get our deer, and get out."

Elliot walked over and stood next to Jake, combing over the map, studying it intently.

I licked my lips. "Levi said to avoid the silent spots."

"Yes, always avoid those," Elliot agreed. He pinned me with a serious look. "The air is foul there in places. Still. It doesn't move. If you find yourself in those places, get out. Go to where you can feel a breeze."

Our gazes felt attached to a tightrope that he eventually snapped with a brisk smile. "Let's pack your bags up so you both can get home."

Jake put his knife down and crouched to help Tia and me fill our bags with plenty of jerky, rope, knives, and ChapStick, which was his idea. He also tucked a smaller axe into his pack, which he said was lucky, and which I could only pray was actually true.

We tucked the emergency flares in along with zip ties that Elliot said always came in handy. Elliot folded two thick tarps and wrapped a bungee cord around them.

"What are those?" I asked.

"Game tarps," he replied. "I got them for you. They're thicker than a normal tarp. You can make a sack to carry the meat back or a sled if you have to. We have a sled here but it's going to be too cumbersome in the Trapper's Forest." He paused, turning to look at the group with a sobering gaze. "If you get your deer and you're stuck there another night, use these tarps to tie the game up in the trees. Other predators are going to smell the blood and come looking for it. Try not to be there any longer than you have to."

The screen door slammed against the frame and we whipped our heads around to see Levi storming through the kitchen. He stomped to his room in a silence that was anything but subtle; seething rage flowed off him in waves that drew a whimper from Tia. He banged his door shut. Tia jumped.

Derek walked in, gently closing the screen door. His eyes looked brighter, but they were still tired. Still drained. He smiled politely at us. "Do we have any blood thawed out?"

"Yeah," I answered.

Elliot stood, a hand stilling me from rising. "I got it. You pack up."

Derek winked at me, then murmured something in Elliot's ear. Elliot shook his head and walked to the fridge, pulling out a blood bag that he poured into a wineglass followed by actual wine. Derek took it, kissing him quickly.

Tia stood up. "I should go."

I nodded, hugging her tight to me. "We'll be fine."

She nodded against my shoulder. Jake nudged her shoulder with his fist. "She's right, Ti, team shitheads is going to hit it and quit it before anyone knows what happened."

"I can't." She tossed her hands up, shaking her head at him.

He carried her bag out of the house for her. Both of them paused at the edge of the forest to wave before disappearing into the thick of the trees. Elliot busied himself with the dishes, surreptitiously watching Derek sink into the couch. He patted the space next to him. When I sat, he tossed his arm around my shoulder, pulling me to his side.

"Are you ready for tomorrow?" he asked, his voice slightly hoarse, as if he needed a glass of water.

"Yes." My beast stirred. She was ready—both of us were.

"Good," he answered.

I tilted my head toward his cup. "It's a bit early for wine."

He scoffed through his nose. "It is most needed."

My voice dropped to a whisper. "What happened?"

"They didn't come, Ethan and Evan." He took another sip, eyes cast forward, staring at the television that was playing a rerun of a soccer game.

I frowned. "What the hell?"

"Said they were busy and couldn't make it last minute," he said, his tone clipped.

"That's so rude."

He laughed under his breath. "Well, it was technically informal. Payback will be fun, though."

"How's that?"

He grinned, his fangs showing. "Because Levi will make it formal. Pack to pack business they can't ignore."

"Is he okay?"

Derek shrugged. "Pissed mostly. We ran a good long ways to wait around for nothing. Evan had a bit of an attitude over the link as well, but he was always a cheeky brat." He pressed his lips to my cheek. "Not to worry, you have enough to focus on."

"Over the link? You can link?"

His eyes grew with excitement. He leaned closer, and a cold line tapped on the corner of my mind. After a few taps I let it in, grasping the line that felt almost liquid.

"Those created by the moon can."

"Witches?"

He shook his head. *"No. Just wolves and vampires."*

"Well, this is fun."

He winked. *"Elliot is going to be jealous I did it first."*

I leaned my head back against his shoulder. *"We should have done this before."*

"We should have."

"I missed you," I told him.

He sighed, pulling me tighter to him. *"Not as much as I missed you."*

Elliot urged me to go to bed early that night. Derek had made us a full spread of stuffed manicotti that I would normally inhale, but my nerves had chased any appetite I had away. The feeling of the encroaching darkness of that forest drove my anxiety wild; I lay in bed and found myself staring at the ceiling for what felt like hours and hours.

Blinking, I searched for the link I felt, half guilty about

reaching for it. Tapping into it, I murmured, *"Andrea? It's me."*

It was quiet for a few moments and part of me hoped she was sleeping. It was well into the night now.

"Are you all right?" she asked.

"I'm fine," I replied. *"I just . . . I'm sorry, I shouldn't have woken you up."*

"Well, I'm awake now," she groused. *"I didn't sleep the night before my hunt either."*

"Yeah?"

"Yeah," she breathed with a laugh. *"Dad tried to get me to sleep but nothing would work."*

"How long did it take you?"

"Five days too many," she said. *"You'll be fine. Handle your business in there, then be done with it. That's what my dad told me before my hunt."* I didn't say anything to that because I wasn't sure what business the shadows had planned for me. Thinking about it wasn't going to help my brewing anxiety. *"Well, in non-hunt-related news, I may be moving."*

"What? Really?"

"Really," she replied, almost bitterly. *"I can't stay here. I love my pack, I love Talia. I've been here for so long, but his memory is everywhere and it's starting to make me resent this place that I love."*

"Where will you go?"

She sighed. *"I don't know. Dad already thinks I'm coming back home to Hemlock with him, but I'm not so sure. There are some packs on the other side of the mountains I was thinking about, but Talia mentioned that I should talk to Levi—"*

"And come here?"

"*Maybe,*" she replied with a breathy laugh. "*Who would have ever thought.*"

"*Well, you'd at least know people if you came here, so you wouldn't be totally alone. And I'm here. And I know where Levi hides all the good booze.*"

Chuckling, she replied, "*You make a good pitch. I still have to talk to Levi about it, but Thunderhead is next door to Hemlock, so I could see my dad more. And Levi's booze is pretty enticing.*" She paused a moment. "*Thanks.*"

"*For what?*"

"*Listening,*" she quietly replied. "*I never thought I would be starting over again. Timber has been my home for so long, but I don't know. I'm kind of looking forward to being on my own for a while. Talia calls it 'protecting my peace,'*" she added with a laugh.

I hummed in agreement, although I found myself ruminating on the thought. I couldn't deny the pull between Liam and me, but I also found myself liking the idea more and more of being on my own in a home that I have been fighting to have. A home that was mine—not Nate's or my lonely old college dorm room, but mine.

"*Don't worry about the Hunt,*" she told me. "*Trust your instincts, they seem pretty good, so trust your gut. I'll be there for a few days toward the end. They do a bonfire every evening until all the teams are home.*"

"*You're coming?*"

"*All the packs in the region are invited. Talia is coming for Tia, and, well, I am betting on your team.*"

"*What's the bet?*"

"*That you make it.*"

The morning of the Hunt I found myself sitting on the front porch, watching the sun rise over the trees. The sky was bleeding shades of red, like streams curling through the sky. There was a faint line in the middle of my palm, something I found myself hoping would never fade. I could feel the bond, pulsing like a faint heartbeat within me. My own beast was close, settling in comfortable nearness while we both enjoyed the songbirds waking the forest.

I could feel him before the door opened. The smell of him rolled toward me in a gentle tide. Levi took careful steps on the creaky wood stairs that probably needed to be repaired soon. He sat, taking a sip of coffee from his mug.

"You ready?"

What waited in that forest was a fog to me. We could run into a trap. My mind drifted to the pit as memories of the suffocating blackness laughed like cackling demons. Maybe Tia's grandmother was right? Maybe it did twist your mind. Either way, I didn't care, because I wanted this. I wanted it so bad that I could taste it, ached for it. My beast pawed in the back of my mind; she was ready for the chase, and I was too.

I turned my palm up, the faint scar showing. "Yeah."

Levi slapped his palm in mine, squeezing it before putting his arm around my shoulders. "Are you sure?" he asked, like he would drive the getaway car if I so much as breathed any doubt.

I tilted my head toward his. "I'm sure. I want this."

Levi breathed a laugh. "Well, we better get moving then."

Elliot carried my saddlebag to the entrance of the normal training grounds. Dozens of people were gathered. Derek gave my shoulder a squeeze before walking over to Lander and shaking his hand as they broke into conversation. Levi grumbled before following him, interrupting what seemed to be friendly conversation.

Elliot stood with me, his arm around my shoulder. Claire waved to me. She jogged over and gave my arm a squeeze. "Good luck. We'll have tequila when you're done."

"Thank you," I told her.

Lyle looked at me then waved someone forward. Penny walked over, her cheeks red. "Go on," he told her.

Penny scowled at him then slipped a bracelet on my wrist. "I made it for you. It's good luck."

Lyle took Penny's hand, and started to drag her away. "Don't die!" he called to me.

Elliot inspected the bracelet, made of small rainbow-colored stones. My heart melted looking at it. "Tuck it in your bag so it doesn't snap when you shift."

Nodding, I placed the bracelet in a pocket that I knew it wouldn't fall out of. Looking across the crowd, I found Liam standing with the lanky brunet boy on his team, along with Ali and Anamaria. Ali was checking everyone's packs, her smile wide as she spoke to the team.

She and Ani turned, waving to me. I waved back, smiling at them before wistful silver eyes caught mine in a heated stare.

I ripped my gaze away and found Tia. She had her hair in two French braids that almost reached her waist, one of them ribboned with silver from the lightning-like streak in her hair. Her saddlebag was slung over her shoulder, a golden firefly charm hanging from one of the clips. Jake was right behind her, cracking his neck as he approached. He tossed his bag across his forearm.

"Hey," she said, smiling at me. "Ready?"

"Yeah," I told her. "You?"

Tia bit her lip, her eyes full of excitement. "Yeah, although I barely slept."

"I slept like a baby," Jake drawled.

Elliot gave my shoulder a squeeze. "You all better get up there," he said, nodding to the front.

"Let's go," Tia said, trying to contain the high pitch in her voice.

As I took a step, Elliot caught my arm. He reached into his back pocket and pulled out a large, folded knife with a cherrywood handle. He opened my saddlebag and tucked it in. "It's always brought me luck."

I pressed my lips to his cheek, then followed my team to where the other groups where standing. Jake stepped aside and let me stand between him and Tia. I could smell it before I saw it—paint.

Bowie jogged out of the woods with Remi on her heels. Both of their arms were covered in bright sky blue, tangerine orange, inky black, and fire-engine red, all of which dripped down their arms.

Bowie smiled, exhilaration shining in her eyes. "All right!" she called over the crowd. "Let's get a move on it."

The audience around us quieted. David walked over to her and handed her a revolver. She took it and inspected the rounds before pushing the cylinder back into place. With her free hand, she wiped some sweat off her brow before counting each of the four teams. A pleased smile curled on her lips.

"Well, you probably noticed that we are properly covered in paint." She laughed, the crowd echoing back soft chuckles of its own. "There is a deer for each of your teams! The deer is painted in your team color. Here are the rules." Her purple eyes grew serious. "There are three emergency flares given to each team. If you use them, someone will come for you. If someone comes for you, your hunt is immediately over.

"Should you link anyone in this pack for help, your hunt is over. Should you not find your deer within the week, your hunt is over. And should you die, your hunt is clearly over.

"If your hunt ends, you will not be accepted as a tracker and you will have to do this next year. At the end of seven days, if a team is not back, we will come looking for you," she finished, her voice dropping with that dark, teasing promise that drew goose bumps over my skin.

"We will begin the Hunt at the count of three." She took a few steps back and held the gun to the sky. "Don't worry, it's a blank round, everyone." Laugher murmured around us. "One!"

I gripped my bag, squeezing the straps of the leather. I felt Jake stiffen next to me as a wind flowed out of the forest. It was cold, like water running down from the mountains and into the creek.

"Two!"

Turning, I caught Levi's silver eyes. He said nothing. His eyes held mine as he nodded. I wasn't sure what he would do while I was gone, but I knew he would be waiting for me day and night until I got back.

"Three!"

The gun went off. We jogged into the training forest that had become an old friend to us. After running a few yards, we stopped and waited for Jake to catch up.

"Okay," Tia said, eyeing me. "You guys go first, I'll follow behind."

"I'll be on your right," Jake told me. "What do you think?"

"I think we need to find the paint before the trail is gone, it's going to be the easiest way," I answered.

Jake hummed in agreement. "Let's go."

We jumped into our fur, letting our beasts come forward as we powered through the training grounds. Jake and I picked up the pace, leading the way, with Tia close behind.

The whole run, I kept looking for any sight of red paint that could give our deer away. But in my gut I knew that Bowie would not make it so easy as to let the deer go in the training ground.

We pushed on, running farther into the thickness of the trees. Darkness felt like it was falling upon us. I could have sworn the sun was setting, but when I looked up, it was only the canopy growing thicker.

The air around us grew colder. Something gnawed at the back of my mind as my paws dug into mud that felt clammy, slimy, and sick.

We turned a corner and ran farther until Jake skidded to an immediate stop, his toes a breath away from a line of white chalk on the ground. I shifted to my skin when I realized where we were. Jake let out a long breath and leaned forward to rest his hands on his knees.

"We're fucking doing this," he said to himself, looking down at the chalk line.

Tia stepped next to me as we stared into the darkness. Into the quiet. I paused to listen. I could still hear the sound of birds wings flapping in the air and leaves falling to the ground.

"It's safe. I can hear," I told them.

"So many people have gone mad in there," she murmured, clenching her fists.

Jake stood, shaking his arms out. "Not us. Not today." He clenched his jaw tightly as he walked into the dark woods. Tia let out a long breath, nodding to me. "Let's go," she said, following Jake.

I gazed into the darkness that felt like it was so eager for me enter. In a shaft of sunlight, a leaf drifted slowly to the shadowy ground.

"I'm not afraid of you," I whispered to the woods, letting my feet carry me forward across the chalk line.

CHAPTER TWENTY

The lanky trees in the forest reached to the sky with their iron bar limbs, locking us away from the warmth of the sun the farther we ran in their midst. Surging forward across the cold ground, I let my beast's instincts fully take over so we could take in every sound, every smell, and every small track.

My beast tipped her nose into the air, letting the stale air marinate while we tried to pick out pieces of the scent to find a needle in a haystack. It smelled like rain, old cardboard boxes, and the decay of something small nearby. Pushing her nose to the dirt, she ran a few steps, desperately digging her nose far into the ground until we found it. Something acidic that made her lips curl.

Paint.

There was no telling what color it was; all we could smell was the pungent perfume, but seeing as we hadn't picked up the scent of a deer, it was the best lead we had.

So we followed it. We hurled toward the scent down a hill covered in slick rocks that felt like it was designed to hurt upon a fall. Whipping around a boulder, my beast skidded to a halt when her eyes spotted something on a bush about twenty yards away. Yipping to the others, she ran forward as pride surged through us.

The dainty leaves of a baneberry bush were dripping with crimson paint. Half of the bush looked covered in it, like the deer had run right through it. I lifted my eyes, spotting more drops rolling down tree bark, like rubies.

Tia shifted to her skin, eyeing the leaves, but careful not to touch them.

"Nice work." She beamed as Jake shifted to his skin, kneeling down about ten yards ahead of us.

He pointed forward. "Looks like it's running scared."

"Hopefully it's not from the forest," Tia murmured.

Trotting forward, my beast stopped to look at the broken limb from a young tree he was holding, covered in red. He pointed to where red frantically decorated a path forward for us.

He tapped the limb. "It's sticky. Probably been here for around an hour."

Tia hummed in agreement. She pulled a knife out of her saddlebag and marked an X on the tree and a line pointing in the direction we had come from. "Where is it headed?" Tia asked, looking around the area, which looked like miles and miles of the same.

I sat back on my haunches, tipping my nose to the sky. I could still hear the sound of birds, and the light breeze dancing on the top of the canopy, almost as if it was begging to be let in. *"It's not a silent area,"* I told them. *"We've been going west. Northwest I think?"*

Jake gave Tia's shoulder an encouraging squeeze. "Keep marking the trees." He nodded to me. "Let's go."

With that, I flew through the forest, following the trail of red laid out like an erratic brick road. It was as if the deer was desperately trying to find a way out—a way to fresh air.

The breeze was becoming harder to feel, which meant it was going to be harder to smell anything until we were close to it; no breeze would be carrying the scent to us.

I tried to assure myself as I charged forward through the ghoulish trees. The scent of paint kept my beast and me going, as did the patch of fur that I later found caught in a hedge. Tia picked it up then held it up so Jake and I could smell it before tucking it into her bag. She made another X with a line pointing home on a nearby tree, then ran after us in her skin.

Soon the paint started to become less frequent. I found a set of tracks with red drops littering it. They were wet, like fresh blood on the ground. My beast stilled while we scanned the area in front of us. Jake tipped his nose to the air.

"It's close," he said.

I agreed. I could smell the same faint scent that its fur carried, laced with the pungent perfume of the paint.

Jake's head nudged my shoulder. My paws quietly crept across the cool ground like the wings of a dragonfly fluttering at night. The only thing I could feel was my own breath rolling out of my snout and over my lips while the musky scent of the deer grew stronger and stronger until we were only a few yards from it.

I could see it between the small leaves of a shrub that hid our bodies. It was standing like a statue on top of a stage of moss that looked more like a rotten, sticky green mold. He was a large buck with a crown of antlers that counted eight. This wasn't his home; anyone could see that in the wide, dark eyes that sparkled with a terror I understood all too well. Red covered his entire body and face—caked and crackling all over him, with only a few drops still running down his belly. The paint would dry soon. Part of me wondered if he would ever be able to get it off on his own.

Jake stopped beside me while Tia held her position behind us. I fell to my belly, letting my beast's instincts roll over me as we watched the deer search frantically around the area.

"*Follow me,*" I told them.

"*I have your left,*" Jake answered.

I felt Tia's head nudge my leg. "*I've got the flank.*"

The buck turned his head to look to the left, and when he did, we sprang into action. He jumped into the sky right as my paws hit the moss, soaring into the darkness of the forest.

My beast snarled. We weren't about to let the forest consume him when he was ours to have. The buck darted left and right, but Tia and Jake were there to stop him from escaping. Instead, he hurled forward in a furious gallop. We ran together in a perfect pyramid, as my legs felt like fire soaring over the ground. We were closing in, closer and closer, when the buck jumped over a fallen tree.

I tracked where he would land before I even stepped on the tree. Fear ripped through me, because when he landed, his hooves caught a line that was reflecting in the small crumb of daylight dripping down from the sky.

Dirt skidded around me as I stopped, panic rolling over me in waves. I shifted to my skin, sliding in the dirt as I turned on my heel. "Stop!" I screamed to the others.

But we were too late.

There was a whistle then something screaming through the still air at me. I leaned out of the way, but whatever it was sliced right across my cheek, burning like I had been the box a match was struck on.

A cry ripped past my lips. My legs moved on their own, running back the way I had come. "Stop! Go back!" I yelled.

Jake fell in next to me while Tia sprinted, her arms pumping, alongside on our right while arrows tipped with silver sliced through the air.

"Don't look back!" Jake bellowed. "Keep going!"

I didn't dare turn around to see why it sounded like the wind was carrying sharp cries from hell. I kept my eyes forward even when something grazed my shoulder, burning a line as it cut through my skin. Gritting my teeth, I kept going.

Tia shrieked as she curved her torso out of the way of an arrow. They whizzed past us, but we kept moving, following Tia, who was flying forward. She leaped over a patch of moss before hurtling through a set of trees, running until I couldn't hear the sound of whistling arrows.

"Tia, stop!" I called, slowing my pace.

But she never slowed. She kept moving through the trees, farther away from us.

"Shit," Jake spat. "*Tia!*"

He snatched a branch and chucked it at her. She stumbled a few feet, her hiss echoing through the forest, reverberating around the trees as if it was bouncing against walls. I skidded to a stop.

I couldn't hear anything. There was no breeze. No sound of scampering creatures or even a crack or a snap from an old limb falling.

Cold terror rolled over me. "*Stop!*" I screamed, quickly snatching Jake and yanking him to me before he could pass by. Tia pulled up with a sharp gasp.

The cold of the darkness felt like it was breathing down my neck, laughing at me for walking right into its mouth. The beast in me pushed closer, rolling over me in waves while she paced.

"Charlotte?" Jake whispered.

I heard Tia suck in a breath. She was wiping something off her arms that was drawing blood, like little mosquito bites. I looked up slowly, dreading what I knew in my gut was there.

They looked like spider sacks, easily glanced over. There had to be hundreds of them above where Tia stood. All of them were closed, but they were attached to lines that wrapped down the trees and hid in the cover of the leaves on the ground.

"Fuck." I wiped my face, spotting one that looked like it had started to crack, a few silver flakes falling like misty rain to the ground where Tia was standing. I traced the lines that laced the ground until I could see where she had somehow stepped into a pocket in the middle of them.

It was a miracle she'd avoided them.

Jake shook his head. "Tia, don't move."

"Close your eyes!" I shouted.

"What?!" she shrieked. Why?!"

She started to turn around. Jake and I jumped forward. "No!" we shouted together.

I took a deep breath. "Tia, don't move. Okay?"

Her body was shaking. She turned her head toward us. "Guys? Guys, what's happening?" she hissed again, wiping her cheek as silver hit her. "Oh—oh god, it's—"

"Close your eyes! Now!" Jake yelled. He stepped back, his hands tugging his hair. "Fuck, fuck, fuck, fuck, fuck."

Tia clamped her eyes shut. "There's sacks of silver dust above you," I told her.

"What?!"

"Tia," I said, struggling to keep my voice even. "Keep your eyes closed. And pinch your nose. Okay? Take shallow breaths. Keep your head down."

"Charlotte . . ."

"Do it, Tia," Jake snapped. He sucked in a breath, trying to hide his panic.

She nodded, pinching her nose then pulling a braid across her mouth for good measure. Jake leaned back, looking at me with wide eyes. He tapped his temple.

"What the fuck do we do?" he groaned.

"How did we not smell it?"

"Or hear it?" he added before he shook his head slowly. *"Billy warned me this forest was fucked-up."*

I looked back at the ground. *"I don't know how she didn't set off more lines."*

"She can't open her eyes. If more of that falls from the others it's going to blind her."

I looked at the lines again. *"Do you think we could direct her? Tell her where to step?"*

Jake knelt to examine the traps. *"She's not the most graceful."*

"You have one of the blankets in your pack. Right?" I asked out loud.

"Yeah." He ripped his saddlebag open and pulled out a thin blanket with a shiny copper side that we each had stored in our packs to keep us warm at night if needed. He handed it to me. "What are you thinking?"

I licked my lips. "Tia?"

"Yeah?" she said, sobbing as the silver carved shallow streams down her cheeks.

"How do you feel about following where we say to step?"

She started to shake. "Charlotte—"

"Okay," I said quickly. "It's okay. Okay? We're going to get you out."

I pulled the blanket around me. Jake looked at me with wide eyes. "What the fuck are you doing?"

I let out a long breath. "Look, I can make it through. I know I can. I can go to her, get her on my back, and then carry her out. We'll put the blanket on her to cover us."

"No, absolutely not."

"What else? She's shaking so bad—she's going to step on a line and that shit is going to get in the air and fuck us all up," I retorted.

He blew out a long breath. "Fuck it, fine. What do you want me to do?"

I handed my pack to him. "Be my other set of eyes."

"Okay," he huffed, his jaw clenching before he nodded to me. "Fuck it, okay."

I turned, clutching the blanket over my head. "Tia? I'm going to come get you. Okay? You're going to get on my back. Do not move at all. I'm going to come to you."

"Char, I don't think that's a good idea," she stammered.

I clutched the blanket tighter around me. "Well, yeah, you're not wrong. But we're going for it. Stay still."

She sniffled as her toes squirmed into the dirt while silver flakes trickled around her.

"Here goes nothing," I said, taking a careful step between the dangling lines. "Jake?"

"Yeah?"

"I'm not going to look up, so I need you to tell me if they're going to fall," I told him, taking another careful step.

I kicked some leaves out of the way, exposing three easy gaps I could safely step in.

"You're good," he told me, his voice struggling to stay even. "It's just that one over her."

I stepped into another gap and had to keep myself from jumping straight up. "Fuck!" I wheezed. I didn't have to look to know I had stepped on silver. It felt like fire on the heel of my foot, a fire that wasn't about to settle.

Lucky for me, I was used to biting back the pain.

Gritting my teeth, I kept walking, stepping in a sickly hopscotch until I made it to the gap that Tia was standing in.

"Hey." I breathed shallowly, my beast frantically pacing back and forth in the back of my mind.

Tears ran down her cheeks alongside the tears of blood the silver had drawn. "Hi," she said with a tiny sob. "I'm so sorry."

"It's okay," I quickly replied. "We're going to get you out and cleaned up," I told her, trying to assure her and myself. The beast in me pressed closer, pulsing through me while I looked around us. "I'm going to hand you this blanket. We're going to put it over your head."

She nodded. I slipped the blanket over her head, and the minute I did, I wanted to start scratching my neck. A few flecks of silver fell right behind my ear, carving an edge as they trailed down to my shoulder.

Biting back a snarl, I made sure the blanket covered her shoulders. "You cannot take a step at all. You're a few inches from lines on all sides."

She nodded, her nose almost brushing mine. I tilted my head toward my shoulder. "Jake?"

"You're good. Get out of there." His voice was steady but I could still hear the panic.

Swallowing, I looked back to her. More flakes fell onto my shoulder blades, raking down them in a way that felt like too many nights I had spent with Nate.

"When I turn around, I'm going to crouch. I want you to slip your arms around my neck first. You're going to crawl onto my back and hold that blanket over us. Okay?"

"Yeah," she whimpered. "We can do this."

"We can," I agreed, silently praying that this plan would keep us from being melted alive.

Slowly turning around, I reached my arms back and grasped her waist. "Okay, I am right here," I stated. "I'm kneeling down now."

Squatting, I gave her leg a tap. "Reach your arms over."

Silver hit the tip of my knee as she slipped her arms over my head. My leg shook from the sparkly flake that found its way down the slope of my skin. I bit back a growl as I reached back to tap her right leg.

She pulled the blanket forward, covering our heads. "I'm going to grab your right leg and stand. I want you to hitch the left around me. You ready?"

"Yeah, let's do it."

"Charlotte, hold still," Jake's voice raced out, shaking in a way that made Tia and me freeze, her with her right leg halfway around my hip.

Tia gurgled back a sob. "Jake?" I could hear him breathing. It was loud, like he was about to have a panic attack. "Jake?!"

"Go, go fast."

The forced evenness of his voice kicked me into gear. "Now, Tia."

Standing, I yanked her leg around me while she latched the other around my waist. Turning quickly, I locked eyes with Jake. He curled his fingers forward, pointing up with his other hand. I didn't ask questions, didn't dare look. I could hear the silver singing its sizzling song as it floated down from above us.

I stepped carefully where I had stepped before. A stream of silver dust fell a few feet from me. My beast was howling, pushing me to keep moving. I was trying to stay light on my toes, which was easier said than done when it felt like my toes were hopping from one pit of knives to the other with each step I took.

Jake held his arm out as we neared, like a parent reaching for their child swimming in a pool. I took two long steps before jumping across the last line, letting him catch us.

We stumbled backward a few steps. He pulled Tia off my back and tore the blanket away from her. He desperately scanned her face. "Don't open your eyes," he said. "You've got it all over your cheeks."

I didn't see his arm reach for me. He grasped the strap of my sports bra and yanked me forward, studying every inch of my face. "You good?"

His eyes gave away nothing, but his voice wavered slightly.

I nodded. I wasn't okay, but I knew how to function while not being okay. How to bite it back, choke it down, swallow without spitting, like a good fucking girl because that is how I survived then—a past I wanted the sacks of silver to melt away.

I looked around us, the beast in me starting to pace again. All I could hear was us and the silver. "We need to get out of here. It's too quiet."

"I'll carry her. Let's find water and clean you guys up. It's too dangerous to keep moving."

"The deer?" Tia bit back a sob.

"Fuck the deer right now. Tia, you'll go blind if we don't clean you up." Jake picked her up. I rubbed my temples, watching the silver fall like glitter, as though we were in some twisted nightclub.

Jake tipped his nose in the air as his back twitched. "This way," he told me.

Every step I took behind him felt like I was walking on that silver all over again. He shoved through bushes, not minding the talon-like thorns that cut his arms, protecting Tia from the brunt of it. He whispered hushed reassurances to her while she cried softly against his chest. The silver was running down her cheeks in red streams that mirrored the ones I could feel on the back of my neck.

We neared a small pond that a little creek sleepily trickled into. Jake set Tia down to lean against a tree while I swallowed the pain and cased the area, carefully looking for anything that could kill us before I smelled the water.

My eyes rose to Jake's. "It smells clean. I think this is safe."

He dipped to smell it, too, then scooped a small pool of it into his palm before he carefully sipped it and swirled it around in his mouth. Spitting it to the side, he grunted in agreement. "Safe. Let's get you two cleaned up."

We didn't have tweezers but we had rags and knives that Jake had packed, which we used to carefully lift all the flakes of silver off us that he could spot. Together, we cleaned off Tia's face first. I helped her to the pond and leaned her backward to wash any bits of it out of her hair before we would let her open her eyes. She blinked a few times then broke into a quiet sob. I didn't say anything. She buried her face in her hands as Jake started to lift the silver off my skin. "It's in my feet too," I told him.

Tia wiped her face. "We're so stupid. We should have thought about where we were going."

"You shouldn't have run past us," Jake scolded her. "We have to stay together. It's not safe, Tia."

"It's not her fault." I hissed as he dug a flake out of my neck. "We're all right, yeah?"

Tia wiped her eyes again. "I'm sorry, guys."

I took her hand, squeezing it. "Hey, we're all alive and safe. We're okay. It's okay."

Jake pulled the last flake out of my neck. When he moved to my feet, I had to bite my fist to stop the screaming. Tia cried quietly and held my hand. When he was finished, he wiped my foot off then repacked his bag.

"Thank you," she whispered again to me.

I nodded. "You're welcome."

Jake stood up, pulling his bag around his waist so that when he shifted it would easily slide onto his back. "We need to go. We still have daylight."

Leaning forward, I drew a rectangle and circles that I had memorized—the general area of the forest from the map. Jake knelt down while Tia scooted forward. I drew a line that ran into a circle with lines across it. "We were in a silent area. That's where the silver was. I couldn't hear a thing. Not a sound. I couldn't even smell it."

Jake's eyes grew dark. "Me either."

Nodding, I looked back at my drawing. I drew a star northeast of the silent area. "I think we were on the edge of it. Where we chased the deer wasn't silent. That deer went north, I think?"

"It did." Tia blew her nose into a rag and shook her arms out, her eyes focused on my makeshift map. "I saw it run a straight path."

"We don't know how many more traps are in that area. We could go back, but there may be more there. I say we curve around then try to pick up the scent again and push north."

"That's pushing close to another silent area," Tia pointed out. "And mountain lion territory."

I bit my lip. "The deer isn't from the forest. It's going to look for water and a way out."

Jake rubbed his chin. "If we can cut it off from going east, that would be ideal. There are too many traps and silent areas that way. I would rather deal with bears than silver." He drew a wider line around the one I had made curling east. "We should pick up the trail and try to herd it west."

We all hummed in agreement before standing. The sun was still high but it wouldn't be for long. Tia dusted off her hands on her shifters. "You good?" Jake asked her.

She nodded, determination filling her eyes. She pulled out her knife then walked to a tree and marked it with harsh cuts. Snapping the knife shut, she turned to us and said, "Let's go."

"You lead," I told Jake, my feet still burning from the silver.

Jake nodded then shifted into his fur, the sandy color looking like ash in the shadow of the forest. I let my fur roll over me and ran close behind him. I caught sight of Tia's paws next to me. They had small stripes of red running down them. Her eyes were hard focused, but her feet were frantic. I tried to keep calm, but I couldn't help but wonder what other scars this forest would leave on us.

CHAPTER
TWENTY-ONE

Jake was careful to lead us around the silent area and farther around where we had almost been killed by the silver arrows. When the burning had stopped in my paws and lessened to a dull throb, my beast cut around his and led the way, stepping lightly as she ran forward. Our eyes studied every tree, every rock, every blade of grass for a sign of danger.

The trees here were twisted and twirled with lanky limbs that looked like they would snatch us at any second. I was jumping over a fallen branch when the scent hit me—the deer. Hope filled me. My beast yipped at the others then ran forward at an easy pace. We spotted red on a tree where the buck must have hit it during his escape.

Jake was running next to me now, the two of us zigzagging

through the area in search of traps while my nose followed the scent farther into the winding trees and hanging moss. I looked up and spotted nets hidden in the tree canopy, silver threads glimmering within them. Sliding to a stop, I spotted a trip line that had already been broken—the unfortunate soul who'd broken it was a mess of bones dangling from the branches above.

Tia stilled next to me. *"Charlotte . . ."*

"Don't look up," I told her, breaking into a run.

But the more we ran, the fainter the scent grew, and the fewer tracks we spotted. Paint wasn't anywhere to be found and no one had picked up a whiff for some time. All we could see were trees and trees for days. We doubled back to the last track that we had seen, running around the area before we decided to head in a direction Jake suggested was our best chance.

But all the twisted trees looked the same.

The air grew thick, the breeze nonexistent.

The sounds of twigs cracking and leaves rustling were so faint it was as if I was hearing them at a distance. I shifted back to my skin. Sweat pooled under my breasts. The air felt humid, heavy. There wasn't anything to circulate it between the swamp of trunks.

Shifting to her skin, Tia ran to a tree with faint markings of red paint rubbed on the bark. Jake snarled. He shifted to his skin, his eyes hard. "We've been here before."

"No, we haven't. We haven't—" she started to say, when her eyes locked onto a tree. She marched to it, her fingers shaking as they traced an X she had carved. "Jake, you've been taking us in circles!"

"The fuck I have!" he growled, his eyes glowing. "I can't fucking think in here."

Tia leaned back, taking in a deep breath before shaking her head. "We're lost. Fuck, we're lost!"

"We need to get out of here," I told them. I'd noticed it was becoming even quieter. The shadows felt like they were enclosing us. I blinked, unsure if the air was making me mad or if my eyes were trying to deceive me. "I need air. We need fresh air."

Part of me wondered if it was as a trap, a gas that the poachers used a long time ago. Shaking the shiver away, I looked up. I could see small tendrils of fading daylight peeking through the canopy. "Jake? Help me up. I think I can climb it. I can get up and see where we are."

"If it's safe then we should all go," Tia said, a hopeful twinge in her voice.

Jake set his pack down and joined me by a tree, taller than the ones around it, with branches wrapping upward like a slippery spiral staircase. He knelt down and gave me a boost, tossing me a little so I could catch a low-hanging limb. The minute I pulled myself up, I climbed, and didn't stop climbing until I punched through the canopy.

Cool, fresh air washed over me like water. Sucking in a long breath, I slowly let it out, sobering while wind playfully danced around me as if it was celebrating that I'd made it.

"Thank god," I gasped. *"It's safe! The air is amazing. Come up!"* I linked them.

I could feel the tree shaking as they climbed, and clung to the narrow trunk near the top. The sun was setting, and orange coated the sky. I scanned the horizon, where the sea of leaves rolled like the waves of a warm ocean.

To my west there were the mountains with snow on the caps. They looked cold, harsh, and unforgiving as they cast a shadow over the land. In the distance, in the middle of the forest, there was something that looked like white limbs tangled with bright-green leaves waving like flags. I was cocking my head, trying to focus, when Jake punched through the canopy.

He gulped the air like he had been held captive underwater. Tia broke through next to him, sucking in a large breath as well.

"I hate that fucking forest," Jake growled. "Fuck that tastes good." He took another deep inhale, like he was tasting cold water for the first time.

Tia closed her eyes, letting the sun roll over her red-streaked cheeks. She looked at me with a smile that turned into a laugh. My lips curled, and before I knew it, I found myself laughing with her. Jake rolled his eyes. "You guys have lost it." He looked down through the limbs, slowly shaking his head. "No wonder people go mad down there. The air is so foul. Like there's no moon. Too bad we can't catch a deer up here."

"Well, can't we?" Tia looked around, her eyes studying the area. "We're farther east."

"There wasn't a sign of it," I groaned. "The trail went dry."

Tia pointed forward. "It probably went west, then. We should push west." She turned around and pointed to a set of mountains to the south, the sunlight glimmering off them.

"That's the glacial range the pack land backs up onto, and those," she explained, pointing to the snowy mountains in the west, "are the silver mountains that border the Hemlock Pack."

A grim frown formed on Jake's face. His eyes were wide, scanning the mountains like he was sure they would attack. He blinked. "We should push west then. It's only been a day. We don't have much daylight. We push until we get somewhere safe and make camp. Start again tomorrow."

Tia hugged the tree. "Can we just sit here a minute?"

I pointed to the strange white tree I'd noticed. "What's that?"

Jake followed my gaze. "The oathing tree for my pack."

"It's in this forest?" I asked, unable to tell where the normal forest started and ended within the sea of leaves.

"It is," he confirmed, his eyes growing hard before he looked down. "We should go. We're almost out of daylight."

We all took a few more breaths of the clean air before we descended into the shadows. Once my feet hit the ground, I snatched my bag and tossed it around my waist. We all shifted to our fur without a word, not daring to stay any longer than necessary in the stale air.

Our group kept pushing west, but there was no sign of the deer. Although at the moment, my priority was getting us out of the stagnant thicket.

Twilight had swept through the forest by the time we crossed over a set of boulders that broke through the line of trees. They stood proud in the fading sunlight, the stone warm and comforting to touch. Trotting to the top, I let the breeze comb through my fur like a friend trying to reassure me that we could survive the shadows. My beast darted forward, galloping across the ground before her paws locked in place. Our breath caught.

Silver sang in the air around us. I shifted to my skin with a shudder as my hand flew over my mouth, a sob threatening to escape.

In the ground there were six pits looking back at me like open mouths. I could smell the rot, the decay—the death. A skeletal hand was reaching over the edge of one, bony fingers lying in defeat on the ground.

My feet moved on their own, carrying me until I was at the edge of one that had a silver net lining it. All that was left was a rusted collar with blunt silver spikes facing inward and bones. So many bones. I didn't dare walk to the other pits.

A tear slid down my cheek. I looked up at the moon, my mouth open and wondering how She could have sat there and watched this happen.

A cold wind laced over my shoulders, but this time instead of feeling dread, bitter anger pulsed in me.

"Screw you," I whispered to the encroaching darkness, refusing to look back at it as I marched to my team.

Jake and Tia were almost down the boulder when I held a hand up to stop them. "Come this way. That way's not good," is all I said before I led them down the other side.

We curved between the trees that lined the upslope of a hill, where I'd caught sight of ruby red on the side of a tree. Darting to it in my fur, I stuck my nose to the ground as Tia pulled out her knife and marked the tree while Jake did a wide circle around the area.

"It was here then went that way," Jake said, pointing through the thick trees.

Jogging over, I picked some dirt up and smelled it as well. The scent was strong, tracks visible in the dirt ahead. "I think that's west."

Tia looked up at the encroaching night sky and rubbed her face. "Shit, it's almost dark. We should camp."

Reluctantly, I agreed with her. I had no desire to venture through these woods at night.

Jake made a small fire for us under a rare opening in the thicket of the trees. The smoke curled up to the sky where we could see the moon. We agreed that we needed to sleep where we could see the sky, where fresh air could easily find us.

I bit off a piece of jerky and quietly swallowed. Tia rested her head in my lap, while I ran my fingers mindlessly over her braids. "We should have slept up there," she said, pointing to the canopy.

Jake scoffed. "With our luck, we'd fall out."

She hummed in agreement. "Or you would, you log."

He chuckled, tearing off a piece of jerky with his teeth. "Speak for yourself."

She playfully threw a pebble at him. We watched the flames crackling, the white noise I needed to calm my heart, which couldn't stop racing in my chest. Soon I could hear Tia's breathing even out, her eyes closed. I could feel my beast shaking her head in the back of my mind. There was no way I would find sleep in this forest.

The edges of Jake's face looked sharper with the contrast of shadows and flames dancing around us. "What did you see earlier?" he asked, eyes never leaving the embers in front of us.

I swallowed. "Six pits. It was a graveyard. It was—" I shook my head. "No one should see that."

"No one should die like that," he said, his voice tight. "I fucking hate these woods."

He turned his head back to me, meeting my questioning gaze. The fire crackled in front of us. Jake's chest rose with a breath; he looked like he was struggling to stay calm. "They took my parents, the rogues that came from these woods." A sick feeling ran over me. I hadn't seen or smelled any sign of rogues, but then again, Levi said that they'd never found anything. I scratched at the scabbing cuts on the back of my shoulder. "Billy sent me to live with Andrea at Talia's pack for a while, until it was safe for me to come back to Hemlock. He took me in after that." He gestured to Tia. "It's how I met her. She was staying with Talia for a bit when I was living with Andrea."

"I'm so sorry." I struggled to keep my voice even.

"It's how they got so many packs at once. They hid in these fucking woods." He looked down, his jaw ticking. "And now I'm camping in them," he added with a wry laugh.

"Mine are gone too," I told him. "I barely remember my dad. My mother died in a car accident."

His brows knitted, the hard line of his lips softening. "I'm sorry."

"It was a long time ago."

He hummed. "Doesn't meant it doesn't still hurt."

The fire sparked as it nipped at the dry leaves. I glanced into the woods, finding a handful of red eyes watching us.

A squirrel scampered down a tree, crawling closer to us on bony limbs. Jake followed my gaze over his shoulder. A growl vibrated off him and sent the squirrel back into the darkness.

We said nothing. Instead, we continued to watch the fire until I found my eyes growing heavy. Jake said he would keep a watch first then wake me. I closed my eyes only to find dreams consumed with darkness yanking me under their depths. I watched my mother walk above the surface, her face colored in horror as she screamed for me. She beat at the surface, but it was like ice—unbreakable.

I woke covered with sweat.

Deciding the forest was a better option than my dreams, I switched places with Jake. I took my post leaning against a tree in front of the fire, which I stoked back to life.

For hours the sounds of the woods brought me a strange comfort. For hours they seemed to steady my heart, even as the night carried on.

I kept listening until I found that I was struggling to hear again. The beast nudged me. She was anxious. Both of us could feel something coming, but all we could see was a serene stillness around us.

A whisper of silence came—a hush that would be tranquil to many, but I knew better. I felt the cold again, the desire to chase it peaking to life. I dug my fingers into the ground, holding firm as bitter air flowed over my face, as if someone was breathing on me.

"Charlotte," it called, almost like it was a lover murmuring to me between soft sheets. I lifted my eyes to the dark, where leaves were scuttling in front of me, creating a path that led down a tunnel of shadows. It felt like they wanted me to follow them.

My hands reached for the trees, fingernails turning into claws that helped me pull myself up as I climbed. Frantically, my hands reached for branches, my feet pushing me forward until I reached the canopy. Fresh air hit my face. The beast paced in the back of my mind, both of us unsure if there was something in the forest or if our minds were melting in real time.

"Just breathe," I told myself. "Deep breaths."

But the sweet night air barely settled my racing heart. Looking around, I spotted the mountains that Tia had pointed out before, the ones that had the glacier. Home wasn't far from that glacier.

My beast nudged me, inspiring me to look down. Leaning over, I focused on where the swirling leaves had been leading, following the trajectory forward, getting a sense of the general direction before I let my gaze trail up from the ground to the tops of the trees.

My breath hitched. I was facing due west toward the silver mountains. Toward the Hemlock Pack.

I felt my beast paw at the back of my mind. "I know," I told her. Something made my stomach curl, but we couldn't worry about that now. We needed to focus on this hunt and getting the hell out of this forest.

She relented, agreeing with me before I took one last breath of fresh air and descended. Tia was awake when I jumped down from the lowest branch. As she wiped her eyes, they started to pulse with a glow. "Are you okay?"

Kneeling next to her, I studied Jake's sleeping form. He

was out cold, snoring peacefully. I swallowed. "Did you hear anything earlier?"

"Hear what?" she whispered.

I shook my head. "Never mind."

"This forest is foul." She gulped audibly. "Gran told me if you hear something calling, it's best not to answer it. Gran always said to let the dead rest."

CHAPTER
TWENTY-TWO

The morning felt like it had already dwindled away by the time we tore out of camp. It was as if the forest was trying to keep us lulled in our sleep. But the only way out was finding our deer.

Tia was more diligent today about marking the trees on our route, and Jake and I were more observant of traps. Traps that we found easier to avoid in theory than in practice. But we were lucky.

We were lucky when we dodged more pits, and lucky when we avoided the tree limbs that had been turned into whips. Deadly hammers with spikes fastened to them sizzled in the air as they sliced past us, a breath away from grazing my skin at one point. We were even luckier when we spotted tree bark that had been rubbed with rose-red paint.

I plucked a piece of hair from the bark and smelled it.

"Nice work," Jake said.

"Follow me," I told him, shifting to my fur and darting down the scent trail the deer had laid for us.

The deer had been trying to rub the paint off. That was evident with every tree, every boulder, every edge that we saw as we pushed west. The paint must have been itchy, coated thick so it most likely crusted over and was irritating the skin underneath.

We followed the trail to another pond, where Jake quickly leaned down to drink, only to be stopped by Tia. Silver flakes glimmered from the bottom of the seemingly serene water. I froze, frantically searching for the sickly-looking pouches in the trees, but to our luck, there weren't any.

Tia snarled. "They must have littered water sources."

Jake looked around, the hair on the back of his neck rising. "Let's catch this fucking deer."

He shoved off the ground, storming ahead. I stepped behind him, holding my pace as Tia fanned around to walk next to me. Her fingers squeezed mine.

Tia looked at me, her eyes struggling to hide her worry. "You have the trail?"

"Yeah," I confirmed. "We're pretty far west."

She nodded. "We are. There's a silent area, if I remember correctly, north of here. If we keep pushing west we'll run into bear territory."

"We'll deal with it." Jake cracked his knuckles. "You coming or what?"

"Go on, Char," she said.

I let out a heavy breath and jogged past him, shifting to my fur and following the trail the deer had left. The traces of red we were graced with were becoming few and far between, but the scent became stronger. Fresher. Alive. We were close.

My beast yipped at the others, running forward over the roots of trees and leaping across sharp rocks, pulled by a scent that felt like a hand wading through easy waters. Jake faded left, paws pounding the ground as we passed an area where the grass was laid flat, a nest where the deer had slept evident to us.

"*We're close,*" I heard Tia say in our group link.

Her black paws still striped with red faded to my right, the three of us quickly made pace through the trees. Jake pressed harder, soaring past me. At first, my beast wanted to howl at him, cheer him on as he led us closer to the kill. That was, until she saw a line gleaming in the light.

"*Jake! Stop!*" I screamed, but I was too late.

His sandy front paws hit the line right at the ankle. A shrill whistle cut through the air. Tia shifted to her skin, her legs pounding the ground as she hurtled toward Jake. She reached forward and grabbed the scruff of his neck, tossing him out of the way just as a hammer covered in wooden spikes whipped around and lodged itself in her side. She had tried to lean out of the way, but it'd caught her with the edge of its barbs and flung her back.

I shifted to the sound of her screaming as she flew through the air. She hit the ground with a loud crack. Another line went off. It sounded like someone frantically reeling a fish in. Jake shifted to his skin, tearing past me. Tia's leg lay perfectly over the mouth of a bear trap. The silver jaws were concealed under leaves, but I could see one of the teeth poking through, ready to strike.

Tia was writhing on the ground, shrieking in pain as she clutched her pierced side, sobs tearing out of her mouth.

"Jake, her leg!" I screamed. My arms pumped faster, desperation powering my legs. "Tia! *Tia!* You have to move!"

Tia rolled. Jake dove.

There was another scream. I think it was mine.

When I blinked, Jake was holding the trap open, his hands burning against the silver while Tia struggled to get away. Blood ran down her torso. Tears streamed down Jake's face as sweat beaded on his forehead.

I dove forward and looped my arms under Tia's, yanking her out of the silver jaws. Jake released the trap with a twisted cry and snatched his hands to his chest.

Tia lay on top of me, screaming while frantically reaching for her side. I rolled out from under her. "Oh Jesus— okay, okay, hold on," I told her before running to Jake.

He was shaking on the ground, the palms of his hands burnt like he had set them on top of a grill.

"Fuck!" I hissed.

"This is my fault," he hissed through his teeth. "Help her! Go!"

"Shit," I panted. "Shit, shit, shit."

I ripped open one of the packs and pulled out a blanket, a canteen, and some balm Derek had whipped up for us before we left. Running to Tia, I rolled her flat on her back. "I'm sorry," I told her before dumping the water on her side.

Her screams made my eyes water. I blinked the tears away as I held her down and desperately inspected the area. The spikes had been made of wood but I didn't trust them to not have silver. I dumped more water over the wound, holding her like she was a fish flopping on a deck gasping for air.

"I'm sorry," I said, struggling to contain a sob. I pressed the blanket into her side. "Hold this tight."

She sucked in a sharp breath. "Okay."

I nodded and ran to Jake. He was sweating, his hands still clutched to his chest. I clumsily opened the jar. "Open your palms."

He cursed under his breath as he lowered his hands, treacherous tears leaking from his eyes. I scooped the largest glob of balm I could then spread it over one of his palms. The skin was done bubbling, but it was burned almost off.

"Jake."

"Fucking fix it and wrap it up." My eyes went wide, lifting to his. His jaw clenched. "We're so close. Patch me up." He turned to look at Tia before cursing under his breath. "Ti?! Tia! Fuck. I'm sorry, Tia."

"I'm okay!" she cried. "It's okay. It wasn't silver."

"We can't leave you," I called back to her while I went to work coating his other hand.

"You can!" I heard her say, her voice gurgling.

She was clutching the blanket to her side, and it was soaking through, red with her blood. She kicked backward, sliding until she was close to a tree. She used her free hand to push herself up to sit. Tears fell from her eyes while another cry tore out of her lips. She pressed the blanket harder into her side.

"We didn't come this far to quit," she wheezed.

I rubbed my face. "You need stitches!"

She shook her head. "We're wolves. We heal fast. It's not that deep, those spikes weren't that long." She sat a little straighter. "In a few hours, I can walk."

Jake shook his head slowly. "Tia . . ."

"No." She snarled as her amber eyes pulsed as if they were catching fire. "We're not going home. We keep going. Besides," she said with a wry laugh, "where else will I go?"

I shook my head and started to tear strips from the blanket. Jake slowly stood. "Let me shift, then wrap my paws up."

I felt my shoulders give. Jake leaned closer with a look of determination that I recognized all too well. "She's right. Wrap me up and let's go."

"Okay," I conceded.

After he shifted I made quick work of wrapping his paws up and securing the bandages so he could still use his claws. I wasn't sure if it would work, but I knew Jake would never admit if it didn't. Jake stayed in his fur while I pulled all the packs over to Tia. I used the rest of the blanket I had ripped up to wrap around her, ensuring that the bleeding had enough compression to stop.

"Go," she told me, her eyes hard. "Bring back that fucking deer."

I wiped my hands on my shifters and reached into my pack, pulling out the knife Elliot gave me, then pressed it into Tia's hand.

She held it firm. "Go," she said, shoving me away.

A new spark in me was starting to sear, crackling along my veins like wildfire. Jake dipped his head at Tia before breaking away into the forest. I ran after him, letting my beast explode through my skin.

Jake and I tore through the forest with a new fury, a new sharpened focus on blood and only blood. He cut around me as a breeze flowed past us. It was fresh, crisp, smelling of wildflowers and new grass. Light peeked from between the trees. I didn't dare question it. Relief poured through me, because I hadn't seen light like that in days and in that moment I more than welcomed it.

Bushes grew taller the closer we got to the green grass that swayed in the breeze like friends welcoming us home. The scent was stronger, permeating the air with the deer's musk. I pushed forward, jumping over a fallen log and darting around a thicket of blackberry bushes until the aroma of iron twisted with the scent of the deer.

Slowing to a jog, my beast tipped her nose up just as sunlight broke through the branches to coat our face. In that moment, stepping into the sunlight, I felt nothing but pure warmth along with pure terror.

"*Fuck,*" Jake said.

There was a bear, a female grizzly bear, with her muzzle dug into the torso of a deer painted red. Our deer. She lifted her head, chomping with thick smacks on the meat as crimson ran down her snout, making it impossible to tell what was blood and what was paint. But it was her eyes that were the definition of pure horror: red veined and swirling with clouds of madness.

Angry scars marked her body, one cutting across her chest. The forest had corrupted her all the way down to her claws, which looked like rusted needles.

"Fuck," I found myself echoing.

My beast curled around a tree. The bear kept feeding like she was at an all-you-can-eat buffet and this was her third time refilling her plate.

Looking to my right, I could see all the trees along the edge of the forest painted with silver at the bases. Across from them, boulders were painted with green. The bear was comfortably on the other side of a boulder with a giant green circle painted on its smooth surface.

The bear—and our deer—was over the pack line.

Jake nudged my shoulder. Blood had started to seep through the bandages on his paws.

"It's over the line," I said.

"This is my pack land, and Bowie didn't say anything about that." He nipped at me, snapping my gaze back to his. *"Better to ask for forgiveness than permission."*

"How long do you think we have before their patrols see?"

He scanned the horizon. *"How fast can you move?"*

"Fast."

In that moment, I knew that if I chose to keep going, there was no turning back. Looking at the deer, a cool rage rolled over me. That was our goddamned deer. And I hadn't made it through this fucked-up forest for some fucked-up bear to rob us of our prize.

"I'm with you," I said. *"What do you think?"*

It was as if I could feel him smiling through our link. He licked his lips. *"You distract the bear. I'll steal the deer. We need to lead it to a trap. Where Tia got hurt there are more lines still on the ground. We can lead it there and let the forest have it."*

My beast liked this idea, as did I. My canines itched for blood.Our paws dug into the ground.

Jake crouched, readying himself to spring forward. *"Wait,"* he told me as the bear took another filthy crunch from the buck. Flesh ripped through its teeth, bones cracking under its jaws.

My beast pawed the ground.

"Wait," he said.

My eyes snapped up and saw red eyes looking back at me. The bear's jaw had stopped. Flesh and entrails fell out of her mouth while her eyes narrowed with anger. A growl rolled out of her and danced across the grass to us.

"I'm with you," I told Jake.

"Now."

CHAPTER
TWENTY-THREE

I went first, running like a tidal wave, hurtling toward the bear. Every fiber of my body was afraid, but my steps weren't slowing. The beast and I knew what we had to do. I let her take over, her instincts like adrenaline pulsing through me, a sweetness on my tongue from the taste of it.

My wolf neared the wild-eyed bear, snapping her jaws in a taunt that made the bear snarl through her bloody lips. My beast slowed to a trot then dropped to a couch, crab walking to the side like she was teasing a pup. The bear growled lowly, showing her teeth, which looked like a row of freshly sharpened knives.

My beast snapped back, clicking her teeth together so the bear could hear what waited for her. We crept closer, light on our paws, dancing toward the monster in front of us as a gentle wind rolled through the grass that waved like a crowd in a colosseum. Something vibrated off us, something that shook the grass. The bear widened its wild eyes. My beast hopped forward again, then retreated, daring her for a chase.

The bear lunged, taking the bait.

Jake sprang into action as I galloped for the forest, confident the bear was on my heels. But when I checked over my shoulder, she had planted her feet like she was frantically braking an eighteen-wheeler. In a second, she whipped around and lunged at Jake. Her teeth found his leg, biting down on the upper thigh until crunching drew an ungodly cry from his muzzle.

We didn't even think. We sprang forward while Jake locked his jaws on the bear's head. The bear's teeth released his leg as mine snapped around the extra skin on Jake's neck, yanking him back toward the trees as he shifted to his skin with a blood-curdling howl that took the breath from my lungs.

My skin rippled over me, hands replacing my paws so I could drag him back to the tree line. The bear stood over the deer, pawing at the ground. A bull ready for the matador.

Blood oozed out of his mangled leg. I was almost sure I could see part of his bone.

"Run," he wheezed.

A roar ripped the air. The bear had risen on her hind legs. The fur on her stomach was patchy, her flesh covered in scars. I looked back at Jake. It was in that moment that his eyes, which never gave away anything, gave away everything.

Because that bear would chase us down. Find us. I could drag Jake into the forest, but the bear was fast and that godforsaken place was her home. I would have to pray we were lucky and could run her into a trap.

But today wasn't the day to bank our lives on luck.

I had options. There were always options, even if they were all bad. My beast surged closer to me, a sentiment running through her that I felt as well. A sentiment that had me choosing the path I never thought I would walk.

I stood up and said, "Stay."

Jake rolled to look at me, clutching his leg. "Charlotte?!"

I stepped around him and wiped the sweat from my brow.

"Charlotte? No! Charlotte!"

The soft carpet of grass hugged my toes with each step I took. A breeze danced around me, whipping around my fingertips.

"Charlotte! Stop!"

Electricity crackled over me and sang through my veins in a cold fire that made my skin twitch. A delicious feeling chipped away at the fear, replacing it with something else with each step I took.

The beast was ready. Pacing. Snapping her jaws in the back of my mind while she pulsed in me. There was a calmness about her that I felt, a focus that centered us. My eyes flickered down to the line across my palm, which reminded me how very acceptable it would be to get good and pissed off right now.

"*Char!*" Jake bellowed.

Pausing, I looked over my shoulder. I said nothing. Frantically, he shook his head. "No."

I gave him one last glance before turning toward the bear, who was watching me, still on her hind legs. She timbered forward, paws hitting the ground like a tree slamming the forest floor. Her lips curled, a roar ripping through the air as spittle flung from her mouth.

But I wouldn't stop.

My chest vibrated as something snapped in me. Something cold and sweet, like jumping into a pool on a hundred-degree day.

I let the beast in me charge forward. A growl ripped through my own lips, rippling through the grass, disrupting the peaceful wave.

The bear's eyes widened. I paused.

She pawed the ground. I dug my toes in.

Then I ran.

She lunged and I let the beast surge through me, fur rolling over me in a wave that had become as natural as breathing. My paws hit the ground as my veins crackled with an ignition that combusted to life with each step.

Because in that moment there was no beast, no me—there was us. We were a team running together as two intertwined souls powered by the blood of the moon igniting in our veins. There were the memories of every tear that I ever spilled. Every broken heart, broken nose, broken bone, and the fragments of my broken soul.

But there was also the hope that filled my heart every time a new sun rose in the morning, and the magic that came with looking at a sky full of stars. There was determination, the kind that keeps you looking forward when all you want is to turn around and watch cities fall. Most of all, there was pure, sweet rage coursing through me without consequence—the kind of rage that is quiet, that seethes and bides its time so it can be the fuel to the fire of a well-deserved fight. The fight I was currently hurling myself toward.

In that moment, I knew I wasn't a human. I would never be human again. My past was fucked-up, but my past is what made me who I am. What had brought me here. And I would not trade each step I'd taken for the world. Because a different past, different decisions, would perhaps not have lead me here. To this pack. To my friends. To Derek and Elliot. To Levi.

Because for the first time in my life, I knew what I wanted. The life in front of me had teeth, and claws, and blood. And I wanted that life. I wanted that life so damn bad. And I would be fucking damned if I let this thing in front of me stop me.

Lunging into the air, my beast collided with the muscled mass of chocolate brown. Our jaws sank into the flesh, biting mercilessly until we felt something hard—something that would crunch under our teeth. Our teeth didn't stop clamping down until we hit the fucking bone.

But the bear's claws had found the skin of my back, raking across it in a gruesome hug. We shoved off her as blood slid through our fur. The bear licked her lips and started to circle us. It looked as if she was almost laughing; her breaths were sharp, almost jagged, falling out of her flailing lips.

Unfortunately for her, pain was my old friend.

I mirrored her steps, letting a growl of my own slice through the grass with a cold storm of vehemence as it rumbled off my chest. Her eyes pulsed with red. She snarled again, coating the grass with a spray of spittle. A last warning.

A warning I didn't give a rat's ass about. Instead, we charged forward, ducking the bear's swipe and nipping at a tendon on her unharmed back leg. She stumbled as she turned to snap her large teeth at us.

But we were too fast for the large bear's movements. We nipped at her front paw, then darted around and raked her belly with our teeth—that one really did it. She stood on two legs again and roared at us. She was huge, this female. The size alone was enough to be insanely intimidating, but we were so consumed with the hunt that it meant nothing to us.

"Charlotte!" I heard Jake desperately cry.

Standing on two bad legs was stupid. I could feel a smile flowing from my beast as she looked the bear up and down.

Charging at her, we tore at one hind leg, yanking at the tendons and bones as hard as we could. The bear crashed down with a sickening cry, but not before she kicked us off her leg like a seesaw.

We skidded across the ground but quickly picked ourselves up as she hurtled toward us, legs pounding the ground like war drums as they galloped forward. A set of rocks was a breath away. Jetting toward them, we leaped onto one then springboarded onto the bear's back. We sank our teeth into the flesh that connected her back legs to her belly and ripped without mercy at it.

The female let out an enraged, growl-like moan, but we didn't let go of her. We weren't done, but she was. Her paw reached around and threw us hard off her, her claws slicing into the skin covering our ribs and down one of our front legs.

The rocky ground showed us no mercy when we landed. We bit back a pained moan. The bear dipped her head, growling with devious satisfaction while blood trickled out of her mouth, as we lay bleeding in the grass.

Jake was still screaming my name. I could hear the wind rolling through the valley and feel sunbeams on my face, as if they were cupping my cheek. My head rolled on the hard ground, finding Jake's panicked eyes looking at mine.

Rolling back, I felt my skin ripple over me.

I turned to look at the bear. Her wild red gaze connected with mine. It was in that moment that two foes recognized something we could both agree on—that one of us would die. One of us would not leave this field.

I felt the beast rumble in me as together, we agreed that there was absolutely no going back. Because the feeling of pitiful helplessness, poisonous shame, and toxic self-pity dissolved the moment I stood and embraced what it was that I had become.

I was a monster.

I was the thing that fairy tales warned you about.

And that thought alone drew a smile to my lips.

Because this was one monster I was more than willing to become. To embrace. To dive headfirst into and never again look to the surface.

Something burned over me, my fingers twitching at the feeling. The bear stepped sideways, as if she was confused. Then ire swirled in her red eyes. Her body shifted into a run, the sound like a stampede roaring for me.

I blew out a long breath and steadied myself, holding firm until the moment was right. She kept hurtling forward, and I waited. Waited and waited until my legs kicked into gear. Running on two legs, I sprang into the air before the bear's feet could lift her to meet me and let my shift roll over me.

Crashing into her front, I sank my teeth into her neck. The bear clawed at my back as she started to fall sideways. My beast dug her teeth in, grinding and grinding until the stream of blood we drew became a waterfall. Until the bear grew limp, paws slowing and balance wavering before her body finally collapsed.

My beast didn't let go of the bear's neck until she hit the ground. Even then, she ripped out a long piece of flesh before sinking her muzzle in and ripping out another piece with a frantic need to make sure the thing below us wasn't ever going to spring back to life.

It was my turn to nudge her, to yank her back. She scooted back on her hind legs as the shift overtook us, my skin greeted by cool, gentle air.

Blood rolled down my skin. The deer was only a few yards away. I sucked in a breath and stood, wiping the sweat out of my eyes.

Turning, I looked for Jake. His mouth was open, his hands still clutching his leg. I turned forward, looking at what lay before me. Instead of feeling horrified, I was proud.

Because I had killed more than one monster with that bear.

CHAPTER
TWENTY-FOUR

Kneeling next to Jake, I inspected his mangled skin. The bleeding had stopped but I still felt a shot of panic at the sight of it.

His hands stopped me. One caught my chin, slowly turning it to look directly at him.

"Do you realize what you just did?"

"Jake?"

He breathed a laugh. "You're fucking nuts." He shook his head as his eyes grew heavy, like two pools of pure relief. "Thank you. You saved my life. Thank you."

I brushed his hand away. "We're a team, right?" He snorted. I turned my attention to his leg. "This is pretty bad."

"Have you seen yourself?" My face fell. Adrenaline was

keeping me from feeling the pain, but I knew that would wear off soon. Blood ran down the claw marks on my left thigh, matching the ones oozing on my back. It looked awful, and I knew it would leave a scar, but it didn't look nearly as bad as Jake's leg.

"Okay, fair," I agreed. I turned over my shoulder, scanning the hill. It was still just us, still quiet.

Jake cleared his throat. "Go find Tia. We need to move before other bears catch scent of the blood or before the Hemlock Pack's patrols find us. We're lucky they haven't already." He shoved me away with a firm nod. "Go, I'll be fine."

I ran hard to Tia in my skin, the adrenaline in my body falling as pain whispered through me. Tia was standing, dragging a log, like the one that had whipped around to hit her, over to our bags. Freezing, she turned to look at me with tears in her eyes.

"Praise the Moon," she beamed, her arms catching me in a hug. "Jake told me—I'm so happy you're okay. I was so worried."

I clutched her like she was holding on to me, as if we both were afraid this was all a dream. "Let's go home," I murmured to her. "How's your side?"

She gave me a one-shouldered shrug. "It's better."

I pulled the bloody blanket that she had pressed to her side back. To her point, it had stopped bleeding.

"You sure?"

"Charlotte, have you seen yourself?" She pulled the blanket around her back into place. "I'll be fine. Once I could stand, I started to cut down the logs on the traps. They're clean, no silver. I thought we could use them to make a sled for Jake."

"Yeah, there's no way that Jake is walking back."

"And we have to bring your bear back." She grinned at my surprise. "You didn't think we were going to leave that?"

She waved me forward.

"Come on, we need to hurry. I can smell blood on the breeze from here, which means something else probably can too."

Together, Tia and I carried the logs she had chopped off the traps back to Jake. He had propped himself up against a tree. We dropped the supplies and ran to him. Tia knelt by his leg and covered her mouth. "Oh Jake—okay, we need to move fast so we can get you somewhere safe to clean this up." She scanned me too. "Both of you."

"I'm fine, let's get out of here. This blood has been out here too long, something probably caught wind of it by now," Jake told us. He nudged his chin to the deer. "It's pretty chewed up, Ti. The bear was deep in it when we got here."

She wiped her brow. "I'll see what I can do. Come on, Char, let's move fast."

I made quick work using the zip ties and rope to create a makeshift sled with the game tarps that Elliot had packed for us while Tia handled the deer. The bear had done some work chewing through it, and we didn't have a ton of time to decide on it. Tia moved fast and took the head and the front quarters of the animal. We wrapped the meat in our game bags and tied it down at the bottom of the sled. The bear was another story.

We speculated that the meat was bad, that no one in

their right mind would want to eat it. The thought of its reddened eyes made my lips curl in a grimace that deepened once Tia opened the bear up. A foul smell tore out, as if the meat was already well past its expiration date.

Tia held an arm over her nose. "This smells awful."

"I think I should wash my mouth out," I uttered, my stomach rolling.

"We'll find water," she promised with a grimace. "We don't have time to properly cape it, I can carve out what I can now, but we need to move. I can cut away more later."

"I'll start packing up," I told her, leaving her to cut as much as she could while I got our things ready to go.

We laid the bear face down so Jake could lie on its fur. I thought it would make him more comfortable with the shape his leg was in, but he needed a pack doctor, and I doubted the blanket we wrapped around his leg was going to do him much good.

Walking to the front of the sled, I picked up one of the two ropes I had attached to each of the logs and tossed it over my shoulder.

Only a blanket of red remained on the grass where the bear had lain. I couldn't tear my eyes away from it.

Tia stepped next to me, taking the other rope over her shoulder, a tired smile on her lips. "You ready to go home?"

I was more than ready. "Yes," I answered.

"You good, Jake?" Tia asked.

"Yeah, you remember the way?"

Tia nodded. "X marks the spot," she said. "I can get us home."

With that, Tia and I towed the sled together. Looking

over my shoulder, I spotted the trail of blood the game was leaving, and prayed that nothing would find its way to us on our return journey.

Jake was the worst patient. Tia and I almost tied him to the sled to keep him from trying to walk. That, and he also didn't want me to apply any more balm to his leg, insisting that the pack doctor would fix him up and he would be fine. At one point Tia looked like she was ready to drop him into a stream.

Thank god Tia had marked the trees. We followed her trail, avoiding the traps, and making better time than I would have thought considering what we were carrying. Familiar tracks led us through the woods, where the dwindling sunlight was glimmering. Tia paused, tipping her nose in the air. She dropped her rope. "There's water this way. Let me check for traps first."

Breathlessly, I nodded. My body was crying for relief, muscles on fire while my fresh wounds screamed in pain. Tia jogged off, returning a few minutes later to lead us to a gurgling stream. I practically threw my whole face into it, letting the water coat my neck while I took long gulps.

Leaning back, I wiped my face. Tia was holding a canteen up to Jake's lips. "I think we should camp here. We need to clean you off, and we're running out of daylight."

I pointed to her stomach. "We should do you too. I think there's tape in one of the packs. We should try to use that for ourselves."

Jake pushed himself off the sled with a groan, dragging himself across the ground until he could lean against a tree. Tia rolled her eyes. He took the canteen from her. She walked over to the stream and splashed water on her side.

I dug into one of our packs. "Hungry?" I asked Jake, pulling out our bag of jerky.

His eyes flickered to his leg. "I don't think I can eat. That bear smells like ass."

"Well, try?"

He took a piece of jerky from me and bit off a small piece. I turned and pulled up a small flap of blanket to check his leg. "Don't worry, pack doctor will have me good as new," he tried to assure me.

I didn't care how fast we healed, the look of his leg made my nerves flame with worry. I knew Jake was a tough guy, but there was no hiding the pain he was in. He barely finished his jerky while Tia and I built a small fire as night set in around us.

I cut strips from the last clean blanket we had while she washed my back with one of them, the water stinging like tiny icy nails digging into my flesh, before she moved to my side. The blood had dried along the edges. She was careful around the split flesh that felt like it had a thousand nerve endings. "We should try to lighten that bear up."

I touched my shoulder where the rope had bitten into my skin. "It's only for another day. You're going to cut everything out?"

"As much as I can but the heart. You're supposed to save that on big hunts and offer it to the moon when you return as a thank-you," she explained. She handed me the roll of duct tape that we had packed. "Tear."

I tore while she patched me up in DIY butterfly bandages. After she was done I made her lean back so I could do her side for her. Jake was out cold behind us. I wasn't sure how he could sleep in the shape he was in, but he looked so peaceful with his eyes closed that I didn't dare wake him.

I checked the punctures in her. It looked like the skin was trying to heal itself. She offered me a weak smile. "We mend fast. You will too."

Securing tape over a bandage, I reached for another strip of blanket. "Doesn't mean it doesn't hurt."

She swallowed, both of us falling into a heavy silence while I smoothed the tape out. "I'm glad you're here, with me." Her eyes were glassy. "On our team."

My lips pulled into a soft smile. "Me too," I affirmed, securing the last bandage on her side. "You should sleep."

She shook her head. "No, you go first."

"I can't." Not even if I wanted to.

"Me either," she confessed. "I'll work on the bear."

"Should we tie the deer up in the trees?"

Pausing, she nodded. "We can't be too safe."

I tied a rope that suspended the deer safely in the air, then found myself staring into the familiar darkness while Tia carved away at the bear. She was silent in her task, and when she was done, I urged her to try to get a few hours in, but she wouldn't budge. She sat with me, watching the forest that looked at me like dark open water where sharks lurked just out of sight. The aroma of blood saturated the air around us. My gut told me that the darkness waiting in those woods could certainly smell it.

My beast crawled forward. I could feel her starting to pace. The sound around us faded enough to make the hair on the back of my neck rise. Little glowing eyes appeared around us. I could make out the shape of a bird perched on a tree, eyes like red clouds.

I felt Tia's hand on my arm. "Charlotte?"

I sucked in a breath. "How far are we from the finish?"

"With the sled?" She bit the inside of her cheek. "Another solid day. Why? What's wrong?"

I couldn't hear the wind anymore. The silence had inched closer. "We need to go. Now."

Tia's eyes pulsed with a glow. She stared forward into the blackness that felt like it was licking its lips at the sight of us. "Charlotte, those silent spots don't move."

I was already standing. "I think they do." I held my hand out for her. "Better safe than sorry. Let's get the deer down."

She sucked in a breath and let me pull her up. We put our fire out, got the deer down, and put Jake back on the sled with the bear, marching fast out of camp on the trail she had made. Jake somehow didn't wake until the sun broke through the night. We stopped once to check his leg. It looked like it had started to heal itself in the night, but with each bump we hit I could hear a hiss from his lips that told me the pain was still very much real.

Tia's puncture wounds looked better and my back was starting to sting less, but both of us were wearing matching rope-burn stripes on our shoulders. We tied the two ropes in loops so we could wear them around our waists and give our arms a break, but eventually, the rope burned against the skin of our stomachs too.

We pushed through the day, not daring to stop or rest in

the forest that felt like it was waiting for us to finally let our guards down. A light fog trickled in with dusk. It made my beast anxious. Tia was no better; her jaw was tight while she trudged next to me.

"I think that's the training ground?" Jake said.

I wiped some sweat from my brow. He was right— through the gangly trees I could see the edge marked with a white chalk line on the ground where we had first stepped into the Trapper's Forest.

"Praise the Moon!" Tia exclaimed.

I picked up my feet in an eager jog with Tia until I was walking alongside healthy-looking trees with warm, welcoming branches that gladly let the fading light of the sun through. The vibrant sounds of squirrels and critters almost made me cry. Tia laughed a sob, turning to me with a wide smile. "I hate that forest."

I bit back a laugh. "Me too."

"Fuck that place," Jake chimed in.

She blew out a long breath. "It's not far now."

But it took twice as long to get back with the sled. Sweat beaded off me and rolled down my skin, somehow always finding the areas where makeshift bandages were sliding off. I bit back a whine while Tia gritted her teeth. Her wounds wept blood when the skin was ever-so-lightly stretched, which was easy to do in our task. But we were close to home, and that alone was enough for me to block out the pain.

By the time we punched through the forest, it was dark. We paused at the edge where we had first met. The clearing rolled into a hill where a bonfire lazily burned, a large group of people gathered around it. My breath caught. Tia's hand reached for one of mine, squeezing. She called over her shoulder, "Jake! We're here! We made it!"

"Hell, yeah!" He twisted to look at us, smiling as the reflection of the fire glittered in his eyes. "Let's go, my leg fucking hurts."

I could spot two other teams. Their deer were slung over a wooden fence post set near the fire. Black painted the side of one, and orange another. Which meant that there was still one team left in the forest: the blue team. Liam's team. I shivered; I had no desire to spend another night in that place and could only hope that Liam and his team weren't far behind us.

Laughter and drinks flowed around the crowd. Lyle was chasing Penny through the people; she screamed as she darted out of his reach before they disappeared behind a group of women. I could see Tia's grandmother, sitting on a log next to Andrea and Talia, watching the fire.

But it was Elliot who saw us first. He was sitting next to the other team's deer, laughing at something Gran had said when he looked up, slowly meeting my gaze. His mouth parted. He reached to tap Andrea, never taking his green eyes away from mine.

It was then that I saw him step into my line of vision. Silver eyes. He smirked, laughing under his breath. Levi tilted his head and muttered something to someone the fire was hiding.

It was quiet. I hadn't realized how quiet it was until the snapping of the fire pulled me away from Levi's gaze. Dozens of eyes stared back at us as we approached. A break in the circle formed for our small brigade as we pulled the sled closer to the fire, which I could feel faintly warming my skin.

Tia and I stopped a few yards from the group and dropped our ropes. I heard gasps as the light of the fire revealed us and our cargo.

Jake smacked my leg. "Get me up."

Tia wiped her tired face and leaned over to Jake, pulling him up so he could stand. I untied the head of the deer and offered it to Jake. He looked at it before he shook his head, and tossed his other arm around me. "Before I change my mind."

Tia's eyes watered. Together, we walked forward, taking all of Jake's weight with each step. "You so owe us," Tia hissed.

Jake snickered with a wince. "Probably so, Ti," he answered. "But you both did make me ride on that smelly-ass bear the whole way here."

Bowie jogged around the fire. She studied every inch of us before she spotted the sled. We stopped a few paces in front of her.

"We had a few hiccups," I explained.

Her face broke into a wide grin. She nodded, a bright laugh shaking her chest. "Well done."

I handed her the deer, carefully placing the head in her hands. She stared at it, her eyes growing soft.

The crowd erupted around us in cheers. Tia laughed, a few tears spilling down her face. Talia ran around Bowie, looking us over. She went to Tia, holding her head in her hands with a teary-eyed smile. Tia murmured something to her. Talia nodded and took Tia's place holding Jake up.

"Ti?" I asked.

"I got him," Talia told me with a soft smile.

"Wait," Jake told me, his hand clutching my shoulder.

Tia walked around to my side. In her hands, she had a heart. A purple-red mound of muscle. The heart of the bear. Smiling, she held it out for me. "I saved it for you. It's yours to offer to the moon."

Talia nodded to me encouragingly, taking all of Jake's weight so I could take the heart from Tia. My breath hitched as the beast in me crackled forward. My eyes watered staring at it.

I looked up at Tia. "The moon isn't who prepared me for this."

My feet knew where to go. The steps I took were sure.

In my short experience with the moon, I couldn't say She had protected me. She never sat through my night terrors with me or let me cry over and over until there were no more tears to be shed. And She never scraped me off the ground only to teach me that I could do it on my own.

I stopped in front of Levi. I held out the heart to him. He shook his head. "That's yours."

My lips tugged in a half smile. "No, it's not," I told him, and placed the heart in his hands.

He was still, staring at it like he was seeing a ghost. His eyes started to glow, a soft smile forming on his mouth,

Without words, he stepped around me and tossed the heart into the fire. Pausing a beat, he turned back to me. "Come here," he said, pulling me into a tight hug.

My eyes watered again as I hugged him back. "I'm glad I didn't die."

"Me too."

The fire crackled again, and then a scream ripped through the night. In a blink, Ali hurled herself across the grass and toward the tree line. Levi locked gazes with Lander for an instant before breaking into a run after her. Andrea was suddenly next to me, her arm around my waist, holding me steady.

Panic flamed in me. "What's happening?"

Andrea's golden eyes grew heavy with a knowing look that sent a chill down my spine. "I'm glad you made it," she murmured to me.

There were only two people emerging from the forest: Liam and another young male, looking just as rough as our team did. They carried a dead girl on a makeshift gurney fashioned out of game tarps and logs. A large hole gaped under her eye, the skin around it burned. Even from yards away, I could smell the familiar singe of silver.

David was yanking a hysterical Ali away from Anamaria's lifeless body.

Andrea shook her head remorsefully. Liam collapsed on the ground, his head down and chest shaking violently in haunting sobs. Lander dropped to his knees in front of him before wrapping his arms around his son. Elliot put his hands on the other male's shoulders and tried to speak to him, but the guy only stood there, frozen in shock. Levi stood over the body, his back so stiff I thought it would snap.

Bowie's head dropped. She blew out a breath before taking a step toward them. Their Hunt was over.

CHAPTER
TWENTY-FIVE

Five days had passed since we returned from the Hunt. Within three days, my body stopped looking like mangled meat, the wounds slowly healing. The only caveat was where the silver had singed my skin—that would leave scars, tiny white lines that I would never be rid of on my shoulders and behind my ears. Elliot said that it was the same for vampires.

Two days after we returned they had a funeral for Anamaria. They built a pyre stacked with wreaths and flowers on top of a cliff overlooking the glacier. For days after, I swore I could still smell the smoke from the flames they'd lit at sunset.

Bowie had torn through the forest to where I'd found the pits and brought the bones back to be laid to rest. But they never found the silver sacks. Tia and I drew multiple maps, but eventually Bowie said that those would remain the forest's secret whether we wanted them to or not.

Levi insisted on making a blanket out of the bear. He pulled one out of the attic to show me as an example of what it could look like. It had Lucas's initials in it. I told him I would love a blanket. He left Lucas's on my bed.

Two weeks later Bowie was on our front doorstep with a toothy grin, the afternoon sun starting to fade behind her. I set down the pair of shifters I was mending and walked to the front door.

"Hey, you." I smiled, pushing open the screen door. "Want to come in?"

She rocked back on her heels. "No, you're coming out."

"Pardon?"

"I'm making margaritas at Claire's and you're coming. No arguments. I'm technically your boss now, after all."

"Did someone say margaritas?" Elliot sauntered over and tossed an arm around my shoulder. "Now, you're not going to tell me I'm not invited?"

Bowie waved him off. "'Course you are. I made spicy ones just for you." She turned her gaze back to me. "Come on, it's Claire, me, Gran, a few other girls. No excuses."

"Is Ali coming?" I asked, hoping we could convince her to come out even for a little bit. She hadn't left her home since Anamaria's funeral, and I couldn't blame her.

Bowie shook her head with a sad smile. "She'll come around on her own. Now, come on, I used the good tequila."

"I mean, I can't turn that down," I conceded. "Let me go grab some clothes to change into."

She nodded while I dashed back to my room and threw my jean shorts, a T-shirt, and some slide-on sandals into a saddlebag. Elliot met me at my door, holding his hand out to take my bag from me.

"I got it," he said with a wink. "Should be fun. Derek and Levi are going to be gone a few hours anyhow."

I slowed. "Why's that?"

Elliot inched closer to me. "They're trying to do another meet with the nephews on the border."

I arched a brow. "They didn't come last time."

"Right," he acknowledged. "But this time David put in a formal request to their Head of Security, Billy, that requires him and the pack second to be there. Ethan is the pack second and isn't stupid, and Evan's hotheaded enough that he won't let Ethan go alone."

"Lander's idea?"

"No." He snickered. "Levi's."

I found myself chuckling lowly. "And their pack lead is good with this?"

He nodded. "Told Lander if he wasn't out of town he would have brought the popcorn."

I rolled my eyes. "Well, hopefully it goes well."

He put an arm around my shoulders as we walked in step down the stairs. "Regardless, we're going to get good and sloshed."

"Just don't let me take my clothes off."

"Same for me, love," he answered, shrugging casually. "Even after all these years it still makes me act a fool. Come on," he said, tugging me to the woods, where we followed Bowie past the pack house and cabins to a house tucked away on its own in the middle of thick trees. The log structure looked welcoming; wind chimes hung from the awning and dozens of flowers and herbs lined the small footpath that led to the front door.

Claire pushed the door open and waved us forward with a warm smile. "Come on in!"

I shifted to my skin and took my saddlebag from Elliot, jogging quickly into her arms for a hug. "Thanks for hosting."

She pressed her lips to my cheek. "I'm glad you came. You want to run upstairs and change?"

"Please," I said breathlessly, following Bowie into the house.

She pointed up a set of cream-carpeted stairs. "There's a bathroom up there. First on your right."

"Thanks," I replied, jogging away from the laughter in the kitchen to the second floor, where the walls were covered with memories. There was one image of Liam from when he was not much older than Lyle, holding a fish up in front of a pond. His cheeks were red from the sun and dimples showed as he beamed a smile.

Something twisted in me as I remembered the haunted expression on his face at the funeral. I had tried to link him and check on him, but he'd been quiet. I wasn't upset about it; anyone would need space after that. I had needed days after the Hunt to decompress and sort through what had happened to my team. I couldn't imagine what he was feeling, so I'd kept my distance, which was probably a good thing.

I changed into my other clothes then followed the sounds of gabbing, gossip, and laughter into the kitchen. Elliot was already pouring two glasses from a pitcher of margaritas, laughing with Gran, who was sitting on a barstool.

"There she is!"

Tia lunged at me. I caught her with a laugh. "Ti, I saw you yesterday."

She had been over almost every day after the Hunt. The first day she walked in and announced that we were hanging out. Levi thought it humorous until after a few days she had made herself at home and snuck some of his ice cream. Which I may or may not have encouraged.

She tossed her long braid behind her shoulder. "We're doing these new face masks I got tomorrow. Don't argue."

"I want in," Elliot said, carrying over our cups.

Tia beamed. "'Course. I got extras."

Elliot pressed his lips to her temple. "You're a sweet one, love."

I took my drink then clinked my glass with his before taking a long sip.

Claire was opening the oven, checking on what looked like nachos. She sighed. "Not crispy yet."

Bowie tossed a chip into her mouth. "How's the queso?"

"Shit!" Claire dashed to the kitchen island and opened the lid of a Crock-Pot. "Oh, we're good. It's good."

Bowie frowned. "I don't believe you."

Tia giggled. She took my hand and tugged me forward. "You won't believe who came."

We walked around the counter to the kitchen table facing a giant window that looked out on a backyard, where Talia and Andrea were seated. Talia rose, her silver hair moving like mist behind her.

"What are you guys doing here?" I asked, quickly hugging Talia. "Her First," I added for good measure.

Talia rolled her eyes. "The acceptance party and ceremony are in a few days," she said, with a knowing smile. I blushed. I was hoping this whole pack admittance thing could be something Levi and I did in the backyard over a bottle of whiskey, but apparently, we had to make a show of it. They were doing it during their annual summer party, which meant, of course, other packs in the area were invited to come. "I have business with Levi, but figured I would come early."

"I'm going back with Auntie after," Tia explained. "School will start soon enough and I want to spend the rest of summer with her."

I playfully shoved her shoulder. "And leave me? Bitch."

Talia and Tia laughed with me before Talia stepped aside for Andrea. She eyed me for a moment. "We can hug."

"Okay." I laughed, letting her briskly hug me. "And you're just tagging along?"

"Sort of," she stated, swirling the ice in her glass. "Do you—can I talk to you?"

"Um, sure."

Andrea nudged her chin at the back door. Talia squeezed my shoulder then took Tia's hand and dragged her over to the island where Bowie was pouring shots. I licked my lips, took a long swig, and followed Andrea outside.

The crickets were chirping around us, and the grass was soft under my feet. I followed her over to a swing set. She turned and sat on of the swings. Pausing a moment, I opted to sit in the one next to her. She was watching her feet, her chestnut hair flowing around her like streams of warm caramel.

I took another sip of my drink. "You good?"

"Is anyone?"

I laughed into my glass, and took another drink. "Fair."

She tucked some hair behind her ears. "So, I'm moving here."

My beast perked up. "You decided?"

"There's nothing there for me anymore. Everything reminds me of him." I knew that feeling too well. "Dad wanted me to move back home, but, well, it would be me, Dad, and Jake. I talked to Talia about it, Thunderhead was actually her first suggestion. She came with me to talk to Levi, we met with him this morning. He approved it and David has a spot for me on the guard that I can jump right into."

"So will you be—"

"Getting sworn in with you? Sure am," she answered before taking a long sip from her glass, almost finishing her drink. "Look, I—well, I don't want to live with David. He's like my second dad and I love the guy, but I need space. Gran is going to go back with Talia and Tia after the party to spend time with Tia, then she's going to go stateside with Tia to move in with her daughter, Tia's mom. I think she wants to be closer to them, but that means her house will be open and Lander didn't seem like he was going to let me have a place all to myself, so I'm going to need a roommate," she explained, eyeing me expectantly.

I leaned back a hair. "Are you asking me to live with you?"

"Yeah, I am," she admitted. "I haven't told Levi yet. I wanted to ask you first."

My brows furrowed. "You want me to be your roommate?"

"Are you daft?"

"Maybe?"

She smirked. "I don't have a lot of friends. All my friends were his friends, and when everything happened, a lot of them faded away. The ones who are left don't really understand. It's hard to connect with them."

Blowing out a breath, I told her, "I get it."

"I know you do," she replied with a small smile. "Which is why I'm asking you."

I tugged my hair. I hadn't ever had a place of my own. I went from my college dorm to Nate's and now to Levi's—which was my home. A good home. But the beast in me—and I couldn't help but agree on the fact that a part of us, a big part of us—liked the idea of having a home of our own. Something that was just ours. Although even if I moved in with Andrea, I knew I would be at Levi's every morning for breakfast.

But still, after everything, leaving him—Levi—I wasn't sure about any of it.

"I need to think about it."

"Of course," she replied. "I wanted to ask before the party. I'll be moving here not long after, so I wanted to give you time to think it over."

"I'm bad at laundry," I found myself blurting.

"I'm a terrible cook."

"Me too." We both laughed quietly. I dug my toes into the dirt. "You sure you don't want to move in with your dad?"

She shook her head. "I love him. He's all I have. My mom was only his bondmate and died when I was young. He's had others here and there, but I feel like he tries to overcompensate—hovers. I need space."

I hummed in understanding. "I'm sorry that happened to you," I told her. "I know I'm new to this world, but it's fucked-up, and I'm sorry."

Her golden eyes pulsed a glow. "Everyone thinks it's how it should be, because it's your 'true mate,' but it is fucked-up. Someone gets hurt." She finished her drink. "If we live together we can't be this fucking depressing."

I laughed in agreement. "I'm not going to make any promises."

"Me either," she replied quietly.

"Let me think about it?" She nodded, looking at my cup, which was now empty. I followed her gaze. "Definitely time for another."

Andrea stood with a laugh. She offered me her hand and pulled me off the swing. Back in the house, Bowie shoved shots into our hands. She clinked her glass with mine. "Bottoms up."

Andrea tossed hers back like it was water while Bowie had to pat my back as I coughed out what felt like an entire lung. She roared with laughter before handing me another margarita. "You'll get better."

I grimaced. "I don't think I want to get better at that," I croaked.

Tia managed to help Claire salvage the nachos, but I ended up eating so much queso Elliot was convinced I should bathe in it.

We were on the third pitcher of margaritas when Talia slid next to Claire, giving her a long, questioning look. Claire's shoulders slightly fell. "They tried," she murmured.

Talia shook her head. "The world would be better if they just let us run it," she quipped. "It's such a shame."

Tia looked up from her nachos. She nudged Elliot, who already had his sights trained on the conversation. Andrea inched closer to me. I could feel our link sizzling to life in my mind.

"What happened?" I asked.

"The meetup didn't go well," Claire answered diplomatically.

"Derek used very different words to describe it." Elliot gave her a tight-lipped smile. He leaned forward, resting his forearms on the counter.

She held Elliot's gaze. Anyone could see the battle she was having with herself. "Can you blame them? They're hurt—they've been hurt."

Elliot clicked his tongue. "Relationships go both ways. They're adults now and they know where the pack line is."

She nodded, quiet for a moment. "Well, they're going to have to work it out. Both of them. It takes time to rebuild trust."

"He would never have hurt anyone," I found myself saying, because the worst thing about Levi, the scariest thing, was the myth built around him.

"That wasn't always the case," Claire gently pointed out.

I tilted my head. "True, but the last few years? No, he wouldn't have." I knew that in my gut. He may be insane at times, rough around the edges, to say the least, but he wasn't out of control. Even when I first met him, he was never out of control. If he hurt anyone, it was because he fucking wanted to do it, not because he couldn't control himself.

"She's right." Bowie stepped forward, leaning her forearms on the island in the middle of the kitchen. "I caught Remi by Levi's more times than I could count. He could have easily come after him, but he never did. He would have never hurt him. I know that."

Claire pushed some hair that had fallen out of her braid behind her ears. Her eyes were growing tired, the weight of the last few years heavy on them.

Andrea steadily sipped her drink then said, "They need to stop acting like children."

Claire gripped her cup a little tighter. "Well, they are men, what did you expect?" She laughed nervously before finishing her drink.

Gran arched a brow. "You needed that. Tia, get her another."

Talia shook her head slowly, her eyes locking with Andrea's for a moment. Elliot slid off his stool and walked around to Claire, pulling her into the hallway.

Andrea nudged her chin to Talia. "Sad you missed the party?"

Talia scoffed. "No," she answered before walking to the bathroom.

I took a sip from my drink then nudged Andrea's shoulder with mine. She tilted her head and arched a brow at me. *"Ask."*

I looked back at the hallway where Elliot and Claire had disappeared. It seemed like neither side of the equation was totally free of fuckups. And I hated that for Levi. If they were truly the only family he had left, well, I can't imagine he didn't still love them.

"Why won't his nephews see him? He's trying. Anyone can see that."

She brushed her hair behind her ears. "They feel like he walked out on them. The boys and Evangeline, his niece. He lost his whole world and then secluded himself, and I think they felt abandoned. Like he chose to be selfish and stay in his misery rather than try for them."

"I heard Ethan tried to come see him."

"Once," she confirmed. "It was too early. Lander warned him. We all did. It did not go well. He said Levi looked like a rogue." My gut clenched because I remembered the haze around his eyes, but it wasn't his fault. He couldn't help the heartache. "To be fair, I think Ethan's the most levelheaded about it, but his siblings are another story. Evan's a hothead and Evangeline was and still is too young to understand what happened. It's just bad blood. You know?"

I licked my lips. "I feel like, considering what happened, they would understand a little more."

Andrea nodded slowly. "One would think, but hurt tends to cloud reason. I think they were in so much pain they just wanted the only piece of family they had left, and forgot to consider what he was going through too."

"So they don't interact with the pack at all then?"

She shook her head. "They have to for pack-to-pack business but not really for anything social anymore."

"Levi's not going anywhere."

She chuckled under her breath. "I know. Dad warned

them as much. But you know, most men have rocks for brains."

I bit back a laugh. We ended up finishing the last pitcher of margaritas before I told Elliot that he needed to take me home; otherwise, I would fall asleep in the grass. We said our good-byes and ran home.

The quiet of the night was broken by shouting when we neared the house.

Derek jogged down the steps and met us halfway across the lawn. His smile was tight, eyes heavy with exhaustion. "I need to feed." Elliot watched him a moment before nodding. I took my saddlebag from him. Derek offered me a weak smile. "I'll see you when I'm back?"

"Yeah," I replied. "You okay?"

His dark eyes softened. He pressed his lips to my cheek. "Don't worry about me," he replied. Elliot took his hand and zipped with him into the forest.

Levi was standing in the window, his arms crossed over his chest. He opened the door and walked onto the porch with a glass in one hand and a water bottle in the other. I strode over, swaying slightly as I tried to take the stairs.

Levi shook with an amused expression on his face. "How many did you have?"

"I think Bowie's a fish."

He chuckled into his glass. I walked across the porch to sit next to him.

"It didn't go well?" I asked. He handed me the bottle, eyebrows raised in question. "Claire mentioned it."

"Did she?"

I took a long sip of water, knowing I would have to drink

two more and potentially take some Advil to have a chance of beating the hangover I would have tomorrow.

I shrugged. "She's like Lander, she says a lot and nothing at all."

Levi barked a laugh that startled me. Then he sighed. "They can hate me all they want, but Lander is right. If we do turn up something we're going to need their cooperation."

I tapped on the bottle. "Did you ever think about going to them? Before?"

"So many times," he answered, his voice lower, almost a whisper. "I never didn't think about them. At some point, I figured they were better off."

My heart twisted. "You wouldn't have hurt them. Anyone could see that."

He smirked. "Lander told Evan that."

"And?"

"Little shit slugged him in the chin." My hand froze, the bottle halfway to my mouth. Levi chuckled darkly. "Lander laughed. He laughed harder than I'd heard him laugh in a while then told Evan to start running." He turned to me, eyes starting to glow. "Lander can be a scarier piece of shit than me at times."

I took a long sip of water, almost finishing the bottle. "You good?"

He leaned back in his seat. "I think I may have fucked up too much."

"Everyone deserves a second chance, especially when they didn't do anything wrong."

"I did plenty wrong, Charlie girl."

"We all have," I countered. "That doesn't mean we should hold things over someone's head. It's not right."

"Maybe," he agreed.

"Did they know anything? About the rogues?"

He shook his head. "No, it doesn't seem like it, so keep your fucking mouth shut." He took a swig from his glass, which was almost empty. "Claire's was good?"

"Yeah, Tia burned the nachos." He snorted a laugh. "Gran was there. She's a riot."

He nodded. "She's seen a lot. Sharp as a whip still."

I finished my water and picked at the edges of the label while I thought about what Andrea had asked me. I wasn't sure if I was ready to leave him. My beast whined in the back of my mind, both of us oh-so-aware of Andrea's position—of how hard it had probably been for her to ask us to live with her.

"What is it?" he asked, cutting his eyes to me.

My mouth opened and closed a few times. It wasn't the time to talk about this, not after the night he'd had. "Nothing."

"Bullshit, what is it?"

Turning to him, I waited a moment. "Really, Levi—"

"Charlotte, just say whatever it is."

I blew out a breath. "Andrea was there with Talia. She said she talked to you about transferring."

"She did," he replied with a nod. "She's always been a good one. Got a shitty hand dealt to her."

"She asked me to live with her. She mentioned something about Gran moving . . ." My heart started to pick up.

Levi turned to me. "What?"

I bit the inside of my cheek. "She asked me to move in with her."

Something pulsed in his eyes. "I'm not doing this tonight," he said as he stood, leaving me alone on the steps.

The door slammed behind him. Blinking hard, I groaned, letting my eyes lift to the sight of the almost full moon. "You're not the most helpful, are you?"

CHAPTER
TWENTY-SIX

Derek was twisting my hair up into a half updo for the party. I wasn't sure it would work since he had also chopped an inch off it earlier today, leaving the length in a blunt cut above my shoulders, but he said he was determined to make it work for tonight—for my pack initiation. I didn't want to dress up, but Derek forced me to put on a bright-yellow sundress with light-blue flowers on it.

Levi shook his head at me. "How the hell are you going to run in that?"

I narrowed my gaze at Derek. He shrugged, a sly grin on his lips. "I guess we're all walking."

Levi grumbled curses then walked back into his room. Elliot grinned. "We're going to be late!" he called to Levi, who returned shortly in a clean navy shirt and jeans that didn't look ripped at the edges. The ponytail even looked neat.

I leaned against the counter. "Are you asking someone out?"

He narrowed his gaze at me. I tossed my hands up and jogged outside with the vampires, who were in the best of spirits tonight, a mood that followed us all the way to the pack house. The lights inside glowed in the evening sun. I could hear laughter and music in the air, which was a sweet summer breeze combing through the grass. Derek smiled, taking my hand. "I love a good party."

"And I love shots," Elliot said. "You're carrying me home tonight."

"Am I?"

Elliot winked. "Oh yes, very much so."

Levi scowled at them. "Come on," he said to me.

I broke away from the vampires and followed him into the house, where it seemed the entire pack was spread about. Kids ran through the living room while a team fussed in the kitchen, setting food out. We walked to the backyard, where tables had been set up around a small dance floor in front of a four-person band.

A firepit was lit up yards away. I could see Lander laughing with a group of people.

Tia ran over and threw her arms around my neck. "You wore a dress! And your hair!"

"It was Derek," I said, shaking her off.

Derek playfully nudged her cheek. "And don't you forget it! Is your aunt here?" he asked Tia.

"Mhmm," Tia hummed, nudging her chin over her shoulder. Talia was sitting with Max, who was bouncing a small baby on his knee. He had his father's eyes but his hair was silver, just like hers. "She brought some people with her. I'll take you," she offered.

He winked at me then fell in line with Tia. Elliot jogged after them. He slipped his fingers through Derek's before whispering something that made Derek's neck turn pink.

I was walking across the lawn when long legs and chestnut hair found me. Andrea put a hand on her curvy hips clad in yoga pants. She looked comfortable in her oversized sweatshirt.

She motioned to my dress. "What the hell?"

I held my hands out. "What?"

"We did not agree to dress up for this."

"I didn't think we were coordinating?"

She crossed her arms.

I rolled my eyes. "Sorry, next time I'll send you a memo."

She snorted. "Come on, Jake was asking for you."

I laughed and let her yank me forward. She pulled me halfway across the lawn to a set of tables next to rows of coolers and kegs. Jake was sitting at one of the picnic tables. It was shocking how quickly his leg had healed. Tia and I had checked on him almost every day, and while he told us he was fine, he never complained about having us fret over him.

He pulled me into a stiff hug. "Don't read into it," he said.

Andrea rolled her eyes. "You big softie." She snickered. "Dad said you cried on Charlotte's shoulder the whole hunt."

Jake grumbled into his glass.

"We won't talk about it, I don't want to ruin your rep." I laughed under my breath.

"You're a dick," he told me.

"And you're a twat," I countered.

He snickered. "Congrats on today, by the way."

"Thanks," I said, taking a seat next to him. "How's the leg?"

"Good," he answered. "I can shift tomorrow. Billy is coming up to run home with me, which I know is going to break your sweet heart."

"Moon bloods don't have hearts, we eat them. Didn't you know that?" I replied, keeping my face completely stoic until Andrea snorted a laugh, breaking my facade. I ended up laughing so hard with them that I spilled part of my drink on the edge of my dress. Jake poured some of his drink on the edge of his shirt to match me.

"I'll get us another," he offered, walking away from the table.

Andrea bit her lip. "So . . ."

"So . . ."

She pushed her hair out of her face. "Have you decided? You know, about moving in?"

Guilt rolled over me. There was no way I was telling her how Levi had reacted. I needed to talk to him when he wasn't in a foul mood and figure out what I was doing, because it wasn't fair to keep her waiting.

I shook my head. "No, I'm sorry."

She nodded slowly. "Look, I know it's going to be hard leaving Levi. I don't blame you if you don't want to."

"It's not me not wanting to, I'm just—" Worried about him. I realized that part of me was probably as worried about him as he was about me.

"Lander won't let me have a house on my own," she explained.

"I know," I answered, blowing out a breath.

"And if I lived with David, I might as well be alone." Her smile was bitter. "There's nothing worse than constantly coming home to people who look at you with pity, like you're a hurt animal about to lose it."

"I get it," I told her. Levi had never looked at me like I was anything but a person—and sometimes a pain in his ass—but never with pity. I couldn't have handled the pity even when it was what I thought I wanted.

"I know. You're the first person in a long time who's looked at me like I'm normal. Like I wasn't damaged goods."

"You're not damaged goods, Andrea."

"We all are, Charlotte." She finished her drink. "You just don't think less of me because of it."

My heart twisted for her. I could feel my beast whining in the back of my mind. I lifted my hands. "I promise, I'll make a decision soon. I need to talk to him about it. I'm sorry, I'm not trying to drag this out."

She nodded with a small smile. "It's all right, it shows you give a shit."

"About what?"

"Him," she answered. "It's good Levi has someone to look out for him."

Jake approached the table with two drinks in hand. He

set them down then pointed forward. "You guys better go, it's almost time."

My heart fluttered in my chest. "Right."

I had known they were going to do this, I just hadn't realized how many people would be here. Lander motioned for everyone to quiet down. Conversations trickled to a stop as people turned to look where he stood next to the fire.

Jake ran his hand through his hair. "Hey, worst you can do is pee your pants in front of everyone."

Standing, Andrea fanned around the table, nodding to me encouragingly as we walked forward. My cheeks heated. I felt like I should have put more deodorant on. I could feel my thighs sweating with every step I took.

Lander waved us forward. "You ready?"

"Is it just us?" I asked.

"Looks like it," he answered.

I scanned the crowd. "Seems like a lot for two people."

He snorted. "Hey, we needed a good excuse to have a party."

"Glad to be your excuse." I laughed.

Lander chuckled and walked us close to the bonfire raging in the middle of the yard. From the corner of my eye I could see Remi and Liam sitting on picnic tables with a front-row view. Liam's gaze was locked on me—eyes soft, smile easy. I turned my head and looked ahead to where Claire was standing with a group of women who were wedged next to Talia. Claire beamed a smile back at me.

Levi walked around the firepit to stand next to Lander.

"All right! Everyone!" Lander bellowed to the crowd.

I was so aware of the eyes watching me that I felt my toes squirming in the grass. At least Levi looked about as uncomfortable as I did. He was rigid, the hair on the back of his neck rising to stand.

"Welcome to our summer bash!" Cheers howled into the night. Lander clapped his hands and rubbed them together. "Now, we usually have a whole song and dance for this, but seeing as we have only two new members, we're doing a combo—"

"It's not a goddamn drive-thru, Lander," Levi snapped.

Snickers rolled across the lawn. Lander looked back to the crowd. "Today, we're going to initiate Charlotte and Andrea into the pack." More cheers erupted. A whistle caught my ears, and turning, I could see Derek beaming at me with glassy eyes like he was watching my first ballet performance.

"All right, you know how this works! Council—shit, where's—"

"We're right here!" Bowie called. She was sitting on top of a picnic table next to David to our right. Penny was sitting on her dad's lap. Bowie shook her head at Lander. "Well, go on, don't let us hold you up."

Lander rested a hand on his hip. "What say you then, our Head of the Hunt?"

"Yes, My Second," she said, tipping her red Solo cup to us. "Clearly."

David arched a brow at Lander. "I already told you this morning." He taunted Lander with a cheeky smile. The crowd broke into laughter. "My vote is also yes, My Second."

Lander went from playful to serious in a split second. He turned to Levi, whose eyes cut to his. "My vote is yes, My First."

Levi let a breath out through his nose before looking at me. "I don't know why you're asking." Fits of laughter were yanked out of the crowd. Levi tossed his hands up. "All right, let's finish this up."

He waved Andrea forward. She took two steps up to stand in front of him. I heard him say, "Repeat after me," followed by both of them uttering words to each other that I should have listened to, but the beat of my heart and the murmurs around me were louder. Levi leaned forward, watching Andrea, until her breath caught.

Levi squeezed her shoulder. "Welcome to the pack, Andrea."

She sucked in a breath before breaking into a big smile. "Thank you," she said, rubbing her temple. She stepped to the side, offering me a small smile.

I stepped forward. His brows furrowed. "You didn't pay attention to any of that, did you?"

"Was I supposed to?" I heard snickers and a murmur of laughter behind me.

He broke into a deep laugh before shaking his head. "Repeat after me: I, Charlotte."

I took a deep breath and let it out. "I, Charlotte . . ."

"Pledge myself to this pack, just as this pack pledges itself to me."

Licking my lips, I nodded. "Pledge myself to this pack, just as this pack pledges itself to me."

Levi smirked, eyes pulsing in a glow as something

tapped on the inside of my brain. I cocked my head as it knocked louder, demanding to be let in.

A link burned through, like heat lightning dancing between clouds in the summer. My breath caught as dozens and dozens of voices chimed in with hellos of their own.

"Oh my god, it's so loud," I groaned, as the pack link pulsed in my mind.

Laughter reverberated around me. Levi shook his head with a tired smile. "Welcome to the Thunderhead Pack, Charlie girl."

Claire was the first person to hug me. She barreled through the crowd and lunged into my arms. It was then I felt tears fall down my cheeks. Claire rubbed my back, saying nothing.

We pulled away, laughing. She rubbed the tears off my cheeks with a bright smile.

"Wait! Pack shots!" Remi jogged over to me with shot glasses in his hands. "Pack shots!"

He shoved a glass into my hand. David walked over and poured tequila into it before filling up everyone else's glasses. Lander laughed at me as I stared at the generous helping with wide eyes.

David raised his glass in the air. "Welcome to the pack, ladies!"

Two tequila shots later, Andrea was forcing me to drink water. "You're not going to make it to the run and I am not carrying you."

"You're a party pooper."

"Do you want to run in the full or not?"

"Fuck, fine," I grumbled, chugging the bottle of water. I rubbed my temple again. "This pack link is so loud."

Andrea snickered. "You'll learn to block it out."

Remi strode over to us. He clinked his glass with my water bottle before turning to Andrea. "Dance?"

Andrea's brows rose. She watched him a moment then said, "To hell with it, why not?"

Remi looked like he had won all the goldfish at the fair. I was laughing into my water bottle when a familiar presence sank down by me. Liam's silver eyes were glowing. They raked over me, holding a heavy heat that would make anyone's toes curl. "Can I steal you now?"

"Liam." I shook my head. "No, I don't think it's a good idea."

He furrowed his brows before laughing a little. "Come on, let's dance."

"No," I said again, the thing I should have said so many times before to stop something that had had no business getting carried away.

"Charlotte."

I looked around. "We need to talk."

He closed his mouth, smile fading. He offered his hand to me. I didn't take it; instead I walked alongside him into the woods until we were far from prying ears.

He was quiet. Silent. Eyes watching mine with a plea. "Charlotte," he murmured, his hand reaching for mine.

"No, Liam. I can't—" I paused and searched for the words to say, but I knew nothing about this was going to be eloquent. "I don't want this, not right now. I need to be on my own. I want to be on my own. I've never had the chance to do that, and I owe it to myself to try for a while."

His hand cupped my face. "Why? I know you feel this too."

"Being someone's mate, their bondmate," I said, the words harder to say out loud than I'd thought they would be. "It's serious, Liam, I know you know that. I'm not ready for serious. I'm just not."

"Charlotte," he rasped, his eyes pleading with me.

"You need to respect my wishes," I said, my voice growing stronger. "Levi is right, if we feed this, it will grow. And I am not ready for that—"

"I can wait—"

"Listen to me!"

He stepped back, eyes wide.

I held my hands up. "Listen to me," I repeated, softer and gentler, because I felt like I was watching an egg crack in my hands. "I am not ready for something serious, and if you are, you need to be with someone who absolutely is. And, Liam, your true mate may show up. I won't do that to you—I will not do that to myself. I've worked too hard for my peace."

"Some people never find them," he hotly countered.

"Andrea?" I tilted my head. "David?"

Liam bit back a curse. "Don't with the excuses." He looked at the ground, shaking his head. "We're diff—"

"No," I retorted. "No, we are not different. We're not fucking special. The laws of the world don't care. They are painfully objective." I took a step back, my resolve unforgiving. "I want to do this for myself. I need to be on my own, and fanning this flame between us is only going to hurt us both. You need to respect that."

He stepped back and leaned against a boulder. Hurt painted his face. I had nothing more to say, and the sound of heartbreaking silence between us was only going to brew into something harmful. So I turned and walked back to the party.

Remi was handing Andrea another beer. He looked up, his lavender gaze glancing over my shoulder. He tipped his chin to me. "They're going to run soon."

The beast in me was starting to paw at the corners of my mind. I was glad I'd worn my shifters under this dress because nothing had ever sounded so enticing—so right for us to do.

"Let's go." I walked in steady steps back to the bonfire, where I could see Levi laughing with Lander.

I could smell Remi behind me. The clouds over the moon were starting to break. I could feel her pushing against the thin layer of skin between us. The hair on my arms stood as a familiar tingle ran along my neck and to my fingertips.

Lander tilted his head back, eyes glowing as the moon came into full view. "It's time."

Something rolled off of Levi. He turned to me, nudging his chin over his shoulder. "Let's go," he said before stepping away and falling into his fur.

Bowie's eyes gleamed like amethysts. A smile broke over her face, her fangs showing. "Run with me," she said, taking my hand.

Remi jogged next to us. I could see Andrea from the corner of my eye, and in front of me Levi and Lander ran together, almost twins in the night. Closing my eyes, I let the shift roll over me, the beast lunging forward into the pure moonlight while howls sang around us.

It was addicting. I could understand why there was such love for the glowing globe in the sky. Nothing felt as serene as sprinting across a field while moonlight combed over my fur. Her rays felt like a mother's hands brushing my hair back, and Her light was as sweet as watching the sunrise after a night of storms.

I found myself running hard, chasing Her rays in a desperate attempt to catch them. But I hadn't looked at where they were taking me.

I didn't realize that I had fallen away from the pack until I stopped a few feet away from a darkness where Her light couldn't be found. I shifted to my skin, the beast drawing a whine from my lips as silence slithered around us.

The wind had been silenced. The grass was still. The trees' limbs were jagged, disjointed like broken bones trying to escape a prison as they reached to the sky. Cold air laced around them, nipping at my skin.

My lips curled involuntarily. It felt like if the shadows of the forest could speak, they would call me to them. But instead of the whispers that I had expected, all I heard was silence.

"Charlotte?" Whipping around, I found Levi's silver eyes staring back at me. "Charlie?"

"This wasn't here before." My voice was low, a whisper that I tried desperately to conceal from the forest. I knew where I was. I was close to where we had exited the forest at the end of the Hunt. There wasn't a silent area there.

His eyes never faltered. "I know."

My jaw dropped a hair. "What do you mean? How is that possible?"

He nudged his chin over his shoulder. "I'll show you."

"What?"

His steps were steady as he approached the trees. "See for yourself," he said, stepping into the darkness. "Walk exactly where I do."

I nodded and carefully followed him through the shadows where the only light was our glowing eyes. Shadows danced around us. The silence was thick, sucking up all the sound we made.

He paused and turned to me. "Focus, what do you notice?"

I shook my head. "It's quiet." It was too quiet. Like before. I wanted to run. The beast in me was scratching at my skin, wanting to take me back into the safety of the moon's light.

Levi tilted his head. "What do you smell?"

I frowned, knitting my brows. Closing my eyes, I let a long shaky breath out of my lips. The scent of the forest was all too familiar—something that felt like it had been sitting still for far too long.

"Focus, Charlie."

There was the scent of squirrels nearby, and water. If I could smell running water, there had to be a stream. It had a fresh aroma, something crisp and alive.

But there was something else there.

Something so faint that I wasn't sure if it was real or if the darkness was playing tricks on me.

"What does it smell like?" he asked, his voice unnervingly calm.

I licked my lips. "Burnt sugar." My voice was hushed, quiet so as to not disturb whatever could be near. "And . . . iron?" I opened my eyes. "It's old. It's like bad breath. Stale."

There was no way I would have smelled it before. During the Hunt I was too focused on getting out of the area to pick up this scent.

"It's remnants of blood magic," Levi explained. "They used a fog. It was like a black box. You couldn't even hear yourself screaming."

I looked around. "But it's faded, barely here. It's still quiet, though."

His eyes glowed brighter. "Blood magic takes a long time to die. The silent areas are spots where the blood magic lingers. What remains of it sometimes stays in one place, but sometimes it moves like this. It's best not to stay near it long. Blood magic corrupts—it *wants* to corrupt." The thought made me want to puke. "It's created from defilement, anything sprouting from it is evil through and through."

"Why would anyone give up their blood?"

His eyes pulsed with a glow. "Who said they had a choice?" My breath caught. "Fur trade wasn't just about taking pelts. They took something that plenty of witches would pay a good price on the hidden markets for. Whether that blood was given willingly or not is another story. But you have to remember, Charlie girl, everyone has a price they're willing to pay for what they want." He kicked the dirt in front of him. "My father always said it was best to learn yours before someone else does. Blood has power in it. All of it, from both humans to nonhumans. And moon bloods?

Even the purest witch can be tempted with a few drops of moon blood." His eyes pulsed.

A shiver raked down my spine. "I don't want to be here anymore."

"Me neither," he replied, walking next to me as we both found our way back to the light.

I woke the next morning to the sound of the worn coffeepot gurgling to life and the scent of cinnamon flowing from the kitchen. I wiped the sleep out of my eyes and poured myself a cup of coffee. Levi was sitting on the front porch, sipping from his own steaming mug while reading a book.

"Morning," I greeted him.

"It is," he replied. He set the book down on the end table next to him.

I took a seat in the chair next to him, scanning the vibrant green yard full of life. It was hard to think that not very long ago the whole thing was covered with so much snow that I'd been sure we'd never see the grass again.

"You sleep?" I asked, breaking the silence.

He shook his head. "No." He paused, then turned to me. "I rarely sleep on fulls."

"Why?"

He shrugged. "Hell if I know. Bowie swung by earlier, she wants you to come to the pack house this morning so she can start getting you oriented to things."

I took a sip of coffee. "It's happening . . ."

"What is?"

It was my turn to shrug. "I don't know, I just—" I laughed quietly under my breath, shaking my head to look at him. "I guess all of this—it's weird when you work and work for something and then you finally get it."

He hummed next to me. "You did work your ass off, more than most, to be in this pack."

"I did," I agreed, leaning back in my seat. "I'm really pack now."

He snorted a laugh. "That you are, Charlie girl." He took a sip of his coffee. "I talked to Andrea last night."

"Levi—"

He held a hand up to stop me. "All of this—you know when you first got here, you could barely decide whether you even wanted to breathe or not?"

"Yeah," I murmured with a small laugh, as the memory of him in my room, gun in hand, offering to put me out of my misery floated to mind.

"I told you that you need to make your own choices," he said, like he was telling himself rather than me. "It's your choice to make. As long as it's not going to get your ass killed, I'll support it," he said. "Besides, Gran's house is barely five minutes away, and it doesn't mean you're getting out of helping out around here because we both know you two are probably going to be eating over here all the time since you can't cook worth shit."

I sat up in my chair. "I'm not that bad . . ." He gave me a long look. My beast huffed in the back of my mind, agreeing with him. Little traitor. "Okay, well, I'm getting better."

He barked a laugh. "You keep telling yourself that." His laughter quieted, eyes growing heavier. "She's going through it, Andrea. It's not fair what happened to her, but when it comes to the moon, I stopped trying to understand her logic a long time ago." He paused and took a sip of his coffee. "She's a good person and I know Billy is worried as hell about her—I would be if it was my kid. But if you want to move in with her, well, I think she could probably use a friend like you."

I took a long sip of coffee, thinking about what she had said to me. Thinking about the idea of having a home of my own. I felt my beast paw at me in excitement. She wanted to create a den for herself, something that we could both be proud of.

"The other night, though, when I brought it up—"

"Was a shit night," he said with a wry laugh. "You're an adult, Charlotte. If it's what you want . . . is it what you want?"

I bit my lip before nodding slowly as a tiny smile pulled on my lips. "It's just—this has been my home."

"This is always your home," he told me. "But there's nothing wrong with wanting to step out on your own, and like I said, you'll be close. In case your ass happens to set the damn place on fire or something."

I shoved his shoulder, laughing next to him. "Andrea will be excited."

"She'll be good for the pack," he added. "I think a fresh start will be good for her."

I hummed in agreement; I could feel my beast smile in contentment.

"So I'm just getting oriented today with Bowie?"

He nodded. "She's giving Remi more responsibility, so she's having him take the lead on getting you up to speed. It will mostly be getting you familiarized with things, but she'll have you out tracking most likely before the end of the week. She doesn't like a long ramp-up for things."

I arched a brow. "Anything I should look for? Be aware of?"

He smirked a laugh. "That's your job now."

"What is?"

"You're a tracker now, Charlie girl. Your job is not just to track things like game or lost pups, but to find things that need to be found. You're the eyes to the forest and beyond. So from now on, it's your job to tell me what we need to find."

EPILOGUE

Around two weeks after the full moon, on a perfect summer morning, Remi and I set out together into the woods. Dew covered the grass, sending chills up my legs like cold butterfly kisses as the trees swayed in the wind.

Levi had reluctantly agreed to let me help Remi with tracking possible rogues. He and Lander had been arguing one night over it—they didn't want to tell more people but needed extra help going into the Trapper's Forest to ease Bowie's workload, what with the upcoming summer hunts. Considering I already knew what they were doing and was now a full-blown tracker, it was a solution that even Lander sided with me on.

Remi and I had started this morning in the normal

forest, running down the line where trees were painted from the base up with silver. He had already cased the eastern borders with Bowie, and together, he and I were making our way west.

"So," he asked, eyes teasing as he cast me a side-glance. "You gonna hook me up with Andrea or what?"

I groaned, shaking my head. This had to be the hundredth time he had asked since I told him I was moving in with Andrea.

She was ecstatic, to say the least, when I told her that I would move into Gran's old place with her. Claire and the vampires had helped me clean most of it out. Remi declared our new home "The Hen House," and even carved a wooden sign for us that I'd hung on a post next to the bed of wildflowers that I'd promised Gran I would look after.

"Rem . . ."

"Come on." He laughed. "You're supposed to be my wingwoman!"

I tossed my hands to the side. "You're like my brother."

He gave me a playful shove. "Whatever, I'm your best friend." Which wasn't far from the truth. Bowie had given him the responsibility of getting me up to speed, which meant we had spent a lot of time together. While he took his role seriously, we also had grown close, which usually meant that he stole my hair ties and we exchanged details about the latest in pack gossip.

"Liam asked about you," he said tentatively.

"Yeah?"

"You're doing the right thing." He shrugged. "Better to cut him loose than lead him on. He told me what you said."

My eyes went wide, cheeks flushing. Remi held his hands out. "I told him he needed to respect your wishes and listen. We're young. Too young to settle down. And if it's not what you want, and it doesn't feel right, then that's your answer, and he can get over it."

I arched a brow at him. "You don't have a sweet spot for someone?"

Remi barked a laugh. "When I can have armfuls of hunnies?" Rolling my eyes, I shoved him away with a laugh. Remi fell back into step with me. "He'll understand one day. When he's done licking his wounds he'll stop being such a dick about it. Back to Andrea—"

"No!" I laughed. "She's working through some things."

He waggled his brows. "She can work through them on me if she wants."

"I think I may throw up."

Remi laughed while we continued our steady walk, until we were stopped, staring directly into the Trapper's Forest. We had been here before, carefully combing through it. But each time we entered it felt like stepping into a haunted house for the first time.

Remi took a few steps then tightened the hair tie holding half his hair up, like mine. "You good?"

"Yeah." I breathed out. "You?"

"Yeah, let's be quick. You remember our route today?"

I nodded to him. "You have your watch?"

Our goal was to run as far as we could alongside the boundary line until the alarm on the watch went off. David had a list of the times when the patrols for Hemlock would do their normal morning sweeps down the line. The alarm let us know we had about half an hour to get out of there and cover our trail before they showed up.

He tapped the leather saddlebag he had tossed over his shoulder. "Safe and sound. Skin?"

"Skin," I agreed as we silently stepped over the line of white chalk and into the Trapper's Forest.

We were quiet as the sounds of the morning coming to life took the place of conversation. A large gray owl flew over us. He came to a stop, his talons grasping a low, thin hanging branch that wavered with his weight. His turned his head almost all the way around, hooting raspingly as his red-shot eyes watched us.

Remi tossed a rock at it. His mangy wings spread and carried him back through the trees. "Never eat anything from here."

"I know." I shook my head at the memory of the rotten meat from the bear. "You would think they'd stay away from danger."

He shrugged. "It's not dangerous to them anymore."

I shivered at that thought as we continued walking down the line, dozens and dozens of red eyes watching us from their shadowy corners.

Shaking my head, I walked forward while the beast in me pressed closer. I could hear Remi talking, but something had caught my attention, something that made the hair on my neck rise.

I hadn't noticed that my feet had stopped moving. I hadn't noticed that it felt like the wind had died or that the birds had stopped their chirping. As I turned slowly, a familiar darkness looked at me through the trees. An oh-so-familiar stillness.

Cold slithered across the ground. My lips curled at the soft touch of it on my ankles.

"Charlotte?"

"It's quiet," I whispered.

Remi walked to stand next to me, staring into the void. "It is," he answered, his voice low.

I swallowed. "Are there silent areas here?"

He shook his head. "Not known ones. They're usually not on the lines."

"It's one of the moving ones, then," I murmured.

His lavender eyes pulsed. "How do you know about that?"

"Levi taught me," I answered.

"We try not to talk too much about it around the pack," he explained. "It freaks them out."

The sound of a twig snapping echoed through the darkness. Both of us whipped around, looking slightly west of the pack line. Remi held a finger to his lips then tapped his temple.

"There's something out there."

He wasn't wrong. It was quiet but it was like I could feel it. Cocking my head, I let my beast come closer and let her senses run over me.

There was a crack, like someone had stepped on a dried twig.

My breath hitched.

"Fur."

"Fur," I echoed, and we were running.

The shift rolled quickly over me while Remi and I darted between the trees. I let him run ahead while I kept watch around his flanks for traps. I had no desire to end up in a pit today.

The farther we ran, the thicker the silence felt around us. It was almost as if the sounds of our feet pounding the ground were being sucked up.

"Keep pushing," he said. *"We're close."*

"To what?"

"I don't know."

I let my beast charge ahead until she was neck and neck with him. She tipped her nose in the air, letting the scents of the forest flow to us. She inhaled another breath, and a familiar fragrance skidded us to a stop.

Something that was foul, like decay, and that reeked of death.

Remi whipped around. He tipped his nose in the air as I shifted back to my skin. I heard his bones crack next to me while I frantically searched around us.

"Rogues," he panted. His nostrils flared again. "It's not new."

"But it's not old either," I pointed out. "It's so quiet, Rem." My voice grew quiet, almost like I was trying not to wake what was around me.

His jaw ticked. "This is what we do. Yes?" He turned to me, lilac eyes glowing.

"Yes," I answered, as my beast pressed forward, pawing at the back of my mind in a show of solace.

We sprinted forward in our skin, following the faint scent trail of rogues. The track had started to fade, almost as if it wasn't there to begin with. Remi surged past me until he broke through the tree line.

I ran after him, leaping over a bush until I was out in the sunlight, where grassy hills flowed in front of us. Slowing to a jog, I turned back to the forest. Silver was painted on the bases of the trees all the way down the tree line that eventually faded into rolling hills.

In front of us were boulders painted with Hemlock's color, green, as if they were in a standoff with the forest.

"What the hell?" Remi shook his head.

I leaned back and closed my eyes. My beast was close, the two of us desperately searching for the scent, but it was gone. Only the scents of fresh grass and wildflowers permeated the air.

"It's gone," I agreed. I frantically searched the ground for something—anything that could be helpful, but there was nothing. The trail was completely gone.

Remi tugged his ponytail. "What the fuck."

I looked back at the forest, following the tree line that dissipated down rolling hills. From there I could see green and silver flags facing each other, waving in the wind as if they were waving to old friends. Turning, I searched the opposite end of the line.

Silver trees continued to stand off with green-painted boulders for miles and miles as the Trapper's Forest curled around the hills, as if it was pulling them to its breast in a side-hug. In my gut I knew not far in the distance was where I had met the bear.

"Come here."

His voice was hard. Whipping around, I found him standing next to one of the boulders painted green. He was looking down, nostrils flaring again.

He pointed to the ground. "They were here."

"Wha—" Pausing, I closed my mouth and focused.

My beast was pacing. A breeze snaked through the grass, the sound of it like rain falling easily in the summer. It grazed my cheeks, as if I was being touched by the wings of fireflies, when the smell hit me.

Immediately, I dropped to the ground and tipped my head to the grass. The scent had picked up exactly where we were standing. It was faint, like a fog fading away, but it was there.

Rogues had been there.

"Holy shit." I stood up, tugging my hair.

Remi looked both ways before jogging ten yards ahead. He tipped his head to the air before squatting down on the ground. "It's here, it's still fucking here," he called, nostrils flaring.

Walking slowly back, he paused a few feet ahead and took a handful of dirt from the ground, smelling it again. "How is this possible?"

Walking back to me, he handed me the dirt. I arched a brow and held it to my nose, the pungent scent of rogues strong. "Oh my god," I gasped. "There's no way—"

I marched back to the tree line of the forest, carefully letting my beast take in each note to confirm that we were not losing it, that the scent, in fact, did die between the two pack lines and pick up at the boulder that Remi was leaning against.

Licking my lips, I asked, "Shit, what do we do?"

He kicked at the dirt. "We can't keep going. We're at their line. We'd have to notify them if we wanted to cross."

"What if they walked across the line? What if they are in their pack, Rem?"

"Their trackers haven't seen anything. I asked already," he answered.

Turning back to the forest, I searched the thick trees. "I mean, it just died . . ." My gaze traveled across the grass and back to Remi. "It's like it skipped over the grass. That's not possible." I knew that I was still new to this, but logic would suggest that, even for this world, that was unreasonable.

"I know," he groaned, slowly shaking his head. "But the rules are the rules. We can't go on their territory unless we want to drag them into this. We need to get my mom out here and see how she wants to handle it. I doubt we're going to be able to do much unless they want to notify Hemlock, and as of right now I don't see that happening. We don't have much more than a weird trail, not enough to prove that there's any real threat here."

Exhaling a shaky breath, I found myself staring past the boulder. "It doesn't feel right."

"I know," he agreed. "Let's double back through the forest. Maybe we'll find something else."

Tugging my hair, I asked, "What do we do about this trail? Just let it go?"

"No." A sly smile crept on his lips. "We need to find another way in."

ACKNOWLEDGMENTS

It's crazy to think we're here, on book two of the Moon Blood Saga. Every day I am so incredibly grateful for this opportunity and for the ability to keep writing Charlotte's story, and so very, very lucky to have an amazing support system behind me.

There are so many thanks that need to be given out, and I definitely know I will not be able to thank everyone who is on this journey with me, but I do owe a large thanks to a few folks.

To my family for supporting me and being an incredible support system. Thank you to my mom for always believing in me, even when things seemed bleak, to my stepfather and father for both being the best dads I could have ever asked for and making amazing subject matter experts for this book, and lastly to my sister—your ability to persevere to get what you want is second to none. I'm glad I took notes from you.

To the people who sat in the trenches with me, who watched me write this series, through every trial, tribulation, and triumph. To Alex, who has been my springboard since day one, and always down to hear me rant or brainstorm out loud. To Will, Lyndy and Justin, Lauren, Rachel, KaylaKat, Cynthia, and Steph for supporting me and being my biggest cheerleaders. You guys have no idea how much it means and how much it is needed during challenging times. Lastly, to Bex, who told me that this would happen one day. I should do better by just believing her, because more often than not, she's right.

A huge thanks goes to the entire team at W. Thank you all for keeping me on track, believing in me and this story, and continuing to champion me. Special thanks to Monica, Rachel, Maeve, Olivia, Anna, Deanna, and Margot. I cannot express how grateful I am to you for believing in this series and for your abundance of kindness, patience, and confidence in me. I am so very grateful for you all.

Lastly, to all of my fans, who have supported me for longer than I deserve. You all are the reason this is a real thing we can all hold in our hands. I will never cease to be humbled, honored, and completely enthralled by you all. Your loyalty, compassion, and excitement motivate me and continue to power me forward. I'm forever grateful for you all, as is Levi, who wishes that I would stop stealing so much of his whiskey.

ABOUT THE AUTHOR

Z.W. Taylor is a writer and Watty Award–winning author who cannot believe the stories that once lived only in her head, on sticky notes, or in random Word documents have become something she now gets to do professionally. Taylor is the author of *The Bite* and *The Hunt*, the first two books in the Moon Blood Saga. She lives in North Texas with her thirteen-pound cat, who does not need a diet contrary to what others may say, and works in digital marketing. When she's not writing, she can be found hanging out with her friends, trying to tackle her TBR list, being active outdoors, or doing the thing she cherishes most: spending time with her incredible family.

**KEEP READING FOR A SPECIAL
SNEAK PEEK OF THE NEXT STORY IN
THE MOON BLOOD SAGA.**

What else will Charlotte find in the Trapper's Forest?

And what surprises await her at the Hemlock Pack?

CHAPTER ONE

The stake Remi had just driven into the ground was bright red, like an alarm blaring a warning through the fog of darkness around us. A small rabbit with jagged front teeth and mangy ears scuttled closer to it. I let out a low snarl, chasing it and other curious red-eyed creatures back into the darkness from which they had come.

Following the rotten stench of rogues that clung to the ground like mold, I drove another stake down close to a tree that was painted silver at the base, like the ones as far as we could see through the darkness. It was the border of our Thunderhead Pack territory. The trees across from us were painted bright green, marking the Hemlock Pack's line within the Trapper's Forest.

Over the past year we had been combing the woods with our small, secret rogue-hunting squad, and had only found whispers of scents, nothing concrete. Nothing like a year ago when Remi and I had found a trail that tracked all the way to the Hemlock line before it disappeared.

There had still been sightings of rogues, although they were rare. Levi speculated that was because of the winter months that had passed, noting that it was hard for anyone to move around with the weather. There had been one sighting in late autumn, at the ports close to Talia's pack. She'd tracked those rogues back stateside to Washington, but the trail had dried up after that before disappearing completely when the snow hit.

However, once the snow melted a few months ago, a pack on the other side of the mountains, the Cache Pack, had caught them: rogues on a human hiking trail in a populated area that was known to be for tourists.

I drove another stake into the ground where the scent lingered before dying only a foot away. It was like the smell was contained to a single area, just like Remi and I had experienced before.

"How far away is your mom?" I asked Remi.

"Maybe two minutes," he noted, slamming another stake into the ground. He wiped his hands on his shifters, bicycle shorts that hugged his skin.

I leaned against a tree and looked around, spotting one that had notches carved into it. They looked like markings one of the teams from this year's Hunt had used to find their way home.

"No one on the Hunt reported anything," I mused while

my beast crept closer, taking in more of the details around us. "But this scent is maybe a week old. The Hunt was only over a few weeks ago."

"I don't like it," he said.

"Levi is going to be pissed."

"He already is," Remi told me as his glowing lavender eyes met mine.

I felt my beast paw at me with an observation of her own. "They slept here."

He hummed in agreement, pointing to grass that was folded over. "For a while, it seems."

Cracking sounded behind us. We whipped around to see Bowie shifting out of wolf form to her skin. I wasn't surprised the Head Tracker had come up on us silently and unnoticed. Her long dark hair swayed behind her as she strode with long steps over to the stakes. Wordlessly, she walked the perimeter of the stakes, which wasn't more than ten feet, before stopping at the one I had stuck in the ground next to a silver-painted tree. Turning, she walked across the line a few feet, then paused a moment.

Her nostrils flared, her eyes glowing brighter in a violet storm that illuminated the new tattoos of tiny flowers under her right ear. "It's like the scent trail is boxed in?"

"Yeah. It literally feels like it's being held in, but there's no blood magic here from what I can tell," I noted, because that had been the first thing I'd looked for when Remi and I arrived.

"It has to be some kind of magic, there's no other explanation," she stated, walking back to us on the Thunderhead side of the border. "The witches are coming soon to retune the borders. Leave the stakes here. I'd like to have one of them look at this."

"Is this like last time?" I found myself asking.

Shaking her head, Bowie murmured, "No."

I blew out a breath, trying to ignore the shiver racing up my spine.

"Good work, you two, now get home." Bowie was our boss, so that was an order.

"What about Hemlock?" Remi asked. "It's on their border, Ma. They're going to notice if the stakes are here."

She chuckled under her breath. "They rarely come to this area of the woods, as you know. They're too afraid of the little rats scampering around here," she added with a snarl of her own as she kicked at a squirrel that looked more like a skeleton venturing too close to her toes. Tapping her temple, she told us, "I'm updating our council. Go home, I'll let you know if there's any news."

Remi dipped his head in obedience. "Run fast," he whispered to her with a soft smile.

The tension in her shoulders left. "Like the wind," she replied with a gentle smile of her own.

I grabbed my saddlebag off the ground and trotted after Remi, letting my fur roll over me.

We made our way through the gloom of the forest until we curled around a boulder where the trees thinned out and green was abundantly clear in the light of the afternoon sun. I felt my beast let out a long breath of relief. Neither of us enjoyed the darkness that always felt as though it was taunting us—calling to us in a whisper I tried to ignore but that somehow found its way into my dreams.

Remi followed me back to the familiar lawn that led to a quaint log home. A post in the ground next to the small footpath had a wooden sign that read THE HEN HOUSE. Remi had carved the sign himself, and Lander and Elliot had helped lay out the footpath of smooth stones. A warm breeze stirred the beds of wildflowers in front of the house. Andrea and I had promised Gran before she moved away that we would care for the garden.

Remi shifted first, jogging up the wooden steps with ease. Andrea and I joked that he was practically another roommate, considering all the time he spent at our place. I shifted, my toes curling into the soft grass. The wind chimes on the small greenhouse tinkled an easy melody.

Andrea was inside at the kitchen sink, washing blood off her toned arms.

My heart skipped a beat. "What happened?"

Remi immediately grabbed some ice from the freezer and wrapped it in a towel.

Turning the sink off, Andrea told me, "I had a day. There was a fight on the Hemlock line."

Remi went to her and tried to dab her freshly split lip. She swatted his hand away, her golden eyes narrowing. She snatched the ice from him. He tossed his hands up in defeat then helped himself to a beer from our refrigerator.

I stood across the counter from her. "What do you mean a fight?"

She tossed her long chestnut braid over her shoulder. "Ali got into it with their guards."

Remi's brows rose. "Ali?" he asked, handing Andrea an open beer.

She nodded, taking it from him. She took a long pull then turned to me. "I got a link earlier about a mountain lion sighting close to the northern border. I took one of the trackers with me to find it, and we followed it all the way to the line, where we found Ali, some of our guards, and their guards in a full-out brawl.

"Our patrols called the cat in, and apparently Ali caught the trail and followed it a little less than half a mile into their border—"

"Aw, fuck," Remi groaned. He took a seat at our small breakfast table, nested alongside the wood-paneled wall. "And she didn't alert anyone over there?"

Andrea blew out a breath. "No, she told me later she forgot because she was trying to find the mountain lion."

"Poor Ali," I added with a grimace of my own.

It was one thing to go a few yards over a pack line. Usually the patrols didn't care as long as you weren't trying to provoke anything. It was another thing to go that far onto another pack's territory without letting anyone know. Levi had warned me that was a recipe for trouble.

"Yeah, and instead of stopping her and escorting her back, like they should have done, I guess they got into an argument, and then the next thing you know I have a split fucking lip," she grumbled.

"I don't understand. Our relations with them have gotten better," I noted, drumming my fingers on the counter.

Our pack wasn't chummy with Hemlock Pack by any means, but the working relationship was better. Over the past year Levi had been able to get his nephews, Ethan and Evan, to actually meet with him. He usually ended up back at our place after each meeting, drinking our liquor. He'd said it wasn't sunshine and rainbows, but it was cordial enough, which was a start. At least that's what I told him when I tried to reassure him.

Remi shook his head. "I mean, if she was tracking a mountain lion—what the fuck?" He paused a moment and rubbed his temple. "Is Ali okay?"

Andrea shrugged. "She's fine but she's upset. She was trying to help, obviously. I talked to Jake. I had linked him before we set out. He got there around when we did. He apologized to her and us and said he would handle the guards himself, but something's going on over there."

"What do you mean?" Remi asked before taking another sip of his bottle. I arched a brow at him. Half the reason we had beer in the fridge was because he drank it.

"Jake pulled me aside and told me that they were tightening up the borders because of bears—"

I barked a laugh and walked to the refrigerator, grabbing a beer for myself, which Remi uncapped for me with a quick twist. "That's such bullshit. That's not how that works."

From what I knew after a year of tracking, we only added patrols in the area when predators like bears and mountain lions were known to be aggressive—like during mating season and when they were coming out of hibernation. But adding extra people to an area of the border was different than totally locking it down. "They don't lock things down for a bear."

Andrea shrugged. "Jake said Ethan was wound up this morning and I guess some people are tense because of it— it's not an excuse. I know Jake doesn't buy it, but he doesn't

7

know more than that. He would have told me." She dabbed at her lip again. The bleeding had almost stopped. "So, did you find anything by that spot I told you about? I wasn't sure, there were whispers, but it seemed off."

Remi nodded. Andrea had been inducted into the rogue squad early on, mostly because each time I came home after going out with Remi, she had this look in her eye like she was onto me. Andrea, I had come to learn, was one of the most observant people I had ever met, and had more street smarts than the best hustlers out there. There was no lying to her. When she'd asked me about it, I'd been honest, and told her I couldn't say anything because I had promised Levi.

So her solution had been bringing it up to Levi. She'd offered to help, and sworn an oath to him that she wouldn't tell her father. And she hadn't. Like Levi, to her a promise was sacred.

"It was like the first time we found it on the Hemlock border," I told her. "It took us an hour after we found your spot until we got to an area it looked like they'd been sleeping in. But it was so strange, it was like the scent was being contained to that area. It completely died off within a foot of the perimeter. And there was no blood magic—I couldn't smell any."

"Me either," Remi chimed.

"I can't believe you two can even smell it." She took the seat opposite Remi and leaned against the wall. "It's always been silent to me."

I shrugged. "You have to get past being scared," I found myself admitting.

"So it was on the border?" she asked.

8

I nodded, meeting her golden gaze. "We put stakes up. It was literally right next to the marked trees."

She groaned into her beer. "My dad needs to know."

I offered her an apologetic smile. Her dad, Billy, was the best. There was no arguing with that. The week we moved in, he came up and stayed with us and, alongside Levi, helped us get the house in working condition so Andrea and I wouldn't "burn it down."

Andrea was the spitting image of her father: legs that could run for days, rich chestnut hair, and golden eyes so molten they were almost unsettling. The man also has the best laugh in the world and Andrea's name tattooed over his heart.

It was hard for me to keep secrets from him too. He stayed with us often. Andrea was his only child, and they were close; and he was kind and so very generous.

But I'd made a promise to Levi, and I wasn't going to break it.

Remi's eyes went unfocused for a moment before turning to Andrea. "Mom just confirmed that Hemlock is coming to the party tonight, and they agreed to meet beforehand. Mom said Levi wants to try to talk to them about the rogues and see how it's received. I mean, it's two cases in less than a year on our borders. They can't ignore it."

I bit the inside of my cheek. "This is progress. Them coming to a social event." Turning to Andrea, I said, "And your dad is coming. So he'll be there and will get to talk to Levi."

She hummed in agreement but I could tell by the worry in her eyes she wasn't satisfied by that answer. She nudged her chin to Remi. "You think they'll listen?"

He shrugged. "Ethan is usually fair and he's not a dumbass, so he can think what he wants, but he knows my mom and he knows she isn't crazy. Evan's not an idiot, either, but he's hotheaded. Having Billy there will help. He always smooths things over."

"Dad always was the peacemaker." Which is what he had tattooed on his knuckles.

"It's not going to be about whether they believe Levi or not," I pointed out. "Levi told me that they probably would. It's whether they want to admit it out loud, because that means they'll have to do something about it. I guess we'll see if they want the burden of truth of not."

Remi finished his beer and stood up with a long stretch. "I gotta head back and freshen up."

"Why? Who are you trying to impress?"

He turned and gave Andrea a wide grin. "Just say the word, babe."

Andrea tossed a dishrag at him. "Get out of my house."

Laughter followed him as he jogged out the door, leaving Andrea and me to the peace of the home we had worked so hard over the last year to make ours.

It was easy to live with her. We were so much the same—we both loved mornings, were pretty awful cooks, and wore almost the same size, which meant that we could share closets.

It had been hard at first to not be at the cabin with Levi, but both Andrea and I often ended up over there for either breakfast or dinner since we ruined half the things we tried to cook, and Levi made himself at home in our new house. He even brought in a recliner one day because he said we had "shitty seating." Only he used the recliner.

We had left our mark on this home. The walls and surfaces were littered with pictures and mementos of the memories we had created—the peace we both had made for ourselves here. In our home. A home that my wolf and I were more than proud of, because it was ours, and we had done this for ourselves.

I walked over to the small table and took a seat across from her. She laid her hand out palm up for me. Smiling, I slapped mine into hers as she asked, "My day was shit, how was yours?"

I snorted. "I hate that forest."

"Yet you are always going into it," she pointed out, releasing my hand to test the skin on her busted lip.

"It's what we do," I answered. "Do you think any of them know what's going on?"

"At Hemlock?"

I nodded.

"I don't know. I really don't. I haven't heard anything from Dad. Jake would tell us, he tells us everything." Which was true. Usually when Billy came to visit, Jake did too. Which meant Billy got the nice air mattress and Jake got our lumpy futon. "What about in your secret emails with Ethan?"

A small cackle found its way out of my mouth before I was snorting with laughter.

Last summer, when Levi resumed his role as pack lead, I offered to help him with some administrative things while he got back into the swing of things. I told him if he called me his assistant, I would dump all his whiskey onto the lawn. Apparently, I was too good at "helping," because now

I was officially in charge of scheduling, spreadsheets that he couldn't filter to save his life, and answering his email. Including an ongoing correspondence with his nephew Ethan, the Hemlock Pack second-in-command.

"He really hates 'Charlie.'" I laughed, finishing my beer.

I couldn't blame him, but "Charlie" was thorough and did not love Ethan's snippy attitude when we were "just following up," or directing him to "refer to the previous email for the attachment that he needed," or scheduling a meeting between him and Levi on a Friday morning because you know, there's only so much attitude "Charlie" can take before they become a real dick.

"Look," I said, "he totally started it. The second email I ever got from him he literally tried to pull a 'per my last email' on me. And the guy must not actually read anything that 'Charlie' sends him because he always asks for things that are clearly stated or attached in the emails above. Like, read the fucking email!"

"You egged it on and you know it," she teased. "You basically told him to fuck off in the last one you sent. What did you say?" She paused, looking off to the side for a moment before turning to me with a grin. "'While that is a creative solution, we're going continue with the current plan,'" she said in a voice that sounded like a monotone customer service recording system.

"It was not creative. He literally kept reiterating his idea over and over with different words. I know what a synonym is."

Andrea leaned her head back with a laugh. "He's going to die when he realizes who you are and that there is no Charlie."

"Absolutely not, we're taking this to the grave. It's too good, and Levi loves it." He encouraged it half the time. He told me last week I should fuck with Ethan and "circle back" a few more times. "Anyway, maybe they'll work it out tonight, or at least make headway on the rogues."

"I hope so," she agreed. "I'll feel better once my dad knows. We're not dressing up tonight, are we?"

I cringed at the thought. "God no, but we can't look like swamp rats."

She waved me off. "We never do."

"That's debatable." I chuckled, because there had been mornings after too much wine with Bowie and Claire when it looked like we had crawled out of our graves.

She rolled her eyes. "We'll 'try.'"

"Fine."

"Fine." She snickered. "Now, come on, we gotta get the air mattress out. Jake wants to stay with us. Dad's staying at David's because he wants to be able to go to bed before seven p.m."

"Billy cannot hang," I said with a shake of my head before leaning back against the wooden panels.

I turned to watch the wildflowers sway in the breeze outside the window, my heart still beating too fast for comfort. I felt my beast pace in the back of my mind, both of us still thinking about the scent we had found earlier, deep in the dark of Trapper's Forest.

"What's wrong?" Andrea asked.

I rubbed my chest. It felt tight. It had felt this way all day. Honestly, I had been feeling anxious that week, but I assumed it was from the venturing into the Trapper's Forest that Remi and I were doing. My beast pawed at the back of my mind, but I wasn't sure why. "Nothing."

She dipped her head, catching my gaze. "I know when you're lying to me." She cocked her head and asked, "Did you hear anything in the forest today?"

I couldn't look away from her, but I wanted to. I felt like a kid caught with the extra Halloween candy they had hidden under their bed.

"Andrea—"

"Charlotte." She held a hand up. "We both know I know you hear something. You look at the darkness in there like you're expecting it to talk to you," she added, her voice growing a hair quieter.

I wasn't ready to admit that to anyone yet. Not to her. Not even to Levi. I felt like Remi suspected it, because there were times when I heard the whispers call to me when I was out there with him. He only heard the wind, but I heard something calling me farther into the trees.

"No, it's not that . . . I don't know. I think all of this stuff with the rogues—I don't have a good feeling about it."

"I know," she agreed. She stood up from the table, tapping her bottle on it once. "Remember what I told you. If you hear your name being called by a voice in the forest, don't answer it."

DON'T MISS THE NEXT BOOK IN
THE MOON BLOOD SAGA
BY Z.W. TAYLOR

Coming soon from
W by Wattpad Books!